ADVANCED READE

A NOVEL BY

ROD C. SPENCE

Publication Date: February 2018
Format: Jacked Hardcover
ISBN: 978-0-9990879-0-9
Retail Price: $24.99 US
Paperback ISBN: 978-0-9990879-1-6
Retail Price: $17.95 US
E-book ISBN: 978-0-9990879-2-3
Retail Price: $9.99 US
Ages: 12 and above
Length: 355 pages
Trim: 6 x 9 inches
Classification: Action & Adventure,
Techno Thriller, Science Fiction,
Fantasy, Young Adult

GALLANT PRESS   *Los Angeles*   2018

For information, contact us at:
publicity@gallantpress.com

UNCORRECTED PROOF

If any material is to be quoted, it should be
checked against the bound book.
CIP information to be included in bound book.

Copyright © 2017 by Rod C. Spence

All rights reserved under International and Pan-American Copyright Conventions.

Published by Gallant Press, Los Angeles.

War World is a work of fiction. Names, characters, places, and incidents either are the product of the author's imagination or are used fictitiously. Any resemblance to actual persons, living or dead, events, or locales is entirely coincidental.

JACKET ILLUSTRATION by Antoine Collignon
ILLUSTRATIONS:
Zyad Kadri – pages: vii, 1, 12, 24, 31, 46, 65, 93, 97, 106, 118, 128, 133, 152, 193, 207, 247, 254, 264, 273, 282, 289, 294, 317.
Anthony O. Yoingco - pages: 63, 74, 150, 178, 198.
Adeel Khan – page 230.
Antoine Collignon - page 164.
James Coates - page 334.

Library of Congress Cataloging-in-Publication Data has been applied for.

ISBN 978-0-9990879-0-9
ISBN 978-0-9990879-1-6 (Paperback)

Manufactored in the United States of America

www.gallantpress.com

To Maria for all the care and love.

For Claud, Gail, Vicki, Craig and Bruce -
because family is where it's at.

Bombs and Liquid Memory™

"After nationalizing the manufacturing of military arms the United States will find themselves controlling a fragile monopoly. 'Black market' dealers and arms manufacturers, hiding behind corporate shells and scientific research, will multiply like cockroaches and create a whole industry hidden from public inspection. Mankind always finds a way..."

Alistair Bambridge
Journal of World Economics

"The HUMAN BRAIN... is the future of technology. When scientists learn how to create an organic, biological based, liquid memory, the old age of computer chips will give way to frightening possibilities. If man can learn to program the brain itself then what about DNA? Someday, the word 'human' may refer to a specific brand of being..."

Dr. Megan Ziu
United Nations internal report

INTRODUCTION

THE RISE OF TERRAGEN

THE DEMISE OF TECH STOCKS at mid-century was the result of two factors: intense competition within the industry as more and more startups popped up all over the globe coupled with the flood of cheaper products from the east. Years of expensive research and development gave birth to stillborn products that were quickly pirated. Stories of overnight billionaires from tech startups became a thing of myth. But like the unstoppable force of water through rock, investors weren't dissuaded. Another technology was found that promised even greater rewards.

The biotech race was on.

Smart phones, data pads, entertainment portals the size of your palm…these technological pursuits gave way to medical mining: the pursuit of the next multi-billion dollar pharmaceutical treatment. Scientists in labs created heart regeneration cell builders and genetically created killer cells to eliminate cancerous tumors.

But their pursuits weren't just limited to medicine. Hair regeneration stem cell treatments were discovered. DNA editing surgeries eliminated mutations. Analysts predicted the lifespan of a human being would surpass the century mark. One insider boasted, "Want to live to a hundred and twenty? No problem! And by the time you reach your seventieth year, the last frontier of the brain will have been discovered and then we'll talk to you about financing the cost of your immortality!"

Yes. The word *immortality* was being used as the carrot to entice more and more money into the biotech world. From birth, a human being could finance their eternal life—who *wouldn't* give up fifty percent of their income for life for the chance to live forever? Investors salivated at the possibilities.

Some critics called it the rise of the modern slave system. They pressed Congress to limit the scope of the biotech companies future power. But money found its way into the naysayer's pockets as well and eventually their voices went silent.

Other biotech companies sought a different kind of immortality: the power to download a person's consciousness… much like you would download a complex computer program, or the latest movie. Brain sequencing was considered the holy grail of bio technology and companies were snapping up college graduates—literally physically snapping them up in India and China in some cases—to give themselves the competitive edge.

T HE ONE SILENT PLAYER in the biotech race was the government.

If you could create a new heart in a lab you could also create a stronger, faster human. The pursuit of the *super soldier* created a windfall of money for those biotech companies whose bribes secured the lucrative contracts. And politicians callously turned a blind eye toward those companies.

New players were added to the government's list of contractors every year. One such company in the midwest secured billions of dollars in research after they showcased the world's first quantum computer. TerraGen Universal went from an obscure pharmaceutical startup to one of the world's biggest players in the biotech field overnight.

TerraGen's arrival created intense competition and technological espionage replaced terrorism as the lead story in every news broadcast. Security was every corporation's fear. Navy SEALS and Special Forces veterans were hired as watchdogs. But the thievery continued.

One of the new *tech mafia* companies was a little known startup in south Texas. MetaUniversal Genetics hired the best hackers and corporate raiders and they quietly filed patents on stolen technology in countries other than the United States. Possession was nine-tenths of the law. Who needed the U.S. market when buyers in Europe and Russia were willing to pay.

"Secrecy was an obsession," one CEO recounted. "Here we are trying to push the envelope, discover the next holy grail of science, and all the while we're being attacked by other biotech firms and the United States government."

Biotech companies were bending every rule and the elected Senators and Representatives passed laws in a vain attempt to control the ethics of new science.

Money always finds a way.

Like cornered animals, the biotech firms looked for other areas on the globe to flex their research muscles. Countries that would turn a blind eye. The common thought amongst the biotech corporations was singular: "What you can't see won't hurt you."

Oh… but it always does.

PROLOGUE

BIRTH OF A BIOWEAPON

EYES BLINKED. CONSCIOUSNESS. Something had awakened… *it*.

The creature stood upright, held in place by *magnafoam* and protected by two inches of high-tech, blast proof *plastasteel*—clear as glass and tough as steel, courtesy of the research department at TerraGen Universal.

Eyes blinked. It wanted to swivel its head, but was locked in place by the magnetic foam. Sound registered.

Soft taps. Distant.

It didn't have many thoughts to dwell on; the creature's entire life experience had been inside this cocoon. Standing just over six feet tall, it was male in sex with two legs and two arms, torso, neck and head were humanoid but distinctly reptilian—a flattened nose, thick skin covered with scale-like flecks and black eyes with vertical slits that were now dilated in the darkness of its surroundings. He'd been created as an alpha-predator and now his genetically designed muscles twitched in anticipation of the hunt. Every sense—smell, eyesight, hearing—was heightened beyond a normal human's and now he heard more tapping—sensations only because it had no frame of reference for words like *tapping*. He now sensed two beings from the sound waves that triggered responses in his infantile brain.

Light exploded in front of the creature and he gave a pitiful bark of pain, pupils becoming pinpricks. This had happened only once before in the creature's short life and he'd almost died from shock. But this time was different.

He'd learned.

Two boys—one seventeen and the other sixteen—stood before a bank of computers in the restricted laboratory. Sneaking their way onto TerraGen Universal's high tech and very secure campus had proven uneventful…almost too easy. The elder boy, Patrick, was a computer prodigy and he'd been hacking into the company's security system since he was twelve. The younger boy's name was Jeremy and, although he wasn't an internationally known hacker like his partner, he made up for his deficient computer skills with an equally high IQ mixed with guts, athleticism and fearlessness. He'd always had a rebellious streak and this break-in was his idea.

"Are you in?" Jeremy asked.

"Firewalls—passwords—you'd think these eggheads would try to protect their grandiose experiments with a little more than the basic encryption," Patrick replied, his fingers a blur on the keyboard.

"If I hear Leo open his big mouth one more time," Jeremy growled. The restricted lab they'd broken in to belonged to the father of Leo Tyrannus, a fellow student at Lewisville High School and a science prodigy. "You never hear me blabbing about my Dad's work!"

"Nor about mine," Patrick said without looking up.

Jeremy stared through the glass partition and saw nothing—the room on the other side was completely dark. "Leo kept going on and on about the latest bioweapon," Jeremy said. "Like his father works directly for the government. What a putz!" High school was a dangerous minefield for teenage psychological trauma. Some kids elevated their status through physical threats. Others spun webs of power by creating reputations from words. Both of *their* fathers worked for TerraGen and both had stellar reputations throughout the world of science. Leo's constant boasting of his father's experiments didn't sit well with either boy.

"Done!" Patrick said triumphantly.

Only a single, blue light turned on in the other room. Looking up, Jeremy noticed that even the outer room they were in failed to have the typical fluorescent lighting of most laboratories—just a single strip of blue light. Strange.

"What is that?" Patrick whispered.

In the middle of the inner room a single, coffin-like object was illuminated—standing in the center of the bare, sterile room that looked more like a maximum security cell instead of the high tech lab TerraGen had spent millions of dollars creating. "Let's take a look!" Jeremy said, eager to see this *advanced weaponry* Leo was so proud of.

"Two layers of security," Patrick was speaking to himself as his fingers continued working on the computer's keys. "There…one down."

The inside of the coffin began to glow, revealing the outline of a body suit, but the lighting was so dim it was hard to see.

"Armor...of some kind?" Jeremy ventured.

"To be sold to whatever country will pay the most," Patrick said, his eyes still focused on the computer screen.

"But...this belongs to the company."

"Please! What rock have you been living under?"

"The company pays Tyrannus a fortune!"

"Greed is never satisfied."

"Same as your ego," Jeremy said, lips curling in a smile.

"Ooh...witty banter from the football jock."

Jeremy turned back to study the body suit, wondering what powers it gave the wearer. Does it make you invincible? His body ached from a vicious hit he took in the fourth quarter of the football game the previous night. Invincible body armor would've done him a lot of good. "Still, it's not right to accuse Tyrannus of stealing just because his son is an arrogant twit."

"There are lots of rumors about our Dr. Tyrannus," Patrick said grimly, glancing up briefly to study Jeremy. "and none of them good. I've given up trying to hack into his finances to see what amounts of money he doesn't report to the government and where he stashes it. His encryption software is a good as the CIA's—and I managed to hack into their site—"

"And spent the past year under house arrest."

"True." Patrick's fingers continued to fly across the keyboard. "Bottom line...Tyrannus paid a fortune to protect his server—which tells me he's hiding something."

"Leo's father would risk his job—his *career*—to sell that body armor?" Jeremy asked, pointing to the block of glass.

"For hundreds of millions of dollars? Abso-freaking-lutely!"

Impatient, Jeremy turned back to the older boy, "Are you almost done? Security in this place is bound to detect what you're doing eventually—"

"Eventually can mean seconds...or hours—"

Jeremy was about to continue when there was a sudden hiss from the security door that barred their access to the inner room.

"Now we have just seconds," Patrick said with a wink. They walked into the inner room just as a second hiss of air sounded from the coffin's front panel.

The armor was dark and had a lifelike, skin-looking texture. A salty, toxic odor filled Jeremy's nostrils and his face twisted in disgust. Beads of moisture traveled down ripples of muscular accents that had been sculpted into the suit's membrane.

"Some bioweapon this is," Jeremy began..but then his voice caught in his throat—two orbs glinted and turned their gaze to him...from *behind the glass*. The orbs suddenly blinked and Jeremy shouted, "That's not armor!"

Patrick had also detected the movement and was now pulling at Jeremy's shirt, dragging him back through the doorway. "I'm gonna kick Leo's butt!" Patrick blurted out, the fear palpable in his voice.

They went quickly back at the computer, Jeremy unable to drag his eyes away from the...*creature*. "Secure it! Lock it back up!" Jeremy shouted.

Patrick's fingers pounded the keyboard. "I'm trying!"

"But what?!"

"Something's jamming it," Patrick cried. "The system keeps giving me an error message!"

"There!" Jeremy cried, pointing to the coffin's front panel. Two razor-sharp claws were protruding from beneath the glass panel, preventing its closure. "What do we do?" he shouted. He'd never felt this kind of fear before. Death lived behind that glass panel, and now it was getting loose. He turned, looking for some kind of direction from the older boy.

"Run!"

They burst out of the laboratory and heard the security door snap closed behind them. Their footsteps pounded on the tile floor as they retraced their steps to the building's entrance. Now they wished—no, they *begged* for TerraGen's security to become alerted to their presence. They'd opened Pandora's box, and whatever bioweapon Dr. Tyrannus had created would now be hunting them.

Jeremy's sore leg muscles quickly warmed as his feet pounded the floor. The sound of heavy breathing behind Jeremy was becoming more and more distant, and he realized he was leaving Patrick behind. Stopping, he turned and looked past his friend to the far end of the corridor.

BOOM.

Panting beside him, Patrick also turned to look.

BOOM. BOOM. BOOM.

"It hasn't learned to open doors," Patrick observed.

"Uh…I'm not staying to find out if it does!" Jeremy shouted before turning and running again.

They burst through the double doors into the foyer. The security station was empty. *Empty!* The two boys shared looks of horror.

"What are we gonna do?" Jeremy squealed, his voice an octave higher than normal.

A loud crash—distant and muffled—came from the corridor.

"Think, think, think…" Patrick hissed over and over to himself.

"We have no weapons to kill it," Jeremy said.

"Thinking—I'm thinking—"

"If this gets out…Jeremy started, realizing the implications of their actions with horror, "I mean, if whatever that *thing* is leaves TerraGen, the town—"

"Got it!" Patrick shouted. "Follow me!" The spindly geek raced down an adjoining corridor that led to another section of buildings and Jeremy hurried after. The long hallway connected to a massive building. Big, bold letters at the building's entrance proclaimed: IMAGINARIUM. Another set of double doors—

"Hey! Stop!"

Both kids whirled around.

A security guard stood at the security station, now fifty yards distant, buckling his belt as if he'd just come from the toilet. "This is a restricted area!" the security guard continued, voice echoing in the corridor.

"RUN!" Jeremy and Patrick shouted in unison, both pointing somewhere behind the guard.

It moved gracefully out of the secured hallway—dark and silent—suddenly standing beside the security guard. *It was human...yet, not human,* Jeremy observed. From a distance, it looked alien. Jeremy felt himself moving forward, trying to see more—the bulging pectorals of the upper torso, legs of knotted muscle, hands tipped with long claws.

The guard tried to speak but couldn't. His lips moved nervously while his hand groped for the pistol holstered at his belt. Like an inquisitive bird, the alien bent its head at an angle, studying the security guard as a predator would its prey. Nervously, the guard managed to unsnap the holster, sliding the pistol out and jerking it upward—

But the guard's sudden movement triggered a fight-or-flight response in the creature and it lashed out, right hand extended and it's movements a blur.

Staggering backward, the guard's body began to tremble. There was a loud clatter as his pistol hit the floor. There was something white on the alien's fingertip, something that hadn't been there before...with a disgusting *slurp* it disappeared into the creature's mouth and was quickly swallowed.

Jeremy went white, knees trembling from the shock of violence—the white object had been *one of the guard's eyeballs*. Blood streamed out of the guard's left, now-empty eye socket, and he let out a guttural scream of pain.

His scream was quickly silenced—the alien's jaws attacking the guard's exposed neck like a vampire...ripping, tearing, causing a spray of blood.

Hands pulled Jeremy backward and Patrick whispered urgently into his ear, "Quick! Before it sees us!"

They turned and ran, banging through the double doors into a spacious foyer—a room with murals, sculptures of prototype machines, displays of futuristic worlds—sculptures, models and art designed to look like the entrance to a ride at Disneyland. Sprinting through the foyer, they entered a large, airplane hangar-like room five stories in height.

Patrick led him across the dark expanse to the literal *feet* of a two-story, metallic robot. "One of my Dad's inventions," Patrick said, fighting for breath.

"Don't we need a place to hide?" Jeremy asked, looking over his shoulder—the foyer was dark...and quiet.

"Inside the *rocktrawler*, we can both fit," Patrick said. The massive giant had two legs, a central chassis and two arms made of titanium—it looked powerful. "It's designed for mining...on the moon," Patrick continued as he moved to the rear. Footsteps sounded on metal as they walked up a mobile step-ladder.

Click. Click.

The sound echoed across from the foyer—*a door opening and closing*. Above him, Patrick had entered the robot's chassis and his dark form was now gesturing for Jeremy to follow. With light steps, Jeremy went up the ladder and moved in beside the older boy. They fit...just barely. Patrick closed the rear hatch the suddenly cramped space amplified the sound of their breathing.

Jeremy leaned close to Patrick's ear and whispered: "It's inside."

Thick *plastasteel*—clear as glass and hard as granite—covered the front of the chassis and they looked down at the floor. A shadow appeared from the foyer, head moving side to side, then cocked—listening and sniffing like a dinosaur hunting for food in an ancient, primordial forest.

"Can you kill that thing?" Jeremy asked.

"Kill? Maybe."

"We can't let it out of here!"

"I thought self-preservation was first priority," Patrick remarked. And then his voice became resigned, "You're right, of course." His fingers pressed a series of buttons and lights appeared followed by the soft hum of electronic motors. Across the room, the alien went rigid. It was looking at them…and Jeremy realized the machine's interior lights were illuminating the two boys. Although safe inside the robot, he still felt exposed.

Rumbling. The whine of motors. Suddenly the robot stood taller.

Below there was a blur of movement.

WHAM!

The alien's face and shoulders slammed into the plastasteel window, inches from their face, rocking the robot. Falling backward to the floor from the impact, the creature lay stunned, unmoving.

"Now!" Jeremy shouted in terror.

"First time in the driver's seat! Sorry!" Patrick answered, hands grasped around a steering wheel that looked like it had been salvaged from an airplane. Gears were pulled back and suddenly the robot lurched forward as it took a ponderous step.

The alien was gone.

Suddenly there was a rapping sound—metal resisting force—sharp tools scraping on metal—*behind them. It was trying to open the rear hatch!*

Patrick also sensed the danger because he suddenly threw one gear forward.

"Hold on!"

The rocktrawler walked backward and crashed into the rear wall. Almost immediately there was another blur of movement on their left—the alien vanished into shadow, then reemerged, flying through the air.

CRASH! Rocking on its right leg, the robot tipped sideways.

"Shift your weight!" Patrick cried and Jeremy threw himself left. The rocktrawler settled back on both feet. Jeremy's face was two inches from the plastasteel where *reptilian* eyes stared back at him. The creature was grappling with the robot, eyes searching for a way inside.

"Screw this!" Patrick snarled. The robot's chassis swiveled violently and Jeremy saw the alien thrown high into the shadows. Gears shifted—motors revved—the rocktrawler moved into the middle of the room. It's arms lifted, and suddenly flames shot out of both.

"Now we're talking!" Jeremy shouted.

Shadows vanished in the flamelight, revealing the alien crouching twenty feet away, it's eyes tiny slits.

WHOOSH! More flames spewed out of the robot, easily covering the distance and creeping up the building's wall. A scream of animalistic pain sounded from outside their compartment.

Gears whined as the rocktrawler swiveled in the other direction. Flames continued to shoot out as Patrick, eyes wide open with panic, tried to catch and incinerate the creature as it sped across the room. The alien disappeared again.

Scratching. Again, it came on the access hatch behind them.

"It's trying to get in!" Jeremy shouted. He twisted around—very difficult because of the cramped space—found the door's handle, and searched. *There's no locking mechanism!* Jeremy's mind screamed.

Fuel—the smell of fuel filled the compartment as the flames spewing out of the rocktrawler's arms suddenly sputtered.

"It's cut the fuel lines!" Patrick shouted.

"That can't be good," Jeremy said, pointing over to crates containing metal cylinders.

Crates now engulfed in flames.

Crates stamped with the words...

HIGHLY FLAMMABLE.

Strange liquid covered the creature as he clawed at the rear of the rocktrawler, his razor-sharp talons fighting for traction in the tiny groove surrounding the hatch. It was a new smell, the liquid, but it wasn't so strong as to mask the smell of the two beings inside. The hunger for a fresh kill drove the beast to madness. He even felt their blood pulsating—

WHOMP!

Suddenly, a bright light and flash of heat—the creature's head snapped to the right. He felt the heat of the flames—remembered the scorching he'd just endured from that bright gas—and yet...he was powerless to give up the hunt. He didn't know what an explosion was—his young brain ignorant of that kind of danger. Flames washed over the creature and ignited the fuel that had soaked every last pore in his body. Less than thirty minutes after being born, the creature disintegrated in a ball of fire.

CHAPTER ONE

THE TERRAGEN KIDS

JEREMY AUSTIN BENT FORWARD, his head in his hands, and his eyes glazed as his mind worked through the events of the past few weeks. Around him, the gymnasium shook with the pounding of feet. On the gym floor the pep squad performed to loud, fast-paced, beat-thumping music, shaking pompoms and moving their hips in a manner that probably wasn't appropriate for high school students. The pep rally was meant to stir up excitement for the big football game: the Lewisville Raptors versus the Knights of Mohattan High. But Jeremy saw none of it. He was overwhelmed with bitterness. Anger. Nothing made sense.

A month ago his father said goodbye before going on an expedition out of the country. "Where?" Jeremy had asked him.

"That's classified and you know it."

Typical. Four weeks and still no word from his dad. *That's what I get for being the black sheep,* he thought gloomily. Always kept in the dark. Two months in juvenile detention didn't help the trust factor either. The one-year anniversary of the TerraGen disaster was quickly arriving and still, no one had believed their story of the alien killer. The explosion of the high-pressure fuel canisters had destroyed the Imaginarium and all evidence of Dr. Tyrannus' secret experiments. He and Patrick had only escaped death because the rocktrawler was impervious to fire. Jeremy shuddered involuntarily at the memory.

"My fingerprints are permanently in the government's database," he mumbled under his breath. "Awesome…"

Still, his delinquency didn't give his father the right to vanish with no word—no status report—*no nothing!* Dr. Victor Austin was one of the world's top geneticists. *Since when did geneticists go on expeditions?* They lived in sterile labs and played golf on the weekends. Now seventeen years of age, Jeremy was a junior and playing his first season as the number one wideout on the football team thanks to a probation deal worked out with law enforcement—*and his dad was missing everything!*

He shook angry thoughts from his mind and carefully moved down the bleachers, stepping through students and picking his way toward the gym floor. The music banged to a climactic finish and the pep rally erupted in applause. Students crowded around the floor, including a group of cheerleaders. One cheerleader, sandy haired with a striking face accented by large, hazel eyes reached over and tugged Jeremy's elbow.

"Where do you think you're going?!" she asked.

"YOU never take *no* for an answer!" He replied, trying

hard to avoid looking at the soft pout of her lips. "I told you. I won't *act* in one of your skits!"

"You did last year—"

"And I'm still scarred—"

"It would make me very happy," she said, giving him a coy smile. *She was so…so hot in that cheerleader outfit!*

Jeremy mentally slapped himself and scowled, "My humiliation makes you happy. Great!" He really had been scarred the year before—*dressed as a pregnant alligator for the dumb amusement of the student body*—FBI interrogation was a breeze compared to that.

But Helene Colbert could be very persuasive. "You're on the football team. It's your duty! And…it's principal's orders." Her lips pursed in a sly smirk, casting a shadow of mischief on her beautiful face, and his heart skipped a beat.

"Don't be ridiculous!"

"Alex has already agreed."

"Figures… the egomaniac. Give him a microphone and a spotlight and he would do anything!" The heat of his words and the flush on his face revealed the intense hatred he felt toward Lewisville High School's richest bully. The bully was also his quarterback and Jeremy had to stomach the boy's ego every afternoon at practice.

Slender feet in white tennis shoes tapped impatiently on the gym's wood floor. "I'm waiting," Helene said with a confident smirk.

Jeremy suddenly found himself running out of excuses. "And… well, your skit's lame."

Helene stood there, unfazed. And Jeremy knew he was beaten.

"Oh, all right!"

She kissed his cheek and smiled, ever businesslike.

"Good. That's an obedient meat-head."

Twenty years ago, Lewisville was a town of five thousand. TerraGen Universal Corporation arrived with a billion dollars in funding and over the first decade a steady stream of the world's most celebrated experts in geothermal, bioengineering and genetic sciences became citizens of Lewisville. The town expanded and put in an airport, and after the second decade Lewisville boasted a population of over one hundred thousand. TerraGen's campus became an industrial complex while tract homes, shopping malls, multi-screen theaters and skateboarding teenagers became the norm in town.

Loud cheering rocked the gymnasium. One thing Lewisville had never experienced during its growth spurt was a state football championship. A month ago that's all Jeremy could think about. But today his mind wouldn't silence the memory of his father driving away.

She stared into his eyes, seeing his worry.

"Still no word from your dad?"

"No. It's not like him."

"He's gone *007* before, right?"

"Secret trips? Yes. But this one made him nervous."

"What has your brother said?" Helene asked.

Jeremy shook his head bitterly, "Erik? He won't say anything! He's a slave for the company—spends all of his time in the lab. And how hard is it to answer a cell phone?!"

"*Impossible* if the company's in lock down," said a new voice. Jeremy turned and stared down at a short, squat, thick-fleshed boy of sixteen. "Your brother didn't go on the," the boy paused, holding up two sets of fingers in air quotes, "the... uh, 'secret mission.' Which means he's been sequestered on TerraGen's compound. No calls in or out."

Jeremy just blinked. Leo Tyrannus always had the answers. The son of Dr. Kaiser Tyrannus had a boyish face but his eyes revealed the ridiculous IQ within. A straight-A student with no social life usually spelled NERD, but Leo had money and a level of self-confidence that intimidated kids his own age.

"My guess?" he continued. "Our parents are NOT on some scientific expedition to a third world country."

"You think they're hanging out at the mall?" Jeremy asked sarcastically.

"Don't be stupid," Leo's beady eyes narrowed. Theirs was a polite friendship; Leo had rightly suspected that the accusations of corporate espionage made against his father were because of Jeremy's break-in one year before. The prank had cost Jeremy his junior year of football while Leo was forced to endure an FBI investigation, but the younger boy showed no resentment. Leo's voice was playful as he continued, "You've never been one to pay attention to details—something I'm really good at—"

"And you obviously know something I don't," Jeremy said, not bothering to hide his scorn. "Your dad doesn't have higher clearance than mine."

"Sure, our dads aren't exactly best buddies and they both like to keep secrets."

Jeremy knew full well the rivalry that existed at TerraGen: Dr. Victor Austin, the world's top geneticist was always getting the honors and publicity, and Dr. Kaiser Tyrannus, also a top geneticist, had worked in Austin's shadow for two decades and had a reputation for pushing legal barriers. Kaiser Tyrannus was never happy being second place to Victor Austin. But strangely, no real animosity had crept up between Jeremy and Leo. Though never close, they had grown up together and shared the bond of being one of the "TerraGen kids."

But Leo seemed to know *something* and Jeremy was curious.

"OK… if not South America or Southeast Asia, then where?"

Leo gave a mischievous look, "Definitely *not* on this planet."

Jeremy looked at Leo and laughed, and even Helene giggled. *Not on this planet?* Jeremy never took Leo for a drug crazed, hallucinogenic hippie…but *that?* Shaking his head, Jeremy started moving toward the back of the gym.

"It's not so crazy!" Leo was following after him. "TerraGen needs a secure place to do all its top-secret experiments. What better place than another planet?"

Top secret. Those two words were responsible for most of the problems between Jeremy and his father (blowing up the Imaginarium was on a totally different level, of course). What are you working on, Dad? *Top secret.* You created a new vaccine to cure cancer? *Top secret.* The Russians and Chinese are sending their best secret agents, killing anyone who stands in their way to steal the technology you've created that will bring about world peace? *Top secret!*

"Top-secret experiments?" Jeremy stopped and turned to Leo and Helene. "The TerraGen Corporation has expensive labs and a security force working twenty-four-seven. They don't need another planet or a third-world country! Whatever medical cure they're cooking up can be done right here in Lewisville."

"No government regulations...very tempting," Leo half smiled.

"They could buy a small country—"

"A virgin planet would be cleaner."

"But the aliens...what about their rights?" Jeremy was enjoying this—not that he cared—he'd killed an alien just twelve months ago—

"Another planet would provide secrecy—"

"There is no other planet! Space travel doesn't exist."

"And if you *owned* a planet, you ARE the government! No one controls you!"

Jeremy stifled a laugh.

Helene caught his look and turned away, covering her own smile. What disturbed Jeremy the most was not the two dozen zits dotting Leo's face, but the wide-eyed certainty of his beliefs.

"My dad is one of the original founders of TerraGen. There's nothing *illegal* he needs to hide."

Leo cleared his throat, "TerraGen has entertained visits

from U.S. government officials—four in the last six months—and they weren't from the FDA."

Jeremy had heard it all before. "Yeah, the Department of Defense…big deal. At least *my dad* wouldn't make biological a weapon."

"Not knowingly," Leo replied, unfazed.

"Not ever," Jeremy returned flatly.

"If you believe *that*, you'll believe *anything*," came another voice from behind.

All eyes turned and stared at a tall, black-haired boy wearing a letter jacket. Alexander Leach, Jr. had a perpetual sneer with an upturned lip that marred his handsome features. His blue-blood arrogance and a bottomless line of credit in his father's bank account made Alex the most desired "best friend" in school… or the most hated.

"What's that supposed to mean?" Jeremy challenged.

"Of course your dad is squeaky clean," Alex said with sarcastic contempt. "The great Dr. Austin would never do anything wrong."

"My father doesn't run TerraGen."

"He still throws his weight around."

"But he isn't president of the company. That would be *your* dad!" shouted Jeremy over the noise of the pep rally.

Alex suddenly spied Leo cowering and trying to blend in with the crowd. The big jock's muscles suddenly flexed. "Where are you going, little man?"

"P-please, Alex," Leo stammered.

Alex towered over Leo, a wild look in his eyes. Jeremy grabbed at Alex's arm but the bigger boy just shrugged him away. And that's when Jeremy smelled the alcohol. Alex reeked of it.

Several other boys, all football players wearing letter jackets, emerged from the mass of students and stood behind Alex. The "Mighty Six" was Alex's crew, and they had a reputation for drinking, partying, and chasing girls. And they were also Grade-A bullies.

"Dr. Kaiser Tyrannus, with his secret experiments," Alex bellowed, "is a bigger screw-up than *his* old man!" Alex's finger pointed to Jeremy. "Jeremy's dad likes to spend millions trying to save the world," his finger swung back to Leo, "but yours is always getting into trouble with the government."

"You don't know anything!" Leo shouted defiantly.

"Tyrannus the dangerous—"

"Shut up!"

"Tyrannus the big insurance risk—"

"Pig!"

Alex's hand shot out and pushed Leo backward into a crowd of students. Jeremy glanced at the rest of Alex's crew as they moved in behind their leader.

Leo steadied himself, eyes darting left and right for a path of escape but the "Mighty Six" surrounded him.

"What kind of dirty genetics is your dad creating in his secret lab, baby Tyrannus?" Alex snarled.

"No one talks about—"

Alex pushed Leo again and Jeremy moved forward, grabbing the larger boy's shoulder. Alex whipped around and threw Jeremy backward to the gymnasium floor, his head bouncing off the polished wood. Stars flashed in Jeremy's eyes as he tried to blink away the pain. The world blurred and the sound of students chanting the school's fight song clashed with the blood pounding in his ears. He felt Helene's tug on his hand and he shook the confusion away. Getting slowly to his feet Jeremy glanced around, trying to find Leo but the smaller boy was hidden behind the wall of the Mighty Six. Two of the bullies, Matt Gilroy and Fern Hernandez, had their eyes on Jeremy, hands on their hips, daring him.

"You lie!" Leo's voice was barely heard above the music of the pep rally. Alex and his crew had Leo boxed in behind the bleachers and out of the eyesight of the teachers.

"I'm getting the principal!" Helene's voice snapped Jeremy out of his fog and then she vanished into a crowd of students. The noise of the pep rally had died down. Jeremy tried to move around Gilroy but his two-hundred sixty-five pounds of offensive line bulk easily shoved Jeremy aside. But then a raven-haired girl shot past Jeremy and embraced Gilroy, hugging the surprised bully in a tight embrace.

"That is NOT true!" Leo's voice cracked above the noise.

Jeremy moved quickly, darting past Gilroy who was struggling to extricate himself from the raven-haired girl's embrace. Jeremy saw Leo, hands raised defensively and failing to block the wicked slaps from Alex. In that moment, all Jeremy saw was a defenseless friend being attacked. Jeremy lowered his head and slammed into the back of Alexander Leach. Both boys went to the floor with Jeremy landing on top. His years on the wrestling squad paid dividends as he deftly pinned Alex's arms with his knees and began slamming punches into Alex's face and body.

Strong hands suddenly latched onto Jeremy and he was yanked backward.

Silence filled the principal's office. Jeremy rubbed his sore knuckles and stole a glance sideways to where Alex sat. The son of privilege had lost his arrogance, and now his face was cold and sullen.

WHACK!

Jeremy jumped violently in his seat and quickly looked up.

Coach Wilton Hayfield's hand rested firmly on the principal's desk but his eyes blazed fire at Jeremy. "Pep rallies were made to motivate us to play," he growled. "NOT to go around fighting like a bunch of street toughs!"

Jeremy gulped.

"Our biggest game of the season and now I've got to bench two of my starters!" Both Alex and Jeremy looked up at the coach in surprise. His face was hard and unforgiving as he turned and looked down at Alex. "My quarterback…"

Hayfield's eyes then swiveled down to Jeremy, "and my number one receiver…the both of you will sit the pine until the second half."

Jeremy vaulted to his feet, "Second half?! But—"

"That's crazy!" Alex was equally defiant.

Hayfield's face remained cold. "Say another word and it'll be a one-game suspension." He moved past the two boys toward the door. Turning the doorknob, he paused and looked back. "Because of your selfish, gi-normous stupidity, if we're only down by four touchdowns at the half I'll count myself lucky!" The door slammed and the sound of Hayfield's angry footsteps echoed down the hall outside.

Jeremy and Alex looked accusingly at each other but a tactful cough brought their heads back forward. Principal Robert Flores studied the two young men from where he sat behind the desk. In his early fifties, Flores was well versed in all things TerraGen. He played at being a politician and knew the advantages to keeping Lewisville's number one source of revenue happy. Jeremy didn't trust the good Principal one bit.

Flores' right hand absently patted an Express Mail package on his desk. He exhaled in a petulant sigh, "Coach Hayfield is a lot more generous than I would be. In my book fighting would've landed you both a one-week suspension." Flores turned his eyes toward Jeremy, "And you, Mr. Austin, am I supposed to notify the Juvenile Court of this? They might lock you away for good."

Jeremy stopped breathing as a chill dripped down his spine.

Flores glanced briefly at Alex, then returned his gaze to Jeremy. The intensity of the principal's gaze caused Jeremy to shift nervously on his feet. Flores blinked, "There's a school bus waiting in the parking lot. I want you both on it—"

"Bus? What gives?" Alex's question stank of impertinence. His father was president of TerraGen and Alexander Leach, Jr. knew he had a certain amount of power over Flores.

"Uncertainty can create stress."

"Stress?" Jeremy asked, completely confused.

"And left unresolved, stress can lead to punches being thrown under the gym bleachers. You TerraGen kids have a lot of questions. Well, the company has decided to give you some answers. So you, Mr. Austin," Flores looked at Jeremy and then turned to Alex, "and you, Mr. Leach, *Junior*... will be going on a field trip."

"We have a game tonight—" Alex began but Flores cut him off.

"You MIGHT have a game, and that's IF you get on the bus and stop running your mouth! Now leave!" The principal's face was red with anger, and Alex beat a hasty retreat out the door. Jeremy started to leave, but the principal's voice stopped him.

"Austin!" Flores' voice echoed in the room.

Jeremy looked backward, the fear of punishment foremost in his mind. But Flores was holding out the Express Mail package.

"This arrived for you," said Flores.

"Me?" Jeremy took the package. Upon looking at the label, he recognized his brother's handwriting. "That's strange. Why would Erik send me a package at school?"

"My thoughts exactly," said Flores. Jeremy once again found the principal looking at him with an intensity that made him nervous. Flores suddenly held out a pair of scissors, "Best open it here."

The package felt light in Jeremy's hands. He turned it over, aware of the principal's fixation on the package, his brain fighting for words to buy time. "It's really well sealed, sir," Jeremy ventured.

"The scissors?" Flores said pointedly, moving forward.

"Later, I think," Jeremy stammered, "after the field trip. But thanks anyway." Jeremy rushed out the door and was down the hall in a flash.

Flores stood in the doorway, his eyes still on the

Express Mail package under Jeremy's arm. He closed the door and went back to his desk, picking up his phone and dialing. The sound of a distant *buzz* came from the phone…and then a *click*.

"Flores," he said then listened. "I've done my part and now they're your problem."

He hung up the phone.

Chapter Two

The Diary

J EREMY STEPPED ONTO THE BUS and was surprised to see
not only Alex, but the rest of the TerraGen Kids—
all *five* of them.

"The gang's all here," said Leo as Jeremy took a seat
at the front of the bus. Leo sat in the middle, and a good
distance from the rear seats where Alex, always trying to be
cool, lounged pompously, trying to look bored. Leo sported a
bruised cheek but his self-confidence was unquenched. The
squat boy leaned forward and whispered, "Remember...
space travel."

"The only space I know of is between your ears—"

"Cute. Even for a Neanderthal jock like yourself."

Jeremy forced a smile. "If you wanna see space travel— watch a movie." *The kid's delusional for someone with his IQ.*

The school bus rumbled out of the school parking lot and soon they were heading through the heart of Lewisville. Trees lined the street on both sides. They motored past an elderly couple walking their dog, the bus kicking up leaves.

"Hey, Jeremy," waved a raven-haired girl three seats back—the same raven-haired girl from the gym. Jeremy suddenly realized it was Marissa Torres who had provided the interference that allowed him to get past Alex's goons. Only 16 years old but wise beyond her years, Marissa's dark lipstick and "indie girl" look disguised the no-nonsense debate team captain who took special pleasure in making intellectual mincemeat of her opponents. No girl was more feared in school, and heaven help the wayward cheerleader who mouthed off to her.

"Thanks for the help...you know, in the gym," he said.

"You were outgunned and outmatched. Someone had to step in!" She smiled before looking back at Alex and sticking out her tongue.

"What?" Alex sneered back at her. He slouched in his seat and tried to look disinterested.

"Can I get you anything for the trip, Mr. Football? Some coke to go with that Jack Daniels?"

"Shut it, Hag-wort reject—"

"How 'bout some nuts to replace those you lost at birth?"

"How 'bout I show Principal Flores where you hide your crack pipe—"

"I'm drug free and a vegan," Marissa spat back.

"Drug free but not a vegan. I know two guys who've visited your secret place—"

She let out a burst of laughter, "Vegan AND a *virgin*, STD for brains!" Then Marissa seemed to remember the presence of Jeremy. A wash of red flooded her face and she turned in her seat and stared out the window. Jeremy had always known that Marissa secretly had a crush on him. Her dark lipstick and black eye shadow might impress the grunge crowd or fellow vampires, but if Jeremy were really honest with himself, it scared him.

Behind Marissa sat an 18-year-old Asian girl with eyes glued to the data pad in her lap. Dressed smartly in the latest designer wear, Selene Choi had only one career aspiration: to be a "professional buyer." Whether that meant working for a wealthy widower, an advertising agency, or using her future husband's credit card, she didn't care—Macy's, Bloomingdales, Amazon—those destinations occupied Selene's attention. Jeremy guessed she was currently shopping online.

The final member of the TerraGen Kids sat slumped in his chair, knees propped up on the seat in front of him, staring out the window. Dark skinned like his father, an immigrant from Tamil, India, 18 year old Sudarshan Prasenjit 'Patrick' Korrapati was the smartest of the group. Tall and thin with the haggard look of a teenager spending all-nighters hacking into forbidden computer networks, Patrick was a brainiac with an IQ a hundred points higher than Jeremy's. Two months in juvenile detention had made Patrick even more anti-social and aloof—they'd spoken only a handful of times since the disaster at TerraGen. Patrick seemed to sense Jeremy's attention and a flicked a bride glance in Jeremy's direction. He raised an eyebrow then returned to staring out the window, safely ignoring the other students, his eyes absorbed with the passing trees as they headed through town.

Lewisville was a contrast of two different worlds, the old and new: buildings of brick and mortar built fifty years earlier sat next to glass-walled, steel-framed monstrosities reflecting the prosperity of the past few years. A medium-sized passenger jet flew overhead on its approach to Lewisville Regional Airport. Lewisville had been a forgotten blip on a map until the arrival of TerraGen Universal Corporation transformed it into one of the most powerful technological destinations on planet Earth. The influx of money could be seen as the bus made its way through the town's suburbs toward the company's industrial complex to the south.

The bus bounced over a pothole and the package almost slipped out of Jeremy's hands. His fingers gripped the square box and he wondered why Erik would've overnighted a package when mailing to the house would've been a lot simpler. Erik was 30 years old, an accomplished geneticist in his own right, and a high-ranking research director at TerraGen. But Erik Austin was more like a distant cousin— Jeremy's older brother was always away at university or interning abroad.

"What'dya get?" Leo craned his neck to see what was in Jeremy's lap.

"A book I ordered," Jeremy lied.

"You? A book?" laughed Marissa.

Okay, so I'm more of a jock than nuclear scientist—Erik had inherited more than his fair share of their father's DNA and Jeremy must've gotten his from…*Mom*. It had been so long since he had thought of his mother. She had died giving birth to him. He had grown up looking at photos and watching vacation videos featuring Erik, the dutiful son, and the smiling faces of mother and father. The memories awakened old pangs of jealousy he felt toward his older brother.

Why send me a package at all?

Jeremy glanced around. Finally, no one was paying attention to him. He feigned disinterest while his hands went to work on the package. Erik must've used an entire roll of tape because it took Jeremy a good ten minutes to get it open. With a cautious glance around the bus he slowly reached into the package and pulled out a black, leather-bound diary.

"That's an old book." Leo was suddenly standing on his chair and peeking over Jeremy's shoulder.

Jeremy hastily shoved the diary back into the package. "Autobiography. Some old football player my brother's crazy about. I guess Erik's making an effort to *bond*."

Leo shrugged. "Figures."

Jeremy's hand went back inside the package and his fingers found a folded piece of paper that must've been pressed under the diary. He opened it and again recognized Erik's handwriting:

> *Jeremy,*
> *Father has disappeared. Before leaving he asked me to give you this diary but the company has me locked up tight and I haven't been able to leave the campus.*
>   *Keep this in a safe place!*
> *Thirty years of our father's research is in this diary and let me tell you, a lot of people would like to get their hands on it. It's the key to our father's work and it will determine which group will own Genesis.*
> *Father is in trouble and he has many enemies… even inside TerraGen.*
>
> *-- Erik*

The number of patents filed by Dr. Victor Austin was ridiculous, and many scientists were jealous—Jeremy had seen how much his father had aged over the past few years from the infighting within his own company. *Enemies, though? That's something more than just envy,* Jeremy thought.

"Austin! Your dad's the reason we're in this mess!" Jeremy jerked up from reading the note. He twisted in his seat to find Alex leering at him from the rear of the bus. "All the secrets, a forbidden expedition, the U.S. military's involvement—"

Jeremy was going to respond but another voice cut in. "Oh, stuff it down your pants, Leach, Junior!" Patrick Korrapati stood up from his seat, pointing straight at Alex.

"Your father keeps more secrets than Dr. Tyrannus!" Patrick patted Leo on the shoulder as he walked toward the front of the bus. "No offense, Leo."

"Alleged…secrets," Leo responded without emotion.

"Nothing alleged about it," Patrick continued as he moved down the aisle. "Every scientist in TerraGen keeps a book of their best experiments—all top secret—even my own father." Patrick sat down in the seat opposite Jeremy.

"Don't forget who signs your dad's paycheck," hissed Alex weakly.

"Alex, everyone has a right to their own stupidity," Marissa shot out, "but you're making a joke of it."

Patrick chuckled and reclined casually in his seat. "That kid's a whack job!" he said, gesturing to Alex with his thumb.

Jeremy laughed. No one ever challenged Alexander Leach, Jr. except Patrick…and, well, Marissa. The older boy wasn't a physical threat to anyone, but when it came to battles of wit, Patrick could be devastating. His hair and clothes may have been sloppy, but his mind was sharp as a razor.

"But seriously, what IS going on?" Patrick's gaze was as intense as principal Flores, but not as creepy. "You don't think it's related to…uh, you know…last year?"

"Don't think so, but I'm in the dark like everyone else," Jeremy said as he quietly stuffed Erik's note back inside the package.

"Did Dr. Austin send you something?" Patrick asked, pointing to the Express Mail package.

Jeremy shrugged, hands covering the diary. "Some old sports book."

"My dad always finds a way to contact me," Patrick said.

"Same here."

"Our bad luck," Patrick leaned forward, smiling, "would be that our parents are stuck in the Congo somewhere and we have to go save them!" The smile left his face and he started to whisper, "Either way, I don't trust the company.

Something about TerraGen isn't adding up." He stood to his feet, wobbling in place as the bus made a sharp turn. Patrick gave Jeremy a knowing wink and then went back to his seat.

Suddenly, Jeremy became very conscious of the package and his father's diary. With a sideways glance, he took the black leather book out of the package and silently stuffed the diary into the waistband of his pants.

The school bus came to a stop at a security checkpoint. Jeremy looked out through the front window nervously—almost twelve months had passed since he'd last stepped foot on this campus. He stared at the ten-story executive office building that dominated the center of the compound. On the building's front face was the TerraGen logo that covered two stories: the symbol of a lunar eclipse, with a small sphere inside a larger sphere. Six high-tech laboratories spiraled off from the office building like the 'double helix' of a DNA strand—his father's lab was in one of these. A dozen satellite dishes rose out of the trees behind the laboratories.

Two things stood out to him: the rebuilt Imaginarium and the squad of armed security officers that patrolled the grounds. Where there used to be one guard at the front gate… *now there were four*—and the additional three stood outside the gatehouse with assault rifles slung over their shoulders. His mind raced—*was he to blame for the beefed up security?*

A hand tapped on his shoulder and he felt Leo's breath as the boy leaned close.

"Lockdown…see? TerraGen is totally on lockdown!"

CHAPTER THREE

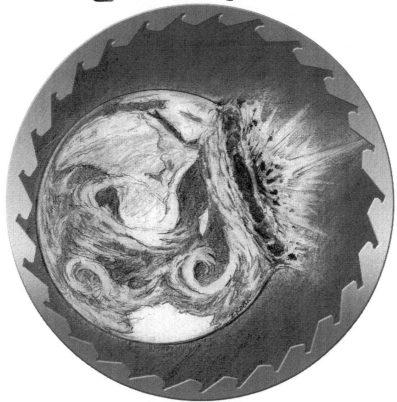

THE TOUR

THEY WERE GIVEN A TOUR of the TerraGen compound—a very boring tour led by Research Director, Dr. Rudolf Hicks, a pudgy, out-of-shape egghead in his early 50s who was always wheezing and gasping for breath. He had too much brain and not enough fashion sense to make himself look presentable. Jeremy couldn't take his eyes off the pile of dandruff resting on Hick's collar and the crumpled look of his suit. One thing was obvious: Hicks rarely left his office for anything other than to grab coffee and a few dozen donuts.

"There! That was exciting, yes?" Hicks beamed at the

six kids, and six dull-eyed faces stared back. Ten floors of office cubicles didn't excite the senses.

"Doctor Tyrannus' lab...I'd like to see *that!*" Alex said and gave Leo a smirk.

Jeremy tried to ignore the comment, his mind reliving the nightmare of the killer alien. *Never again*, he vowed inwardly.

"Oh, you know that's restricted, Mr. Leach," Hicks said reprovingly, and then turned to Leo for support. "Right, Leo? When have you ever been allowed in your father's lab?"

"Never," Leo replied, and the bitterness in his voice spoke volumes.

Patrick glanced sideways at Jeremy—both exchange wide-eyed looks of guilt—but then a smile touched the corner of Patrick's mouth. Jeremy laughed.

"Exactly. The very thought!" Hicks huffed in mock outrage. He cast a glance in Jeremy and Patrick's direction, "Of course, there have been rumors..."

Smiles vanished and both returned sheepish gazes. Neither boy taking the bait, Hicks resumed his tour. They now found themselves outside the main office building, and following a sidewalk leading to the nearest research laboratory.

"This will be a lot of fun!" Hicks exclaimed and led them inside.

Cool air washed over Jeremy's face as his eyes adjusted to the building's interior. Letters made of polished steel hung over the lobby proclaiming: *TerraGen Geophysics*. Floor-to-ceiling murals and sculptures depicted various stages of planetary development, details of the earth's core, volcanoes and earthquakes, and vintage geophysics instruments were also on display.

"I thought we created medicine?" Jeremy asked.

"Oh, my, my..." Hick's eyes twinkled, "we're so much more than that!"

What followed was a succession of high-tech, sterile

laboratories, a massive greenhouse two football fields in length, and more cold storage vaults than Jeremy could ever remember.

But everywhere they went, there was the constant presence of armed security guards.

Next was the newly rebuilt *TerraGen Imaginarium*— both Jeremy and Patrick went pale and shared a look of dread. *At least it looks safer in daylight,* Jeremy mused. The lobby was redesigned, but still like an amusement park entrance. Still, Jeremy couldn't shake the memories: running for his life… the battle in the rocktrawler…the fire. The Imaginarium was still the domain of Dr. Sudarshan Korrapati, and it took the collective breaths away from the other TerraGen kids. They stared up at a massive machine three stories high that Hicks called the *TerraGen Terraformer*.

"It creates massive amounts of oxygen…VERY high tech! We're going to put one on the moon, just you wait!" said Hicks.

Ten minutes into the tour, Patrick had begun a running dialogue with Dr. Hicks that was at first, innocent. Jeremy shook his head—Patrick loved to sniff out BS. And now, walking through his father's workplace and the tour script from Hicks remaining neutral and sanitized, Patrick's questions become more pointed. "Terraformer? Is the company planning on taking over Mars?"

Hicks laughed.. "Mars? There are a million planets in the universe, why would we settle on Mars?"

"Proximity. Mankind still hasn't solved interstellar travel."

"There's always more than one way to skin a rabbit," Hicks retorted.

"Rabbit? Yuck! Don't make me gag!" said Selene. The older girl rarely spoke up but she reacted to the strangest things.

"Terraformers, geological experiments, pharmaceuticals…" Patrick persisted. "I don't get the connection,

Dr. Hicks. My father's worked here for twenty years and I still don't understand—"

"Understand what?" Hicks was genuinely befuddled.

"The... the *why*."

"Ah... that," Hicks sighed. And suddenly his face had changed from TerraGen scientist to benevolent father, and he gave Patrick a knowing smile. "You've already pinpointed the essence of where TerraGen has been headed for two decades: three groundbreaking discoveries..."

Hicks paused and led them out of the huge Imaginarium and into a dark, cavernous tunnel where vehicles of all types were parked: jeeps, transport trucks, huge digging machines and forklifts. Long strips of glowing light lined each side of the tunnel. The smell of gasoline and rubber tires filled Jeremy's nostrils. Most of TerraGen's sprawling campus had remained a mystery to Jeremy and he longed to explore every square foot.

"If you only knew what your parents were really up to..." Hicks trailed off and continued at a quick pace, and the kids hustled to catch up with the doctor. Footsteps echoed against the concrete walls.

"Three discoveries?" Patrick prodded.

Hicks maintained his quick pace, but his face was suddenly serious. "Yes, yes. Three... each distinct and important technologies in their own right, yet... each related to the other." He stopped in his tracks, and the kids almost ran into him. He then approached Selene Choi, who looked pale in the tunnel's light. "TerraSynth: developed by two sisters... Dr. Midori Choi—"

"Mom?" Selene blinked in surprise.

"Yes, and working with your aunt, Dr. Hitomi Zheng."

Hicks then stood in front of Patrick.

"Next, GeoSynth...know all about it," Patrick deadpanned.

"Of course you would," Dr. Hicks said with a forced smile. "GeoSynth, developed by Dr. Sudarshan Korrapati."

Hicks then turned and stood in front of Leo and Marissa. "And finally, BioSynth: developed by Dr. Kaiser Tyrannus and Dr. Geraldo Torres. Three discoveries that will change the course of human history."

"What about my father?" Jeremy exclaimed. He felt slighted. Dr. Victor Austin was world renowned in the field of genetics as well as geophysics!

Hicks chuckled and patted Jeremy on the shoulder. "Where do you think these great scientist got all their research from? Who do think *created* the synth process? Every breakthrough at TerraGen has filtered down from the greatest scientist we'll ever know: your father."

"Don't get a big head," said Alex.

Jeremy glowed on the inside and couldn't suppress the smile on his lips as Hicks slapped him roughly on the back. The doctor started walking at a swift pace again and the kids had to rush to catch up.

T HEY WAITED AT A SECURITY CHECKPOINT where two armed guards stood in front of a large metal door two stories in height. Hicks tapped his shoe and checked his watch nervously. Boom. *Whoosh. Clack.* Jeremy looked up expectantly as the metal door started to open. He was amazed at the thickness of the door—like that of the entrance to a bank vault—and the silent precision with which it opened.

Clackity—clackity—clackity.

Two figures walked out of the doorway's shadow. The first was a fierce-looking woman in her late forties, wearing a business suit and carrying a sense of authority. She looked surprised as she saw the kids. She shot Hicks and angry look.

"Kids, Ms. Barbara Yossarian, Vice President of the company," introduced Hicks quickly. Behind Yossarian was a very imposing, thick-chested, African-American, ex-military looking man in a security uniform that Jeremy recognized as Benton Keene. It was Benton Keene who'd found them one year ago amidst the burning hulk of the Imaginarium. The jaws-of-life had to be used to open the melted exterior of the rocktrawler. Inside, Benton Keene had found two high school boys—safe but shaken. Fierce and warlike with rippling muscles, Keene stabbed a disdainful look at both he and Patrick—like a prison warden greeting two escapees. Jeremy looked behind Keene and saw another large tunnel that seemed to stretch on for miles, lit only by the strips of glowing light.

The unhappy expression on Yossarian's face didn't change as she continued to glare at Hicks. "Didn't you get the memo?"

"Memo?"

"The tour was cancelled," she said.

"Cancelled?" Hicks confusion was genuine. "Then why send a bus to their high school?"

"*Here* is not the place to discuss recent events," she said. The expression on her face changed to one of compassion as she looked at each of the kids. "My apologies."

"Is there something I should know—?" Hicks began, but Yossarian interrupted him. Her head swiveled to face him with irritation.

"Yes. It was in the memo." She looked back to the kids and her face softened again. "Let's finish the tour in the conference room. Everything will be explained there."

A nearby door opened and a harried, breathless scientist in a lab coat rushed out and approached Yossarian. He had sweat pouring down his face. "Sorry for my tardiness, Barbara. Have I missed anything?"

Annoyance flashed across her face again. "You didn't get the memo either?!"

"I'm here to take them into, you know, the—" the scientist started with obvious fear.

"Enough with the tour!" Jeremy blurted out. "Where *are* our parents?"

"And please," Marissa said, her voice cracking with belligerence, "expeditions to Bolivia, or southeast Asia? That's a *load of crock* so don't waste your time."

"I thought they went on a vacation..." Selene added.

Yossarian was clearly troubled, and Jeremy could see she was thinking hard about her response. She gestured at the scientist. "This is Dr. Nielssen, one of our astrophysicists. When the tour is *rescheduled,*" she looked pointedly at Hicks, then Nielssen, "Dr. Nielssen will show you the single, greatest discovery in TerraGen's history. But now, it's the conference room for you kids."

And with that, the vice president turned and walked away.

D R. HICKS, STILL STUNNED over the sudden change in the tour, watched Benton Keene lead the kids back toward the Imaginarium. Hicks glanced at the visibly shaken Dr. Nielssen and whispered, "What is this memo she's talking about?"

"Beats me," said Nielssen. "Such a pity. The Portal is finally showing activity..."

CHAPTER FOUR

TERRAGEN'S LITTLE SECRET

"**I** DON'T BELIEVE IT!" Jeremy heard the words echo in the room. "I don't believe it!" What he didn't realize at first was that *he* was the one shouting them.

"It's a harsh reality...I'm sorry," said Barbara Yossarian without emotion.

But Jeremy wasn't looking at the vice president— his eyes were on the distinguished man in his mid-sixties, dressed in a very expensive suit and sporting a head shock full of white hair: Alexander Leach, Sr., President of TerraGen Universal.

They were seated around a large, polished conference table and the mood was grim. Marissa sat, stunned, with tears streaming down her cheeks. Selene was slumped over the table, face buried in her arms, her shoulders shaking from deep sobs. Leo sat quietly, looking out the expansive window in a daze. Even Patrick was speechless, but his eyes showed the deepness of the loss. And for once, Alex Leach, Jr. wasn't boasting or making snide comments. The football quarterback sat next to his father with glazed eyes, trying not to look at the others.

"I won't believe it!" hissed Jeremy angrily.

"The scientific breakthroughs your parents performed at this company will change the course of human history," said Alexander Leach. "They will be missed."

"My father never mentioned going to an island—"

"It was top secret, he wouldn't have," Alexander Leach responded evenly.

"Top secret... secret from what?!" Jeremy's face was red with fury.

"Corporations, hackers, the governments of Russia, China, India... even the United States," said Alexander Leach. "Technology doesn't belong to everyone, but to those who discover it first. When it comes to billions in profits, the word *fair* doesn't exist!"

"So you bought an island?" asked Marissa through her tears.

Both Leach and Yossarian nodded their heads.

"So tell me," this came from Patrick whose voice rasped painfully, "how does an ENTIRE expedition of the world's best scientists end up DEAD?!"

"More than just a few scientists are...gone." This time the voice was Benton Keene's. The massively built security man stepped over from behind Yossarian. "There were engineers, carpenters, masons, miners, doctors, nurses, technicians, security personnel... *five hundred people lost!*"

"But how?" Patrick persisted.

Alexander Leach cleared his throat. "Here in Lewisville, our campus is one of the most advanced in the world—twenty years of development—with enough power to light up a major city."

"Nuclear?" questioned Patrick.

"Sanctioned by the U.S. government," broke in Yossarian.

"We found an island in the south Pacific and hoped to recreate *this* campus," Alexander Leach continued. "The expedition to Taraga Island was the completion of eight years of planning. The island is very remote and can only be reached by ship."

"You said the word *lost*," said Patrick, eyes riveted on Benton Keene. "So they might be alive somewhere—"

"I misspoke," returned Keene quickly. "My apologies." Keene stepped backward as if in retreat.

Alexander Leach shifted in his chair. "There was a nuclear meltdown yesterday." He looked at each of the TerraGen kids in turn. "Everyone on the island perished."

The kids took the news in silence.

"The only survivors were out at sea on one of our ships," said Alexander Leach. "A hazmat team has already landed on the island and confirmed the fatalities...and that includes each of your parents."

"I want to see her!" burst out Selene.

"Sorry. The radiation would kill you," Keene interjected.

"Because of the amount of radioactivity, all bodies will be cremated on the island," Alexander Leach said formally, as if addressing the Board of Directors. "The facility itself will be off-limits to...well, to mankind for the next one hundred years."

"Was it sabotage?" asked Leo in a quiet voice.

"Impossible to tell. Not a living soul escaped from Taraga,"Alexander Leach said, and rose to his feet. "We're providing grief counselors. Barbara was kind enough to contact—"

"Kind?" Patrick jumped up from his chair. "You killed *my* dad—and *his* dad—," he pointed at each of the others in turn, "and *his* dad—and *her* dad—and *her* mom! I could do without a little of your kindness!" Patrick stormed out of the conference room.

Alexander Leach opened his hands in surrender. None of the others looked up from the table... each of them too absorbed by grief.

Jeremy looked up at TerraGen's President, "Excuse me, sir, but... *where* is my brother?"

D<small>R. R</small>OBERT N<small>IELSSEN RODE</small> a golf cart down the long tunnel, lights flashing by intermittently. His nose twitched in irritation. He always hated the cold, dank smell of the tunnel. The high-pitched electronic sound of the cart's motor echoed in the semi-darkness behind him. His mind replayed the rebuke by Yossarian. She had been so angry, yet, almost frightened. *Strange.* They were so close to salvaging the grand expedition, but it seemed they were panicking too early—throwing in the towel while the expedition's outcome wasn't even close to being decided.

Very strange.

Nielssen slowed the golf cart as he approached Checkpoint Alpha. Another massive steel door blocked his way, and a bank of security cameras swiveled as they trained on the cart.

"Dr. Nielssen...you're late," said a voice from a hidden speaker.

"Don't you start," muttered Nielssen.

A low rumble sounded in the tunnel as the door started to swing open. Nielssen pressed the accelerator and the cart motored through the gap and into a large elevator. He tapped his foot impatiently as the elevator began its descent, three hundred feet below ground, until a *thump* sounded and the elevator doors opened.

"Daddy's home," he said, and pressed the cart's accelerator. He entered the cavernous Portal bay, which was so huge that it always reminded him of an airport hangar. Gray walls and ceiling masked the granite rock that had been excavated over a decade ago. The Portal's Control Center rose three stories in height from the floor to the cavern's ceiling, with rows of mirrored, bullet proof windows looking down upon the Portal bay's floor where Nielssen parked his golf cart next to a dozen others. To the side of the Control Center was a huge wall with a jagged line traveling vertically down its middle—this "wall" was actually a large hangar door with huge interlocking teeth.

Nielssen jumped out of the cart and hurried toward a small door and Checkpoint Beta where a security camera tracked his progress. The sleek metal door whisked open, revealing three heavily armed security officers.

"Let's be quick about this," said the astro-physicist as he held up his TerraGen badge.

"Out partying all night?" queried one guard with a smile.

"Very funny. You know we're in lockdown," said Nielssen. Still stressed by Yossarian's anger, he blew by the security officers, muttering under his breath. For the last month he'd been sequestered on the TerraGen campus and forced to live in the dorms—four weeks of separation from his wife and daughter, paying bills, watching football… and his nerves were seriously frayed.

This had better be worth it, he thought as he approached the next metal door. *They were so close and no matter what the problems were, they shouldn't give up now.*

J EREMY SAT ACROSS THE CONFERENCE table from Alexander Leach, Sr. The door was closed and the two of them were left alone in uncomfortable silence. Jeremy's heart still beat rapidly, but the realization of his father's death was still something remote, shut off from his emotions. There had always been a separation between them both—Jeremy always felt inadequate in his father's presence—the great Dr. Victor Austin, world-renowned genetics scientist and physicist. Not since Einstein had one man changed how the world viewed science in such a profound way.

Gone. Dead.

Having an older brother who was just as much a science celebrity didn't help Jeremy's self-confidence any better. Dr. Erik Austin had received every one of their dad's genetic predispositions for scientific genius. Erik's research had been published in all the top science journals and TerraGen had accorded him many of the same security privileges as their father.

"You sent him to China?" Jeremy asked.

"He's directing the hazmat team," said Alexander Leach with a thread of compassion in his voice. "Erik is a valued member of TerraGen and we needed his assessment of the true extent of the damage."

"But the radioactivity—"

"Radiation suits, and only the best—"

"Why can't I speak to him?"

"He, like everyone else in the company, is under communication silence until we find out what really happened," said Alexander Leach. "Once we have our answers, I assure you, Erik will be contacting you first thing."

"But *when* will that be?" said Jeremy, rising to his feet.

Alexander Leach stood up and gave Jeremy a look of pity. "First—thing." And with that, Alexander Leach opened the conference room door and walked out. Jeremy started toward the door, but the hulking figure of Benton Keene suddenly filled the doorway.

"One last item," said Keene. "It seems your father's research diary has come up missing. Before he left for China, your brother asked me to help track it down."

"A diary?" Jeremy ventured innocently.

"About yay big," Keene held his hands out in about the same width as the diary in Jeremy's waistband, "and bound in black leather. Erik was very distraught over it."

Heat rushed into Jeremy's face, and it took every ounce of self-control to ignore the diary hidden beneath his clothes. "Don't think I've ever seen it. My father rarely allowed me into his lab."

"But your house—"

"I'll certainly check, mister…uh…."

"Keene, Director of Security. You don't remember me from the events of a year ago, Mr. Austin?" asked Keene. Jeremy looked defiantly away. Keene's eyes bore holes into Jeremy, then he changed the subject. "Your father didn't have a home office?"

"Years ago, but it doesn't look like an office now."

"How it looks is of no matter," Keene said, flashing white teeth in a broad smile. "The company requests an opportunity to do a search."

"It's no longer an office—as you would know an office, sir—"

"Five minutes—"

"It's not an office! My father allowed me to transform it…so I turned it into a man cave. You know, video games and all," lied Jeremy. *Why* he was lying Jeremy couldn't fathom, but he knew Erik had wanted him to have the diary. Plus, Keene was studying him like a python studies a mouse. Erik warned that elements within TerraGen couldn't be trusted. Jeremy suspected this man might have an agenda that was drastically opposite that of Dr. Victor Austin.

"I promised your brother," Keene added with a hint of impatience.

Promised? What a crock! "There're nothing left of my father's work in the house," Jeremy said smoothly. "Why don't you search his office here?"

"It's secured behind his personal, encrypted code,"

Keene stated flatly, no longer smiling. "But you would know that."

Jeremy shrugged, "Sorry. If I stumble across it I'll let you know first thing." Jeremy didn't trust the Security Director. He moved past Keene, conscious of the diary rubbing against his belly. He and Erik had never been really close, but his older brother had always drummed home one important lesson into Jeremy's brain:

Always trust your gut.

CHAPTER FIVE

AN UNWANTED VISITOR

R. ROBERT NIELSSEN STOOD in the operations room overlooking TerraGen's single greatest discovery in its twenty-year history—perhaps the single greatest discovery in human history. The operations room was on the third floor of the Control Center and its vast windows allowed the scientists to observe the Portal's inner chamber below—even though this inner chamber showed only a fraction of the size of the Portal device. TerraGen spent five years and employed over two hundred workers to excavate an underground cavern the size of a small town. Carved out in the shape of a sphere, the outer chamber was perfectly round and a half-mile in diameter. At the exact center of the outer chamber was another sphere—the inner chamber.

"When was the last ping?" Nielssen asked a nearby technician. In his late twenties, the technician was typical of TerraGen's hiring: get them young and locked into a long-term contract and then put the best technology the world can offer at their fingertips.

"Just the one," the technician said.

"Strange."

Nielssen studied the center of the chamber where a metal platform, sixty feet in length and seemingly suspended in space, extended through the middle of the inner sphere from end to end—the *embarkation platform*.

"I think we should inform the sixth floor," said the technician.

The impertinent suck up. "I tried that already," said Nielssen. "They have more pressing matters than a random ping—"

"It came from the other place."

"Are you one hundred percent *sure* of that?" Nielssen demanded.

"Well..."

"Thought so. We've had computer glitches before."

"Not like this!"

"Is it worth your job?" Nielssen was testing him, knowing the answer. "I'll call the sixth floor right now—"

"Forget it!" the technician hissed. He turned quickly on his heels and walked away.

Nielssen was left to his thoughts, nervously biting his lip and turning his eyes to the end of the embarkation platform where a silver, metallic ring encircled the metal walkway. Six feet thick, sixty feet in diameter and made out of a high-tech alloy that was one of TerraGen's best-kept secrets, the giant ring was where all the magic happened.

But, not now.

Now it sat in semi-darkness like a theme park ride in the offseason.

Nielssen cursed under his breath and turned away. *Four weeks!* The longer the Portal remained dark the more likely he was out of a job. He suddenly desired a cup of coffee and began walking toward the break room.

Below, the darkness that filled the center of the Portal ring suddenly shimmered with silver light.

A loud *PING* reverberated throughout the Control Center. In the hallway, the sound stopped Nielssen mid-step. He pivoted and raced back to the operations room.

A red light flashed overhead as Nielssen crossed to one of the windows. His hands slammed into the thick glass, his eyes looking quickly toward the Portal ring.

Nothing.

But there had to be!

And then he saw it. Standing in the darkness at the center of the Portal ring was some…*thing*. It was over seven feet in height and dressed in dark, leathery armor, but… it definitely wasn't human.

Waaaah! Waaaah! Alarms sounded throughout the facility, alarms that signaled activity within the Portal. They were meant to alert technicians of the return of expedition members. But none of the corporate manuals would've prepared the technicians for this… *being*… a creature that was anything *but* human. It looked more like something out of a horror movie.

Doors opened and four security personnel armed with assault weapons stormed onto the embarkation platform. A sharp bladed weapon appeared in the alien's hand, and then it *vanished*.

Nielssen blinked his eyes.

Cries of pain sounded from the security guards, and Nielssen realized the alien was among them. The creature hadn't vanished, but moved *so fast* that in the fraction of a second one guard was lying dead and a second was being knifed by the alien's blade. The two remaining guards panicked and began shooting wildly, raking fire back and forth.

But the creature was too quick.

The third security guard crumpled under the alien's blade, and the fourth tried to make it back inside the Control Center. The alien covered the thirty feet—*like a blur*—and to Nielssen's dismay, he watched the creature as it caught the remaining guard inside the doorway. Both disappeared from view and Nielssen slowly exhaled. He had held his breath the entire... *what was it, six seconds?*

There was a final scream, then... silence.

It's inside the Control Center, he realized and an icy shiver ran down Nielssen's back. His eyes opened wide as he suddenly came to a realization: there was only one-way back to the surface.

He was trapped.

A scream sounded below—*probably one of the Portal techs,* he thought. He fought down panic, knowing he had to move. Another scream. The agony in the voice let the scientist know that the alien was enjoying its work. Sweat trickled down his forehead. Silence. And then he had it!

The access stairway—rarely used and built for the construction workers—led downward into the Portal bay where his golf cart was parked. *If he could just get around—*

Nielssen started forward, willing his frightened legs to move.

PING—

Nielssen froze. *Another alien?*

Waaaah! Waaaah! The Portal alarm moved him into action and Nielssen ran into the hallway. He stopped at the staircase leading to the lower second floor. The sound of heavy footsteps sounded below, muffled by stealth—and then a shadow appeared at the base of the stairs. *This creature is huge!* Nielssen thought absently. One part of his brain appreciated the *perfectness* of the creature and its ability to kill.

Nielssen rushed past the staircase, his flesh pale with fear. He turned into a second corridor and spied the door leading to the access stairway.

ILVER MIST VANISHED WITHIN the middle of the Portal ring. Two men stood on the embarkation platform surveying the bloody carnage. "Ruud-Goth is an artist when it comes to killing," said the older, silver-haired man with an authority that pegged him as the obvious leader of the two.

"He serves our purpose," the second man said, his tall, bulky frame squatting to retrieve a sub-machine gun from one of the corpses.

They stepped past the torn bodies and approached the Control Center's security door. The younger man pulled out an aged, plastic card and swiped it through the card reader. Red lights turned green, and there was a loud *buzz*. They smiled at each other and walked through the doorway.

QUATTING AT THE BASE of the access stairs, Nielssen stared into the Portal bay through a door that was slightly ajar. Nothing moved. The elevator leading to Checkpoint Alpha was just fifty yards away—it was fifty yards that seemed like a mile. The cries had silenced and the only sound was his own breathing. He wanted to run for the elevator but... that *thing* was ten times faster than him!

A whisper sounded behind him and he recognized the sound of leather on concrete. He looked back, and his heart stopped—the creature was at the top of the stairs, blade in hand. He detected a faint smile on the creature's face. A chill went down his spine as he realized the creature was stalking him.

The alien leapt.

Nielssen was out the door and he just managed to slam

it shut before a loud *THUD* shook the door's frame and bent it outward. Panic filled him and he turned wildly, bumping into one golf cart and then another as he ran for the elevator. Terror had filled his chest, his heart beating loudly.

A loud *THUD* sounded again.

Nielssen sprinted the remaining twenty yards and quickly pressed the elevator button. The loud whir of motors sounded, and Neilssen cursed his luck... *the elevator was at the upper level.* He heard the squealing of metal. He turned around.

The door to the access stairway had been wrenched ajar. In the hole of blackness that remained stood the alien. Nielssen dropped to the floor, his view of the creature blocked by the carts. *Had it seen him?* The whir of the elevator continued. It was taking an eternity. One of the golf carts rocked back and forth just thirty yards away. Nielssen slowed his breathing.

PING. The sound registered but—

Yes! The elevator! Nielssen turned to see the elevator doors slide open, and he quickly stood up and raced toward—

Suddenly he felt a sharp pain in his lower back, and then it moved upward. Then he caught the stench of foul air that was unusually warm.

Alien breath.

HE TWO MEN WALKED ACROSS the Portal bay to the elevator where the alien was feasting on the body of the dead scientist. *Ruud-Goth was allowed a treat.* The alien turned and looked up as the two men approached. Blood dripped down from the creature's massive jaws.

But Ruud-Goth's usefulness was over.

The silver-haired man blew a small whistle and the alien suddenly doubled over in pain. The second man calmly raised his assault rifle, aimed for the area at the back of Ruud-Goth's head... and pulled the trigger.

AN HOUR HAD PASSED since the carnage had begun, Benton Keene calculated. He stood in the Portal bay as technicians wrapped up what was left of Dr. Robert Nielssen, astrophysicist and loving husband and father. A buzz of activity from the Control Center meant the technicians were bringing the rest of the bodies out—four security guards and eight Portal technicians, all butchered by this... *creature*.

Directives from the sixth floor—Alexander Leach and Barbara Yossarian—said the alien was to be preserved at all costs. *Experiments and research. Dissection.* It lay in front of the elevator door in a congealed pool of its own blood.

Fine. But the Head of Security for TerraGen had other ideas. Keene reached into his coat pocket and pulled out a very thin, high-tech camera. He turned his head one way and then another, making sure none of the technicians were looking in his direction. Swiftly he raised the camera and quickly snapped several pictures of the dead creature. He returned the camera to his pocket.

Perfect.

CHAPTER SIX

THE COMPETITION

HE SAT FACING THE NINETEEN SENATORS that made up the U.S. Senate Appropriations Subcommittee on Defense, and they were in a nasty mood.

"This is the *third time* this year that China has been caught buying secrets! Why don't we just sell them our technology and *make* something in the deal?" the senator from Massachusetts asked in voice bitterly sarcastic. "I feel like a used car salesman robbed of my commission..."

"We fund the research, and they simply wait to steal it," said the New Jersey senator who always liked to say the obvious.

"The leak must be coming from your department—" shouted Illinois.

His hand slammed down on the table in front of him, silencing the very people who were responsible for paying his salary. Robert Morton wasn't a patient man, but nor was he particularly athletic. His bony hand throbbed with pain. "I won't have you disparage my people," he said, staring down each senator in turn.

"Then *who* sold the Chinese our quantum network?" This came from Alabama.

"You've had my brief on MetaUniversal Genetics," Morton began. "A very sly and very crafty company, they've funneled millions through off-shore accounts—virtually untraceable—buying and selling technology, arms, drugs... you name it."

"Why do we allow them to exist?" pressed Alabama.

"Our country *still* has a Constitution—somewhat battered, maligned and attacked—but a Constitution nonetheless that prevents us from seizing companies without hard evidence."

"That hasn't stopped us before," said New Jersey.

"I'm glad this is a closed subcommittee," joked the senator from Massachusetts and several of the senators politely chuckled... but not many.

Morton cleared his throat. "For decades we've regulated the private tech companies almost to the point of extinction. I'm afraid we're reaping the whirlwind, ladies and gentlemen."

"The *what?*" asked New Jersey.

"We've forced the private companies like TerraGen and Pharma-Dynamics to go underground with their research." Again, Morton looked each senator in the eye. "They're looking to make profits, and research is costly."

"Oh, cry me a river," lamented the senator from New Jersey sarcastically.

"The biggest danger..." he said, emphasizing *danger*.

Now, Morton had their attention. "The biggest danger is that they *may* go to the Chinese or Russians with their most advanced technology simply because we've outlawed it."

"We can't just let them create biological weapons or clone an army!" protested Alabama.

"Not on their own! But if they were exclusive to the United States... then why shouldn't we give them a little creative freedom?" hinted Morton. His voice echoed in the room, and for once the senators were speechless. Morton was always accused of pushing boundaries too far, but he was also a politician—most of those Senators owed him gratitude for funneling pork projects to their states.

Job security *could* be bought.

THE SENATORS FILED OUT of the room as Morton hastily pushed papers into his briefcase. *He actually might be able to play nine holes after all—*
"Sir?"

Morton looked up to find his loyal lapdog, Pritchard Durant, kneeling at his elbow. Durant was your typical ambitious political assistant: highly energetic, and a master of every nuance of Washington protocol.

"He's outside... waiting," Durant whispered.

OUTSIDE THE CHAMBER, Morton avoided a news crew interviewing one of the senators and spied Lachlan Evans waiting in a stairwell at the end of the hallway. Morton put a hand on Durant's arm, "Stay here and keep the press—and all other curious eyeballs—looking in any direction but mine. Understood?"

"Not my first rodeo, sir" Durant retorted.

The arrogant twit. His young aide was getting a little too familiar. If Durant's father wasn't the owner of an arms manufacturing company, he would've jettisoned the ambitious aide months ago. He walked the few feet to where

Lachlan Evans waited with a smile, and Morton's tone was harsh and petulant. "No word, phone call or email for two weeks. I was concerned you'd gone off the reservation!"

Evans dropped the pretense of the smile. "I promised to never contact you unless I had something concrete."

"Let's not be too literal—"

"Especially when it's *this important*—"

"TerraGen?"

Evans nodded. He lowered his voice and leaned close to Morton. "As we suspected, our friends at TerraGen Universal are setting up a clandestine research facility outside the reach of the United States." He paused, then continued, "They sent out an expedition."

Morton swore and sweat seemed to break out on his forehead. "I've put my neck out for Mr. Alexander Leach and his company more times than I can count. Are we talking outright betrayal, or is there something else?"

Evans shrugged, "Betrayal, autonomy, scientific freedom… whatever the reason, they've invested millions and compiled a team of scientists, construction workers, and ex-military types. It's an expedition that, by my agent's calculations, numbered over five hundred."

"Five hundred? Expedition to where, Bolivia?" Morton looked around, fearing that his voice had carried down the hall.

"That's the million-dollar question: it appears their expedition has gone missing." Evans let the statement settle in Morton's brain before continuing. "They're in a heightened state of panic."

"Millions of dollars, five hundred people lost on an expedition, all for what? I hardly think they're trying to cure cancer!" said Morton.

"Bio weapons."

"Not that again!" Morton looked at Evans with disdain. "I've told you a thousand times, Dr. Victor Austin would never develop weapons—"

"Maybe they are still in the testing phase, but their next genetically engineered, bioweapon—*a super soldier*—just killed half a dozen of their employees," said Evans.

"A super soldier?"

"What would the black market pay for something like that?"

"That's all we need... a billion Chinese peasants genetically turned into some futuristic killing machines," said Morton.

"My agent is getting me additional—"

Morton stopped Evans mid-sentence with a strong grip on his arm. The Pentagon's expert in bioweapons tried his best to put as much authority into his voice as possible as he looked at Evans. "There is no room for mistakes, Lachlan. If you have to call in the army, I'll authorize it, just *get me* the information I need to bring TerraGen to its knees. If anyone deserves the next super soldier... it's *me!*"

"Understood." Evans nodded to Morton and disappeared down the staircase.

Morton snapped his fingers at Durant, who obediently rushed to his side. "Pritchard, get me everything we have on TerraGen's competitors."

"I can search online and have that in five minutes—" began Durant.

"Were you this sloppy at Yale?" Morton interrupted scathingly. "Dig deep—use one of our moles in the CIA if you have to—but make a list of all the companies who would benefit if TerraGen were to go belly up. I want to make sure that we are the only players in this game!"

T HE FLUORESCENT LIGHT ILLUMINATED the color photographs laid out on the CEO's desk. Each picture showed the alien—head, hands, feet, the sword-like blade—and each picture was worth a fortune. Benton Keene smiled and looked up at the faces of the three most powerful people who controlled MetaUniversal Genetics—M.U.G. for short. Keene was the scientific equivalent of a double agent— he worked as TerraGen's Head of Security, but in reality, he'd been on MUG.'s payroll since his honorable discharge from the U.S. Army as a member of the Special Forces.

"Was that thing ever human?" asked MUG's Chief Executive Officer who was studying the photo of the alien's face.

"Reminds me of my ex-mother-in-law," said MUG's legal adviser.

Keene smiled, not at the jest, but because he knew he had captured gold with those photographs. He distrusted the science community, hated their manipulation of the human body and rebelled against their air of superiority. But now he was in his own element: espionage.

MUG's majority investor—a southern, matronly woman in her late-sixties who looked sweet and innocent but was in actuality the most ruthless person in the office— she looked up from one of the photos with a frown, "Their genetics research is decades ahead of ours."

"We don't know if this life form actually was human… or some alien race they discovered on Genesis," said Keene.

MetaUniversal was TerraGen's biggest competitor, with a merciless desire to acquire all technology created on planet Earth. MetaUniversal had one advantage over TerraGen: they had research labs in southeast Asia, the Congo, and one in the mountains of Chili—all outside the reach of the U.S. government and the feeble shouts of the United Nations. TerraGen may have had the brightest minds on their payroll, but MUG's geneticists were the most devious—they were willing to take risks. Their experiments made the Nazis look like compassionate health care workers. For MetaUniversal, the ends always justified the means.

"Genesis?" the lawyer asked.

"Is this some kind of history lesson?" asked the CEO.

"This is about the future," said Keene. "Unofficially, we have black market laboratories in third-world countries—"

"Off the record, and I hope this isn't being recorded," said the lawyer, who was looking up at the ceiling where a security camera hung in prominent view.

"The future of what?" asked the matron lady.

"Scientific freedom." The room became suddenly quiet and Keene had their full attention. "While we're sending our scientists to mosquito infested sewers called third-world countries, TerraGen is operating with total freedom millions of light years away."

"Poppycock," the lawyer sneered.

Keene's finger tapped one of the photos of the alien. "These photos prove my point, ma'am," Keene said, looking straight at the matron. "What if TerraGen *owned* a planet? No government regulations, no human rights councils... everything created on the planet is property of the company." Keene looked at each of them in turn. "Cloning, the cure for cancer, harvesting organs for sale here on earth... the financial opportunities would be endless. And there would be nothing the U.S. government could do or say because the company—"

"Yes, owns the planet," said the CEO.

"Sounds like science fiction rubbish," chided the matron.

"Is this some kind of Hollywood stunt?" asked the lawyer as he tossed one of the alien photos across the table.

"What you're telling me is that the manpower, the machines, the technology necessary to take advantage—" began the matron.

"All—left—this—planet... *four weeks ago*," said Keene. Somewhere, a figurative pin dropped, and it was loud.

"To this... Genesis?"

"The official total was a team of over five hundred scientists and support personnel. I'm guessing is was three or four times that."

"Why?" she asked, her voice less skeptical.

"Because of the amount of equipment—*fifty electrical generators*—array after array of quantum computers and enough construction equipment and materials to build a town the size of Topeka. Not to mention the cows, pigs, horses, sheep… a veritable Noah's ark, and enough medical equipment—all top of the line—to refurbish Johns Hopkins many times over." Keene finished, out of breath.

"Excuse me," said the skeptical CEO, "but I don't live under a rock. There was no mention of space ships blasting off to outer space on any news program I watch."

"I won't bore you with all the technical details—we'd be here for a week—but I'll summarize: by using quantum computers, particle acceleration and a lot of scientific mumbo-jumbo, one of TerraGen's astrophysicists discovered he could create a wormhole—a wormhole to other galaxies. That was over ten years ago," Keene paused to let the information sink in. "But a wormhole to outer space is of no use unless you can direct it to a place you can actually travel to… like a planet."

"What'd they do?" inquired the matron, eyes now bright with excitement.

"They built a Portal."

"Like a doorway?" the matron asked.

"That would be a very crude description," Keene smiled. "The science is beyond my comprehension, but for simplicity's sake, what I'll say is that the Portal focuses the wormhole and allows the quantum computers to guide it, looking for habitable planets. It took a year for them to find the planet they were looking for."

The CEO laughed and shook his head. "Nothing was ever published—"

"Of course not! Why would they?" said Keene. Inwardly the military man despised the CEO, knowing him to be small-minded, arrogant ox. The CEO threw around wads of cash whenever he wanted to get his way. He hadn't the brains to be crafty.

"A Portal to a planet called *Genesis?*" asked the lawyer.

"Not the most creative of names but it's a reflection of the man who actually runs the company," said Keene. "He's a purist."

"Alexander Leach?"

"No... Leach is only a figurehead. The real power at TerraGen is Dr. Victor Austin," said Keene. "The technology they're taking to this planet is Austin's—"

"Technology?" asked the CEO, "What type?"

"DNA engineering, brain mapping, nano technology, terraforming... I mean, the man's a genius," said Keene, his admiration for Austin unmistakable.

"And he's beyond bribery," lamented the matron.

"Many have tried... unsuccessfully," said Keene with a nod. "But we might be able to get access to a work-around."

"A what?"

"A diary."

"Of his research?" asked the matron, her excitement renewed.

"Thirty years of research—all of it." Keene let the words settle in their minds. "And I think I know who has it..."

"Before there was order… chaos reigned.

Light begat light;

Darkness rose in the south

and the Shadow Lord was born."

SACRED KADIMAH SCROLLS – Chapter 1:14

CHAPTER SEVEN

BIG BROTHER

JEREMY SAT IN THE LIVING ROOM of the Austin family home. Set in a residential neighborhood south of downtown, the two-story house was built in an old, Victorian style, and for Jeremy it was now empty of life... a dead thing. His missed the late dinners with his father and the rare occasion when Erik would surprise them both by showing up with ice cream and a movie. Now, the fact that he would never hear his father's voice again, never get a pat on the back for good grades or for his exploits on the football field...

His eyes became fixed on a photo sitting on the

fireplace mantel: his dad embracing Jeremy in a tight bear hug. The tears started welling in his eyes, and Jeremy stood up, breathing deeply and trying to comprehend the enormity of his loss. *If only Erik were here. But he's heading toward the island in the south Pacific wearing a hazmat suit.*

Another photo: Erik receiving one of his many international awards for his genetic research. Jeremy studied his older brother's face, the natural good looks, the clear-eyed stare that seemed to penetrate your very soul—*oh yes...Erik was incredibly intimidating as an older brother*—and his business was *here*, taking care of the household and not off solving problems for the company.

The wind outside whipped tree branches that rapped against one of the windows. The distraction caused Jeremy to look at the coffee table where his father's diary lay. Jeremy picked up the leather-bound book, worn and aged. He opened it, seeing his father's handwriting, and the tears started anew.

Knock knock.

Rapping at the front door jolted Jeremy out his grief. He craned his neck to look through the front window and saw two shadowed men standing on the front porch. Jeremy quickly jammed the diary behind a cushion on one of the chairs and then went to the door.

Two men in suits stood facing Jeremy in the open doorway. One held up a badge. "Lachlan Evans, Central Intelligence Agency. Are you Jeremy Austin?"

"Yes."

"Perfect."

The two agents walked past Jeremy into the house and sat down. Waves of indignation at their assumed authority caused color to flood into Jeremy's face. A threat had just entered his house and his first thought was to the diary hidden just out of sight.

YOU'RE IN DANGER," Evans began with feigned concern.

"Danger? From what?" asked Jeremy warily.

"The TerraGen Universal Corporation." Lachlan leaned forward in his chair. "There are elements—scientists within TerraGen—who are developing biological weapons and selling them to the highest bidder."

"My father?"

"No. Your father was above reproach," smiled Evans. "But others, more unscrupulous and greedy for profit, have taken Dr. Austin's research and used it illegally."

"Wow, that's a relief. I mean, about my dad—"

"I think you would agree that having weapons of mass destruction developed in your father's company—"

"Ridiculous!"

"Of all people, I'm surprised to hear you say that," Evans said and exchanged a look a chagrin with his partner, a fierce looking man with ex-military written all over him. "One year ago, you told police that an alien had killed a security guard—"

"And been laughed at," the kid retorted.

"Local police. Imagination isn't their strong suit." The CIA man smiled and Evans pasted the most endearing and compassionate look on his face. Lachlan Evans leaned forward. "The name of Dr. Victor Austin—his research and legacy—are in danger of being corrupted by traitors inside TerraGen. And they'll stop at nothing to sell your father's research," said Evans in a low, conspiratorial voice. He was was pleased to see Jeremy lean forward in response.

"Such as...?"

"Kidnapping, torture, death," said Evans. "Let's just say they don't take *no* for an answer." To Lachlan, the boy seemed to fidget nervously in his chair. Now in his early fifties, Lachlan Evans had decades of experience manipulating others to get what he wanted. Life in his twenties had been spent as an agent for the CIA, but his thirties brought disillusion and he decided that being a free agent was more profitable. Now he was a liaison to the Pentagon…off the books, of course.

"Geez," said Jeremy, looking from one agent to the other.

"What about the diary?" asked Evans.

The boy seemed to hesitate and then, "The what?"

"Your father's diary—his research," Lachlan stared at Jeremy. *The boy knows something.* Lachlan had deliberately thrown out the diary reference to get a response. "Our sources inside TerraGen told us about it." Lachlan looked across at the youngest son of Victor Austin. He meant to break the kid, to force him to reveal the location of Austin's diary. He would then take the famed scientist's research for the greater good of the United States government. At least that was the story he was going to tell the boy.

Lachlan had other plans for the diary.

"The security guy, Keene… big, muscled, fierce-looking guy, he mentioned something but…" Jeremy shrugged his shoulders, "I haven't seen it. I doubt I would recognize it if you hit me upside the head with it."

The boy seemed genuine, but he had hesitated earlier. "You've searched the house?"

"No. Why would I? Dad never brought his work home," said Jeremy.

Lachlan was disappointed, and he tried to put on his best poker face. *Still, the kid could be hiding something.* He had to put the fear of God in the boy. "Your father's death—the entire expedition—wasn't by accident, I'm afraid."

"You know this?"

"We're sending men to the site as we speak, but my source has verified it was an act of sabotage," said Evans, noting the real fear on Jeremy's face. The CIA man motioned to the other agent sitting next to him. "Jeremy, this is one my best men…"

Evans watched the boy turn and study his associate.

Whereas Lachlan Evans had the look of an out-of-shape, corporate executive, his "pet killer" was the opposite: swarthy, heavily muscled with spiky, black hair, and black eyes that would stare right through his victims. If the Grim Reaper wore a suit, this man would be his twin. "Duarte Vega is a former S.E.A.L.," Evans continued, "he can look after you."

"As in protection? No…sir! That's okay—"

"There are some very bad people out there who *will* kill you—painfully, I might add—then take your father's research and sell it on the black market." Evans couldn't help but smile as he described himself.

"I don't need a nursemaid. Taking care of myself is something that I've had a lot of practice at," said Jeremy. "Are we done?"

Lachlan stared at the boy. *This kid was going to be tougher than he thought.*

JEREMY WATCHED THE TWO CIA MEN drive away in their nondescript, average-looking car. He closed the door and looked down at the leather bound diary in his hands. A cold shiver ran down his back.

How many people would kill for his dad's research?

The diary seemed to grow hot in his sweaty hands. He scanned the room—no…*the perfect hiding place needs to be out of sight, difficult to find*. He turned and started toward the staircase leading up to the second floor bedrooms.

THE CAR TURNED ONTO a side street and Lachlan pulled in behind an unmarked van parked at the curb. The passenger door opened and he looked over at Duarte Vega who was stepping out, "The kid knows where the diary is. Don't let him out of your sight."

"As good as done," Vega said with a nod.

The door closed and Lachlan watched as Vega got into

the passenger seat of the van where another gun-for-hire sat behind the wheel. *These killers are expensive, but well worth it,* thought Lachlan. He accelerated his car into the street and headed back to the Lewisville airport and his private jet.

J EREMY STARED INTO HIS BEDROOM. *Too obvious.* Erik's room? *No he's a target.* His father's bedroom... *again, too obvious.* The hall closets? *Maybe.*

The diary in his hands felt heavier all the while. There was a fourth room on the second floor—his father's office—and he walked over to where the door stood open. This room actually existed, and wasn't the *remodeled man cave* he had told Keene about.

"What a mess," he whispered.

Stacks of papers crowded the ornate, wooden desk. Four filing cabinets lined one wall and a dry/erase board covered the other. French doors behind the desk led out to a balcony where his father used to drink his morning coffee. *It would take an intruder just seconds to tear up a bedroom or the living room...but this? It would take them hours to sift through this mess!*

He moved around the desk and sat in his father's chair. One, two, three desk drawers were quickly opened but Jeremy wasn't satisfied. He went to the filing cabinets and quickly opened the four drawers, one by one, and found each drawer packed with papers. The second filing cabinet yielded the same. But it was the third cabinet that drew his attention. At the back of bottom drawer was a space big enough to fit the diary...except the space contained a manila folder with the name "Jeremy" written at the top.

"What the...?"

Jeremy reached for the folder, which was yellowed from age. He quickly opened it and a photo fell to the floor. Picking it up, Jeremy stared down at a picture of a baby lying in a crib. Scrawled at the bottom was the baby's name: *Jeremy.*

He quickly pulled several documents out of the folder and the words at the top stopped his heart.

ADOPTION.

DUARTE VEGA SAT WITH HIS PARTNER in the unmarked van several houses away from the Austin home. Both men were bored.

"Kid hasn't shown his face in four hours," Mats Kennet said from behind the steering wheel. Vega looked at Kennet and saw the killer's eyes fluttering, fighting off sleep. *Amateur.* Vega shook his head in disgust, and then glanced back at the Austin home. He rammed his elbow into his Kennet's ribs and the man jolted awake, reaching for his gun. Vega didn't bother explaining himself, he simply pointed a finger toward the house.

JEREMY LAID THE ADOPTION PAPERS on the desk. The color had long since drained from his face. The shock was over-whelming, accompanied by a feeling of betrayal by this new knowledge.

Adoption? Dad, why didn't you...? Did Erik know?

He heard the muffled closing of a door downstairs, and he stiffened. The hair stood up on his neck and a surge of adrenaline coursed through his body. Breathing deeply, he inched toward the open door. He slowly took off his tennis shoes and stepped into the upstairs hallway. The carpet muffling his steps, he approached the staircase and looked downward into the front foyer... nothing. He stepped down and the creak of the stair jolted him. *Slowly!* He took a second step, carefully balancing his weight, and this time the creak in the stair was fainter. Jeremy fought to control his breathing as he moved downward.

The cold hardness of the granite floor was a welcome relief, and he looked around. The front door remained closed, nothing moved in the living room and there was nothing in the hallway leading to the garage. He moved around his father's huge aquarium toward the kitchen. Empty.

Suddenly, arms closed around his neck and a pair of legs wrapped around his torso in a fierce grip! Panic filled Jeremy and he moved to crash his attacker into the wall—then stopped—the scent of perfume arresting him.

"Gotcha!" shouted a feminine voice.

"Your Chanel saved your life," exhaled Jeremy. And he wasn't kidding.

Helene Colbert slipped off his back and stood looking at Jeremy quizzically. "It was just a joke! I didn't think you were the scaring type."

"How'd you get in?"

"Door was unlocked," Helene said. "Pretty sloppy if you ask me. Any thug could've snuck in here and stole you blind." The look on her face changed from teasing to concern. "Say, you really look like someone did a number on you! I'm sorry—"

"You didn't hear?" He searched her face, which was a mask of confusion.

"Yes. The coach is making you sit out the first half," Helene said. "Of course, Alex deserved it but not you!"

That seemed so long ago...and yet it had been just this morning.

"You might want to sit down," Jeremy said.

HELENE SAT IN SILENCE for a long while. Face pale and eyes rimmed with tears, she buried her face in Jeremy's shoulder. "Your father... dead... it's all so unbelievable!"

Jeremy wanted to respond, but his own tears had returned, and he was too embarrassed.

"Jeremy, regardless of what you've found... your dad loved you!"

"And kept secrets."

"I'm sure he had his reasons." Her voice trailed off. She felt awkward after stating the obvious, but it was all so overwhelming. Jeremy losing his father was traumatic enough, but not knowing who your real parents were...

"What's more, Erik is on the other side of the planet."

"You've tried calling him?" Helene asked.

"Goes straight to voice mail."

She pulled away from her embrace, looking into his eyes. "We've got a spare bedroom and my mom's a great host, why don't you stay with us tonight?"

He glanced upstairs, then looked back at Helene. "I can't. It's important I hang around here for a while..."

T HE SOUND CAME THROUGH his headphones with startling clarity. Duarte Vega sat in the back of the van, listening and writing on a notepad.

"*A lot of stuff is going on that I can't even tell you about—top-secret TerraGen stuff,*" came Jeremy's voice through the headphones. The microphone they had trained on the Austin house was state-of-the-art and could penetrate walls. The sound of a kiss caused Vega to smirk and wink at Kennet.

Then came Helene's voice. "*I'll see you in few.*"

Vega's head whipped around, straining to look through the van's front window. In the distance, Helene walked out of the house toward a black sedan parked in the street. The sun overhead beat down through scattered clouds, casting the Austin's porch into deep shadow. Vega moved closer to the front of the van. Squinting through the sunlight he could barely detect Jeremy in the front doorway—*was the kid looking at them?*

CHAPTER EIGHT

THE GAME

T WAS TWO MINUTES into the second quarter and the Lewisville Raptors were already down 17-0. Star wide receiver and star quarterback sat on opposite ends of the bench in sullen silence. Every few minutes Coach Hayfield would glance back at them with a disgusted look on his face. Even the other players refused to look at the two ashen-faced misfits. Alex, his face a mask of bitterness and frustration, spent his time fixated on the game, refusing to even look at Jeremy. For his part, Jeremy was more than happy to be ignored. He sat lost in grief. When the rug of your life has been pulled out from under you it's acceptable to be a little shell shocked…right? Adopted by a dad who's body is lying cold on a distant island. Closing his eyes, Jeremy tried to block out all thought.

Raptors, Raptors, you're the ones! Beat the Knights to kingdom come!

The sound of the cheerleaders broke into Jeremy's grief, and he looked behind him. Helene, pompoms at the hips, was performing high kicks—she saw Jeremy and winked at him with a smile. There was movement behind Helene—Patrick stood at the front of the bleachers, waving his hand at Jeremy.

The crowd erupted, and Jeremy jerked around as one of Lewisville's return specialists ran down the field with half of the Mohattan Knights chasing after him. The touchdown created pandemonium on the sidelines where Coach Hayfield stood surrounded by cheering players and coaches. Nearby, Alex kicked the water cooler in frustration.

Jeremy looked behind and Patrick was still there, earnestly beckoning him now with both hands.

JEREMY WALKED CALMLY TOWARD the bleachers. Patrick glanced around at the cheering fans and the exultant players on the sidelines, then leaned down toward Jeremy.

"Why did you lie to Keene, that security guy at TerraGen?" asked Patrick.

"It's none of your business," Jeremy said defensively.

"I think it's ALL of our business," Patrick said. They stared at each other. "Listen, I don't believe the whole South China Sea expedition, mysterious island, nuclear holocaust story! It's all a pile of horse pucky!"

Despite his mood, Jeremy grinned.

"My father loves scuba diving," began Patrick. "He keeps a journal with pictures of every dive he's ever been on. Heck…he's dragged me on more dives than I can list!"

"And the point you're getting to?"

"My father's journal and his scuba gear are with me at the house."

"So he left it behind. It was probably forbidden—"

"The diving in the south China sea is incredible. The water so clear you can see hundreds of feet down," Patrick said. "My dad would never leave his journal behind because he'd find a way to strap on his oxygen tank and go diving. It was an obsession."

A little flame of hope ignited within Jeremy. "If you think my dad's still alive—"

Patrick leaned even closer to Jeremy. "We need to talk... like, tomorrow!" He gave Jeremy the hand signal for *phone call* before turning away and disappearing into the crowd of cheering Raptor fans.

Jeremy turned and made eye contact with Coach Hayfield, who wasn't happy. Jeremy began walking quickly toward the bench, but as he walked, soft fingers stuffed a folded note into his hand. He looked sideways to where Helene gave him a seductive smile. Golden curls and a flash of her sexy cheerleader uniform and she was rushing back to join her squad.

"Don't make me bench you for the second half, Austin!" Coach Hayfield screamed—Jeremy hurriedly returned to his seat on the bench. Alex snickered where he sat at the opposite end, his lips locked in that perpetual sneer.

Jeremy slowly opened Helene's note:

> *I'll be at your house after the game.*
> *I expect you to skip the after party —*
>
> *And that's an order!*
>
> *Love 'H'*

Jeremy smiled.

PATRICK KORRAPATI'S BEDROOM had the look and smell of a bio-waste treatment facility. Dirty plates and decayed food were stacked on top of the dresser, piles of dirty clothes were strewn everywhere—*was that underwear?* Marissa Torres kept pinching her nose, almost to the point of drawing blood. The smell of curry and other Indian spices had greeted her when first coming into the home but upon entering Patrick's room *curry* left the party and was replaced with smelly, teenage boy funk.

"There… it was called the *Free Technology Initiative*," said Patrick. He was seated in front of his laptop computer, fingers moving in a blur as he did what he did best: hacking. "Government regulation was strangling research, so fifteen years ago TerraGen's board of directors started looking throughout the globe for locations free of interference."

"Like an island?" Marissa asked.

"Remote, accessible only by boat… very plausible," Patrick said. He noticed the girl's upturned nose and continued, "My room doesn't smell *that* bad."

"A lot of people hold on to their dead pets—and I'm not talking memories—and my humble guess is that the carcass of *Fluffy* the cat or *Tiger* the super dog is buried under those…" Marissa quipped, finger pointing to a pile of dirty clothes.

Patrick huffed and raised an eyebrow, his version of a sarcastic rebuff. He returned to the computer where he was deep inside TerraGen's computer network, and incredulity was evident on his face. It had taken Patrick only half an hour to hack into the site and he had found the Tarraga files easily… too easily. The images on the computer showed the pacific island from all angles—from land, air, and even satellite images. Pictures showed the construction of huge laboratories and the beginnings of an airstrip. But it was all too polished.

"Your mother lets you get away with this room?" Marissa asked.

"We have an understanding," Patrick said. "I do all the chores, inside and out, and she doesn't invade my space."

"Your space is being invaded all right. Bacteria, most likely."

"Shhhh!" Patrick hissed. He was going deeper into the network's code, looking for hidden files. "Tarraga Island… I don't believe your story one bit!" His fingers danced over the keys, his eyes searching. "Ahhh…"

"Found something?" Marissa leaned forward and peered over his shoulder.

"Barbara Yossarian, you were clever—very clever," Patrick said. A series of folders were arrayed on the screen under the general heading: TG-FTI-Exploration. "TerraGen Free Technology Initiative Exploration," Patrick said, beginning to hum under his breath. He began opening one folder after another, revealing cost reports, construction projections, and a list of members of the expedition. He found his father's name near the top of the list.

"That's a lot of people," Marissa said. "A lot more than five hundred!"

"And a large percentage are ex-military—"

"Well, with China being so close—"

"Please, that story is so suspect," Patrick said flatly.

The computer screen flashed momentarily and a pop-up screen appeared: INTRUSION WARNING. Patrick's fingers began to move faster.

"They're tracking you!" Marissa shouted.

"Not quite," Patrick frowned. "I have my own software that's monitoring their network. They know someone's in the system but they haven't come close to finding me. We've got time."

"How much?"

"Ask me in ten minutes," he said, and continued working swiftly. A folder popped up on the screen, and Patrick's eyes widened in surprise. The folder was labeled simply: FTI ALTERNATIVE.

THE GLOW OF THE STADIUM LIGHTS cast his body in shadow as Jeremy walked out of the gym locker room. He wove a path through packs of Raptor fans and received pats on the back and loud congratulations for the come-from-behind win over Mohattan High. His eyes darted around the school campus, giving off the appearance of being carefree... *not the hunted young man that he was.* In the celebration after the game, with hundreds of fans jumping up and down on the football field, Jeremy had noticed two men sitting in the bleachers—two men who didn't celebrate, and whose attention seemed to be focused on the sidelines.

Duarte Vega had looked right at him.

The diary.

Jeremy picked up his pace and darted quickly into the school cafeteria. Faces turned and there were more shouts of congratulations. The cafeteria tables were loaded with cakes, pies, and soft drinks in preparation for the game's after party. Jeremy passed by the well-wishers without comment and exited through the door on the opposite side. He immediately threw himself backward and into the door's shadow.

Vega and the other man were standing fifty yards away, scanning the crowds of fans heading to the parking lot. A loud air horn sounded and their attentions were drawn away from the cafeteria. Jeremy swiftly crossed the sidewalk and darted between a row of cars, keeping his head low. He used the crowd of people as a shield between him and the two watchers. Although his heart beat rapidly, he managed to keep his pace controlled so as to not attract attention in a crowd of slow-moving, happy fans.

Jeremy stopped behind a school bus, spotting his car parked thirty yards away on a street bordering the school.

POP—POP—POP!

The firecrackers almost made him jump out of his skin. He jerked around, looking back toward the school.

Duarte Vega had separated from his partner, both spreading out in the parking lot in opposite directions. They were more overt now, looking aggressively through each pack of students as they passed.

Jeremy turned and sprinted toward his car.

THE POP-UP SCREEN SUDDENLY changed to: DETECTION IMMINENT.

"Prison time is gonna really suck, ya' know?"

"Your lack of faith is duly noted," Patrick countered.

"Faith? You were a genius up until two seconds ago," Marissa retorted. She was rocking back and forth in her chair, hands clenched in fists.

Patrick willed his fingers to move faster. The software on his computer showed the entire globe. Pings of red light began to appear in cities around the world, one after the other. "There. I just bought us another half hour." The pop-up screen suddenly disappeared.

"Still a genius. You made us proud," Marissa relented with a grudging smile.

Patrick's attention never wavered from the screen. "I just routed my ISP address in a continual loop through four hundred cities around the globe." Just then, he gasped. On the computer screen, a three-dimensional diagram popped up—a circular ring with a walkway bisecting its center—and it turned slowly in a 360-degree arc. He bent forward. The writing under the diagram was very small and kept moving.

"Is that some kind of monument?" Marissa asked.

"No. Something very top secret," Patrick said.

"Surprise, surprise."

"My dad's finger prints are all over this."

The ring began to animate on the screen. White light filled the inner part, and then the image started to pulse. Then a whirling, tornado-like tube appeared behind the Portal. Patrick sat back in his chair in amazement.

Marissa, having never seen Patrick impressed by anything, suddenly leaned forward in fear. "What is it?"

"The Einstein–Rosen bridge."

"Looks more like a tornado to me."

"That's because you have an infantile brain—"

"You would know."

Patrick ignored her sarcasm and leveled a serious gaze at her, and his voice was hollow, "They've discovered a wormhole."

J EREMY CLOSED THE FRONT DOOR, surprised to find the house dark. Helene always played her music loud whenever she cooked dinner at his house. No light came from the kitchen and there were no accompanying smells of cooking. Instead, it was dark and quiet as a tomb. He took a step and almost tripped over several books and a letter jacket… Helene's. He smiled, remembering the surprise she gave him earlier in the day. *Not this time!* His smile turned into a grin as he tiptoed into the kitchen.

His fingers found the light switch. Light filled the room.

Helene sat tied to a chair. Her face was bruised and her mouth was gagged.

Jeremy stood still in shock, his brain trying to comprehend what he was seeing.

With her whole body strapped to the chair, Helene could only rock back and forth. She tried to shout through her gag, and her eyes kept darting behind Jeremy.

CRASH! The sound came from the upstairs office, and Jeremy's head jerked around to look.

A large man came out of the shadows from behind— all Jeremy could see was the wicked smile on the man's lips. Move! But Jeremy was quickly grabbed by strong, muscular hands and violently thrown across the kitchen. He slammed into the cabinets and pain lanced up his side.

Suddenly a knife was at his throat.

The man's face came into view, leering with smug confidence. Jeremy, breathing in shallow gasps, couldn't pull away from his attacker's eyes. They were startling in their clarity, but what really stood out was their clash of color: the man's right eye was a vivid blue, and his left a radiant green.

THE SCHOOL'S PARKING LOT was now mostly empty. The stadium lights systematically began to shut off until the only light came from street lamps along the road. The two watchers sat morosely in their nondescript car parked near the school's entrance. A few stragglers from the game's after party drove past them.

A light began pulsating and Duarte Vega put his cell phone to his ear. Seconds later, the car's engine roared to life and the two men sped away into the night.

MARISSA'S CAR MOVED cautiously through downtown Lewisville. She glanced at Patrick seated next to her. He inserted a power cord into the car's cigarette lighter and the black box at his feet suddenly came to life. With the cockiness of your typical computer genius, he whipped open his laptop and smiled to see that he was still inside the TerraGen network. "Wireless is a godsend."

"I still don't see why we have to drive across town," Marissa said. "Jeremy has a girlfriend, remember?"

"It won't be the first parade I've rained on."

"Punk."

"Dr. Austin's name is on, well, everything. I need to ask Jeremy some questions."

"How about tomorrow? A girl's gotta get her sleep—"

"Tonight." He said with finality. He glanced at her with indifference and she responded with a snarl on her lips.

"Fine." She continued to drive, then stole a glance at Patrick whose face glowed from the light of the laptop.

Patrick was poring through one computer folder after another, and was now deep inside the history of TerraGen's

Portal facility. Here he found the discovery of the wormhole by physicist Brogan Riga using their massive particle collider, the development of the world's fastest quantum computer, five years spent refining the computer's matrix to bring control over the wormhole, and the final discovery of planet 7005TG401...code named *Genesis*. TerraGen's board of directors chose to keep the wormhole and planet 7005TG401 a secret, and spent ten years planning an expedition to establish a research base on Genesis.

"They want to own a planet!"

"Who?" asked Marissa.

"Our parents!" Patrick looked at her with genuine shock. "The company wants to own an actual planet. And your father and mine were up to their necks in this!"

Marissa pulled the car to the right where it skidded to a stop at the curb. Her look at Patrick was one of total bewilderment. "Wait. They're not on some stupid island in the Pacific? That was all a story?!" Her eyes flashed in anger.

"Hey, easy—"

"NO! I *hate* being lied to!" she retorted angrily.

"But you're missing the obvious, Marissa—"

"Don't use my first name."

"Huh?"

"You sound just like my father," Marissa said, her anger abating. "Wait, what's obvious here?"

A slow smile came over Patrick's face. "Our father's aren't dead."

For the first time in hours, Marissa found herself smiling too. On the laptop's screen below Patrick the pop-up screen returned, but this time the words flashed spasmodically: SECURITY DETAIL DISPATCHED. Her smile vanished. "You want me to drive faster?"

HE NONDESCRIPT CAR SPED along the darkened streets through Lewisville. In the passenger seat, Duarte

Vega calmly fitted a silencer on the end of a wicked-looking, Russian-made successor to the Ruger Mark II handgun.

THE KNIFE WAS SHARP AGAINST his throat, and a trickle of blood slowly made its way down his neck. Jeremy stared across the kitchen through eyes pale with fear. This wasn't a video game—this was life and death and it was obvious the man holding the knife was used to killing.

"Your father's research. His diary. Tell me where it is." The speaker was a second man, older... in his mid-sixties was Jeremy's guess. He had long silver hair that fell to his shoulders. This man had ransacked the second-story office, but had failed to locate the diary. Something about the man seemed very familiar. Cold eyes studied Jeremy like a wolf relishing its kill.

"TerraGen. That's where his office is," Jeremy lied.

"Okay. That's *one*," the silver-haired man said. "You get two more tries and then I slit your girlfriend's throat."

Jeremy jerked upward in response but the ropes binding him to the kitchen chair held fast. Next to the silver-haired man was Helene, still gagged and tied in her chair. Her eyes pleaded with Jeremy, and he had never felt despair like this before.

The knife flicked at Jeremy's neck and jerked sideways at the sudden pain. The stocky man studied him from above, lips turned in a frown. He turned to the older man. "Kid doesn't think we're serious."

"He will," the silver-haired man said.

Jeremy struggled to get his hands free, but the effort was a waste of energy.

The silver-haired man stared at Jeremy with a hint of a smile, eyes boring into Jeremy. "We worked with your father once... a long, long time ago. He didn't take us seriously either."

The knife at Jeremy's throat quivered as the stocky man chuckled, "You won't be seeing his face again in this lifetime."

"What about my father?" Jeremy asked. "You were on the island?"

The question took the smile off the silver-haired man's face. "Whatever are you babbling about?"

"TerraGen's island in the Pacific, a big expedition, the nuclear meltdown..." Jeremy faltered, looking at both men with a sudden realization. "You sabotaged the reactor!"

The stocky man began laughing but the silver-haired man just stared at Jeremy.

"Do you think we're playing games here?" The silver-haired man's eyes darkened, and his voice took on a dangerous tone. "Where we came from, young Jeremy Austin, you won't find on any map in this world. Pray I don't take you there and feed you to the reptillicoths!"

"I would like to see that," the stocky man said.

"Now, that's *two*," the silver-haired man said. He beckoned to the stocky man. "Brogan, come take the girl's eyes out. The boy needs convincing."

Brogan took the blade from Jeremy's throat and crossed to where Helene began to frantically jerk up and down in her chair. She whipped her head sideways, away from the blade, her eyes wide in absolute terror. Brogan viciously grabbed her head with one hand and slowly moved the blade toward her right eye with the other.

"What do you want with my father's research?" Jeremy shouted.

The blade stopped.

"Dr. Victor Austin, if he's anything, he's a perfectionist," the silver-haired man stated. "Our data is incomplete. His work fills a few holes that will allow me to complete my research and change a few rules... rules that will give me an edge back in the old country."

The blade started forward again, and Helene tried to fight Brogan's iron grip.

"My bedroom!" Jeremy shouted. "It's right next to the office—I couldn't think of any place clever to hide it—"

"Let me guess," the silver-haired man said in a silky voice. "Under the mattress."

"Right next to the girly mag's, I bet," Brogan rasped in derision.

Jeremy snarled and jerked upward, bouncing the chair off the kitchen floor.

"At least one member of the Austin clan has some sense," drawled the silver-haired man as he moved to the doorway. He looked at Jeremy and smiled. "You made a wise choice." And then he disappeared into the living room.

HER EYES CONSTANTLY DARTED to the rear view mirror… no headlights. Shadowed trees whipped past the car as Marissa drove out of Lewisville's business district and into the suburban neighborhoods to the south. Sitting next to her, Patrick was still glued to the laptop.

The pop-up screen in the upper right corner still flashed: SECURITY DETAIL DISPATCHED. Below the pop-up screen Patrick followed the progress of one of his computer applications, which was searching through hidden folders in the TerraGen network faster than a normal eye could follow.

"I wrote a program called *Wormzilla*," Patrick said. "It's like a hound dog with a scent. Give it a code word and off it goes, burrowing. It cracks encryption on its own, digs through hidden files, finds whatever you tell it to look for. Basically a security expert's worst nightmare."

"Burrowing… for what?" Marissa asked.

"Lab experiments with no publication date," he replied. "TerraGen actually helped me out on this. Every one of the company's experiments must be published. It's company policy. Failure to publish means getting fired and maybe thrown in jail."

"You're kidding," she said, and then looked at Patrick.

His flat stare was his only response. "Okay, thrown in jail. Got it."

"I know firsthand about some of their secret experiments—"

"That explains why you started the fire last year!" Marissa exclaimed. "You discovered clandestine experiments and inhaled a zombie neurotoxin—"

"Actually... we were attacked by an alien—"

"Save that story for one of the cheerleaders," she said scornfully. She glanced his way and the serious look on his face almost made her laugh. "Oh, please. That hurt puppy look won't sell your alien invasion story." Both Patrick and Jeremy had never spoken to any of their classmates about the night they burned down TerraGen's Imaginarium—*I'm sure his father, who built the Imaginarium, had plenty to say*, she thought soberly. Marissa vaguely knew of the legal injunction that prevented the two boys speaking to local newspapers. In essence, TerraGen had buried the story. Only Patrick and Jeremy really knew what happened that night. *But aliens? Please!*

"My dad always suspected some of his fellow scientists were conducting personal projects—secret, classified experiments, off the books, and definitely *not* published," Patrick said. "It just so happens, I know *which* scientist is hiding his data."

"You're a devious twerp, you know that?" she said.

"Absolutely," he said. "One of my best qualities." He looked up from his computer. "You wanna know one of my worst qualities?"

"Failure to bathe?"

"I'm told I don't have a sense of humor," he stated without emotion.

"Hmmm," she looked at him. "No surprise there."

Headlights appeared in the rear view mirror. Marissa's fingers tightened around the steering wheel. She heard an audible gasp from Patrick.

On the computer screen flashed images of the genetic monstrosity from a year ago—the alien killer straight out of a child's bad dream. "Got you, Dr. Tyrannus," Patrick whispered.

Wow! That actually does look like an alien, she thought… and then checked herself. *No. No freak'in way they're keeping aliens locked away at TerraGen.* "Leo's dad is Lewisville's Frankenstein?" Marissa asked, eyes darting back to the rear view mirror where the headlights were getting closer.

"It's called Project *Wunderkrieger,* some sort of futuristic army—"

Headlights drew larger—the car behind was swiftly gaining.

"The research is years ahead of anything I've ever read about," he continued. "Genetics experiments, DNA programming… it's like something right out of the Third Reich."

The laptop almost flew out of Patrick's lap as the car swerved toward the side of the road. Brakes squealed in protest and the sound of gravel pinging away at the car's undercarriage filled her ears. Patrick glared at Marissa in alarm, but her eyes were glued to the rear view mirror—

Headlights made Patrick's face become obscenely white.

The nondescript car with Evan's two assassins sped past them at twice the posted speed limit. They watched as it turned into a suburban neighborhood and then disappeared from view. Marissa became aware of a loud, ceaseless buzzing.

"You hear that?" she said…a little too loudly—the racing car had unwound her nerves.

A loud gasp escaped from Patrick and Marissa followed his gaze. On the screen of his laptop flashed: COUNTER INTRUSION IN 10, 9, 8…

The look on Patrick's face matched the terror in his voice, "The old mill pond—and be quick!"

"What mill pond?! I'm not a GPS!" she yelled back.

"Follow that car!" Patrick shouted. "And don't drive like your grandma!"

Her foot slammed on the accelerator. The car's tires spun angrily in the gravel, then caught traction. Marissa's car lurched forward and sped off after the two assassins.

OR THE THOUSANDTH TIME, Jeremy exchanged troubled looks with Helene. Gone was the upbeat, vibrant, can-do cheerleader. Now, Helene appeared worn and exhausted, her breathing ragged. Fear and anger boiled inside Jeremy, but he was powerless to help her. Footsteps sounded and Jeremy swiveled his head sideways as the silver-haired man returned.

"What price is paid for advancement?" the silver-haired man rasped. He stood in the doorway, his expression cold. A triumphant smile played at the man's mouth. In his right hand was the diary and Jeremy felt more hopeless than ever. The older man tapped Brogan on the shoulder. "You've been longing for this moment ever since we decided to make this excursion. I know you wanted the other brother but...well, that will be for another time, I guess." The silver-haired man never stopped looking at Jeremy. "Don't keep me waiting." The man flashed a brief, cold smile and then he was gone. Seconds later, Jeremy heard the front door open and close.

The man called Brogan was studying intensely. There was a feral, animal-like viciousness behind the eyes of this man, and Jeremy felt an icy stab of fear go down his spine.

"Oh, son of my enemy," Brogan said, stepping toward Jeremy with his knife twirling in his fingers. "I've dreamt of a million ways to hurt the man named Victor Austin—"

"I don't even know you!" Jeremy shouted.

"How could you?" Brogan said coldly.

"You've got the diary!"

Brogan smiled wickedly, "Yes. But his research was only part of the reason for my visit. I've a grudge to settle—"

"Whatever issue you have with my father—"

Brogan was in front of Jeremy in a flash, his free hand grabbing Jeremy's hair and yanking his head upward. "This is not some petty disagreement, boy! Austin chose to be my enemy—kept all the research to himself and locked the rest of us out!"

"Please," Jeremy pleaded.

Brogan looked down at Jeremy with contempt. "It's fitting that you should feel a bit of the pain... the same pain your father will have to deal with when I see him next!"

"Please..." Jeremy's terror was over whelming.

Brogan released Jeremy's hair, took three steps back toward Helene... and slid his hand across her throat. Jeremy watched as Helene gasped for breath, eyes wide, and then a line of red appeared below her chin as blood began dripping downward. The knife in Brogan's hand was red, and the big man moved toward Jeremy next. "You want to find out where your daddy has gone off to?" Brogan rasped. "Sorry to disappoint you."

Total shock overwhelmed Jeremy, and he lurched upward, still bound tightly to the chair. His weight tipped him forward and he fell head first onto the kitchen floor at Brogan's feet.

Pain... and then blackness.

FTER SLITTING THE YOUNG GIRL'S THROAT, the man named Brogan lusted for more bloodshed. But the kid had panicked and knocked himself out. Now Brogan was in a quandary: kill the boy unceremoniously, or wake him up for the pure enjoyment factor.

CRASH! Wood splintered inward as the rear kitchen door flew open. Brogan's head jerked sideways as Duarte Vega stepped in, his gun raised. Brogan whipped the knife upward, throwing it expertly. Vega twisted sideways, and the knife flew past him and embedded itself in the kitchen door.

He fired two shots, but Brogan had already disappeared. The sound of the front door opening didn't phase Vega as he strode calmly across the kitchen toward the girl. Helene Colbert gasped one last time, and then her pupils dilated, staring into nothingness. The professional killer closed her eyes—collateral damage was always part of the game—and then he turned back to the boy.

Jeremy Austin lay face first on the floor, unconscious but still breathing as a pool of blood grew ever wider under his head.

THE POP-UP SCREEN SEEMED to have encountered a glitch. It kept flashing: COUNTER INTRUSION IN 4, 4, 4, 4, 4.

Patrick's fingers moved swiftly over the keyboard. "Someone at TerraGen is very determined! He... or she... is almost as good as me."

"Good enough to defeat your program?" Marissa asked.

"Maybe."

"They'll discover your identity—"

"Regrettable—"

"The FBI will show up on your doorstep!"

"Not if you drive faster!"

"There's a legal term... it's called *reckless endangerment*," Marissa retorted. Patrick looked down; she had the accelerator pedal almost to the floor.

The neighborhood street they were speeding along suddenly opened into the countryside. The moon overhead reflected off the waters of the mill pond that was set at the base of a rolling hill and lined with dark, towering trees. Marissa's car skidded to a stop and Patrick vaulted out the door. Carrying the laptop under his arm he raced toward the pond, heart pounding in his chest. As he neared the water's edge he suddenly stopped and looked down at the computer.

"You deserve better than this," Patrick said with anguish, gripping the laptop.

He launched the computer into a high arc. It hit the still waters with a splash and sank into the depths.

"Is that gonna work?" Marissa asked, coming up behind him.

"Circuit board has already shorted out by now," he replied. "The water acts as a barrier, cutting contact with the wireless." He sighed in disgust. "That's a lot of wasted money sitting at the bottom of a stinking pond."

"You lost all that research."

"Nah. That laptop's my disposable copy."

A HALF HOUR LATER they were parked several houses up the street from Jeremy's. Blue and red light moved back and forth across the surrounding houses and trees in a jittering motion. Marissa turned the headlights off, her mouth dropping open. Both she and Patrick stared in disbelief through the front windshield toward the flashing lights.

Other neighborhood residents stood immobile in silent witness. In the Austin driveway, two paramedics wheeled a covered gurney toward an ambulance. The body under the black plastic bounced, but didn't move. The flashing lights of two police cars parked in front of the house added to the scene.

"Criminently," Marissa whispered.

Patrick was speechless.

"What was the message your laptop was flashing?"

"Counter intrusion in—"

"No, lunkhead! The other one!"

"Security detail…" he gulped, "dispatched."

Marissa went cold on the inside. "What has TerraGen done now?"

CHAPTER NINE

EAVESDROPPER

ALEXANDER LEACH, SR.'S STUDY was a reflection of his wealth and intellectual curiosity: floor-to-ceiling shelves filled with legal and technical books, several Rembrandts and a Van Gogh hung on the wall with thermal lasers for security, and furniture that once resided in the Versailles palace in the early 1700s. Light glowed off the polished wood surfaces of the walls and floors. Smoke drifted upward from the cigar between Leach, Sr's teeth. But the eyes above the cigar reflected one emotion…fear.

"I don't like it," said a thin man in his late 60s. "The same two men went *back* through the Portal?"

"We can put a name to one of them," said Barbara Yossarian, imposing in her navy-blue suit but looking haggard from the stress of the past few hours. She was supposed to have been addressing TerraGen's Board of Directors in two days, bringing them up to speed on the Portal security issue. But tonight's death of a Lewisville cheerleader at Dr. Victor Austin's house had plunged the TerraGen world into terror. Now she was facing Alexander Leach and the Board without her normal preparation, and her nerves were fraying.

"But it *was* the same two?" came the shrill voice of Logan Scarsdale again.

"Absolutely. We got one set of prints off the Portal elevator. That print matches DNA taken at the crime scene," Yossarian said.

"The girl put up a fight?" Alexander Leach asked.

"I'll put it this way: there was no shortage of skin cells under her fingernails. The skin came from one person... Brogan Riga."

"Our physicist?" This came from Edward Kotts, a Wall Street banker and another board member.

"Astrophysicist, weekend warrior... a muscle-head with a brain," she said.

"A very smart brain," Alexander Leach said. "Discovered the wormhole."

"But I thought the Portal was malfunctioning?" asked TerraGen's remaining Board member, Augustus Gerhardt. "Riga and this... mystery man are going back and forth like they own it!"

"That's because they sabotaged it." Yossarian stated. "Using a very sophisticated computer virus, they've managed to lock our best computer experts out. How they managed to come back from the other side is... well..."

"And the second man?" interrupted Scarsdale.

"My guess? Kaiser Tyrannus," she said. "He's the only one capable of holding Riga's leash."

The phone buzzed next to Alexander Leach, the red

light blinking. Yossarian watched as Leach picked up the phone and turned away for privacy. *This was supposed to have been a giant leap for mankind… and for the TerraGen stockholders, of course.* But the Portal was turning into a disaster that could send every person in this room behind bars. Yossarian shuddered.

"I still can't believe it!" Scarsdale exclaimed.

ALEX QUIETLY CLOSED THE passenger door of his Italian sports car. The sound of crickets and the smell of expensive perfume, coupled with the giggling of a college girl next to him, promised Alex that his celebration after the football game was going to be special. Brenda—Brandy—Beth—*whatever her name was*, bumped into him in the crush of people leaving the stadium. It was an easy conquest—*too easy*. Her alcohol fueled giggling stopped abruptly when she turned and saw the opulent mansion in front of her: two-stories, over 20,000 square feet, and Tudor-style architecture that boasted of money and wealth. The only light shining into the darkness came from a curtained room to their left.

Four other cars were parked in the circular driveway… all very expensive.

Alex recognized the car of Security Director Yossarian, and his brow furrowed with interest. "Don't say a word," Alex hissed to the girl as he took her by the elbow and led her down the stone walkway lined with sculpted hedges and pale lights that glowed faintly.

The 18th-century front door slid silently shut. The foyer was dark except for the light escaping from his father's study further down the east wing. Cigar smoke wafted into him—his father's brand—and his curiosity was piqued. Alex patted the girl and sent her giggling up the winding stairs to the second floor. Like a Navy SEAL, he moved toward his father's study on tiptoe where the door stood slightly ajar, casting patterns of light on the marble floor. Alex heard the sound of a phone being placed onto a receiver.

"Austin's son has been secured," said the voice of Alexander Leach. The sound of his father's voice always made Alex tense and he fought the desire to sneak away. *My father doesn't own me!* At least, that had been Alex's mantra for as long as he could remember. Their father-son relationship could best be described as a formal partnership. The word *love* was never mentioned. His father spoke again. "It's imperative we protect and control Jeremy."

"And his brother, Erik?" Yossarian's voice was almost apologetic.

"You lost him. You find him!" Alexander Leach's voice was sharp.

"He deliberately went off the grid," she began.

"He's our employee!"

"And a genius, or are you forgetting?" Yossarian challenged.

"When young Austin eventually wakes up..." Alexander Leach's voice was suddenly filled with compassion, and Alex took a breath in surprise, "he's going to have a lot of questions. We can't keep telling him that his brother's somewhere in the Pacific."

Alex's mind reeled with the knowledge. Movement within the study jolted him back to reality, and he ran silently to the staircase. He was halfway up the stairs when a single thought jolted him to a stop.

Everything his father had told the other TerraGen kids was a lie.

Chapter Ten

Time Lost

THE MOVEMENT OF HER DRESS *captivated him the entire night. Gold and blue sequins dazzled in the light, almost matching the brilliance of her smile.*

They were dancing.

Her eyes were mischievous — Jeremy couldn't dance for spit — and he knew that mocking look on her face as she inwardly laughed at his awkward steps.

He saw the faces of their friends, laughing, joking...all decked out in tuxedos and sequined dresses. For many kids prom was a night of torture, but for Jeremy and Helene, it had been magical.

The smile on Helene's face faltered, and then turned into a look of horror. Jeremy stepped on her toes but she didn't notice. Her pupils began to dilate and suddenly a stream of blood began to run down from her mouth.

WHOOSH!

He was suddenly watching as a spectator, like a ghost floating overhead—Helene's dance steps stuttered, and he noticed the ribbon of blood at her neck—the person she was dancing with had a vicious grip on the back of her head—the face turned and the leering smile of Brogan jolted Jeremy.

"NO!!!"

He was sitting upright, bathed in sweat. "No! Please!" The shouted words were coming from his own mouth. He blinked and discovered his eyes were wet with tears. He looked around the room—his room. He rubbed the tears from his face, shaking the sleep from his mind.

Yes, his room. The pictures of his father; Erik's photos from around the world; Jeremy's own images—the several high-speed photos of him playing football—they all still sat on his dresser.

The smell of bacon cooking filled him with a ravenous hunger. Morning sunlight streamed through the windows. Clothes were laid out on the chair at his desk. Everything was almost as it was when… Jeremy looked down at his arms and saw how thin they were. He whipped the blanket off and stared down at what was left of his legs. *They look like toothpicks*, his mind screamed in horror.

The sound of activity in the kitchen downstairs brought his head up in alarm. He moved his left leg close to the edge and it fell over the side. He yelped in pain as unused muscles strained in agony. Flames of heated agony shot up his right leg as he brought it around and dropped over the side. Sitting on the edge he looked up and saw his reflection in the mirror over his dresser—face unshaven and body emaciated. He struggled to his feet on shaky legs.

What has happened?!

AFTER WHAT SEEMED LIKE an eternity, Jeremy stood in the doorway to the kitchen—*his kitchen*—where just last night...*but not last night*, the other part of his brain said. A plate of eggs, toast, and a large glass of orange juice waited for him on the kitchen table. Working at the stove was a tall black woman in her early 50s. She turned and eyed him with stern appraisal.

"It's the bacon, right?" she asked. "Nothing motivates my kids faster on a Saturday morning than the smell of bacon frying in the pan."

"Who are you?" Jeremy whispered hoarsely.

"Your minder," she replied.

"My what?"

She placed several strips of bacon next to the eggs and gave him an exasperated smile. "You gonna wait 'till it gets cold?"

He stared at her, but she just stared back, so he shrugged his shoulders and sat down at the table. After smelling the eggs and bacon up close, he was suddenly ravenous. He dove into the food, eating like a starved prisoner of war just released from captivity.

"Freeman," she said. "Mrs. Freeman to you."

He came up for breath between bites. "Why are you here?"

"You needed looking after."

"That's Erik's job. Where is he... my brother?" Jeremy asked.

"The company was hoping you could tell us."

"TerraGen?" Jeremy's suspicions were aroused. He almost lowered the fork full of eggs, but then quickly stuffed them into his mouth. Mumbling, he said, "You're not with the school?"

"Eat your food," Freeman said. "Questions later."

He took a long drink of the orange juice and felt the rush of sugar in his system.

He continued to eat, but questions kept popping into his head.

Something isn't right here.

Jeremy glanced around the kitchen: there were the same pictures on the fridge; ceramic containers on the counter with 'sugar,' 'flour,' 'tea,' and 'coffee' in raised letters... the rest of the counter was empty. Then he realized what was bothering him: everything was *too clean, too tidy.* He glanced over to where Freeman was cleaning the frying pan in the sink. He saw the handgun at once, hidden underneath the apron she was wearing in a holster under her arm. She cleaned the cooking utensils with deftness, every movement practiced, quickly executed...*professional.* She picked up a knife, and suddenly time stood still. A wave of nausea hit Jeremy, and his eyesight blurred. *The knife—*

"It's fitting that you should feel a bit of the pain..." Brogan threatened.

"Please..."

The knife slid along Helene's throat—

A scream.

JEREMY'S EYES BLINKED. He'd blacked out. His forehead ached, throbbing with heat and he realized he must've slammed his head on the kitchen table.

"Don't do *that* again," Freeman said with just a hint of compassion. "Losing you a second time—and on my watch—would be unforgivable. My family needs the paycheck, okay?"

She sat across the table from him...this *minder* called Neriah Freeman—the *company's* minder. Her voice was flat, devoid of emotion... businesslike. "You had brain damage," she began. "At one point doctors thought you'd end up paralyzed. Your brain swelled. They opened up your skull, induced you into a coma, and the swelling went down. Unfortunately, you also contracted a virus and almost died."

Jeremy reached to the back of his head and found the

scar from where the doctors had relieved the pressure on his brain.

"And Helene?" he asked with not much hope.

"I think you know the answer," Freeman said.

"Tell me anyway."

"Dead. Bled out." Her words were clinical. "There was nothing you could have done to save her."

"The funeral?"

"Made the local papers. It was a tragedy." She looked into his eyes, and there was just the slightest hint of compassion. "There were several dozen flowers in your hospital room. We threw them out after a week."

He blinked. "How long?"

"Long?"

"Was I in a coma?" Jeremy stared at her.

Freeman studied him, then… "Long."

Frustrated, Jeremy shifted in his chair and stared through the living room windows facing the street. When he had walked…rather, stumbled down the stairs earlier he had noticed something wrong with the living room. But the problem wasn't inside—*it was outside*. Through the windows he saw what had registered in his unconscious: Christmas decorations on his neighbor's lawn across the street—*and snow!* Shocked he turned to Freeman. "It's Christmas?!"

She shifted in her chair. "You were in a coma for three and half months."

"Three and a half…" he gulped, then continued. "Did my brother visit?"

She simply stared at him.

"What?" he pressed.

Freeman sighed deeply. "Your brother's been missing for over four weeks now. The company lists him as 'going off the grid.' We were hoping you might have an idea of where he's gone."

"Erik went out to an island, off, uh… some place close to China!" Jeremy could feel his blood pressure rising. "You should be telling *me* where he is! It's your island!"

"There was no island trip," Freeman said. "Your brother simply vanished."

Jeremy took his gaze off of her, studying the food remaining on his plate. *Erik wouldn't just leave me!* He bit his lower lip, thinking. *She's not telling me everything.* He looked again at her. "Did the police catch the two men? The killers?"

"What do you remember about them?" Freeman asked.

"You didn't answer my question."

"Correct. I didn't."

Jeremy felt his anger boiling. "Did they catch them?!"

"How 'bout we play a little game of *quid pro quo?*" Freeman said, leaning forward.

"Quid... what?"

"I'll answer your questions if you answer mine."

He thought for a moment, then answered. "Sure."

"Two men?"

"Answer my question first," Jeremy demanded.

She rolled her eyes. "Okay. The two men—I'm assuming *two* of course—broke into your home, trashed the upstairs office, looking for something—"

"Were they caught?!"

"They tied up your girlfriend and waited for you to come home," she stated.

Jeremy inhaled slightly and closed his eyes, fighting to hold back the memories.

"They bound you and put a knife to your throat," she continued. "They wanted something..."

"Were—they—caught?!" he asked through gritted teeth, closing his eyes.

"You refused to cooperate, and they killed her." Freeman's voice was rhythmic. "In your attempt to save her, you fell forward and suffered massive injuries to your brain."

"Please!" He said, and then his eyes snapped open. *It had been here, in this kitchen, and that pitiful cry for mercy...*

"Police found no trace of your killers," Freeman said. "I'm sorry."

Jeremy painfully stood up on shaky legs. He took several steps toward the living room, but stopped next to his father's fish tank. His eyes took in the bubbles of the oxygenator, the various exotic fish, and his favorite: the deep-sea diver in his Jules Verne diving suit that went up and down, blowing bubbles. He blinked tears from his eyes and looked back to where Freeman still sat. "You can tell that security guy, uh... Mr. Keene, that he can stop looking."

"Looking?" Freeman looked at Jeremy with confusion.

"My father's diary. They have it," he said, his voice becoming harder. "And the next time I see a man with different colored eyes, calling himself *Brogan*... I'm going to rip his heart out."

H E WALKED ALONG THE SUBURBAN street in a daze. There was a foot of new snow on the ground, and the various neighborhood yards had different incarnations of snowmen: some with the standard charcoal eyes and carrot noses, and others sculpted to look like comic book characters. Homes were decked out with Christmas lights, plastic Santa Claus figures on the roofs, nativity scenes in the front yards. It all looked so... normal. But there was never going to be a normal for Jeremy's life ever again.

"I let you down," Jeremy whispered as he walked.

He didn't need to look where he was going. He had walked these three blocks a million times in sunshine and darkness. Helene Colbert's house was the third one on the left, a single-story, brick home with four bedrooms and a large backyard where a hammock hung between two trees. How many times had Helene teased him while they drifted back and forth, swaying on the hammock and talking about the future...

The tears rolled off his cheek and his mind snapped

back to the present. He studied the sign firmly planted in the front yard: *For Sale… Sold!* Looking through the front window he could clearly see that the house was empty.

She was really gone.

"You would be alive if it weren't for me," he spoke, barely audibly. *All because of a lousy diary. I should've given it to TerraGen instead of listening to…*

Bitterness toward his older brother welled up inside Jeremy. Erik had been their father's favorite and had graduated top of his class, valedictorian with a full ride to any university of his choice. And Jeremy? Average intelligence with a propensity for losing his temper. Instead of awards and scholarships, Jeremy's numerous trips to the principal's office were for fighting, sleeping in class, and pranking the other kids. And then he remembered his discovery in his father's filing cabinet—adoption papers. *I'm not even a blood relative of Erik. No wonder I suck at math!*

Helene had been so understanding—trying to feed me useless encouragements of how much my father must love me to go through the adoption process. Empty words! And now she's gone—because I wanted to protect my father's precious work! What a moron!

Jeremy stood looking at Helene's house for what seemed like an hour. When he left his house he'd only put on a light jacket over his clothes, and now the cold was beginning to chill him to the bone. He started walking again, turning just once to look back at her house. The footprints he left in the snow looked as lonely as he felt. He walked, not even caring which direction he went.

The neatly laid-out houses with their holiday cheer were only a blur to him as the tears began anew. *I really am alone.* Despair crept up like a sickness, threatening to drag him down and smother him. *This was all my fault!* His father had never allowed him and Helene to be alone together in the house. But after his father left on his *expedition* and with Erik always absent on business trips… well, he had started to bend the rules. Helene had paid the price.

Jeremy didn't even hear the car pull up next to him at the curb.

"Austin!" said a voice.

He turned, and his eyes opened wide in surprise. Seated behind the wheel of a late-model Chevy was Patrick Korrapati. Jeremy wasn't even aware that Patrick had taken the time to get his driver's license.

Patrick seemed to study Jeremy's frail body, his face serious. "Get in the car."

"You finally learn how to drive?" Jeremy asked. Patrick's sudden appearance had put him on guard. *Besides, he's probably only curious about the...*

"No excuses," Patrick said. "We're going to a meeting."

CHAPTER ELEVEN

LAST RIDE TO NOWHERE

HAINS BOUND THE DOORS of Lewisville High School's main entrance. The building lay like a tomb in the deep snow. He'd rarely seen it so quiet. Patrick led him around to the side of the cafeteria where a door stood slightly ajar, a rubber mat wedged from inside. Jeremy glanced once at Patrick, then entered the cafeteria. Closed for winter break, the cafeteria's interior—always the loudest place on campus—was now a sepulcher, quiet and devoid of life. Their footsteps echoed on the tile floors.

Entering the main hallway, they passed through the school's lobby. Floor-to-ceiling glass display cases lined two of the walls, and Jeremy stopped in front of one where a brand new trophy was on display: LEWISVILLE RAPTORS – DISTRICT CHAMPIONS. His eyes were drawn to a large photo next to the trophy—Alex Leach, Jr. stood poised to throw a football. The caption under the photo read: ALEXANDER LEACH, JR. – ALL-STATE QUARTERBACK. *Good for him! There won't be helmet big enough to squeeze onto his arrogant head at whatever Ivy League university he ends up at.*

Jeremy saw the team photo—*his own face missing, of course*—and then he remembered that the team's yearbook photo was scheduled for the week after they played Mohattan High School.

He was about to turn away when his eyes caught the very next glass case; blood drained from his face and he went pale.

"The entire school took it pretty hard, just so you know," Patrick said.

A large, 10" x 13" photograph was placed amidst dried flowers. Dressed in her cheerleader uniform, with the most beautiful smile Jeremy could never forget, was Helene. Next to the photograph was an equally large poster board inscribed with: HELENE COLBERT—WE WILL NEVER FORGET YOU! Tears began anew, trailing down Jeremy's cheeks as he studied the several hundred student signatures.

"My names not on there," came a voice behind him. "Sorry." Jeremy hurriedly wiped the tears from his face and turned around. Leo Tyrannus was standing next to Patrick with a guilty look on his face. "They interrogated all of us kids—you know, from the company."

"What sort of interrogations?" Jeremy asked with alarm.

"Did we know of anyone who wanted to harm you or… uh, Helene," Patrick said.

"And?"

"Well, everyone loved Helene," Patrick stated without emotion.

"She was vastly—VASTLY… more popular than you," Leo chimed in.

"My thoughts exactly," Patrick said. "As for the murderers? Despite your occasional, obnoxious jokes, I can't think of one person who would want to end your life."

"Unless you possessed something they wanted," Leo said, and that was too close to the truth. Jeremy ignored the younger boy and turned back to the display case, his eyes still captivated by Helene's smile and the noticeable gleam in her eyes. Seconds later, Patrick's voice broke through like a thought lingering at the back of his mind.

"We're going to break into TerraGen—let's call it *round two*—and we need your help," Patrick said.

THEY HAD TRANSFORMED the computer classroom at Lewisville High into an expedition staging area. Black canvas bags lay on tables stuffed with MRE's, rappelling gear, ponchos, tents, survival supplies… everything needed for a trek into a hostile environment. Patrick, acting as expedition leader, introduced Jeremy to two other members of the team who were standing at the far end of the room: Marissa Torres and Selene Choi. Selene gave him a wave that registered to Jeremy as: *Hey, haven't seen in you three months because you survived a violent murder attempt and I'm feeling really awkward.* Jeremy didn't wave back.

"When you had your…*accident*, I was in the process of hacking TerraGen's computer network," Patrick began. "I discovered that the company, and our parents, were not exactly truthful with us."

"They fed us a load of crap," Marissa said. "Personally, my dad has a lot to answer for, let me tell you."

"Mine too," Selene added, nodding her head.

Patrick moved sideways and Jeremy noticed, for the first time, a large diagram hanging on the wall: a circle within a circle, and a line intersecting the smaller circle where a third circle—a ring—sat at one end. *I've seen this somewhere before.* Jeremy looked closer and saw what looked like rays of light shooting out from the third ring.

"The crazy thing is, our parent's expedition never traveled more than a mile in one direction—"

"They had a group getaway at the local coffee shop?" Jeremy asked skeptically.

"Cute…and we've gone to a lot of trouble to present our findings to you," Patrick said, his eyes locked on Jeremy and sounding like a college professor. "So, I'll kindly ask you to dispense of the sarcasm."

"My father—your father—they went on a one-mile expedition. Maybe they're waiting for us at a truck stop."

"He's in pig-head mode," Marissa hissed.

"One mile won't get you out of town—"

"I never mentioned what direction," Patrick said with exaggerated patience.

Jeremy just glared at Patrick. He was tired of the mysteries, tired of being weak, tired of having memories of Helene—

"They went one mile straight down."

Down? Jeremy puzzled that in his head. The frustration returned. "Riddles," Jeremy stated coldly, turning from the diagram to Patrick. "My father was great at riddles. Drove me nuts."

"Your dad was… uh, well, IS the world's foremost scientist on cellular programming and genetics," Patrick began. "Mine, on the other hand, is really good at building things." He turned and pointed to the diagram. "He built that."

"A weapon of some kind?"

"Something bigger," Patrick stated, a hint of a smile forming.

"A spaceship." Jeremy's patience was obviously wearing thin.

"Almost," Patrick said, exchanging glances with Leo.

Jeremy saw the look between the two boys, and slowly he turned to face Leo. And then memories of that fateful day three and a half months ago flooded into his mind. *The pep rally in the gym—Leo had mentioned something about space.* And now Leo had a mischievous look on his face. Jeremy blinked twice. "Is that some kind of stargate? You know, a doorway kind of thing—"

"A wormhole, actually," Leo said, a smile broadening on his face.

"They were underground, so I get the wormhole—"

"Geez, lunkhead, were you ever awake in science class?" Marissa stabbed at him sarcastically.

"Wormhole's compress space-time," Selene offered. Every set of eyes stared at the Chinese girl in amazement...as if the white-faced mime in the park suddenly began to speak.

"Wormhole? To where?" Jeremy asked.

"Your grandma's underpants," Marissa quipped.

Leo shot her an angry look, then turned back to Jeremy. "It's just what I told you," Leo said. "They went to another planet."

Jeremy stood, looking at each them in turn. *They were serious.*

"They call it the Portal," Leo said.

Jeremy's eyes swiveled back to Patrick, still skeptical. "So... Dr. Austin goes to Mars?"

"The planet's name is Genesis," Patrick said.

"Genesis? Is this a joke?" Jeremy said. *They're all nuts!*

"Your father didn't think so," said a voice behind Jeremy. "And neither did your brother."

Jeremy turned around, and the hair on his neck stood on end. Standing in the open doorway was Alex. "What's he doing here?" Jeremy asked, pointing to his longtime nemesis.

"How do you think Patrick got access to the school?" Alex said. "I'm student body president, remember?"

"And All-State quarterback—"

"Yeah... that too." Alex's face contained the hint of a smirk.

The two rivals stared at each other.

Patrick cleared his throat. "Dudes, let's not quibble over the past. Football is over." He turned to Jeremy. "You were missed on the team, I'm sure." Patrick's eyes then swept through each person in the room. "What we've got here is the biggest scientific cover up in the history of mankind, and our parents are at the center of it."

A single pair of hands began clapping... and they were Jeremy's. "Where's the hidden cameras? Three months in a coma and this is the story I get?!" Jeremy said. "I'm outta here!" He started toward the door.

"Your dad helped write this story!" Patrick's voice whipped Jeremy around and the intense look on Patrick's face chilled Jeremy. "For some reason—reason for which there is absolutely no logic—your dad, my dad, *our parents*, saw fit to make us a part of their cover up as well."

The heat faded from Jeremy's face. "Us?"

"Creepy," Selene whispered. She glanced around at the others like a thirteen year old watching her first horror movie.

The room was silent. Five pairs of eyes stared at Patrick.

"TerraGen found a pristine planet," Patrick began. "The perfect place to set up laboratories, do cutting edge research—"

"I've heard this story before," Jeremy said skeptically.

"I'm not talking about some stupid island, pea brain," Patrick's look at Jeremy was a scornful as his words. "We're talking a whole planet!"

Jeremy wasn't convinced. "Yeah, and they took an army of soldiers with them. Why?"

Jeremy's question hung in the air. It was Leo who cleared his throat, "Afraid of hostiles, I guess. It's a big planet—most of it unexplored."

"Excuse me," Jeremy said, "what kind of hostiles?"

"I wouldn't know." Leo's voice was hollow.

"What we *do* know…" Patrick continued, pausing for effect, "is that something went wrong. TerraGen lost contact with the expedition and were locked out of their own Portal. That is… they thought they were locked out." Patrick glanced at Leo, and then back to Jeremy. "The two men who attacked you…"

"Brogan… and—"

"*Both* were members of the expedition," Patrick continued. "Brogan Riga is an astro-physicist. He was the one who discovered the wormhole over a decade ago."

"What about the old guy?" Jeremy asked. "He was the evil bastard in charge!"

"The company has ideas, but…" Alex's voice trailed off.

"But?" Jeremy demanded.

Alex shrugged, "They've locked everything up tight. All information related to… uh… *your* attack and the Genesis expedition has been cleaned from all internal emails."

"My best hacking software bounces back like it hit a teflon wall," Patrick said.

"The old guy is…the old guy," Alex said with an authoritative air of finality—like he was prosecuting attorney delivering his final remarks to the jury. "We don't know who the old guy was."

Leo moved toward Jeremy. "We need to go on a rescue expedition to save our parents. You need to go with us." Leo's breathing was rapid, and his intensity made Jeremy take a step backward.

Jeremy couldn't believe their sincerity. "You're all insane!" He turned his attention back to Patrick. "I get it now. *You want to go through this doorway to another planet, thingy?* If TerraGen can't access their own Portal, what makes you think you can?!"

"My birthday was last month," Patrick said.

"Congratulations. Sorry I was stuck in a coma. My bad for missing it," Jeremy stated humorlessly.

"I blew out a non-existent candle on a non-existent birthday cake, opened up my laptop like I normally do, and *presto!* There was a new folder on my desktop," Patrick said. "My dad's a tricky old fart, and he programmed a special present for my eighteenth birthday."

"A secret folder just magically appeared on your desktop?" Jeremy asked with as much sarcasm as he could muster.

"Hey, your dad ain't the only genius on planet Earth," Marissa declared, coming to Patrick's defense.

Patrick exhaled, eyes blinking at Jeremy. "The folder contained documents on every project he's ever worked on." Patrick's eyes flicked to the Portal schematic, and then back to Jeremy. "It was on one of those documents—"

"He found the backdoor codes to the Portal!" burst out Selene. She had a look of wide-eyed wonder… and the look on Patrick's face was nothing but daggers.

Patrick bit his lip, then turned his attention on Jeremy. "Whatever computer virus Brogan and his *superior* loaded into the Portal's computer network I'm confident I can neutralize."

"Neutralize?" Jeremy said with much skepticism. "You're going to break into a tightly secured research facility—okay…you did that once already—it didn't work out so well the last time—"

"We survived," Patrick said acidly.

"And then you're going to disable a computer virus written by a world-class physics genius and go for a casual walk several million light-years across the galaxy!" Jeremy's face was red with anger. "Where's the dotted line so I can sign up?"

His sarcasm silenced the room.

"You wasted a lot of time waiting for me," Jeremy continued, looking each of them in the face. "You should've left a long time ago."

"It would be better if you came," Patrick said.

"No dice."

"Your DNA and *our* DNA—according to my father's documents—*everything* on the other side of the Portal uses programming based on *us*... our DNA." Patrick's words hung in the air. The computer geek picked a binder off a nearby table and continued, "I read through my father's journal—a long read—would probably put you to sleep—"

"Algebra put him to sleep," Marissa quipped.

"And science class," Selene added.

"Your father wanted a back up plan in case something went wrong and we were needed to come rescue them," Patrick finished.

"Did you plagiarize this story from one of your comic books?" Jeremy asked, smiling.

"TerraGen has many enemies," Alex said, "and the company has spies on the payroll. My old man might be a traitor to the company for all I know."

"Dr. Austin and my father didn't want to be left stranded light years from Earth," Patrick said as he placed his hand, palm downward on the binder of his father's journal. His eyes swept the room. "Together, they planned to build genetic codes—fail safes—throughout the security system of the research facility being constructed on Genesis. So you see...*we need you and your DNA.*"

All eyes looked at Jeremy. Their serious looks turned into confused ones as Jeremy began laughing. "There's only one problem," Jeremy said with strained mirth. "I'm adopted. My DNA won't match my dad's...or Erik's."

Confused looks turned to shock.

"Sorry, guys. I guess you're on your own."

No one said a word. *Adoption!* The three Austins were a fixture in their world, and now, with Jeremy's admission, that world just got spun sideways.

Now very uncomfortable, Jeremy tried to look each of the TerraGen kids in the eye, but faltered upon seeing Marissa's look of disappointment. He looked away and found Alex studying him. The sneer on Alex's face made Jeremy boil with anger. "Why are you even here, Alex? I mean, your DNA won't do squat! Or maybe they used your DNA to program a Genesis robot to write checks—"

"Why I'm here is my own business—"

"Daddy issues," Marissa blurted.

Alex chuckled sarcastically, and then the smirk returned as he looked at Jeremy. "You don't wanna go? Well, your brother thought differently. He wasn't afraid."

Jeremy's head jerked sideways as if slapped. Blinking furiously, he tried to comprehend Alex's words. "You better start explaining before I tear your head off—"

"Me and the old man don't often have father-son talks," Alex said, "and why he doesn't trust me I think is obvious—"

"Two unwanted pregnancies and an alcohol problem—" Marissa began.

"Exactly," Alex hissed, casting only a fleeting glance her way. "So most of my intel comes from spying on the old man. Six weeks ago, TerraGen's goons—you know, security— reported that someone had activated the Portal. When they checked the I.D. code used to gain access… it was your brother's."

Silence.

"If Erik could disable Brogan Riga's computer virus, then we can too."

Jeremy presented them with a look of calm indifference. But on the inside he was furious. *Erik goes off without me! How typical. He was always Dad's favorite so why should I be surprised.* Jeremy's heart pounded inside his chest and he suppressed the urge to scream. *They both abandoned me!* Deep-seated resentment toward his older brother bubbled up within him. And that resentment was also aimed at his father. *I was never smart enough for him.* His throat was suddenly bone dry, and he had to cough to clear it.

"That doesn't change anything. All of you, go without me!"

"Wow," Alex said. "Helene's killer is on the other side

of that Portal, but you'd rather stay behind. I didn't take you for a coward."

Jeremy's eyes flared and he started toward Alex, but Patrick's arms encircled him and pulled him back. "Say one more word and I'll put you in a grave next to her's!" Jeremy growled. The violence of his words caused Alex to move backward.

Patrick continued to hold Jeremy. "We're going through the Portal, with or without you. I would prefer having you with us," Patrick said quietly with a touch of compassion.

"Tell him about our window of opportunity," Alex said.

Patrick let go of Jeremy and retrieved his father's binder. "The wormhole is only active at certain periods of time—star alignment or something—but our best opportunity ends tomorrow night. After that, my best guess would be waiting until late summer."

"Great," Jeremy said indifferently. "I don't know why all the rush—"

"Something went wrong on Genesis—could be our parents are dead just like TerraGen reported," Patrick said in a strained voice. "But I'm not taking any chances! My father's not gonna die on the opposite side of the galaxy just because I waited for a more convenient opportunity."

Jeremy felt hollow inside.

"You've got till nine o'clock tomorrow night, sport," Alex sneered. "In or out, I don't care."

T HE MEN ARRIVED IN LEWISVILLE that morning, having been notified of Jeremy's transfer from TerraGen's outpatient facility to the Austin home the day before. The boy had finally come out of his coma. His emergence from the house had surprised them. Hollow cheeks and the way his clothes seemed to hang off his frame painted a picture of months of inactivity. After following Jeremy Austin to the home of the dead girl the appearance of the Korrapati boy had turned a painfully boring morning into a day of opportunity. Now their van was discreetly parked near the high school.

"That's gonna leave a stain," groaned Mats Kennet from the passenger seat. A fresh dribble of ketchup marred the front of his pressed, navy blue shirt. He was working his way through a lukewarm hamburger and none too happy.

Sitting in the back of the van was Duarte Vega. He lowered a pair of headphones from his ears and looked at Kennet. "Get me the Sat phone," Vega demanded. "Our man at Langley needs to hear this."

CHAPTER TWELVE

GEORGE TOBIAS

Attorney at Law

AN UNEXPECTED MESSAGE

THE IMPOSING MRS. FREEMAN was cooking breakfast again. Jeremy studied her from his seat at the kitchen table. The bulge on the inside of her smock spoke of a future threat. *Still packing. Doesn't even bother to hide it. Honestly, I don't feel any safer.* On the kitchen table he spun around a cell phone, flicking it with his fingers and watching it spin like a top. It annoyed the dangerous Mrs. Freeman, and that felt good to him. When Jeremy had returned to the house yesterday he could barely walk from exhaustion, and rest was the only thing on his mind. But he had found an overnight shipping package on his bed. The note taped onto the package from Freeman was very abrupt: "Came for you." Inside the package was the cell phone... and nothing else. *Was it bugged? Had Freeman sent that to him as a means of tracking his movements?*

"How many pancakes you want?" Freeman asked from the stove.

Jeremy took his eyes from the cell phone and looked at her. "Two, please."

She slid two pancakes onto his plate and stood there, staring at the phone. "Strange," she began, "you getting a package the day you wake from a coma." They exchanged looks, but Jeremy simply shrugged his shoulders. Freeman went back to the stove.

She's a pathetic actor, Jeremy mused. *Wait... had Patrick sent him the phone?* The thought of the computer genius inflicted a pang of loss in his soul. *The TerraGen kids are going through the Portal today and here I sit.* Jeremy angrily dug into the pancakes. He had a tremendous feeling of abandonment. *Serves them right if they all get killed!* He forked more of the pancakes into his mouth but his furious chewing couldn't get the images of Patrick, Marissa, Selene, and Leo out of his mind.

"You're gonna choke on them cakes if you don't slow down," Freeman warned. She watched him from the stove, like an over-protective mother hen.

"Sorry, ma'am," Jeremy mumbled.

He became fixated on the cell phone again, and was jolted by the time, which read 9:02 AM. *They're leaving in twelve hours! Why am I still sitting here? I should be packing for the expedition.*

He heard movement at the stove, and for a split second he thought his dad was there, making coffee. The bitterness returned. *I can make my own decisions! Erik and our father were always together... in everything!* In his own house, Jeremy had always felt like he was on the outside. Now he knew why. *Adopted!* Jealous pangs of anger caused his heart to start racing. Still, the emotion of being left behind kept resurfacing, and he felt the temptation to pick up the phone and call Patrick.

BUZZZZZZ!

The cell phone was vibrating with a loud buzz and Jeremy almost gagged on his food. He swiftly grabbed the phone. *BUZZZZZZ!* He switched it on and a text message appeared: 4492 CENTRAL AVENUE, SUITE 207.

Freeman peered at him. "You got a hot date?"

Jeremy shrugged his shoulders. *BUZZZZZZ!* Another text message: 4492 CENTRAL AVENUE, SUITE 207 – URGENT!

"You mind if I see who's texting you?" Freeman asked.

"Actually, I do mind," Jeremy responded, giving her his best indignant look. "I appreciate you looking after me, but as I've already told you, I don't need a nurse."

"Yeah… you did say something like that."

Jeremy kept looking at her until she finally returned to working at the stove.

BUZZZZZZ!

He almost jumped out of his chair and stared a third time at the phone: COME NOW OR SAY GOODBYE TO YOUR DAD AND BROTHER. Jeremy glanced once at Freeman then hastily ate the remaining pancake. A feeling of panic washed over him and he struggled to keep his eyes focused. *Dad and brother…* The last bite was still being swallowed when he shot up from the table and hurried out the front door.

S HE WATCHED JEREMY back the Lincoln out of the driveway and then disappear down the road—and past the white van inhabited by her two coworkers—*the killers.* Letting the drape fall against the front window, Neriah Freeman casually pulled out a cell phone of her own. She hit one button and a man's voice answered on the other end. Freeman's voice was businesslike as usual: "Yes, sir. He's going to meet someone."

THE PARKING LOT AT THE Lewisville Mall was crowded—and crowded was good. Jeremy walked briskly toward the mall's entrance, weaving through people. He glanced back only once, making sure the two men in the white van had left their vehicle. They had. He recognized the muscular, dangerous form of Duarte Vega.

While driving his father's car into town Jeremy noticed the van following him. He'd tried to lose them in the neighborhoods but they were like ticks on a dog. And then he'd thought of the mall.

People moved around Jeremy in all directions. Jeremy was halfway down the mall's main thoroughfare, and standing in front of Lewisville Sports. By appearances, he was looking through the glass window at the latest sportswear. But Jeremy was interested in the reflection in the glass which showed the two men—*TerraGen agents, more than likely*—keeping a safe distance. Jeremy moved further down the mall. He entered a large department store and quickened his pace, hurrying toward the escalator. He was trying to appear natural while keeping the two agents in sight. Riding upward to the second floor he had his back to the store's entrance, but used the mirror hung alongside the escalator's rail to see the two agents rush into the store and spot him. The second his foot touched the second floor tiles, Jeremy began to run.

BELOW, VEGA AND KENNET hastened their pace upon seeing Jeremy Austin disappear up the escalator. They barreled past an overweight couple with three kids and rushed onto the escalator, taking each step in twos until finally arriving on the second floor.

The boy was gone.

THE OFFICE BUILDING AT 4492 Central Avenue was decades old and had seen better days. Jeremy closed the door of the Lincoln and gazed at the building with dismay, still debating on whether to uncover this mystery.

This could be a trick.

At the mall, Jeremy had used one of the emergency exits to get back to the mall's parking lot. He had forced his depleted leg muscles into a sprint and gained the safety of his car wheezing from exhaustion. *Football shape* was a distant memory—every muscle in his body screamed from pain.

He walked into the building and took the elevator to the second floor. The sign for "George Tobias – Attorney at Law" was weathered and partially covered in cobwebs. Jeremy double checked the text message—*yes, Suite 207. This has to be it*. He pushed open the door. The interior of the law office mirrored the outside: old and musty.

Odd. That was the best way to describe Mr. Tobias' office. There was a receptionist desk with no receptionist. The office contained only two doors, one of which was obviously a bathroom—he could see the toilet from the foyer.

"You can come into my office, Jeremy," said a voice from the other doorway.

Jeremy hesitantly stepped forward and entered the inner office where a bald man in his late 50s sat behind a desk. The man wore glasses and studied Jeremy intently as he held out his hand. "George Tobias. Have a seat."

He shook the lawyer's hand, but something in the office was strange. Tobias' desk was empty of papers and, except for a state bar association's certification, there were no other documents or pictures of any kind on the walls. The office was like a museum display—Paul Revere's home in Boston…he'd been there once—something old and preserved but not lived in.

"The text message…?" Jeremy asked, sitting in the chair opposite the attorney.

"Which you obviously got, otherwise, why would you be here?" Tobias smiled at Jeremy.

Despite the lack of interior decorating in the office,

Tobias himself didn't look to be poverty stricken. Jeremy noticed the expensive watch, polished suit, and air of confidence with which the lawyer carried himself. Pulling the cell phone out of his pocket, Jeremy held it up and began reading: "Come now or say goodbye to your dad and brother."

"Cryptic, I have to admit," Tobias said. The lawyer immediately turned and took a large overnight shipping package off the shelf, placing it on the desk in front of Jeremy. "Did I mention that I'm your father's attorney?"

"No. I would've remembered," Jeremy said testily. *This guy's a nut case.* Looking around the office, Jeremy asked, "Is business booming, Mister Tobin? You know, people hiring you for legal stuff and all?"

"Clients?" Tobias laughed. "No! Heavens no. Just one client."

"My father," Jeremy stated and Tobias nodded. "Figures."

"Well… then again, that statement is not entirely true," Tobias corrected himself. "Actually, there are *two other* clients." The lawyer tugged and managed to pry open one end of the package. With great care, he took out a tablet computer and placed it directly in front of Jeremy.

Jeremy's patience was wearing thin. "What does my being here have anything to do with seeing my father or brother?"

Tobias sat down behind the desk. "I haven't a clue. I received this package yesterday with a note from Erik."

"Erik?" Jeremy leaned forward in surprise, his eyes drawn to the tablet.

"Yes. He's client number two… grandfathered in, you might say. And you are number *three*." Tobias gave a half smile. "Erik's note was very simple—I was to text the phone number, and the message had to be very precise."

"I don't understand," Jeremy said.

Tobias shrugged and rose to his feet.

Jeremy made as if to rise too, but Tobias motioned for

him to sit back down. Jeremy stared, open mouthed. "You're leaving?"

"I'm to do one last thing before I..." Tobias paused, then smiled. "Before I take my lunch break." Jeremy tried to speak, but the lawyer put a finger to his lips. Jeremy sat back. Tobias winked and quickly pressed the power button on the tablet.

Jeremy saw the tablet glow brightly as it booted up. *I shouldn't be here! Get up, Jeremy, and get out of this nut case's office!* He looked around the room and into the foyer, but Tobias was gone. Jeremy got up and went to the window overlooking the street. On the sidewalk below, Tobias was walking away, hands in his pockets. A sudden screech of tires caused Jeremy to look to his left. A white van—*the* white van—had stopped in the middle of the street. In front of them, two kids on bikes were shouting angrily with fists raised. *Those two guys again?*

"Hello, Jeremy."

Jeremy's head jerked around.

"I see you've come out of your coma." The voice was very familiar.

Jeremy went back to his chair and sat down, eyes fixated on the tablet computer where, dressed in wilderness gear, was... *Erik!*

"Where are you right n—" Jeremy started to speak, but Erik's voice continued—*a video recording, obviously,* he thought.

"I'm sorry I wasn't there for you the night you were attacked. Helene was a beautiful girl. She meant a lot to you, I know." Erik paused, as if in respect.

"No... you don't," Jeremy hissed bitterly.

Erik's voice was full of compassion as he continued. "The few times I met Helene, I could see her love for you. I'm sorry, little brother. Nothing I could say now will heal the hurt you must obviously feel."

Jeremy felt resentment bubbling up toward his older brother. Erik hardly knew Helene! And he certainly wouldn't have approved of her being at the house.

"The two men who attacked you—"

Jeremy's breath caught in his throat.

"—both men were part of the expedition with Dad." Erik's voice became colder. "I assume they took the diary."

"Obviously," breathed Jeremy. Although dressed is wilderness gear, Erik was filming inside an office... their father's office. *Why there?*

"I'll speak plainly," Erik said, "For the last thirty years our dad has been developing technologies that will virtually save our planet, revolutionize the treatment of all major illnesses, medicines beyond comprehension... and, he's developed a never-ending source of food." Erik paused and Jeremy leaned closer. "People will kill for that kind of technology—people in the government, people in competing companies... people within TerraGen. I'm sitting in Dad's office because it's the only room in the entire complex that I know—with one hundred percent certainty—isn't being monitored, or bugged."

Jeremy sat still, stunned.

"Brogan Riga is one of TerraGen's best scientists." A look of cold fury played out on Erik's face. "He was one of the two men who killed Helene to get Dad's research. *With the diary they escaped to a place you wouldn't believe existed in your wildest dreams—*"

"—Yeah, a planet," Jeremy muttered with a laugh.

"Their destination is code named: Genesis. And it's accessed—"

"—through a Portal. Got it."

"—through a Portal," Erik said, his face becoming still more serious and businesslike. "The fact that you're watching this video means I haven't returned from Genesis."

"—and *you're* the genius—"

"I hate to say this, little brother," Erik said with just a hint of a smile, "But the fate of Genesis—and Earth too, for that matter—may well be in your hands."

THE DUFFEL BAG SHIFTED on the bed as Jeremy stuffed clothes into it. He glanced at the clock on his bedside table which showed 7:30 PM. *I'm running out of time.* One drawer after another was pulled out, and various items of clothing were grabbed and put into the bag. He pulled on his high school letter jacket and grimaced at the way it swallowed his thin frame. *Weight gain, next on the agenda*, he thought ruefully. From time to time he would strain his ears for any sign of Neriah Freeman—she had been absent when he returned from the lawyer's office. Erik's video message had lasted for almost an hour. After a final goodbye to Jeremy there had been a soft, *POOF,* and then Erik's face was lost in a small cloud of black smoke. *Leave it to Erik to have the computer self-destruct.* A pair of hiking boots was the last item Jeremy was going to pack.

Photos grabbed his attention. The collection of pictures on his dresser. His dad's serious face in a lecture at Harvard. His dad's serious face receiving the Nobel Prize in Physics in Stockholm, Sweden. There were a couple family pictures: Jeremy with his dad and Erik. His older brother's smiling face beamed from a collection of travel photos: China, Africa, the Amazon, Japan...

A stirring of electricity began in his stomach, then travelled upward. *His father and brother were on a planet in a distant galaxy.* The photo of Erik in the Amazon—wide hat, camouflage pants and shirt—holding a rare plant species.

What kind of planet is Genesis?

Was it like the Amazon? Green jungles? Deadly snakes? Ancient civilizations?

Excitement coursed through Jeremy's body—the anticipation of the night's adventure calling to him with more force than a football championship game *ever* could have. *He* would be going through a Portal—wearing the latest in survival gear...he must make a shopping run by the local sporting goods store—or is there a wilderness outfitter he should go to? He could go back to the mall.

Weapons. *Hmmmm...* hostile aliens... *Hmmmmm.* A pistol? Rifle? Danger of the unknown made his heart beat faster. He'd watched his fair share of sci-fi movies. Aliens with acid for blood. Alien cyborgs. Alien creatures with two heads. Female humanoids with three... *well, best not think of that.*

Click.

Jeremy turned around.

"You're a busy little beaver," Neriah Freeman said. Her face was cold and emotionless as she aimed her revolver at his forehead. "I guess being in a coma for three months left you with a backlog of errands to run. You've made some associates of mine just a little more than curious..."

I N THE DRIVEWAY OF THE Austin house, the white van was parked. Doors opened. Duarte Vega and Mats Kennet emerged, sliding pistols into holsters as they walked to the front door.

CHAPTER THIRTEEN

EXPEDITIONARY FORCES

NOT ONLY WERE MRS. FREEMAN'S EYES imposing when just making breakfast in the kitchen—her stare alone sent chills down his spine—but those same eyes behind a very businesslike Glock 50 were even more imposing. And now all he could see of Mrs. Freeman was the back of her head as they walked into a large aircraft hangar at the Lewisville Airport. Duarte Vega and Kennet trailed behind Jeremy with flat stares.

A private jet was parked in the middle of the hangar with the emblem of the United States located next to the plane's registration number. Beyond the plane, a small group of people were milling around. Jeremy recognized Patrick at once. And then he saw that all of the TerraGen kids were there—all looking at him with unhappy faces.

"Now that *you're* here," Patrick said sarcastically, "it must be the end of the world." The backpack on Jeremy's shoulder caught Patrick's attention. "They pack that for you?"

"No, dirtbag, I changed my mind. Scout's honor." Jeremy said. He counted Leo, Marissa, Selene and, with his ever-present smirk, Alex—all standing there with forlorn faces. Their backpacks and survival gear were stacked on the hangar floor.

"Finally, we have a quorum," came a familiar voice. Jeremy turned and saw, dressed in black khakis and shouldering a handgun, the CIA agent. Lachlan Evans stared into Jeremy's eyes as if appraising him. "How was the coma?"

"Too long," Jeremy replied. He was suddenly filled with immense distrust of this government agent.

"No one knows that better than me," Evans said, eyebrows raised. He turned and addressed the entire group. "For obvious reasons, let's dispense of word games, shall we? No need for any subterfuge—*but really, officer, we were just going on a camping trip!*—please, spare me the lies."

"Spare me the *act*," Marissa's voice echoed in the hangar.

Evans paused, glancing at the half-smile on Marissa's face before addressing the entire group again, "I know all about your plans: TerraGen's Portal to a distant planet, going off to save mom and dad—believe me, I share your enthusiasm… and this little doggie is tagging along for the ride."

"You're what?!" Patrick's voice boomed.

"We're not going to prison?" Selene blurted out.

"Hardly, Ms. Choi," Evans said, smiling. "I'm joining you on your quest."

"I'll take prison, thank you very much," Marissa deadpanned.

"No one asked you to come along!" protested Alex.

Evans didn't even flinch. "I won't hold that against you. But rest assured, myself and few of my colleagues have signed up, paid our fees, and are joining you wonderful kids on tonight's expedition!" Evans face was buoyant and youthful. He suddenly glanced at his wristwatch. "And time is a' tick'in."

"Colleagues? How many colleagues?" Alex's voice was still defiant.

"Friends… just a few," Evans responded.

"And TerraGen's given you permission?" Alex questioned with a sneer.

"Same permission as yours."

A queasy, sickened look came over Alex, and he began to sweat. "Ours? But…but we've got special permission b-because of our puh-parents!"

"Yes, I know," Evans smiled. "I assure you, Mister Alexander Leach, Junior, that your father would absolutely approve of my tagging along… off the books, or course, to protect TerraGen's liability. The U.S. Government is one of the company's biggest clients." He looked at each of the kids, ending with Jeremy. "And tonight, we're joining forces. We're protecting the government's interest by protecting TerraGen's latest technology." The smile on Evan's face was wolfish.

"Protect? Or appropriate?" Patrick asked.

Evan's turned an appraising eye on Patrick. "Trust me when I say that you're going to *want* our protection." He stepped back. "Three and half months ago, a small army of highly trained soldiers with the latest weapons traveled through that Portal and haven't been heard from since. What did they encounter? Why the silence?" Evans no longer smiled. "Something to think about." The CIA man turned and headed deeper into the hangar, motioning for them to follow with a flick of his fingers.

Jeremy caught Patrick's eye and both shared concerned looks.

They were led into an adjoining hangar. It wasn't

the sight of the two tractor trailers that caused their jaws to collectively drop open—it was the rows and rows of high-tech weaponry that were being packed into shipping containers by over a hundred soldiers. *Private security or mercenaries more than likely,* thought Jeremy. The men barely glanced at the kids.

"You're going to be glad we came along," Evans repeated. The CIA man suddenly looked out the hangar doors on their left, and his expression became bitterly cold.

T HE BLACK LIMOUSINE PULLED up next to the hangar where the two tractor trailers were being loaded. Robert Morton stepped out, smelling the new clothes smell of his very expensive, recently purchased hiking gear. Gravel crunched under the soles of his five hundred dollar hiking boots. Mortan smiled as he studied the grim expression on Lachlan Evans' face as the agent walked up to him.

"Morton, what on earth—?" Evans began.

"Thought you might need a little company," Morton said flatly in a tone that offered no recourse. Stepping out of the limo behind Morton was his aide, Pritchard Durant. The brand new hiking outfit seemed to hang loosely on Durant's wiry frame. The former Ivy Leaguer had a pained expression on his face, glancing furtively to watch the soldiers loading the weapons into two black, semi-trailer trucks.

"But the dangers!" Evans exclaimed.

"If the technology is as extraordinary as you hinted at," Morton said, "then I want to be part of its discovery." The angered look on Evan's face justified every one of Morton's gut feelings. *This pup actually thought he was in charge.*

"Have you ever been in the field, sir?" Evans cautioned. He motioned to Durant. "What about your aide? Frankly, we have no idea how dangerous this Genesis is."

"Put our things next to yours: we'll take care of ourselves," Morton commanded, then gave Evans a measured look. "Don't worry, Lachlan, this is your mission. I won't be quick to countermand your leadership."

Evans' face changed from angry upstart to obedient dog in just a flicker of time—good boy, Morton thought. "Yes, sir." Evans said without emotion...and then turned on his heels and walked back to the hangar.

Morton felt a pair of eyes boring holes into his back, and he turned to look at Durant. All of the color had drained from the aide's face. "Suck it up, Yalie! You can't get anywhere in politics without taking a few risks!" Durant simply nodded wordlessly.

Chapter Fourteen

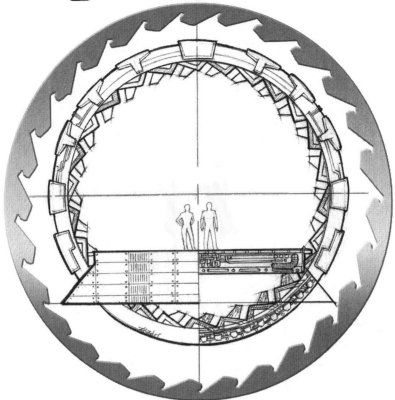

The Portal

TerraGen lay in darkness with just the lights of the parking lot illuminating the grounds. The main building was completely dark, an unheard of event before the first expedition. Now it was like a tomb. Jacked up on too much caffeine and pacing nervously at the security gate was Benton Keene. A veteran of foreign wars as part of the elite Special Forces, it had been many years since Keene had felt the queasy, bowel loosening fear before a mission— he felt it now, and cursed. Too many years and too many strings had been pulled to bring him to this moment. And like a house of cards, he knew the entire operation could crumble with one little mistake. And their window of time was closing fast.

"Time, time, time!" Keene growled, tapping his watch like an expectant father.

The lights of the black tractor trailers pierced the darkness just before the sound of the truck's engines reached his ears. Casting a furtive glance back toward TerraGen's headquarters, Keene watched as the trucks pulled up to the guardhouse, almost blinding him. He licked his dry lips. *Here goes everything.*

The first eighteen wheeler rolled by and Keene saw the face of Lachlan Evans staring down at him. Keene merely nodded. The second truck whipped past him, and he lowered the gate. Keene had dreamt of this day for over three months and it was finally here. *Finally.*

THE TWO TERRAGEN security guards at Checkpoint Alpha merely nodded at Keene as the massive steel door rumbled open behind them. Behind Keene stood rows upon rows of private soldiers and their motorized carts loaded down with weapons and tactical gear.

Lachlan Evans leaned in behind Keene and whispered in his ear. "Everything secure below?"

"My men control the Portal," Keene said. *And for the next six hours I control the TerraGen complex,* he thought with a smile. It had taken Keene the last twelve months to replace Barbara Yossarian's hired security officers with men loyal to him. A year of careful planning had taken place for this six-hour window of opportunity. "Everything is prepped and ready on my end. You have the codes?"

"I wouldn't be here without them."

"Perfect," Keene replied.

The tunnel door swung open and the expectant face of Dr. Rudolf Hicks looked at both men. Hicks stood in the middle of the huge elevator dressed like an African safari guide.

"I thought this place was secure!" Evans hissed with alarm.

"Our good Mister Hicks is my stroke of genius," Keene responded with a smile.

Hicks walked up to the two men, his lips quivering with excitement. "We're actually going through? Really?"

"Not without you, Mr. Hicks," Keene reassured with a smile.

"And the Board of Directors?" Hicks asked. Keene pivoted to reveal the TerraGen kids standing further down the tunnel. Hicks saw Jeremy Austin and Alexander Leach at once. "Marvelous! Alexander's boy as well. I feel so much better, knowing the Board supports the rescue expedition. Perfect!"

Keene's plastic smile didn't falter for even a nano-second. Hicks' enthusiasm was so childlike it made Keene sick.

"I've always wanted to see the other side!" Hicks said with wide-eyed wonder.

THE HUM OF THE LARGE ELEVATOR added to Jeremy's nervousness. Lights flashed upward as they descended. Casting glances at Patrick, Selene, and Marissa, he saw the fear in their eyes that mirrored his own. Alex stole a glance at him, then quickly looked down at the floor.

He's nervous. Jeremy started to smile, then remembered Erik's words from the video. "You think TerraGen is owned by a corporation or by the Board of Directors, or even by Alexander Leach? Think again. Leach is simply a figurehead. Every patent ever filed by TerraGen Universal is registered under the name of Dr. Victor Austin. Our father! You were almost killed because our enemies know that you are heir to one of the richest companies in the world." The concept of wealth was foreign to Jeremy. They had lived modestly, and his dad had always made him earn his allowance.

But wealthy? Stinking wealthy?

If he survived this expedition through a wormhole he would have strong words for his father—well, actually one word—*relocation*. Not that he wanted to flaunt their wealth. But at least an upgrade in their living situation. A bigger house—bigger television—maybe a gym and sauna—

Ding! The elevator came to a stop, the gravity shifted, and Jeremy felt his pulse racing. The wide elevator doors opened and their group stepped into a huge, vaulted room where a squad of armed soldiers met them. Behind them he could see even more soldiers escorting a line of motorized carts, each stacked high with shipping containers that were being funneled through a large, hangar door.

"This is the Portal Bay," Hicks' voice whispered in reverence, resuming his role as tour guide for the kids. "The Control Center is to our left." He pointed to the three-story building with mirrored glass. "Our journey will be programmed in the action station—all state of the art quantum computers with nuclear power—no dangers of power outages there!" And then Hicks' voice seemed to catch in his throat. "And straight ahead... well, let me just say that it's the closest thing to experiencing the supernatural."

Jeremy heard a snicker. He looked around. Alex was staring fixedly at the Control Center, as were Patrick and Marissa. And then came a second snicker, and Jeremy saw that it was from Leo. The stocky boy was shaking his head with mirth. And then Leo caught Jeremy's gaze, and the pudgy boy lifted one eyebrow before looking stoically ahead.

Several of the soldiers glanced at the group of high school students as they walked past. When they stepped into the Portal Chamber, the air seemed to be sucked out of Jeremy's chest. Before them was a long, metal platform that stretched into darkness.

"Go ahead, kids," Hicks said with unabashed wonder. "Step onto the embarkation platform." The smile on the research director's face reminded Jeremy of his third grade teacher, Mrs. McCaffrey (she had always given out stale candy and cheerfully cheesy quotes of the day).

Lights winked on and off along the platform. At the far end he could see a large curved structure made of metal—no, *not* a curve. Jeremy walked to one edge of the platform and looked to the far end. Glowing faintly in a silver light was the largest ring he'd ever seen. The platform, stretching hundreds of yards, intersected the ring a third of the way from the bottom of the circle.

"The Portal," came the voice of Dr. Rudolf Hicks. Jeremy turned and found Hicks at his elbow, looking intently at him. "Your father's dream," Hicks continued. Jeremy looked at the far end, and the Portal's silver glow seemed to pulsate… and he found that he wasn't breathing.

OR Patrick Korrapati, the idea of following his father through a wormhole across the known galaxy was the ultimate irony. He wasn't scared of the wormhole—*easy peasy*—but he was absolutely terrified of meeting his father on an alien planet. Before the Portal ripped a hole in their family three months ago, Patrick had lived in holy fear of Dr. Sudarshan Korrapati. His father was a physics genius and a strict disciplinarian around the house. God forbid he should ever get a grade less than an 'A'. What excuses can you give to the father who was given the Nobel Peace Prize for physics?

Patrick had always attributed his own rebellious spirit to an attempt to climb out from under his father's shadow.

What a crock, he thought now. *I just wanted his attention.*

His dad was now missing. But would Dr. Korrapati welcome him with open arms on the other side of the Portal?

"Dad's gonna kill me," Patrick mumbled.

"Actually, the wormhole might do that for you," Dr. Hicks whispered in his ear.

Patrick looked down at Hicks, but the man wasn't smiling. "How... exactly?"

Hicks leaned even closer to Patrick's ear, and the smell of garlic and onions almost made Patrick's stomach hurl. "At the core of the Portal is the space-time continuum that controls the wormhole," Hicks stated in a hushed whisper. There was then an uncomfortable silence.

"And?" Patrick asked impatiently.

"And? Well..." Hicks seemed to squirm a little. "There is one little issue—"

"That causes death?"

"Death is relative—"

"Relative?" Patrick asked in confusion. "You either exist or you're dead. What's relative?"

"It's *when* you die," Hicks stated. "I really shouldn't say any more—"

"Oh, but you will—"

"Fine," Hicks said with resignation. The garlic was causing Patrick's stomach to heave. "The wormhole does have issues with stability. There! That's all I'll say!"

"Issues with time?"

Hicks leaned away from Patrick and just shook his head noncommittally. "Nothing to worry about, really. They assured me they fixed all the bugs months ago."

"Comforting," Patrick mumbled.

A second voice cut in from his left. "I'll be needing both of you in the Control Center." The look Lachlan Evans gave to Patrick brooked no refusal.

Hicks suddenly seemed to be filled with energy. "Yes! Time to enter the protocol." Hicks turned to Patrick. "You have the backdoor codes, Mr. Korrapati?"

Yes, I have the codes, Patrick calculated, *but would the CIA man put a bullet in my head if I refused? The decision was relatively easy, taking that argument into account.*

Patrick nodded his head in the affirmative.

They led Dr. Hicks and Patrick into the three-story structure that overlooked the embarkation platform. The size and scope of the Portal project had intimidated him… and to know that his own father had built this facility, helped design the quantum computers and the Portal interface… whatever respect he held for his old man had increased a hundred-fold.

Dad, you do good work, he thought.

They entered the operations room where the core of the quantum computers resided within air-cooled chambers. Hicks was quick to lead them to the central console. He turned and looked at Patrick expectantly.

"Make like a rockstar, Patrick," Evans said. "Show us that all of this preparation hasn't been a total waste."

Or what? Introduce me to your little friend…the Glock? Patrick put the thought out of his head and stepped to the console, feeling Evans eyes boring into him. With a deep breath, he calmly entered his father's thirty-digit backdoor code.

On the computer screen, the TerraGen logo spun into view.

Hicks' eyes grew large and his jaw dropped open. "We've waited months for this," he said. The research director moved past Patrick and sat down at the console. The fingers of Hicks' hands tapped quickly. A three dimensional image of the Portal appeared followed by the words: PORTAL TRANSIT REQUEST. "We've begun," Hicks whispered.

Patrick watched as Hicks keyed in the coordinates for planet 7005TG401. The display went black, and then seven letters appeared, each in succession: G-E-N-E-S-I-S. A planet with two moons rotated on the screen. There were multiple continents within the oceans. Mountain ranges ran vertically along the globe… and on the center of the globe, a pinpoint of light pulsated.

"Your dad is there," Hicks said, pointing to the flashing light.

"How far?"

"Two point four million light years, give or take." Hicks replied.

"We just… step through?" Patrick asked, the idea of Portal travel difficult to comprehend.

"They tell me it's like riding a roller coaster without the comfort of being strapped in," Hicks said. He pressed a button on the keyboard and a countdown began: 5:00, 4:59, 4:58. "No turning back now. Come!" He beckoned both Patrick and Lachlan Evans to leave the operations room.

Despite the rush to leave, one question kept nagging at the back of Patrick's mind. "When are we scheduled to return?"

"We haven't even left and you want to return already?" Hicks exclaimed, tugging on Patrick's arm while giving him a condescending look. "Return transit is done at the other end. Nothing to worry about." Hicks gestured to Evans while giving Patrick a radiant smile of absolute confidence. "Our Mr. Evans and the U.S. Government are backing this endeavor. Their agents on Genesis guarantee that the return transit is one hundred percent secure. Now, let's hurry! You don't want to miss what comes next!"

As they left the operations room, Patrick caught a singular motion from the CIA man—Evans right hand had been hidden inside the pocket of his pants, but was suddenly yanked out and now hung casually by his side. As Evans walked by, Patrick glanced a second time at the CIA man's pocket and saw the outline of a pistol.

MARISSA STOOD ON THE embarkation platform with trepidation. The dark eye shadow she wore gave her a deathly look, but, the emotion currently wracking her soul was guilt. *Was it just this morning that she'd hastily written a note to her mother? A pathetic note, she mused. Nothing deep. Nothing personal. Just a quick, "Hey, I'm going out of town for the weekend with a bunch of friends, don't worry!" And that was all. Pathetic.*

Her mother, Camilla, might never see her again. Fourteen year old Tiffany and 11 year old Clarisse—her precious sisters—would be without an older sis to look out for them. *It was her dad's fault for going off on a whacked expedition in the first place!*

She and her mother had never seen eye to eye. But oddly enough, she was more like her mother than her father. Dr. Geraldo Torres had developed breakthrough medicines and was world famous for his vaccines, but it was from her mother that Marissa got her dry, sarcastic sense of humor. Her father trusted everyone. Her mother? Her mother *should've* been busting jewel thieves for Interpol because no one could get anything past her.

Dr. Geraldo Torres had given Marissa an incredibly high IQ—and that IQ was now getting her into a world of trouble. *Wormholes? A distant planet? Hopefully the aliens are cute*, she mused.

Marissa moved to the edge of the platform and carefully looked below—nothing but blackness. The embarkation platform seemed to float in midair. She turned to see Patrick exit the Control Center with Hicks and the CIA creep following. *I don't trust Evans one bit.*

THUMP!

The platform almost shook from the sonic boom, and Marissa had to catch herself from falling over the edge. At the far end, the gigantic ring suddenly began to pulsate with a bluish light.

THUMP!

Inside her chest, fear mingled with excitement— excitement mingled with guilt. "Sorry, Mom," she whispered.

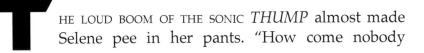

THE LOUD BOOM OF THE SONIC *THUMP* almost made Selene pee in her pants. "How come nobody warned us about that?" Selene whispered to no one in particular. "Geez!" Several of the motorized carts with shipping containers moved past her and she immediately began to review every item of clothing she had packed. *This Genesis planet better have a medi-spa*, she thought.

"Nothing to worry about," Hicks said with undisguised enthusiasm as he walked over to her. "The Portal goes through contractions like an expectant mother. Totally normal!"

I hope Mom appreciates what I'm doing for her, mused Selene. She figured that if her mother could go through this… Portal… then why not her? *Wormhole? Big deal!*

"Those shoes are so unusual!" Dr. Hicks exclaimed.

Selene looked down at the fuchsia-colored hiking boots she'd purchased two days ago, "Thirty percent off," Selene said. "They're durable—a mixture of style and rugged stability." She was proud of her boots, although she knew her mother wouldn't approve. Her mother had no fashion sense, and Selene had given up trying to educate her mother shortly after her twelfth birthday.

Leaves, photosynthesis, fungi, algae, chlorophyll, habitats, soil erosion—these were the elements that meant the most to her mother. Dr. Midori Choi, Selene's mother, was a botanist of some renown and was paid handsomely by TerraGen. *Of course, she's a tree hugger, so what would she know of fashion?*

Her mother treated her like a plant—always digging, pruning, and clipping her wings whenever Selene got too big for her britches. Dr. Midori Choi smothered her daughter— *yes…with love…but smothering is smothering.* And now Selene was embarking on an adventure of her own choosing. *Yes, it was to find her mother, but that doesn't change the fact that this was my own decision. Finally!*

THUMP!

Okay…maybe this decision had been made a bit too quickly, she thought with a fearful groan.

THE FILE OF SOLDIERS and their motorized carts moved past Leo down the long embarkation platform. He glanced to where the CIA man—*Evans, I think his name is*—looking all secret agent and whispering to an older man. *Another government agent, I bet.* Leo moved backward, using Alex to shield him from the two men.

He looked the other direction and saw Marissa backing away from the platform's edge. *Why the harsh makeup? I don't get it.*

Marissa saw Leo studying her. "Don't get any ideas, Tyrannus. Going on this expedition doesn't mean we're close or anything."

Leo simply shrugged his shoulders and stared forward. *None of the other kids in school ever paid me any attention, so why would this be any different?*

"Your dad tell you anything about this Portal?" Marissa's question took Leo by surprise. He felt heat flush on his face, and he averted his eyes from the intensity of her gaze.

"Maybe," Leo said, unable to prevent the smile that played at his lips. He fought to control his emotions, his voice cold and unreadable. "One piece of advice, Marissa?"

"Don't drink the water?"

"No," he said without humor. "Don't take anything for granted."

In fact, Leo knew more than anyone on this embarkation platform what lay on the other side. His father's notebook had been very explicit. A school outcast his whole life, the pudgy, non-athletic genius from the Tyrannus household inwardly patted himself on the back. *Knowledge is power,* he thought and grinned—excitement poured through every cell of his body like electricity and he stifled a laugh.

ALEX WATCHED BABY TYRANNUS talking to the Torres girl, and he couldn't hide the scorn on his face.

What a loser. No, two losers. They'll probably hold everything up—get lost in the woods—get eaten by cannibals—die. The fact that Leo had an IQ in triple digits above Alex really irked—*aren't I the son of Lewisville's most powerful CEO?* The ever present sneer twisted Alex' lips. Alex caught a quick glance from Marissa before the Halloween reject turned away, ignoring him. His sneer turned into one of disgust. Alex had eavesdropped on his father's Board of Directors meetings over the years and knew how much money Dr. Geraldo Torres's pharmaceutical drugs had brought into the company—billions! What happened to the daughter? Alex never understood the subversive makeup trend. Marissa was better suited leading a witches coven than tagging along on an expedition that might prove to be physically dangerous.

"So, why do we have the unfortunate pleasure of Lewisville's most likely to succeed?" Alex turned and found the eyes of the ultra-nerd, Patrick, boring into him. "Why give up partying with your jock buddies—what's your club name? The Mighty Six? *Mighty stoned* would be a better description."

"Don't push me, nerd!" Alex hissed. The one kid at Lewisville High that refused to give him any respect, Patrick was the proverbial thorn in Alex' side—always mouthing off. Alex looked forward to the day he gave the son of Sudarshan Korrapati a lesson in humility. *He ain't so smart.*

"Seriously. What agenda are you hoping to accomplish?"

Alex would never reveal his true reasons—getting out from under his father's shadow in a audacious act of defiance—so he'd rehearsed his pre-planned reason for just a moment like this. "My father approached me—practically begged me to be a part of the expedition. The Leach's aren't just corporate leaders, Patrick, we're actually committed to your best interest."

"Your father signed off on this *secret* excursion?"

As far as Alex was aware, no one on TerraGen's Board of Directors knew of this hostile takeover of the Portal and its wormhole—especially his father. "Yes. Why else would I be here and put up with your filth?"

"Alex' presence is what convinced me to brave the unknown," Dr. Hicks' voice broke into their standoff. The Research Director was standing beside them, brimming with excitement. "I don't normally go *into the field,* as they say."

"I'm not sure what your *normal* is, Dr. Hicks," Patrick said, an eyebrow raised.

"Yes. Quite right," Hicks said with a giggle. "You have your father's sense of humor, young Patrick."

"And his arrogance," Alex sneered.

Patrick ignored the comment, turned and moved away. Alex fumed darkly.

"You two really must learn to get along," Hicks said reproachfully.

"Sell that to someone who cares, egghead," Alex snarled.

Dr. Hicks, with a look of distaste, silently moved after Patrick.

Crackpot, Alex thought coldly. *My days of taking orders is officially over!*

"Wormhole…it sounds so disgusting," Selene Choi moaned. The Asian girl moved into his view, and Alex snickered. The Chinese girl with nothing but air between her ears—she won't last a day. "Is there another way to get us to this Genesis planet?"

"Faster than light travel hasn't been invented yet," Jeremy Austin responded. Alex's gaze shifted to where Jeremy stood and felt a pang of jealousy. Jeremy oozed confidence—confidence Alex didn't feel. He wasn't sure going through a wormhole was the smartest of *life choices.* But Austin's kid was committed to the expedition and so Alexander Leach, Jr. had to put on a brave face as well. Jeremy Austin… every aspect of this expedition seemed to revolve around him. *Why? My dad's the president of TerraGen—isn't he the ultimate authority?*

A figure nearby studied the way Alex watched Jeremy.

"He's going to need your protection, you know." Alex caught a whiff of garlic as he turned to find Dr. Hicks—*again*—at his elbow. Hicks' voice was almost in earnest. "Your father is placing a lot responsibility in your hands."

"Me? Responsible for him?" Alex said incredulously.

"Why else would you be here?"

"Well, uh, why is it so important?"

Hicks turned and stared at Jeremy. "Everything related to Dr. Victor Austin is of extreme importance."

Alex followed the research director's gaze and bridled at the almost worship look in Hicks' eyes as he studied Jeremy.

THUMP! The platform shook again and Jeremy's eyes became fixated on the Portal ring at the far end. Blue and green light flickered along the ring's metal surface. Inside the ring, the air shimmered with silver light, pulsating and growing thicker by the second. Soon, the embarkation platform disappeared behind the Portal as the silver sheen of pulsating light filled the ring.

"Keene!" Lachlan Evans' voice traveled down the platform to where Benton Keene jerked around in attention. "Take the advance scouts through!"

Keene turned and barked orders to the soldiers around him. "You heard the man! Forward scouts on me!" And with that, Benton Keene walked into the Portal. His body shimmered in the silver light and was suddenly swallowed whole. Jeremy moved sideways to get a better view. Two dozen soldiers, machine guns at the ready, marched into the Portal and were also swallowed by the sheen.

"Wait!" Evans' voice halted the next squad of soldiers who were all too eager to follow their comrades. "Count to sixty and then proceed!"

Jeremy felt his own pulse quicken. His heart pounded in his chest, and for a moment, he felt he was going to vomit. *Wouldn't that be awesome.*

A second squad of soldiers filed through the Portal. The soldiers attending to the motorized carts went next. Each soldier seemed to turn into silver light themselves before they vanished.

Heavy breathing sounded behind Jeremy, and he twisted around to see Hicks looking very pale. "This is all so overwhelming!" Hicks wheezed. "Totally unexpected!" Jeremy smiled and turned to find Lachlan Evans and Neriah Freeman standing in front of him.

"Keep to the rear, Mr. Austin," Evans said. "This is your father's creation we're visiting. Wouldn't want to risk a vital asset we may need on the other side." Turning to Freeman his tone became cold. "You'll continue to look after young Mister Austin until I say otherwise."

"Understood." Freeman's tone was devoid of emotion.

The CIA man turned and motioned to the man from Washington. "Let's not keep the men waiting! Kids... follow Mister Morton."

Their footsteps were silent thumps on the embarkation platform, drowned out by the pulsating booms from the Portal. Jeremy was inwardly surprised at the stoic looks on each of his classmate's faces—Patrick, Marissa, Selene, Leo and Alex—each walking with purposeful steps. Behind Jeremy walked Lachlan Evans, bringing up the rear. Ahead, he saw the Washington man, Morton, disappear into the Portal.

"Keep a distance of ten feet!" Hicks voice was strident. "Very critical!" The research director then walked the ten feet toward the Portal. Jeremy heard him gasp in amazement... and then Hicks disappeared into the silver light.

Patrick stepped up to the ring. A slow smile spread over the whiz kid's face, "Cosmic!" And then Patrick stepped through, the light swallowing him whole. Marissa was next, and then the rest of the kids.

Jeremy stepped toward the ring, and then a gasp of surprise escaped his own lips. The silver light was only an illusion. Standing just inches from the gigantic ring, he saw that the light wasn't silver at all. Amidst the hum of electricity that caused the hairs on his body to stand at attention, Jeremy realized that he was staring into: the inky blackness of deep space. What he took for a silver sheen was actually pinpricks of light—each light blurred and moving rapidly from the huge doorway's center point and traveling outward in all directions.

The light whipping past Jeremy became infused with color—the deepest blues, reds, and oranges, which turned into mixtures of all of them—and then galaxies came and went. Quasars, white dwarfs, supernovas, and other celestial bodies blurred past him. He stood transfixed as he gazed light years across the universe, his pupils constricting as the space grew brighter. Fear suddenly shot through him... not from the doorway's light display but from the power radiating from it.

Like a magnet, the Portal pulled at him, beckoning him to step through.

He took a deep breath, clenched his fists, and stepped forward. His foot touched the light and suddenly he was pulled inward. Air exploded from his lungs and he gasped, mind reeling from the awesome gravitational pull. The light became so brilliant his closed eyelids couldn't keep it out.

And then the presence of an alien being entered Jeremy's mind as the light engulfed him.

Jeremy screamed.

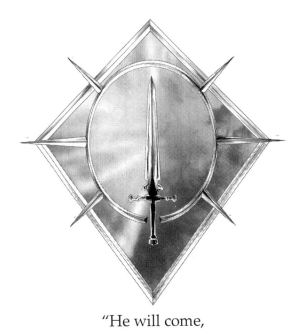

"He will come,

unheralded and without recognition;

into a land hungering for truth

he will bring the sword of light."

SACRED KADIMAH SCROLLS – Chapter 7:8

CHAPTER FIFTEEN

BEWARE WHAT LIES ON THE OTHER SIDE

WHITE LIGHT ENCASED HIM like a blanket. Closing his eyes did no good; it penetrated to the core of his mind.

Something is trying to possess me!

Jeremy fought against the light like a fly caught in a spider's web. He became aware of a probing, the gentle pressure of a foreign intelligence into his brain. The alien force pushed, invaded... and then a gate seemed to open into his mind. Information poured into his mind—alien places, people, history, technology, science—all from this foreign intelligence. His body trembled at the influx of power—a tingling sensation prickled every skin cell on his body...yet, no pain. His eyelids twitched and his hands clenched and unclenched. He felt like his brain was going to explode if it didn't stop soon.

"Aaahhhhhhh!" He shouted, but was unable to stop the influx of information.

Whoosh! The transmission stopped. Jeremy breathed heavily. His body was still surrounded by the white light, electricity pouring through every nerve. The blood in his temples pounded rhythmically like a tribal war dance. And then an image formed in his mind, hazy, indistinct, blurred, and rotating. It took on the form of a man. And then the man came into focus.

"Hello, son. So glad you could make it."

LEX BLINKED. FINALLY HE was doing something on his own—*in spite of the old man!* This Genesis might have some dangers, but at least he was master of his own destiny. He blinked again. After stepping through the Portal's shimmering mist gravity had pulled at him. Now, stars whipped past...and then a pinprick of light grew—*WHOOSH!*—and suddenly he was walking onto a platform and Dr. Hicks was shaking his hand.

"I don't know about you but that quite took my breath away!" Hicks exclaimed breathlessly. Hicks looked past Alex and his face darkened. "Oh dear."

Alex turned and took a step backward in surprise. Five figures hovered in midair, toes just inches off the platform and arms by their sides, their eyes rolled back in their heads. Alex moved to look closer: Jeremy, Patrick, Marissa, Selene, and Leo were *floating in the air* with an aura of electricity surrounding them, shielding them. Suddenly, Alex' view was blocked by a very angry Lachlan Evans who studied the five TerraGen kids.

"What's next!?" Evans hissed in frustration. "We travel millions of light years across the galaxy just so that our five treasured assets can be locked in some kind of trance—"

"A possibility I tried to impress on you—" Hicks ventured.

"Shut it!" Evans wheeled away from the frightened Hicks and moved past him, signaling seventy yards down the platform to where Benton Keene stood at the head of his security force—a force Alex estimated to be over 100 soldiers . "Keene, have you established a perimeter?"

"In progress," the security director shouted back.

Evans turned back to Hicks. "Doctor, it's time to find out how things operate on this side of the galaxy." Hicks tried to reply, but Evans had already moved to join Keene, sidestepping motorized carts and lines of soldiers. One detail jumped out at Alex: whereas the platform at TerraGen was made of solid metal, cleaned and polished to reflect the tiniest of light, *this* platform was covered in dust, as if it had spent centuries in disuse. The only thing providing light were the powered lanterns spaced along the platform, but the light's glow barely reached the cavernous roof overhead.

"Wanna come?" Hicks offered to Alex's surprise.

"What about them?" Alex asked, pointing to his five floating classmates.

"They're not going anywhere," Hicks replied as he turned and followed Lachlan Evans.

Alex glanced briefly at Jeremy and the others and felt a stab of jealousy. Once again he felt like he'd been left out. The sneer returned to his lips.

"Losers."

TWO DAYS AGO, ROBERT MORTON had been sitting in a Senate sub-committee. Now he was on another planet. Beside him, the wiry frame of Pritchard Durant seemed to shrink in fear. The *walk* through the Portal had obviously unnerved his aide. *Soft and weak. Our next generation of leaders.* Morton almost choked on the thought.

"What next?" Durant's voice was almost childlike.

"Stay put and don't anger the mercenaries," Morton said sarcastically. "You'll live longer." Morton saw Lachlan Evans heading toward the opposite end of the platform and he quickly followed after.

N O SECURITY CODE. ODD. Lachlan Evans knew the door leading into the Control Center should've been locked with a sophisticated security code. It was a problem Benton Keene had foreseen, and had counted on Dr. Rudolf Hicks to give them access. But Keene had worried for nothing. Instead, Evans found an open stone doorway with a circular stairway leading upward. The stone steps were made from large granite blocks and reminded him of the medieval castles he'd toured in Europe. His footsteps echoed on the stairs as he went upward. Behind him, the curious faces of Robert Morton and Hicks followed.

S TANDING ON THE EMBARKATION platform Alex felt lost...and alone. His *friends*—that is, his fellow students—were suspended in mid-air in some kind of zombie trance, while all around him soldiers armed themselves, slamming magazines into assault rifles, opening crates with yet more sophisticated weaponry... in short, he was smack in the middle of the next world war. Dr. Hicks disappeared into a stairway and Alex quickly moved to follow after him. *Better to follow someone I know than to stand around a bunch of muscle-heads who might kill me just for looking at them.*

He entered the stairwell and moved quickly upward. Dust kicked up under his feet, almost choking him. It was as if, after several thousand years, they were the first ones to step into the tomb of one of the lost Egyptian pharaohs. Alex reached the top of the stairs and entered a hallway. Hearing voices, he hurried down the dark corridor.

LACHLAN EVANS STOOD in what looked like a control center, but from another era: desks empty of machines but layered in dust, no computers, no monitors or wiring of any kind.

"This place has been deserted for decades… perhaps a century or more," Robert Morton said with disgust.

"I don't understand," Dr. Hicks said. He looked like a little boy who just found out Santa Claus was a serial killer. "The expedition left just three months ago. We should be standing in a simple base camp—"

"What else are you hiding from us?!" Morton asked accusingly, glaring at Evans.

"Enough, already!" Evans hissed. His eyes took in the strange architecture. It was all built from stone. Mortar had been used, but the stones were huge and definitely not cut within the last century. Even the spider webs looked aged and unused. It was all so baffling. "Nothing was mentioned of an alien civilization." He turned to Morton. "You wanted new technology for the Pentagon? Well, I'm guessing you won't be disappointed."

"I'm glad you understand you priorities, Evans," Morton said, eyes filled with mistrust.

Evans suppressed a smile. Any technology they discovered would be sold to the highest bidder—the Pentagon, China, Russia, whomever—and not sold by Robert Morton.

"What interest does the Pentagon have with medical research?" The three men turned in surprise to the new voice in the room. Alex stood in the doorway. "My dad said that TerraGen's expedition came here to create new drugs."

"Of course!" Dr. Hicks was beaming again, but his eyes had a hard edge. "But the company also has to pay its bills. We have many defense contracts—"

"Weapons?" Alex asked.

"TerraGen is a business," Evans' voice cut in. "Your father is very aware that the next frontier of weapons is bio-based. Like the discovery of gunpowder, the next big bang will come from a bunch of scientists in a laboratory somewhere playing with a fungus."

"TerraGen or alien," Morton's voice was like sandpaper. "As long as it comes into my possession and that of the United States."

THE BRIGHT LIGHT HELD Jeremy fast. "As you're about to discover, things on Genesis aren't what you'd expect from a well-organized expedition led by scientists." His father's voice contained a hint of humor, which bounced off Jeremy's cynicism. And then Dr. Victor Austin became more serious. "There were some among us who were only concerned with the profits to be gained by developing biological weapons. Weapons!" Anger travelled into Jeremy through the binding light. "Money lovers! They came for the wrong reasons. Had I known…"

The image of his father wavered has he momentarily looked away. Then Victor Austin looked straight at Jeremy with a fierceness that surprised him. "They went off on their own, took much of our supplies… even some of the soldiers went with them." Jeremy had never seen his father this angry.

"I'm glad you followed after me, son," his father said with solemnness. "But your life is in danger now. Those dogs! They will stop at nothing to pervert my research! Most importantly, they would like nothing better than to kill you…"

BENTON KEENE, TWITCHING NERVOUSLY, watched Lachlan Evans, Morton, and Hicks emerge from the control center. Keene caught Evans' eye and motioned him off to the side. Away from the others, Keene kept his voice hushed, "Lachlan, my instructions were specific. Once through the Portal we were to immediately get outside with our men—"

"What's stopping you?" Evans whispered irritably.

"Those lousy kids!" Keene pointed to where Jeremy and the others floated in a white haze. "They're comatose! And Colonel Glass was adamant, those kids must come with us or—"

"Or what? I thought you had a deal with Glass?"

"Which specifically mentioned the Austin boy."

"And if we can't wake them from their coma, then what?"

Keene stared at Evans coldly. "We never get back to Earth. Ever."

Movement behind them jerked their heads around. The bodies of Patrick, Selene, Leo, and Marissa were lowering to the ground as if by an unseen hand. The white light around them winked out and they stood... still in a trance. Keene felt a rush of hope and he ran over. He got to within a couple of feet and stopped: each of the four kids were mumbling gibberish, their eyelids wide open and their eyeballs moving rapidly from side to side. From behind Keene came other footsteps.

"My heavens," exclaimed Hicks. "They must be in some kind of R.E.M. sleep!"

"We don't need kids with seizures on this expedition," Morton exploded from behind Evans and Hicks, and his voice brokered no arguments. "Send them back through the Portal."

"Those losers are damaged goods anyway." Alex stood just outside the circle of men and he pointed to Patrick and the other *zombies*. "Only... don't send me back with them."

Keene exchanged a dark look with Lachlan Evans and shook his head.

"Going back is impossible," Dr. Hicks said. All heads whipped around and the scientist cowered under their gaze. "We can't possibly send those kids back!"

"Why not?!" Morton pressed angrily.

"Take a look around!" Hicks moved backward, arms opened wide in a gesture to include the cavernous Portal bay. "This complex hasn't been used in ages. See any cables? There isn't any power here to generate a wormhole."

"That's insane!" Morton protested. "We know two men travelled back to Earth a few months ago and killed this boy's girlfriend!" He pointed to where Jeremy still hung suspended in air.

"It's obvious they didn't come from this location," Hicks stated flatly.

Silence. *Finally...the moment of truth*, Keene groaned inwardly. He glanced once at Evans, and then cleared his throat. "Doctor Hicks is absolutely correct. This place where we are standing is called the Arrival Portal."

"Arrival Portal? The expedition built two?" Hicks asked.

"Two... at the very least."

"Mr. Keene, I'm not impressed with how things look on this side of the universe!" Morton's voice had a petulant air and Keene stiffened in anger.

"I didn't build this—"

"Where, pray tell, is the other Portal?" Hicks demanded.

"The Departure Portal you mean?"

"No. The nearest Disneyland theme park!" Morton said, his voice dripping with sarcasm.

Keene didn't like being under the scrutiny of so many. "We have coordinates and a timetable for leaving this planet."

"I feel better already," Morton spat.

"What kind of timetable?" Hicks had a look of genuine surprise on his face.

Keene tapped a bracelet on his wrist and held it up. The display read: 30:10:00 —and it was counting backwards. "Thirty days from now, every person in our company needs to be at the Departure Portal." Keene's words hit them like a sledgehammer. "We always knew this was going to be a snatch and grab." As a sergeant in the Special Forces Keene never had to deal with *personalities*—his word was law, and if you crossed Keene you paid the very high price of pain. He'd grown sick of the TerraGen's corporate politics. Now that he was on Genesis, things would go back to the way they should be. The shocked looks on their faces filled him with warmth.

"Earth days or Genesis days?" This time it was Hicks' turn to surprise Keene.

"Genesis, of course," Keene replied angrily. The grizzled ex-Special Forces man turned his flushed face to Lachlan Evans. "It's imperative that we leave this facility *now!*"

"Or what?" Morton demanded. "We're perfectly safe in here. It's like a fortress!"

Keene looked at the Washington man and snorted in disgust before turning away. *Fools!*

D r. Rudolf Hicks looked at Lachlan Evans' wrist and saw he was wearing the same bracelet as Keene's. Hicks' own wrist was bare and it miffed him to be left out of critical information. Also, he wasn't satisfied with the Security Director's answers. Something was going on here—some kind of hidden agenda. With an IQ of 124, the research director was frustrated that he couldn't figure out Keene's end game. One thing was for certain: he wasn't going to let Keene out of his sight.

Hicks waited, then followed after Keene who was walking toward the end of the embarkation platform. Hicks allowed enough distance behind Keene so as to appear casual. He wove in and around the soldiers, sidestepped opened cases that revealed the latest in high-tech weaponry. *They aren't taking any chances*, Hicks mused.

Keene walked out of the chamber through a large hangar door and into the Portal bay outside. A platoon of thirty soldiers waited in front of a large steel door that reminded Hicks of a bank vault. Interlocking steel rods secured the door. Keeping soldiers between him and Keene, Hicks moved forward and saw the security director go to where some of his men were examining a small security pad to the right of the door.

Hicks smiled upon seeing Keene's evident frustration with the Portal bay's security system. Keene turned and suddenly Hicks realized Keene was looking at him.

"Dr. Hicks? A moment?" Keene said in a voice that made it clear that was an order, not a request.

"Me?" Hicks didn't like being commanded… anywhere. Keene may have brought him into this expedition, but *he* was the senior representative from TerraGen, not this *security director*. Hicks moved slowly to where Keene stood beside the steel door and noticed that the security pad contained only an imprint for a hand.

"Your hand, please," Keene demanded.

"Mine? Why would Dr. Austin use my handprint?"

"What does it matter?" Keene shouted. "Place your hand on the pad, now!"

Hicks took a step back in shock. He had been bullied in high school and the force of Keene's anger brought too many bad memories back. His hands shook uncontrollably. "Mister Keene, you will speak to me with a more civil tone—"

"I will speak to you any bloody way I like!" Keene roared. "Now, your hand… *please*… before I chop it off and use it myself!"

"Yes. Quite right," Hicks stammered as he placed his palm on the security pad. He felt a puff of air and he pulled his hand back in surprise. A trickle of blood seeped from his palm.

Keene watched him, bending over with laughter, "Forgot to mention that part. Some kind of blood test, DNA most likely."

"Didn't seem to work," Hicks said, glaring at the unmoving steel door.

Keene grunted in agreement, "Didn't think it would."

Keene suddenly smiled at Hicks. "It was fun to watch your face, though."

Hicks tried to form a retort, but Keene was already turning away. Through the hangar doorway came a procession of soldiers carrying the son of Dr. Sudarshan Korrapati. The sight almost made Hicks retch: Patrick Korrapati, eyes rolled up and white-eyed, mumbling gibberish. The boy's hand was placed on the security pad, and instantly there was a loud click... and then the creaking of long-unused machinery reverberated in the bay. Open-mouthed, Hicks watched the steel pins of the vault-like metal door slide inward. There was a loud squeal of metal on metal, a sudden rush of air, and the massive door swung inward. Soldiers streamed through the gap.

"I want a perimeter outside this complex in sixty seconds!" Keene's voice boomed.

Rough bodies pushed past Hicks as more soldiers disappeared out the door. The only soldiers remaining were hastily marshaling their motorized carts and directing them into the opened door.

Keene's voice again boomed in the Portal bay, "Hurry now! I want all equipment and gear at the perimeter's edge in two minutes! Now, hustle!"

A shiver went down Hicks' spine as he sensed the panic in Keene's voice. *Surely this facility is as secure as—*

WHOMP!!!

Vibrations shook the Portal bay as a loud rumbling seemed to come from beneath them.

WHOMP!!!

A second shockwave caused Hicks to hastily steady himself. He looked over to where Benton Keene was standing, ashen-faced.

"We were too slow," Keene moaned.

From deep within the structure came a distant *roar*, and Dr. Rudolf Hicks felt real fear for the first time in his life.

JEREMY REMAINED WRAPPED in white light. Seeing his father had shocked him, stirring up raw emotions deep within. The buzzing in his brain had subsided. His father had spoken a long time on the divisions within the Genesis expedition—a split of power. A sudden vibration pulled Jeremy's attention away, and he was aware of a tingling sensation throughout his body.

"Soon you will find out that the animal and plant life on Genesis is... well, different," Victor Austin said with a wry smile. *BZZZRP!* The image of Victor Austin suddenly began to shake violently. "*Deadly* would be an apt description of..." His father's face began to deteriorate. "...certain plants in the southern hemisphere actually have independent thought."

Wavy lines appeared throughout Victor Austin's image. Pixelated spots appeared within the lines, and suddenly his father was gone!

Jeremy remained enveloped in the white light. His father disappearing was sudden and left him conflicted. When first he saw his father the deep resentment had returned, but eventually it had given way to a rush of warmth.

A crown of gold, studded with sparkling jewels, rose into view. Under the crown was hair the color of night, and suddenly Erik was staring at him, dressed in silks that looked... well, medieval. The *royal* look was disturbing and confusing.

"Jeremy," Erik said with a smile, "you've made it safely through. Perfect! Now it's time to begin your education."

Chapter Sixteen

Watchdog

JEREMY TRIED TO COMPREHEND the kingly image of his brother. Light bounced off the diamonds encircling the crown. But still, despite the strange clothes and crown, it was definitely Erik... but older. A ragged scar now marred the right side of his face, from under his eye traveling down to his jaw . Worry seemed to tug at the corners of his brother's eyes. The one person Jeremy had always failed to live up to, and here he was: *a king!* Locked in white light in the middle of a wormhole... and still, Jeremy felt resentment toward his older brother.

"You've come to Genesis, and now, little brother, you

must bear some grown up responsibility," Erik said. His voice was slightly teasing, but then turned serious. "This planet was meant to provide cures for disease, renewable resources. Unfortunately, all we've known is war, death, and attack from every quarter—there are monsters on this planet that kill for enjoyment—and then there's... *him.*"

Erik's face became cold and hard. "His power is in the south, a place of hideous atrocities, and he has an army of the vilest creatures at his command. He goes by the name *Malcator*—Malcator the deceiver—Malcator the killer of children. And with the name of *Shadow Lord* he strikes fear into the hearts of the free lands." Erik paused, as if to contemplate, and then he spoke again. "Back on Earth you seemed to constantly fall into trouble... if only you'd told me what was bothering you." Shame coursed through Jeremy, followed by rising indignation. *What did he know of trouble, Mister 2400 on his SATs?*

"But here on Genesis you will have power and abilities to shape this world and help save it from destruction," Erik continued. "Whatever your inner demons, they will pale in comparison to the real demons you're about to face."

Jeremy fought to comprehend what his brother had just said.

"The Shadow Lord will want your powers, and he won't stop until you are under his control," Erik stated frankly. "Whether or not we ever see each other again largely rests on you, Jeremy. You are the key to saving Genesis and reuniting our family."

H E FELT LIKE A GOD. Lachlan Evans stood in the shadow of a grand temple at the head of a broad staircase that stretched downward for half a mile. The temple stood on a hill overlooking a vast, ancient city—a city that descended for several miles down to the forested valley below. Structures of stone fanned out from the temple in a semi-circle, massive buildings of all sizes that cascaded down the hillside with avenues and staircases interconnecting them. It was a city built for defense—like a medieval fortress—with a stone battlement at the bottom of the hill that looked to be thirty yards in thickness from Evans' vantage point. Towers were spaced along the battlement that curved in a semi-circle around the vast city. A ribbon of blue showed on one side to be a river that must provide the city's rear defense. It reminded Evans of ancient Rome.

But it was a dead city.

Eerily quiet with only the occasional chirp of a bird and the flap of wings. Sweat trickled down from his forehead and he looked up at the sky. The sun overhead had an orange tinge. *We're definitely not on Earth*, he observed.

The buildings lay in tomb-like silence.

No voices called out. Not a single human being stirred. Wind moaned between the buildings, whipping in and out of empty windows. Everything looked old, abandoned. The air smelled of decay. Yet, he seemed to feel the presence of a thousand eyes on him. There was a sense of...*waiting*. Evans' soldiers rushed past him as they set up a defensive perimeter around the temple.

Wings flapped again. Several ravens had nested under a stone balcony of one of the towers, the flash of black wings that quickly disappeared. More silence.

Stone lions were built into the supporting columns of one building. Tigers, elephants, and beasts that Evans didn't recognize decorated other stone structures. Warrior figures and elegant female stone figures had been sculpted into the face of cathedral-like buildings.

Random trees and brushes had grown up in and around the buildings and streets of the city. A grand staircase led down from the temple to a plaza far below. Evans looked closer and saw how the grand staircase was crumbling. Vast cracks and rubble made the stone stairs look like Berlin after the bombings in World War II. What remained of the city streets had now been taken over by vegetation. The city's central park, dominating the main plaza, looked like a dense forest. Through the trees Evans spied a stone statue at the center of the plaza's park: a warrior in plate armor stood with one arm raised skyward, holding a sword. Evans could only guess it was a sword because the blade was missing and only the sword's hilt remained. The statue must have been massive based on how large it was from even this distance.

But whatever people had built and lived in this grand city had been killed off or fled long ago. *Maybe they died by pestilence?*

The stone underneath his feet moved, and then a loud roar sounded from deep within the city and the sound caused Evans to stop breathing. The soldiers around him looked at each other with stricken faces. The ground trembled again, and he had to steady himself.

The former CIA operative found that the pain coming from his chest was the pounding of his heart.

The city of death had awakened. The intruders from Earth had triggered some kind of internal alarm and now the city was stirring—like a spider detecting prey on its web.

A very *big* spider.

HICKS TRIED VERY HARD to keep his thoughts in order. Panic was like a parasite boring into his brain. The bodies of the four TerraGen kids lay at his feet and he move away slightly. They unnerved him. His head jerked upward, watching soldiers running out of the Portal bay, many discarding their carts and grabbing what weapons they could lay their hands on. *Chaos. Chaos was never good.* The research director was sweating from fear, wanting to flee with the soldiers, but feeling the urge to stay with the kids lying motionless on the stone floor.

WHOMP!

Hicks legs wobbled as the ground trembled again. He

felt his bladder weaken.

"Rudolf!" a voice boomed behind Hicks. "Doctor Hicks!" Keene was walking toward him, face red and furious. "Wake up and get moving! I need stretchers for these comatose kids!" Keene pointed to where Patrick, Selene, Marissa, and Leo were lying.

"I don't know—I mean—where would I find stretchers?" Hicks stammered, his brain failing to suppress his rising terror.

Keene came to within a few inches of Hicks' face. "Good doctor, I'm putting our precious cargo under *your* care. Find a way to move them or find yourself left behind! Improvise!" Spittle from Keene dotted Hicks' face. Keene's face radiated fear and if the ex-Special Forces man was scared...

"Of course, I'll do my best," Hicks stammered.

"Stop acting like a bookworm and start using your very expensive brain, Mr. Research Director," Keene snarled. "We need these kids to get off this planet!"

"I kn-kn-know!"

"Trust me," Keene said as he leaned even closer, "you don't want to spend the rest of your life on Genesis, because a garden paradise it ain't." Keene then grunted and walked away.

WHOMP! The stone floor seemed to shift and another *roar* echoed into the Portal bay.

"Oh dear," Hicks murmured. He moved away and began looking in earnest for some stretchers—two poles and a tarp—*anything*—amidst all the military gear.

IS BODY SHIFTED AND HE felt the hard stone under his head. His eyes opened, and slowly his senses started giving him information. A vaulted ceiling, the sound of boots scraping, the smell of... a damp cavern. Patrick rolled onto his side and looked around. Soldiers were hurrying carts through a door. Next to him he felt Selene stir.

Her eyes darted around the huge bay and she quickly sat up. Their eyes met.

"I'm not dead?" she gasped with wide-eyed awe.

"No, because that would mean I would be as well." Patrick got to his feet and he helped Selene stand. Below them remained the sleeping forms of Leo and Marissa, both white-eyed and lips mumbling unintelligible words.

"Are we still in TerraGen?" Selene asked.

Brainless. Patrick tried not to be sarcastic. "You don't remember walking through a bunch of stars and galaxies?"

"Oh, yeah, fer sure," she nodded in agreement. "That was trippy."

Patrick bit off what would've been a juicy, sarcastic retort. Instead, he grinned through gritted teeth and began looking around. At the far end of the platform a figure floated in mid-air, like a magician's assistant in a Vegas show. *Jeremy!* Fear and concern washed through Patrick's emotions. Jeremy Austin lay horizontal in a comatose state three feet off the platform—eyes open wide and showing only two white orbs—his mouth mumbling gibberish. "What is going on here?" Patrick said, speaking to no one but himself. He walked over to Jeremy and tried to find whatever magical device was holding his friend in the air. Nothing.

His feet brushed against something. To his delight, Patrick realized his backpack had survived the journey through the Portal.

WHOMP! The ground shook violently and Patrick whipped around. The last squad of soldiers was vanishing through the open doorway. Suddenly, they were alone. Dust floated down from the cavern's ceiling.

"I wish they'd stop setting off fireworks!" Selene commented, looking at the doorway.

Patrick scooped up his backpack and moved past the Asian girl. "Selene, I doubt they have the Fourth of July on this planet."

"Maybe they are sending a signal," Selene said. She

followed Patrick, and her voice shook as she tried to keep up. "You know, like a, "Hey, were finally here!" kind of thing."

A deep roar sounded outside, causing nearby discarded carts to vibrate. Patrick stopped. "That's no signal from our side," he hissed, looking back at Selene. "That was more like, "Hey, you just woke me from my hibernation and I'm really ticked off!""

Selene blinked. "I like my story better."

Patrick moved out the door with Selene trailing behind him like a stray puppy.

ERIK CONTINUED HIS SPEECH, his voice tinged with anger. "As long as you stay connected, you don't have to worry about *Him*..." Erik had spent a lot of time on *Him*—the Shadow Lord who was obviously the biggest, baddest dude on planet Genesis—sorcerer, evil dictator, and mad scientist all rolled into one unhappy villain. Malcator had descended upon the land like a plague, enslaving races, exterminating those that gave defiance, and using sorcery to pervert the natural into the unholy. Vast armies had marched under his banner and yet there had arisen a band of free warriors—races who had refused to bend the knee to the Shadow Lord. Malcator's armies had been defeated. Now, the sorcerer of the shadows was waiting—building a new army, conjuring more hideous atrocities—Erik didn't know because Malcator had retreated to his lands in the south and stayed silent. Erik continued, "Just watch your back, little brother. The Shadow Lord has some power of his own and his spies are everywhere."

Erik paused and seemed to think about his next statement.

He looked up and a slow smile spread on his lips, the jagged scar becoming less frightening. "We were way too distant growing up. I really do want to see you again. Love you, little bro."

And then Erik was gone and Jeremy almost felt regret. Almost.

EVERYTHING WAS DEAD. Empty.

Alex stared out at the silent, stone structures that glowed orange-white in the sunlight. The sheer vastness of the city made him feel small. Lewisville quickly shrank in his mind in comparison. Alex had seen London, Paris, Rome, Moscow, Tokyo and New York—massive cities with populations in the millions—but none of those had overwhelmed him, and yet…the stillness of this ancient city was oppressive. Wind whistled through opened doorways and arched windows. Soldiers continued to move outward, setting up perimeters… looking for what? Aliens?

Back in Lewisville and among the high school crowd, Alex was a big fish in a small pond. But here? Soldiers were running in all directions, and the son of Alexander Leach, Sr. felt insignificant. Not being the center of attention disturbed him.

"Who's the guy with the broken sword?" came the voice of Patrick behind him.

Alex jerked around, trying to suppress the relief on his face at seeing his nemesis awake from his coma. But the sneer was quick to return. "You took long enough. Got enough beauty sleep?"

Patrick, with his backpack firmly resting on his shoulders, looked down at the plaza at the bottom of the grand staircase with its warrior statue. "Broken sword guy… who do you think he is?"

"What statue?" Alex had seen no statue.

"Hercules," came a female voice.

Alex turned to see Selene Choi hiding behind the nerd. "Hercules carried the world on his shoulders," Alex said with contempt.

"It's not Hercules… we're on a planet light years from Earth. An alien, maybe," Patrick's voice sounded authoritative. Then he turned to Alex. "And… that's Atlas, bonehead."

"What?" Alex tried to bow up, flexing his muscles, but he knew Patrick was toying with him.

"Greek mythology," Patrick said. "Atlas was a primordial Titan—he was forced to carry the celestial spheres on his shoulders."

"Why?" Selene asked.

"Ticked someone off, I guess."

"Loser," Alex muttered.

"You're back!" Dr. Hicks, wearing a tight smile through gritted teeth, was weaving his way past several soldiers toward them. But Hicks was only interested in Patrick. "Mr. Korrapati…I must confess that we borrowed your hand!"

"And left your mark," Patrick raised his palm to reveal where a trickle of blood had dried.

"Had to open the door, you know," Hicks' smile never seemed to fade. "Perfectly by the book. You were never at risk."

Alex flashed Patrick a sarcastic sneer. "You're the Genesis door opener!" But Alex's humor fell with a thud.

"Ah… where are the rest?" Lachlan Evans had come up behind them, and immediately Hicks started shaking with nervousness. Evans' tone and his manner demonstrated extreme impatience. "Have all the kids returned from zombie land?"

"I—I… am looking for—scouring, actually—the entire city for some stretchers," Hicks spoke in a rush. "For the remaining three kids—"

"Still got a couple dream walkers?" Evans said, clearly livid. He quickly began searching the temple area and found Benton Keene surrounded by soldiers. "Keene!"

Alex saw Keene start to turn.

WHOMP—WHOMP—WHOMP—

The earth-shaking thumps were getting too close for Alex, and he began easing himself back toward the temple's entrance.

A loud roar split the air.

BENTON KEENE FELT HIS legs tremble. A queasy sensation spread in his stomach and he realized he was terrified. *WHOMP—WHOMP—*

Soldiers froze with guns raised.

"Keene!" The sound of Evan's voice shook Keene out of his fear, and he whipped around and saw the CIA man was standing fifty yards away with three of the TerraGen kids. "I want three stretchers in the Portal!" Evans shouted. "Get the Austin kid and the other two wrapped, strapped, and carried out!"

Keene tried to process what Evans was saying—
WHOMP!

The ground shook, and piece of the stairs sheared off and began rolling, crashing down the long staircase.

Keene turned to one the soldiers, a former Army Ranger from Chicago. "Take five other men, carry those kids out if you have to!" His voice trembled as he fought to control his fear.

The ex-Ranger nodded and motioned to five other soldiers. They disappeared into the temple, leaving Keene alone. There was a tension in the air, a foreboding air of disaster that made Keene want to escape this city of death at any cost.

Suddenly he realized there were holes everywhere—torn gaps in the sides of many of the buildings, black pits with stone rubble strewn on the ground—everywhere. *Why hadn't he seen these before?!*

Stone exploded outward from a three-story building below Keene. A soldier disappeared in a spray of red. Another was sent flying through the air, his body smacking with a wet thud against the stone wall of another structure before dropping to the ground in a limp mass. A cloud of dust was suddenly whipped away by the wind, and a huge, black hole was revealed in the side of the building.

Keene strained to see the cause… and saw a shadowy hulk suddenly fill the breach.

"My god…" Keene whispered to no one.

A monster lumbered out of the hole.

Keene gasped. The monster stood over fifteen feet tall, walked on four, tree trunk-sized legs, and was covered in plate armor. It looked prehistoric. Massive jaws revealed razor-sharp teeth. A sharp horn jutted out from its forehead where two yellow eyes searched hungrily, and wicked spikes travelled down its spine. The sheer size of the creature dwarfed the biggest elephant Keene had ever seen. When it breathed, the beast rumbled deeply like a Bengal tiger as great globs of saliva dripped from its mouth. Its head seemed to twitch from side to side—*the creature has small ears*, Keene observed, but this didn't seem to hinder the creature's hunting skills.

The beast's mouth opened and it roared, a reverberating scream that belonged in the Stone Age. *Right, we're on another planet.* Keene's military training finally kicked in and he began to look for weaknesses in the creature. He took note of its muscled stockiness and sheer weight. *With that size, we have the advantage of speed.*

A squad of soldiers was just yards away from the monster, and they began opening fire with their machine guns. Two other soldiers made a break for an open doorway. Keene inhaled. With surprising quickness, the monster pivoted and was on the two men before Keene could exhale. *So quick!*

The creature's jaws sank into one of the men with a sickening crunch, and his body was flung high into the air. *One point for the monster… it has speed after all.*

All the mercenaries opened fire. Thousands of bullets, a rain of lethal force, struck the creature… and harmlessly bounced off the beast's armor plating.

Point two for the monster's defenses. It's built like a tank, but better.

The monster was disoriented momentarily as more bullets ricocheted into the stone walls around it. And then it saw the second soldier who was trying to climb up the building's side. Blood dripping from its jagged teeth, the creature stalked forward. But then a third soldier raced from his place of concealment, unloading an entire clip into the beast, trying to distract it.

And then Keene saw the creature's main weapon. "Get back! Get back!" Keene shouted, taking several steps toward his men.

With only a brief glance backward, the creature sent its tail in a sweep toward the *distractor*. It was a tail tipped with a wicked looking spike, and the foot-long spear gutted the hapless soldier. The man climbing upward gave a yelp of fear and scrambled to climb higher to safety.

The monster's eyes had never left the man.

Keene watched as the creature lowered itself in a crouch before exploding upward. It shot twenty feet into the air, easily reaching the escaping soldier. Jaws took the man in another shower of red. The man's scream was cut off violently. The creature landed on the stone floor, and the ground under Keene shook from the impact. The sound of bones crunching almost brought Keene to his knees in fear. The creature seemed to enjoy this kill; it tore the corpse apart, limb by limb.

We were too slow to escape! Keene started backing away. *Live to fight another day.*

Keene, the veteran of two wars, turned and ran to join Lachlan Evans and the protection of his well-armed soldiers.

SOMETHING BRUSHED HER LEG. Marissa's vision was blurred; she blinked furiously, sitting up and grabbing her knees. Marissa's eyes focused, and she found herself on a platform like the one at TerraGen. But this one was...*ancient*. She brushed away some of the dust covering her pants. A crash behind her jerked her around.

Leo was rummaging through empty shipping containers further down the platform.

She stood up. Her legs tingled after the... what was it, an alien intrusion? She had stepped through the Portal, saw some galaxies and stars and then a blinding light had enveloped her and she'd felt a presence enter her mind. Her brain still ached from the intrusion.

A container rattled on the platform. Leo was still digging, looking for something.

"What are you doing?" Marissa asked.

Leo continued without looking up. "None of your business."

And then she saw Jeremy. He was lying face up on the platform at the far end. She moved past Leo and walked to where Jeremy lay. His eyelids were closed, and she could see his eyes moving side to side behind them. His mouth was moving rapidly in a language she couldn't understand. It wasn't gibberish. Marissa had studied Mandarin and Spanish and recognized a flow of words—words in an alien tongue. "Creepy," was the only thing she could say.

"Don't judge," came Leo's voice from behind her. "You were doing the same thing."

CRASH!

She jerked around. Leo had thrown one of the containers over the platform railing.

"Looking for snacks already?" Her sarcasm was laid on thick. "I'm sure there's a vending machine just around—"

"Weapons, brainless! There aren't any weapons!" Leo shouted angrily.

"The last person I want holding a weapon is you."

"You'll think differently in a minute."

She laughed derisively. "In case you haven't forgot, we came here with an army."

"Sorry to disappoint you," Leo began, "but your army is getting their butts kicked outside. Haven't you heard *anything?*"

She remembered something—an explosion—and she had come awake with her body moving back and forth on the platform.

"Don't move," a voice hissed. "Either of you."

Marissa froze. The voice wasn't familiar, but the fear in it was very real. Slowly, Marissa turned around. Beyond the platform there was a huge opening into another room.

Nothing.

"Shhhhh," the voice hissed again.

Her eyes tried to focus in the dim light. The outer room was dark. She could see the dim shapes of discarded containers littering the floor. A body moved beside her, and Marissa flinched. It was the woman who'd been Jeremy's guardian… a Mrs. Freeman.

"Don't move," Freeman whispered. "It hasn't seen us."

Then Marissa saw the doorway.

Dim light filtered in and outlined a large door at the far end of the outer room—the Portal bay. Silhouetted in the light of one of the lanterns stood a *creature*.

Chapter Seventeen

The Hunted

THEY HID BEHIND THE HUGE PILLARS supporting the roof of the temple. *Hiding,* Patrick thought sarcastically, *is a very loose term for what we are doing. Cowering… yes, cowering was a better description.* The monster was currently smashing through stone blocks and killing TerraGen soldiers with relative ease. Protection behind a five-foot thick stone pillar was iffy at best.

"Is it gone?" Selene whispered. She crouched behind him, hands over her eyes. Great tremors of fear shook her body.

Patrick groaned inwardly. *I'll have to carry her out. Sucks for me.* He turned and looked behind him. *Where's the star quarterback?* His head twisted one way and then another, and finally spotted Alex sheltered behind the pillar next to them, conveniently located nearer the temple's entrance. *Figures.*

Only a few soldiers remained visible. The rest had scattered in groups.

"Patrick?" The usual arrogance was gone from Alex's voice, replaced with terror. "Hey! This ain't going so well!"

"Tell that to the guy who just got eaten," replied Patrick.

"I ain't kidding!" Alex shouted, and then whispered, "Dweeb…"

Lachlan Evans was huddled beside a stone wall, shielded from the monster. He spoke animatedly with Benton Keene and Patrick wished he were close enough to hear.

"What are they saying?" Alex asked, seeing Patrick's interest in Evans.

"Don't know," Patrick replied. "Probably our need for a virgin sacrifice to appease the, uh, big monster thingy, right Selene?"

"Shut up!" Selene whimpered.

"We need to stick to Mister CIA, whatever he does," Alex ventured, looking at Evans. "Not that I trust him—"

"By all means, go ahead." Patrick said. "Me? I'm going the opposite direction." He quickly scanned below, looking for a way out of the city, but there was nothing. From their vantage point overlooking the dead city, he saw that the original builders had built the city for defense. Sitting on a bluff, it was built in a circular pattern with towers spaced evenly. In the distance, past the grand staircase and the plaza below, the city's farthest edge ended at a huge, fortified gate with towers on each side. Beyond the gate, Patrick could see a canopy of trees stretching outward for miles. He saw a flash of blue and guessed it must be a river.

Sweat trickled down his face. He looked up. There was a scattering of clouds in the sky and he guessed it was still morning.

"You're gonna get yourself killed," Alex said. The sneer had returned to his face.

Good ole' Alex, Patrick thought. He'd never liked bullies, and just being close to Mr. Leach, Jr. made him want to hurl up the power bar he'd eaten...what was it, two hours ago? *Geez. Crossed a whole galaxy and now face to face with a prehistoric monster—in just under two hours!*

WHAM!

White light flashed before Patrick's eyes. He blinked furiously as a buzzing started in his brain. His head started swimming, and he fell to the ground. *Not again!* His brain had been the target of a massive data download while the white light had held him fast in the Portal. Now, more data was streaming into his brain and the sensation, while not painful, was extremely uncomfortable. The flashes ceased abruptly, but his brain still pulsated with energy, and the tingling feeling made Patrick queasy. Both of his hands gripped the stone underneath, and shaking his head had no effect.

Suddenly, the ground trembled under his hands and knees. Heavy steps sounded, and they were gaining momentum.

Patrick lifted his head. Blood drained from his face in abject terror.

The monster's eyes were fixed on him, and it was coming closer. Bloody saliva dripped from the creature's jaws. But the eyes showed... *intelligence.*

Running would do no good; the monster was thirty yards away and closing fast. He felt a whimper rising from deep within.

The monster leapt upward—

Patrick shut his eyes and waited for his violent end—

...and felt the temple grounds shake violently as the creature landed. He flinched as bits of stone pelted his body. *Close. It's very close*, he thought with a shudder—because Patrick could feel the heat from the animal's body. He opened one eye, waiting for its teeth to cut him in half.

Black, bulbous eyes stared down at him. Like a predator assessing its prey, the monster studied Patrick. It began to move downward toward him when suddenly its big head snapped upward, head whipping from side to side. And then it looked down at him.

Jaws slowly opened. Blood dripped from jagged teeth.

Patrick tensed.

ROOOOOOARRRRR!

The monster bellowed a challenge that shook the stones and caused Patrick to fall flat.

A loud rumble sounded from within the beast. Patrick twisted his head to look up. The beast was staring fixedly at the temple opening, motionless.

THE SWIFTNESS OF THE BEAST stunned Lachlan Evans. And then he saw the son of Sudarshan Korrapati lying face first on the ground—with the monster overhead. Looking left, he saw the Asian girl and Alexander Leach's whelp edging toward the temple entrance. Suddenly, the precariousness of the situation hit him like a ton of bricks. He jerked around to where Keene was concealed behind a massive column. "The kids!"

Keene looked at him, unfazed.

"The kids!" Evans screamed.

Confusion turned to shock, and then Keene stepped from his concealment, eyes going wide. Shock turned to action as the ex-Special Forces commando turned, scanning the area—one of his lieutenants saw the look and snapped at attention. "Assemble the entire team!" Keene bellowed. "Get all of my men back here! Double time!" The lieutenant disappeared down the stone staircase.

Lachlan Evans stared at the beast, barely breathing. Any second and the Korrapati boy would be ripped to shreds. Footsteps behind signaled the return of the lieutenant and the remainder of Keene's mercenaries. However, the monster's attention seemed to be focused on the temple, despite the easy meal at its feet. And then it slowly turned its head, looking past Evans' location. A chill went down Evans' spine...

Leathery, humanoid creatures streamed out of a dozen empty doorways. *Aliens!* Evans' brain shouted in surprise. Metallic, swordlike weapons were held in their hands—it was a small army. But the alien warriors didn't attack. They stood on the opposite side of the grand staircase, watching the beast.

"Sir?" It was the lieutenant. "Might we try—"

Evans saw the flash of an alien's hand whipping downward—a blur of movement past his head—and suddenly a projectile was embedded in the lieutenant's throat. Fighting down panic, Evans turned to Keene, "No time to waste. Let's get the hell out of here!"

"But the kids!" Keene exclaimed.

"We have the tracking device," Evans' expression was hard. "Get moving!"

The kids were on their own.

MARISSA FOUND THAT HER legs were shaking involuntarily. Try as she might, they wouldn't stop. Her eyes were fixed on the creature. Light and shadow played across the alien as it walked through the Portal bay—*like a bird*, she thought. *A predator looking for threats.* Roughly six feet tall, the humanoid had sinewy muscles encased in a strange battle armor. It held a sharp, bladed weapon in its right hand where a dark red liquid dripped from the blade's edge. *No need asking what that was. Blood...*

Movement pulled Marissa's attention back to Freeman. The woman stepped silently past empty containers like a Navy SEAL. At first glance, Freeman had first reminded Marissa of one of the hall monitors at school. But now she moved like an assassin.

A scuffling sound echoed to Marissa's right, and the alien froze. Its head swiveled left, eyes darting back and forth.

From the corner of her eyes she saw Leo scuttling toward an open doorway at the far end. *Cowardly punk! He's deserting me!* Marissa began to sweat. She fought the overwhelming desire to lie down in a fetal position. *Leo's leaving me behind!*

Trying desperately to control her panic, Marissa looked back to Freeman—Leo's distraction had allowed Freeman to gain the protective side of the Portal bay's open doorway. Freeman's hand slid along her back, pulling a handgun free of its holster.

DILATED PUPILS SHRANK BACK to normal. His head ached, and there was a metallic taste in his mouth. He licked his dry lips and sat up… and saw the creature immediately. It moved like a prehistoric dinosaur, but its face was human. Well… ugly human. The alien had a large, flattened nose, pointed ears, leathery skin mottled in grays and brown, sharp teeth, a pronounced forehead, and cat-like eyes that suddenly found Jeremy's. His blood ran cold. The creature's eyes were intelligent and unafraid, studying Jeremy with cold calculation. They blinked. It's head twitched. Lips parted to reveal jagged, yellow teeth. Deliberately, it walked toward the Portal chamber.

Silently, a darkened figure stepped into view, gun raised.

The alien stopped, sensing the new threat, head turning and eyes locking on to Neriah Freeman: cook, guardian, and government agent. Freeman's gun was leveled, and it was obvious she knew how to use it.

Jeremy found his heart pounding in his chest.

"Come on, little man," Freeman whispered hoarsely. "Let's see what you got."

The alien tensed, as if preparing to leap.

The gun in Freeman's hand flashed six times in succession, shots piercing the stillness. Bullets struck the alien where his heart should be, and the alien staggered momentarily.

And then the alien seemed to smile, baring razor-sharp fangs.

Freeman took a half step backward when suddenly the alien moved with the swiftness of lightning. Covering fifteen feet in a fraction of a second, the alien swept its right arm in an arc. Freeman's legs wobbled... and then her head separated and fell to the floor, her the body landed heavily beside the grisly face frozen in shock, blood pooling underneath.

It had happened so fast! Jeremy's mind screamed in panic.

The alien took a moment, and then looked straight at Jeremy.

"Move!" came Marissa's voice. "Run, now!"

But Jeremy was frozen in fear.

The alien tensed... and then stopped, eyes and head swiveling to a point behind it.

Six soldiers raced into the Portal bay, and Jeremy's heart leapt with hope. The soldiers carried makeshift stretchers, which they promptly dropped as they reached for their assault rifles.

Slowly, almost unconcernedly, the alien turned and studied this new distraction.

The soldiers stared open-mouthed at the creature. Fanning out in a semi-circle, they brought assault rifles to shoulders.

The alien attacked.

With amazing speed, the creature killed two of the soldiers, its wicked blade flashing, sending blood spraying in the air. A third soldier panicked and fired blindly—the creature severed the man's arm at the shoulder, and then the soldier's head rolled onto the stone floor seconds later.

Two of the mercenaries panicked and disappeared through the Portal door. One remaining soldier, the group's leader, unloaded a full clip into the creature. Bullets ricocheted off armor but several found flesh, and the alien went berserk.

Move! Move, you idiot! His mind screamed but Jeremy was rooted in terror. He watched as the creature caught the soldier in the chamber doorway. A loud *CRACK* sounded and the soldier fell to the floor in a broken heap. And then the alien was gone.

Coming out of his shock, Jeremy struggled onto weak legs and began hobbling down the embarkation platform. He knew it might only be a matter of seconds before the killing machine returned. He was a stranger in strange, foreign land and he knew of only one place that offered refuge.

Don't look down…especially at the head.

He stumbled past the remains of Neriah Freeman, keeping his eyes focused on the massive door of the Portal bay. The mercenaries' bodies were like broken, bloody rag dolls and he had do step carefully to avoid the unthinkable—*must not step on that hand…oh, and that…* He fought to control a sudden wrenching sensation that boiled in his stomach. Breathing heavily, he moved quick and danced around body parts and gained the chamber doorway.

Horror films will never have the same fascination for me, he mused without thinking.

Outside, the darkened hallway was empty—and then a scream echoed back to him. Seconds later a strangled cry followed. And then he heard a low growl, deep and guttural.

The creature was returning.

THE HIDEOUS ALIEN CREATURE had disappeared back up the hallway. On the stone floor lay the mangled corpses of two soldiers. Alex had long been a *gamer*—playing the most violent of computer games and many against so-called alien races—but this was his first close encounter with the real thing…and now his body quivered in terror. Computer games were *make believe*. The two soldiers lying at his feet were very real.

"You're getting snot all over my shirt," Patrick's voice echoed nearby.

Alex turned. In the gloom of the stone hallway two

figures stood huddled; Selene, standing behind Patrick, had her face buried in his shirt. Deep sobs wracked her body, and she trembled.

Sheesh! I'm shaking just like her! Alex thought.

Patrick's voice took on a note of compassion. "Look, we're fortunate to be alive, Selene. And the only way to keep from being…" He gestured to the corpses in the hallway, but Alex interrupted.

"Cut into little, tiny pieces."

A whine came from Selene, followed by a gurgling snort as she blew her nose into Patrick's shirt.

Patrick glared at Alex as he continued. "To keep from ending up like them, we need to move and keep moving. Focus your mind on what you can change right now. Forget about… *that*."

Selene nodded her head and stepped back from Patrick. Her eyes deliberately avoided the floor. "What was that *thing*?"

"Ain't it obvious?!" Alex sneered. "An alien super soldier! Or we stepped through a Portal into a masquerade ball for psycho killers." Outside the temple, the monster had roared its challenge then disappeared into the tunnel it originally appeared out of. It was then that Patrick had suggested going back after Jeremy and the others… and, like a fool, Alex had followed him. They'd heard the soldiers being killed and had seen a glimpse of the alien retreating toward the Portal. Now Selene was having a mental breakdown and Alex wished he'd stayed with Evans and Benton Keene. Alex turned and headed back into the temple's foyer. Shafts of sunlight hit his eyes and he shaded them with his palm. The foyer was a domed space with gaping holes in the ceiling that let in the early morning sun.

"Where you going?" Patrick called after him.

"I'm making a change."

"We should stay together!"

Alex laughed derisively. "You play nursemaid to the

mental case. I'm going back to the A-team." He ran through the foyer and out the temple doors.

They were gone!

The city was quiet, and Alex was alone. Benton Keene and the CIA man had taken their army of soldiers and abandoned them.

"Not fair," Alex said, and his voice was lost in the wind.

BOOM—BOOM DA BOOM—BOOM.

The sound of drums echoed from within the city, rhythmic and deep, and the hair stood up on Alex's flesh.

EREMY'S EYES QUICKLY STUDIED the Portal bay's large, vault-like door which towered over him, constructed with steel and very thick. No way to close it unless…

A second *growl* echoed from the hallway outside.

He spotted the security access panel with its human handprint. An image flashed in his mind causing his eyes to blink—data from the alien takeover of his mind—he saw a schematic of the door, *this door*, and its wiring—and suddenly Jeremy knew what to do. In high school he was never a straight-A student, but after being zapped in the Portal and suspended in mid-air, his brain was now processing data like a high-speed computer. Placing his hand onto the panel, he felt a puff of air hit his palm. A rumble sounded, and the door started to move.

Jeremy's eyes searched the dim hallway. His breath caught: a shadowy form appeared, moving rapidly toward him. Two orbs glittered in the gloom and Jeremy realized it was the creature's eyes—and the creature was running.

The steel door moved faster, and Jeremy threw his weight behind it, pushing.

Footsteps   pounded—a   bestial   growl—metal squealed—

WHAM! The door shuddered from a violent impact on

the other side. Jeremy's breaths were shallow and relief swept over him… the door had shut.

WHAM! The door rocked again—and then silence.

Looking down at his palm, Jeremy saw a small dot of blood.

"Is it gone?" Marissa asked from behind him.

"Locked out for the time being," Jeremy responded.

"You seen anything like that before?" Her voice still trembled from shock.

"A nightmare…maybe, I guess?" Jeremy ventured. He looked quickly around the bay for another exit, but was not rewarded—the stone walls were built like a fortress with no doors or windows. The huge columns from floor to ceiling were spaced evenly down the front wall, and at one end of the bay the entire wall was covered in alien hieroglyphs, strange symbols from hostile aliens who killed for pleasure. And yet… his father and brother were somewhere on this planet, but what had become of them?

He turned to Marissa, "Where'd everybody go?!"

"Soldiers, creepy CIA guy, and henchmen—gone," she answered. "Patrick, Alex and Selene—gone."

"Uh… who's left besides us?"

Marissa laughed in scorn. "It's just you, me and the cowardly lion."

"Leo," Jeremy said, looking around. "Did he run off on you?"

"Yeah, with killer alien dude coming right for me." Marissa's face was pink with anger. "I didn't know guys with Leo's IQ could move so fast."

"Wait!" Jeremy said. He slowly turned back to the steel door, listening. A rhythmic thumping seemed to emanate from the walls. "You hear that?"

Marissa moved closer and stood beside him. She craned her neck to hear.

"Drums… and very tribal," Leo's voice was behind them, and both Jeremy and Marissa jumped in surprise.

Marissa swung around in fury. "Run off again like that and I'm gonna—"

"Shhhhh!" Leo hissed.

The drumbeats seemed to get louder and more distinct.

"Now might be a good time to power up the ole' Portal and come back at a better time," Marissa deadpanned. "What ya' think?"

"Go back to Earth?" Leo said. "Impossible."

"Impossible?"

Jeremy was oblivious to them. He leaned against the door, pressing his ear into the metal and heard more drumbeats… and then a voice sounded in his head—

"If you don't leave now, you will die."

In a flash Jeremy was hit by dizziness, and he swayed on his feet. Energy surged through his brain, making his eyeballs tingle. He shook it off and looked at Marissa and Leo, but they were too engrossed in their conversation to notice.

"This Portal doesn't go back to Earth," Leo said smugly.

Marissa stared at Leo, open-mouthed. "How would *you* know that? Stumble across any Portal manuals in your haste to flee the scene?"

"Turn on the power and follow me," the voice repeated in Jeremy's mind, and this time he recognized the voice—Erik, his older brother. *But how?*

Jeremy turned to Marissa. "Did you hear that?"

Marissa, pointing her finger at Leo, only spared him a hostile glance. "Drumbeats, yeah, very creepy." Leo pointedly looked away from her, but Marissa wasn't backing down. "How would genius boy here know this Portal doesn't go back to our own planet?!"

"Jeremy! Move or die!" Erik's voice pounded into his head, and Jeremy looked wildly around the chamber. Erik's voice screamed again, *"Now!"*

"Hey?" came Marissa's voice. "I asked you a question—"

Jeremy jerked around, wild eyed. "We gotta get outta here!"

Marissa stared at Jeremy. "No duh. But open that door and *predator boy* will make like a vampire on all of us."

The steel door shook slightly—the drums sounded outside, loud and close.

"What about the control room?" Leo suggested with a shrug.

Jeremy stepped into the middle of the Portal bay. There were no doors to his left and none to his right. He turned back to Leo. "The *Earth Portal*—the one at TerraGen—there was a door to the control center here," he gestured to the cavernous room. "In the outside bay."

"But there was only one exit that I saw: the elevator," Marissa challenged.

Frustrated, Jeremy began walking back to the Portal. "This Portal's different," he said over his shoulder. "Don't know why, but I just know there's another way out..."

"THIS PLACE STINKS," Selene said, her voice echoing against the walls. "Is there a football game somewhere? Those drums are giving me a headache!"

"Yeah, there'll be a football game," Alex's voice was saturated with sarcasm. "Except the home team's gonna be throwing spirals with your severed head."

"They wouldn't do that."

Patrick refused to comment. A hoarse laugh from behind let him know what Alex thought of Selene's optimism. Patrick halted them. They were moving down a circular stairwell, wide enough for ten people, but the farther down they went, the darker it got. Above them, thin windows let in the light, but few rays reached this far down.

"Should never have left the soldiers," Alex's voice was petulant.

"You were lucky to find us as it were," Patrick responded. Alex had coming running up from behind like a kid who almost missed the school bus. The memory made Patrick grin, but Alex had always travelled in limousines to school, so the analogy was flawed and his smile faded. "I waited just long enough to save your sorry behind."

"*Mister Know-it-all*," sneered Alex. "Leading us down the stairway to hell."

"Stop it!" Selene was close to another breakdown.

Angrily Patrick turned and faced Alex who was a good ten steps behind. "You wanna go find the *spook* soldiers? I won't stop you!" Alex was bigger and more athletic than he was but Patrick didn't care.

Alex paused, his mind working. "Not really."

"Good."

"You got some great plan in mind?" Alex's voice had a hint of conciliation.

"Yeah. Get the heck out of—" Patrick broke off, his eyes looking upward through the middle of the stairwell. Six stories up the light was brighter and he could clearly see a group of alien eyes peering down at them. Mouths parted, showing long, sharp teeth. "Right. Time to run." Grabbing Selene's hand, Patrick started descending two stairs at a time, his backpack bouncing up and down on his shoulders. Darkness enshrouded them the deeper they went.

"I can barely see my feet!" Alex roared.

"Just a little further," Patrick said.

"You been here before?" Alex challenged.

"If I had, do you think I'd come back?!" Patrick responded. He was making for an access door at the lower level. *How* he knew that, was the bigger mystery.

"Just saying…" Alex's voice had become petulant again. "You seem pretty sure for a guy making this trip for the first time."

Patrick's brain still ached from the data download in the Portal—what kind of data, he hadn't a clue. After discovering the alien and its kill in the temple foyer, he knew they wouldn't be going back to the Portal chamber. Would they ever see Jeremy and Marissa ever again? Unlikely now. Instead, he'd needed a way of escape—a way out of the city. Then, like discovering an Easter egg bonus in a video game, the schematics of the city had suddenly popped into his head, as if his need had called up the blueprints—streets and avenues—stone buildings that once housed the living—all part of a city that was laid out in a half-circle descending downward to the plateau.

The schematics were amazing in their detail. Patrick just had to focus on one area and suddenly he was inside a factory, or the temple—he'd seen huge mansions that had been built along the city's upper level, facing the river to the north—and deep within the city's bowels were the dungeons and other secret rooms.

But now, with aliens hunting them, he was thankful that at least he had a plan of some kind. Anything was better than being gutted by an extraterrestrial... except that analogy was flawed as well—

I'm technically the extraterrestrial.

Total darkness engulfed them now.

BOOM—DA BOOM! The drumbeats increased in intensity.

There came a clattering above him, and Patrick knew the alien killers were descending the stairs. Somewhere below there was an access door that would provide an escape... except he couldn't see a thing.

CHAPTER EIGHTEEN

THE GOLDEN CROWN

"**N**OTHING BUT DUST," Jeremy said with disgust. Light from the military lanterns showed a control room that hadn't been used in ages. No equipment...just empty tables.

"The secret passageway... don't you see it?" Marissa's voice cut into the silence. Both Jeremy and Leo quickly turned and the look they received was blatantly sarcastic. "Yeah. Neither do I, boneheads."

"Seek the crown," said Erik inside Jeremy's head.

"Where?" asked Jeremy, eyes hastily scanning the darkened room.

"Wow. Talk about slow," Marissa said.

"Jeremy, nothing will happen unless you speak it," instructed Erik. Having his older brother in his head was like the buzzing of electricity, and it was very disorienting.

"I can't see anything in here!" Jeremy moaned.

"The secret passageway was just a joke!" Marissa said exasperatedly.

"Turn the power on."

The words were Erik's, but the logic was blowing Jeremy's mind. Turn what power on?

"Earth to Jeremy!" Marissa said.

"Don't fight it." This time the voice was Leo's. Jeremy turned and the younger boy's face betrayed no hint of joking. "Things don't operate on this planet like they do on Earth."

And then he remembered Erik's words: *Nothing happens unless you speak it.*

"Power: turn on."

No sooner had the words left Jeremy's lips than a great hum sounded. Lights hidden in recess came on, and the room was fully illuminated. A buzz sounded, followed by metallic hisses as the empty desks were suddenly transformed—panels swung inward and keyboards emerged, but they weren't like any keyboards Jeremy had ever seen. They had glassy surfaces, strange icons… they were *alien*.

"Patrick should be here to see this," said Marissa in awe.

"I have to find a crown," Jeremy stated. "That's how we get out of here."

"And you know that… how?" Marissa demanded.

"Just trust me."

"Hearing voices again?" she said with mock sarcasm.

"Yes, and it's giving me a headache."

It took her a second to realize Jeremy was serious. She tried to smile, but couldn't. "Geez. That's… that's, uh… well, wasn't expecting that…"

They scanned the luminous keyboards, trying to spot a crown icon amidst the alien script.

Nothing.

Jeremy stepped back and let his eyes sweep over the room. Again, no crown. He moved into the hallway outside—he could see only three other rooms. Quickly they split up and examined each room, only to reunite outside the control room. Discouraged faces told the story.

"Secret voices can be a sign of mental illness," Marissa said.

"It turned on the power, didn't it?" Jeremy returned, flushed with frustration.

"What else did it say?" Leo said.

"Seek the crown."

"What else?" Leo kept pushing.

Jeremy kicked at the floor, stirring up dust. "We're wasting our time."

"There's something else," Leo said. "Think!"

"I have!" Jeremy turned away, breathing heavily. He closed his eyes in concentration. "Well… he said nothing happens unless you speak it."

"Crown! Show thyself!" Marissa shouted with derision.

The walls echoed with her voice but nothing happened. She laughed.

"No, Jeremy, you try," came Leo's voice again.

Jeremy looked into Leo's eyes and knew he was being utterly serious. *Well, why not try it? This isn't Earth. Things here are definitely weird and probably operate differently.*

"Crown… show thyself." Jeremy's words were the same as Marissa's. For his part, Jeremy couldn't think of anything else to say.

The hallway was the same as before. Only emptiness could be seen around the cold, stone walls and floors.

"Wait." This time Marissa's voice had a tinge of seriousness. "What's that?"

The hallway looked unchanged, but something had

happened. Jeremy was trying to notice what the difference was, but couldn't place it.

"I can't see—" Jeremy began.

"Shhhhhh!" Marissa hissed angrily.

Her voice echoed off the walls. And then the sound entered his consciousness—a persistent beep, beep, beep. They all heard it.

Entering the control room they immediately saw that the alien keyboard had changed: icons that had once been gray were now infused with color—and glowing in gold was the outline of a crown. The crown covered most of the keyboard with three jewels showing on the crown's top. One jewel was flashing off and on in time with the beeping. Jeremy's finger started forward—

"Wait!" Marissa whispered. "It could be a trap."

"Really?" Jeremy said sardonically, and he motioned behind them to the Portal. "We can go back to that big door and try walking out through there—"

"Never mind," she backtracked. "Just push it."

His finger pressed the flashing jewel.

"Good work," came Erik's voice in his head. "You're learning."

With a whoosh of air, the keyboard disappeared and the control room returned to its previous state... empty.

"A trap," Marissa moaned. She tried looking at Leo, but his attention was on Jeremy.

"The way is open," Jeremy said simply.

Jeremy immediately walked out of the control room. Marissa and Leo exchanged looks and followed.

The Portal bay was still littered with the dead bodies of the soldiers. Jeremy tried to look away from Neriah Freeman's body, but a flash of light drew his attention. Numbers flashed on a small bracelet on her wrist—30:09:35. Suppressing the revulsion he felt, he took the bracelet off Freeman's lifeless wrist, and the numbers vanished.

Stuffing the bracelet in his pocket he stepped away from the corpse that used to be his *minder*.

In the Portal bay the large steel door remained shut, much to Jeremy's relief. He turned and walked the past huge columns and made straight to the far end of the bay. The hieroglyphs, once just black holes in the wall, were now glowing with multiple colors. One symbol grabbed his eye immediately: a small crown glowing a bright sheen of gold. Jeremy reached out and pressed the symbol. Air hissed out of the wall as a huge stone block moved inward, revealing stairs leading downward.

"Okay, maybe you're hearing voices, but whatever," Marissa said. "It's working."

Lights flickered on in the stairwell.

"You have one hour to get out of the city," Erik's voice spoke in Jeremy's head. "One hour—stay longer at your own peril."

Jeremy took a deep breath and looked at the other two. "Follow if you dare."

"Is that what the voices are telling you?" Leo asked.

The chamber was suddenly rocked by a massive concussion.

"Stay and die, more like it." Marissa said flatly.

Another concussion.

"Exactly," Jeremy said, and then led them quickly into the stairwell. The block of stone closed behind them with a grinding thump.

Chapter Nineteen

Genesis Revealed

"**S**OMEONE FORGOT TO HIRE A JANITOR," quipped Alex.

"Like, for the last century," Selene agreed.

Dust kicked up around Alex's shoes as he followed Patrick through the passage. They were heading downward into what looked like a dungeon—Alex had never seen a real dungeon, but he imagined this is what one would look like. Every once in a while they would pass stone carvings of strange beasts and tattered remnants of banners and tapestries. *Very dungeon-esque.* Light flickered from recesses near the ceiling, and it was reassuring; it was *that light* that had saved them. They had descended into absolute darkness at the bottom of the staircase with the sound of the aliens getting closer, and then the light had come on and Patrick had found his access door. Now they were rushing through strange passages, hoping the aliens had lost their scent. Alex had lost count of the arched openings they had passed by on either side, the tunnels and stairways leading to unknown horrors in this dungeon they were descending into.

Patrick's voice penetrated the stillness. "This is it." The hallway had ended abruptly. Facing them was stone wall and Alex shook his head in disbelief: *the brainiac had led them their deaths. Trapped in the bowels of a dungeon hell!* In the dim light, only a circular relief showed to be carved into the wall.

"It's a dead end," Alex said sarcastically. "Dead, as in… *us.*" He certainly couldn't see anything special.

"Take another look," said Patrick with a hint of impatience.

Alex stepped back and the circular relief became something more. Stone and metal had been shaped into the wall—it looked like a cog, a huge, circular gearwheel from a piece of machinery. The center of the wheel's spoke was smooth, and he watched as Patrick's finger lightly touched it… and a puff of air issued forth.

Alex reached for Patrick's wrist. "Let me see your hand."

Patrick twisted his hand to reveal a tiny speck of blood on his palm.

"You don't feel anything?" Alex asked, eyes wide with curiosity.

"Nope… just air."

"Totally invasive," Selene said, her voice echoing in the hall.

The wall seemed to shudder with a grinding jolt. The stone cog moved inward with a quiet hiss, and then it slowly turned clockwise.

"How did you know?" Alex asked in a whisper.

The entire stone slab containing the relief suddenly swung inward to reveal a chamber. A buzz sounded and light appeared, reflecting off the ceiling. The smell of damp, musty air filled Alex's nostrils as they walked inside, and he wrinkled his nose. "I don't know why we're wasting our time when we should be escaping this place—"

"Hush!" Patrick's voice boomed in the small room.

"The gremlin faces are out there looking..." Alex began, but trailed off when he noticed that Patrick was ignoring him. And now he realized that this chamber was different from the rest of the dungeon. The temple and dungeon corridors reminded him of the pictures of ancient Rome in his history books, but this room was definitely from modern-day Earth.

It was made of solid metal.

"TerraGen Universal," Selene read monotonously, looking upward.

Alex swiveled around. TERRAGEN UNIVERSAL was stenciled above the doorway's entrance. He turned to see Patrick set his backpack on a flat metal console at the center of the room. "How'd you know this room was here?"

Patrick examined a vertical column that ran along the entrance. He glanced at Alex briefly and answered, "A little birdie whispered in my ear." Patrick's fingers glided over the polished metal and then found a hidden recess. Alex heard a loud *click* and watched as the vertical column moved inward, separated and then moved out of view to reveal an instrument panel with rows of colored stones.

"Wicked cool!" Selene said, scarcely hiding her awe.

"More tricks." Alex couldn't hide his bitterness. Whenever Patrick went into genius mode he always felt inadequate... like an outsider.

"Does it do anything?" Selene asked.

"Without a doubt," Patrick said with confidence, fingers touching one stone and then another, each one glowing upon his touch.

"Pretty," Selene said.

Pretty? Alex almost snorted in derision. *If a prize were given out for the largest cavity of air between the ears…*

Patrick turned around and the light seemed to dance in his eyes.

Alex turned as well, and above the center console a three-dimensional map shimmered, showing mountain ranges, valleys, and rivers floating in the air.

"Where are we located?" Patrick asked.

A point of red light suddenly appeared between the edge of a mountain range and a river. Alex looked at Patrick in surprise—*he speaks and the map answers!*

"What about our parents?" Selene asked.

Patrick shrugged and said, "Show us our parents."

Nothing.

"What about the company?" Alex demanded.

Patrick's eyebrow lifted. "Show us TerraGen." Six additional pinpricks of red light appeared.

Alex shot Patrick a look of disbelief. "Three months on an alien planet and the company doesn't waste any time." Alex had eavesdropped on his father's private meetings with the TerraGen board members, and he knew their ambition. If they'd said the original expedition listed five hundred people, then it was more likely five thousand. "They must've known about this alien race the whole time and never mentioned one word."

"Typical," Patrick said sarcastically.

Selene frowned. "I thought they were coming here for science experiments?"

Alex had heard enough. "Wake up, *numbnut!* They *are* doing experiments! Except it's on a bunch of aliens, and that's why those leather faces are pissed!" Heated, Alex turned to Patrick and shook his head in frustration.

But Patrick continued to study the map. "We're on a planet with an ancient civilization that's particularly hostile…"

"And not very welcoming," Selene added.

Alex followed Patrick's gaze back to the map where the seven points of red lights seemed to wink at them.

Patrick shrugged. "Our parents have definitely left this location and are probably at one of these six base camps—"

"If they're still alive," Alex said darkly. *Someone has to be a realist.*

Patrick turned and looked from Selene to Alex, looking serious, "Getting home might take longer than we thought."

THE DAMP, FOUL-SMELLING air was becoming oppressive. Footsteps echoed in the stone hallway and then stopped. *Another stairwell leading downward... great!* Marissa was unhappy. It seemed that the further down they went, the fouler the air assaulting her nostrils became. They were in the bowels of the great city and had been moving steadily for almost an hour. Marissa brought up the rear, following Leo as Jeremy led them through tunnels, past ancient halls and fortified bunkers... and always with unerring direction. Whatever alien civilization had built this underground network, they had built for defense, and it obviously hadn't worked; because the tunnels and chambers had clearly been abandoned for centuries.

"I'm gonna vomit," moaned Marissa. She looked to Leo for sympathy, but his attention, as always, was on Jeremy. *Following Jeremy around like a puppy dog!* She wrinkled her nose and tried to breathe through her mouth, but that took concentration, and she reluctantly gave in to the foulness. "Fine."

Her muscles were sore and she followed the other two down the stairwell with resignation. A distant roar was getting louder the further they descended, and a damp mist swirled around her feet. She stepped out onto a walkway and all three collectively gasped. A torrent of water rushed past them under an ancient, stone bridge. Three huge orbs hung in the air thirty feet above them, each orb fixed by chains that ascended upward, disappearing into the darkness. The orbs shown a pale yellow light that revealed a huge cavern. Mist floated up from the water, obscuring the opposite wall. The sound of rushing water was deafening.

"Probably their source of power!" Leo shouted, his face lit with excitement.

"We need to hurry!" Jeremy said urgently.

"You keep saying that," Marissa moaned.

The bridge spanning the torrent of water was made of stone and had deteriorated over time. It looked many centuries old. Vast sections were in ruins and debris littered the narrow walkway that arched over the water. Marissa hated heights of any kind. She stepped onto the bridge and looked over the side to where water rushed underneath thirty yards below. She blinked and steadied herself, then followed after Leo and Jeremy. A sudden pain in her groin slowed her progress.

Cramps…

Her period always came at the worst of times, and she gritted her teeth—no painkillers, no box of tampons, no bowl of ice cream—*expeditions suck!* Mist swirled around her, partially obscuring Jeremy and Leo, chilling her to the bone. They crossed the bridge, the roar of rushing water pounding into her ears as they headed toward a dark opening that materialized at the opposite end.

Jeremy hesitated at the opening and turned to look behind them.

"Looks like a great place for a rest, right?" Marissa asked, her cramps sending spikes of pain through her body. A few minutes would—

"Can't," Jeremy responded. And then he pointed toward the opposite side of the cavern.

She turned. Mist still shrouded the stone bridge. And then she saw the movement. Dark humanoid shadows moved in the haze at the opposite end of the bridge. She felt Jeremy lean close to her ear before he whispered.

"We're being hunted."

ALEX WATCHED AS PATRICK's fingers moved across the instrument panel, touching a series of colored stones in sequence. How much he trusted Patrick he didn't know. The math genius was hearing voices, having visions... whatever. But he reluctantly had to admit that, so far, Patrick was batting a thousand. "Any weapons in this place?" Alex's question sounded petulant, even to himself.

"Dunno."

"I could use a weapon."

A hiss sounded. The hologram map vanished and a foot-square compartment appeared on the surface of the center console. Patrick's hands reached in and pulled out a wooden box. He held it delicately for a moment, then set it on the console. Selene crowded beside him as he opened the lid.

Alex moved closer, and saw a piece of paper in Patrick's hand.

"Use this wisely," Selene's voice echoed as she read the words on the paper, "and welcome to Genesis, son." She lifted her head to look at Patrick. "Who's *Big Brain*?"

Patrick didn't answer. Alex realized it was because the little nerd was choking back tears. "Lemme guess... you're wittle bitty brain—"

"Shut up," Patrick hissed. And then the paper disintegrated, falling in pieces between Patrick's fingers.

"Cool! Just like the spy movies," Selene said in awe.

"Not cool... just too much oxygen," Patrick said shakily. "Which doesn't make a bit of sense."

"A computer tablet!" Selene exclaimed as she lifted a black, reflective tablet out of the box. Patrick tried to reach for it, but Selene moved away. "Wait. I want to try it—"

"It's a data pad, and meant for me—"

"One second!"

"You might drop it—"

Selene stopped moving and handed the data pad over to Patrick. "You keep it. It doesn't work anyway."

Patrick's fingers explored every aspect of the data pad. "I didn't break it," Selene said with a shrug.

Losers. Alex shook his head, watching the brainiac try to find the button to turn it on. Something glimmered down inside the compartment that gaped on the console. Alex moved between Patrick and the small chamber, using his body as a shield. With his right hand he reached into the compartment and felt his hand wrap around a small object.

"What's that?"

Patrick's voice jerked Alex upward, face red from guilt. And then his pulse relaxed as he realized Patrick had suddenly found a button on the data pad. Alex carefully stole a glance behind to see what treasure he'd discovered: in his palm rested a black, six-sided gemstone with a design inscribed on its face, a small sphere within a larger sphere— *TerraGen's symbol of the lunar eclipse.* The object was attached to a silver chain, and Alex carefully tucked it into his pocket. He casually turned back and found Selene staring at him. "What?"

Selene was standing in the open doorway. "It's back."

"Back?"

A question formed on Alex's lips, but then he heard it: the *BOOM, BOOM, BOOM* of distant drums.

"I need more time!" Patrick hissed in frustration. The skinny, high school computer geek returned to the instrument panel where the multi-colored lights waited as if in invitation.

"Do you think there's any weapons in this place?" Alex asked.

"Weapons?"

"Guns, laser beams? How about an axe?"

"Axe?"

"Pay attention, numbnuts!" Alex shouted, trying to break through to Patrick who'd become obsessed with the glowing, colored stones, the nerd's face a picture of indecision.

"I need more time!"

"Our friends of the alien persuasion have a difference

of opinion!" Alex said, thumbing to the open doorway where the sound of drums was getting louder.

Patrick jammed the data pad into his backpack. "Crap, crap, crap! Okay, we're leaving!"

"Weapons?"

The computer genius was already heading out the door. "Enough with the weapons! We haven't the time..." Patrick's voice trailed off.

Stepping past Patrick and into stone passage, Alex looked around and then gave the other boy a bewildered look. "What's the matter?"

"Where's Selene?"

The passage was empty except for the two boys. Drumbeats boomed deep within the city.

Alex groaned... *we're so doomed.*

CHAPTER TWENTY

DRANGALL

H E CARRIED HIS PRIZE into the passageway, not bothering to wait for the secret entrance to close shut. He shifted his burden from one shoulder to the other, feet plodding through dust while dodging the various outcroppings of stone that marked chambers on the other side of the hidden passage. The *Zarredkorthund* race was a warrior race—violent, territorial—with a strict hierarchical caste system. In the *Zarkund* caste system Bagut was a *Zarskreyja*, a laborer. The *Skreyes* were the lowest of the low...and to make matters worst, Bagut was the runt of the litter. He used the secret ways because that's what gave him power. *Power* meant being able to move freely throughout the great city—without anyone being the wiser—which allowed Bagut the freedom to steal whatever he wanted, whenever he wanted. And now he had a treasure that would make the *Zartaksu*—the warrior caste and great killers with blades—envious. Sold into the Skreyes by his birth parents, Bagut was excluded from the Zartaksu and ridiculed by those larger, heavily muscled brutes that pulled his ears and stole whatever food he'd stashed away.

"*Thegya Bagut*," Bagut hissed in triumph. "*Bagut pus nil vapna!*"

Bagut had started his day in a foul mood. Horns had sounded, drums had beaten their orders and the warriors had marched off to attack the invaders. Bagut had been left behind...as always.

Let the brutes go to their deaths, he'd snarled inwardly.

So Bagut had decided to explore the old corridors and halls on the city's western side, a place normally forbidden to laborers by the ruling class, the *Zargoorag*, because they were selfish and suspicious. Bagut had slipped into the secret ways and bypassed several patrols, stealing into the western dungeons, heart pumping and expecting to find gold and jewels beyond his wildest imaginings.

Nothing! Not even a strip of copper! Bagut is cursed!

And then the dreaded *forad kringla* had awakened...

He shuddered at the memory. Bagut was considered middle aged amongst his clan. He'd heard stories of the great monster but they were just stories. He and his fellow laborers were warned about venturing close to the city's surface—*bright light hurts eyes, anyway.*

But still... the forad kringla had slept for so long.

Only the old ones—those being prepped for the *great transformation*, where their flesh was given as sacrifice to the greater clans in return for the great Lord giving them rebirth—these ancient Zarkundian's had spoken of a long ago awakening of the forad kringla—the great monster who dwelt in the city. But even their tales had been passed down from other old ones of centuries past. Sure, warriors and laborers would go missing from time to time, but who was to say what had become of them? There were hundreds of places in the great dungeons where the Zarkund could be killed or fall to their death.

Another roar had sounded close, causing Bagut to fall prostrate on the floor. He felt the rumblings of the monster's steps and cursed himself again for straying so close to the surface. But death didn't come. And then Bagut did what frail outcasts do best—he ran. Terror gripped his imaginations and he had run headlong, without thought of direction. The beast would roar, the stones would shake as the creature lumbered in the corridors above him and Bagut would change course and run in the opposite direction. One passageway led to another…and then to another. Bagut had cursed his bad luck, his mind imagining the treasures that were being hoarded so close to the surface—treasures he would never see.

But then his luck had changed.

He'd entered an unknown passageway and smelled the intruders at once, smelled the sweetness that contrasted with the rotted, fetid air that was the norm in the vast dungeons under the city. It was a smell wholly unfamiliar to Bagut. It smelled delicious, mouth watering. Bagut was weak in stature—especially when compared to the warrior Zartaksu— but his smeller was without equal amongst the Zarkund. He'd smelled the blood pumping through the intruder's veins, even imagined he could hear the *thump thumping* of the being's heart.

Laughter rumbled from deep within him as he shifted his burden to the other shoulder. *"Drangall ek lango pleasoln!"* Bagut whispered cheerfully in his raspy speech. *Drangall* was his pet. His pet loved fresh meat.

Snnnnnnnffff!

Bagut breathed in the scent of his new treasure, saliva dripping from the corners of his mouth. His tongue licked at the jagged remnants that were his teeth, fighting back the desire to rip and eat. He thought of his pet and smiled again.

Yes… Drangall would be pleased.

T HEIR FOOTSTEPS SOUNDED HARSH in the corridor, the great pounding of their shoes bouncing off the walls around them. "Wait!" Patrick shouted, stopping dead still in the middle of the passage. Selene had disappeared—kidnapped and taken for dinner most likely. There had been no blood in the corridor and Patrick had figured the girl was still alive. After closing the great cog that marked his father's TerraGen vault, they'd moved swiftly, then turned a corner to find an empty corridor.

"Wasting our time," Alex sneered, panting heavily from behind.

"Shushhhhhh!!!!" Patrick hissed, head cocked, listening.

"Don't hear—"

Patrick raked back with an elbow into Leach, Jr's belly and was rewarded with the expulsion of breath and a gasp of pain. "Listen!" Patrick growled.

Further up the passage there came the faint grinding of stone on stone. Patrick moved forward, light on his feet, mentally trying to pinpoint the source of the sound— *THUMP*—the sound of a stone sliding into place echoed in the corridor a few paces in front. In the dim light that still emanated from recessed cracks in the corridor's ceiling, Patrick strained to examine the stone floor. His breathing was loud in his ears and he tried—tried and failed—to hold his breath.

"She's alien meat," Alex whined.

"There!" Patrick shouted, turning to glare at the spoiled twit.

Alex leaned forward. "It's a wall—"

"The floor, you moron!"

The All-State quarterback muscled past Patrick and squatted near the wall. Alex shrugged his shoulders, "Okay. Probably a secret door—"

"Of course it's a secret door!" Patrick snarled, finger pointing to the curved marks on the floor where the hidden door had slid on its axis. He suppressed his frustration— Selene's life was more important than humiliating this oaf who wore stupidity as if it were a shiny object of celebration. "There has to be a way to trigger it back open."

"Figuring that out is more like… uh, *your* department?"

"Even a muscle-head like you can help!"

"For what? How?"

"Find the trigger!"

"It's a big wall," Alex moaned, hands outstretched to demonstrate how long the corridor was.

"Start by putting to use those precious, million dollar fingers—the same fingers that won our school a state championship—search every crevasse, every hole and find whatever button opens the door!"

"Seems complicated," Alex moaned. He shot Patrick a withering look then turned and began searching.

Patrick bit off a retort, seething on the inside—*it sucks being stuck with a kid whose never worked a job in his life!*

SELENE WOKE AFTER A VIOLENT shake and realized with alarm that she was being carried. *Being carried is so much better than walking,* her bleary mind thought. Her eyes blinked. Dim shadows—stone walls—the constant up and down bobbing was making her nauseous. She felt like a sack of potatoes. But it was the smell that assaulted her nostrils—an alien smell—that clued her brain into the identity of the creature that carried her on its shoulders—not that she was an expert on alien body chemistry, but Patrick and Alex couldn't stink this bad on their worst days! The stench of the alien was like a backed up toilet, two day old fish meat left to rot and rancid body odor all rolled into one.

"Bagut pus nil vapna," the alien muttered in its alien tongue. "Drangall ek lango pleasoln merg Bagut."

Sudden realization swept over her, filling her with terror: *I'm about to be killed and eaten!*

Selene screamed.

Well, she tried to scream but the alien was fast and brutal, clamping a filthy hand over her mouth. Sharp, mottled teeth flashed in the gloom and fetid breath assaulted her nostrils.

"Tekja eitt! Tekja eitt!" the alien hissed. The creature slammed her roughly against the stone wall, covering her with its body like a vise. "Tekja eitt!" it hissed again, hand still clamped over her mouth.

Her eyes scanned her surrounding and saw that they were hidden in a small passage, deep in shadow. The passage ended at an arched doorway, where red and orange light flickered to reveal a large corridor. Firelight, her eyes observed. And then she understood the alien's consternation. *It was fear.*

The sound of marching, scuffling feet grew louder. Torches flashed into view, each held by huge aliens—*warrior* aliens with swords and axes strapped on their backs. She moaned, unable to control her terror. The alien tensed, clamping her mouth so hard it caused a stab of pain in her gums and tears to spring up in her eyes. Her captor silently hissed a warning, dark eyes glaring at her. It looked away, studying the arched doorway and the procession of alien soldiers. A tremor of fear ran through the alien's body.

Hope flickered—an idea formed in her mind—hope grew and became the smallest of flames within Selene. *Her situation offered few outcomes that left her alive, that was obvious. But she wasn't a sack of potatoes nor some alien's piece of meat, either!* But hope is still hope and there was a depth of tenacity within the Chinese girl that would've surprised every one of her high school classmates.

Pinned against the stone wall, she felt its surface. *Diamonds are good for something after all*, she thought grimly—then quietly slid the sharp surface of her class ring against the rough, stone wall.

USELESS. ALEXANDER LEACH, JUNIOR was as useless as an AK-47 in a mud slinging contest. Patrick snorted in disgust and continued probing the wall for the hidden trigger. Alex... well, Alex was doing what Alex does best.

"This is long overdue," Alex gasped. The jock's word's were followed by the sound of a steady stream of fluids against the stone wall. "Yeah..."

"Selene's about to be killed and you're taking a piss," Patrick frowned.

"Helps me focus." Lewisville's finest faced the wall opposite the hidden doorway.

"You could've done your business further down the hall! Geez, it stinks!"

"And get snatched like Asian Barbie? No thank you."

Patrick's finger snagged on a sharp piece of stone and he cursed. He glanced indignantly to where Alex was still facing the wall, head raised, eyes closed in obvious relief.

"Wait a second," Alex said in surprise.

"It's been longer than a second—"

"Wait!"

"You're disgusting—"

"Hush!"

Patrick heard the sound of Alex zipping up his pants and watched him step backward. He seemed to wave his hand in front of the stone wall—*the* stone wall that now shone damp in the dim light. Patrick started to deliver one of his patented and very sarcastic insults. "You showered the wall now it's time—"

"Quiet!" Alex hissed... and then, "I knew I felt a breeze."

"A breeze?" Patrick didn't like where this was going.

A hand waved again. "A cross wind." He turned, one hand gesturing from the hidden door's location and then across the corridor's width to the wet spot on the wall.

Patrick began to laugh.

The jock didn't see the humor. "What?!"

"Congratulations, meat for brains! You just found the trigger."

"Ha ha, very funny," Alex growled.

"No… you did!" Patrick growled back in frustration. "Now press firmly on the stone you just pissed on and let's go save Selene!"

A hiss was quickly followed by a loud curse. And then a plaintive voice said, "Can I use my shoe?"

THE GLOW OF FIRELIGHT still flickered like a firefly in the far distance of the stone corridor. The sound of the alien warrior's marching was muffled now, but the threat of their nearness still sent shivers down Selene's spine. She stayed silent on the alien's shoulder. Her mind had been working in overdrive since waking up as the Christmas turkey for some alien's family. If she screamed, the warriors would take her from her captor and pass her around as some Asian appetizer for the troops. And if she stayed playing the subservient captive…well, the alien had something in mind and Selene knew it wasn't for her betterment. Her mind kept replaying the same movie scene: *alien creature opens door to find his wife and little, alien son waiting hungrily. "Honey, I'm home!" the alien says in his alien speak. "Look what Daddy brought!"*

"Bagut tulle be sothgremere fe!" the alien muttered under its breath.

The alien liked to mutter to himself. *Probably lonely,* she thought. The images of an alien wife and pre-school tyke gave way to something more sinister—what horrible death was this creature planning?

"I really think you should let me go," Selene whispered.

"Tekja eitt!" the alien hissed for the umpteenth time.

Rotted flesh and other nasty smells assaulted her nostrils again and she regretted opening her mouth. But still, this was going too far. "You don't want me. I smell terribly—well, not as terrible as you—"

"Tekja eitt!"

"Tekja yourself!" she said in a louder voice.

The alien tensed and clapped a grimy hand over her mouth. He looked away and she felt the tenseness leave the creature's shoulders. At the far end of the corridor the light was gone. Black eyes turned on her and she could see the faint outlines of its sharp teeth. Eyes blinked. It seemed to study her. Selene was suddenly thrown up and down, the alien readjusting her on its bony shoulders. It began moving, shuffling quicker and sure of itself. Seconds, then minutes passed. The alien stopped and Selene felt a cool, humid breeze brush across her face. She blinked, her eyes trying to make out detail. The recessed lights in this part of the dungeon were weaker. One thing was obvious, they were at the opening of another arched doorway. Stairs, vague and pale as ghosts in the light, faded downward toward the source of the wet, damp air that reminded Selene of the snake exhibit at the zoo.

"Drangall ek lango pleasoln merg Bagut," the alien whispered with evident pleasure.

"Who or *what* is Drangall?" Selene asked, not bothering to whisper.

Upon hearing her use the alien name, the creature twisted its head around. Again its two, black eyes studied her and she could see the forming of a smile on the alien's lips.

"I TOLD YOU THIS WAS a waste of time."

"We're not giving up," Patrick whispered, and winced as he heard the despair in his own voice.

"How much longer can we continue to go sneaking around?" Alex hissed, his words laced with anger. "The natives are restless and we've been lucky to avoid two aliens! Did you see how big they were?!"

"Selene wouldn't let *you* be taken for food without a fight," Patrick said. "So stop with the crybaby act—"

"And do what? You have no clue where she is!"

For once, Patrick had no words. He *was* stuck. They'd been searching this location, where the tunnel bisected a large corridor, for what seemed like an hour—more like five minutes, actually—and found nothing. The large corridor offered two opposing directions that the creature could've taken Selene—which gave Patrick a fifty/fifty decision to make, since splitting up was out of the question. If he chose wrong… Selene was dead. And so they remained, looking for any sign of her passing. But staying at this junction was equally dangerous.

"Chinese chick is gonna get us killed," Alex sneered. Loud, hocking and snorting sounds followed his words as the jock started to build a disgusting wad of phlegm.

The muffled thunder of footsteps reached Patrick's ears just as the hazy light of torches glimmered at the far end of the corridor to his right. Patrick took hold of Alex's arm and yanked him back into the tunnel and deep into the shadows.

A choking sound was followed by coughing as Alex inhaled phlegm. Patrick slammed his palm across Alex's mouth. Strong hands grasped his own, trying to break his hold.

"Aliens!" Patrick hissed into Alex's ear.

The coughing ceased but Alex trembled as he fought to control it. Patrick lowered his palm. Both young men stared behind where the light was growing brighter in the corridor. As if connected by some mental bond, both crept deeper into the tunnel's gloom. Orange and yellow light flickered from a dozen torches as a small group of armed aliens marched swiftly past.

Patrick felt the smooth, cool texture of the tunnel wall and looked down to where it glowed faintly in the torchlight. His heart stopped. Two scratches, each a foot in length, formed an 'X' on the surface of the stone wall. His heart beat faster. Suddenly Alex's hand gripped his shoulder and shoved him further down the tunnel. Looking back toward the corridor he saw a single light bobbing and moving slowly back toward where the tunnel intersected.

A single alien appeared, torch in hand. It's head was lifted, twisting, nose snuffling the air. Both Patrick and Alex stood rigidly still in the gloom, bodies flat against the cold, stone wall. An outcropping of the tunnel wall partially hid them. Seconds passed. Hearts pounded chests as both of their fates were suddenly bound together by the concept of… smell.

Surely, its gonna see us, Patrick's mind screamed. *Or get a whiff of our body odor.*

More snuffling. Patrick had a quick, partial glimpse of dark, alien eyes searching the tunnel. Strong muscles rippled across arms and chest leading up to a neck, thick and taut as its head swiveled one way and then the other. Neither boy breathed.

Suddenly it was gone.

They waited for a good minute, the dark tunnel a welcomed relief. No sound came from the corridor and both young men exhaled in relief.

"We're outta here," Alex snarled with finality in a low whisper.

"No."

"What do you mean… *no?!*"

Patrick patted the wall. "Selene left us a map to where she's being taken!"

THE ALIEN ARMS HELD her fast like a vise and she marveled how a creature smaller and thinner than the other aliens could be so strong. Ignoring the ache in her neck, Selene lifted her head once again and studied the great cavern above them. Her captor had brought her down a long flight of stairs and into a subterranean cavern—pitch black but the way the sound echoed and the smell of dampness reminded her of a cave attraction at Disneyland. Light from the alien's torched showed a slime covered stream winding through stalagmites at the cavern's center. They were deep in the bowels of the mountain upon which the city had been built. Despair had crept back into Selene for she knew that her captor had brought her this far underground for a reason—as a present for something called *Drangall*.

"Drangall ein laarg minn," the alien said. He spoke often to himself and she guessed he was a loner...a hermit alien with no friends. Well, that wasn't exactly true. His one friend was Drangall, who was some kind of *laarg*—whatever that was.

"For the last time, I don't want to meet your Drangall!" Selene spat. She tried to twist around to look at the alien but the creature's bony shoulder had bruised her left hip and she winced from the effort.

"Laarg! Laarg!" the alien croaked and she could see him pointing to the cavern's ceiling twenty feet above them. The subterranean chamber was wider than it was tall. Jagged stalactites hung above them like monster's fangs, pale white in the gloom with drops of moisture hanging on each tip.

"Let me down!" Selene bellowed.

"Tekja eitt!" the alien snarled and she felt a sharp pain in her thigh as it sunk claws into her flesh.

"Okay, okay!" she cried. The pain gradually eased and she breathed in relief.

"Tekja eitt pie laarg var ski lictvid." The words were hissed into her ear and she felt the heat of the alien's breath and smelt the foul exhalations and wished she'd never left her bed back in Lewisville.

A great sucking sound came from somewhere above them.

"Drangall…" the alien whispered.

Fear crawled over her flesh as a presence manifested on the cavern's ceiling. Twisting again and looking up, her eyes detected a blob-like shape that moved past stalactites in a fluid motion. Firelight shimmered off dark, moist skin and she could hear the sucking noise as it scuttled above them. Rough hands grasped her legs and suddenly Selene was sent falling, striking the cavern's rocky floor on her left side. Air exploded from her lungs and a shriek of pain escaped her lips. White heat stabbed at her elbow where her funny bone had struck a stalagmite.

The presence… coming.

Instinct saved her.

Selene rolled over and threw herself backward. Above her a long, sinewy creature plummeted from the ceiling and plopped onto the ground where she had been lying a second before. Resembling a jelly fish, but dark and snakelike, it suddenly rose up on wiry tentacles. Just four feet in height, the creature's head was a massive blob without eyes but dotted with tiny blow-holes that sucked in air.

"Drangall, gor bu sva vel!" her captor shouted, pointing to Selene.

Selene backed away from the *laarg*. It swiveled around, bulbous head supported by thin tentacles that multiplied as if by magic—two tentacles suddenly becoming twelve. Blue-green skin glistened in the torchlight off the head that lifted up, revealing a flap of skin that Selene took for its mouth. Lips parted to reveal a gaping maw ringed with sharp fangs.

PATRICK'S FEET POUNDED STONE, racing from an alien that followed them in the dark corridor. Behind him, Alex's heavy breathing matched his own. They'd gone left at the corridor's junction—Patrick seeing a long scratch on the corridor's wall that he'd mistook earlier as just…well, a scratch on a wall. They'd followed the trail of

'X's left by Selene and then became aware that they were being followed.

The sniffling alien hadn't really left after all. Now he was hunting them.

"Maybe you were just hearing things," Alex whined.

Patrick slowed to check the wall, then sped up again. "No. He's back there."

"Why hasn't he attacked?"

"How should I know?" Patrick growled.

A stairway opened to their right and a waft of foul, moist air assaulted Patrick. A glow from the recesses of the corridor's ceiling cast muted light and he strained to examine the stone wall. Patrick glanced back down the corridor from which they'd come, listening—he heard a shuffling sound... then silence—*sneaky little alien*, he thought. Peering close to the stone entrance he saw a faint scratch—and then another further down where the stairs dropped away into darkness. "Found her," he said.

"Down there?" Alex whined. "You're nuts! We're not going down there!"

"Okay. You stay and deal with our friend, the hunter."

"No. Down there is fine." There was a pause, and then... "Wait. We'll need this." Alex flicked something in the dim light and suddenly a flame appeared above a cigarette lighter.

"At least you're good for something," Patrick muttered. They descended.

T HE TWO INTRUDERS HAD LEFT the corridor and taken the passage downward. The Zarkund warrior hesitated. Curiosity had allowed the two intruders to live this long—the Zartaksu wanting to see what these strange creatures were doing so deep in the mountain. But entering the old ways? The cavern at the heart of the mountain was the ancient entrance used by their people hundreds of years in the past. Used and forgotten.

"Hvat segir ke" the warrior grumbled, not liking this new development.

The old ways had become the *paths of death*. Other creatures had taken up residence in the caverns and the Zarkund had instinctively left the area alone. The ancient race that had built the great city had long been overpowered and eaten for food and so, the Zarkund had remained at the upper levels of the city. No need to travel the *paths of the death* any longer.

A scent drifted upward—intruder scent—and the Zartaksu's stomach responded with a rumble of need.

Needs must be satisfied.

The warrior dragged a flinty device along the wall and a flame appeared. He held a torch in his other hand, hastily lighting it just as a draft of wind blew in from the cavern. Flames took root in the torch, illuminating the ancient stairs built by a dead race.

Licking his lips, the Zartaksu warrior followed after the intruders.

AGUT GNASHED ITS TEETH, watching the intruder dodge away from Drangall. The *laargspurr* was an ancient creature—*his* pet—and Bagut had gone to a lot of trouble to bring Drangall a tasty meal! Of course, Bagut would snap up any leftover scraps… if possible. But now the intruder was trying to ruin his gift!

"Gamla vis et bislinger!" Bagut screamed at his captive.

The captive ignored him.

Bagut snarled, barring his teeth. He whipped out a small dagger and silently slipped around the laargspurr, giving his pet a wide berth.

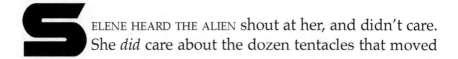

ELENE HEARD THE ALIEN shout at her, and didn't care. She *did* care about the dozen tentacles that moved liked spasmodic snakes in the air in front of her. One tentacle would dash in—she would dodge—and then another—more dodging—she even slapped one and the creature had backed away in alarm.

But not for long.

Hungry little monster, she thought.

Movement to her right. Her alien captor was trying to reach her, but going to great lengths to avoid Drangall. *Why?*

Her hand rested on a small rock. Drangall moved toward Selene. She threw the rock and shouted in triumph. The stone the size of a baseball pummeled the creature's bulbous head, knocking it backward.

"Gamlok vis!" her alien captor screamed again; he was off to her right; she circled to the left, trying to keep Drangall between them. She noticed that her former captor held a knife in his other hand. Alien lips parted in a snarl, showing yellowed fangs—*I guess I've upset his plans,* she mused.

Selene was shocked at her calmness. Thoughts of death and horrible dismemberment assailed her—every twitch of a tentacle shouted her fate—but she forced calmness into her mind...thinking and calculating. She was lucky to be alive and continued to back away and circle left. Selene searched with her hands for another rock to throw, daring an occasional glance to the cavern's floor.

Lucky to be alive but no luck in finding rocks, she moaned.

THE LIGHTER'S FLAME HAD gone out but they'd reached the bottom of the stairs to witness something out of an alien horror movie. Light from a torch held by one of the aliens revealed a dark cavern. In its center they could see Selene, thin and pale, dodging between stalagmites to avoid the tentacles of another alien creature that partially blocked their view.

"What's that squid thing?" Alex asked.

Patrick never heard him, moving silently forward,

eyes scanning the ground for a weapon—any weapon. His foot almost rolled on a rock, cursing his bad luck and thankful he hadn't sprained his ankle.

"We should've searched your father's little vault for weapons," Alex whined from the stairs. "No. You wouldn't listen."

"Not helping, Alex," Patrick growled.

"Freak'in computer pad. Some help *that* is right now. Doesn't even work—"

"Shut it!" Patrick's toe booted another rock forward and he winced in pain.

"Uh... hey?" Alex's voice was plaintive. "Yo... Patrick?"

Frustrated, Patrick wheeled around to confront the whining, spoiled rich—

"Trouble," Alex said, pointing back up the winding stairway. In a twist of the staircase far above, an orange-yellow bead of light was moving downward, bobbing like a malevolent demon.

Instinctively, Patrick stepped backward—and this time his shoe rolled on another rock and he fell the ground, elbows first.

Bloody rocks will be the death of me—

THE HEAD OF HER ALIEN captor twisting, looking back toward the staircase. The nervous flicking warned Selene that there were others in the cavern. Holding off the blob sucker and his alien sidekick was one thing... but if there were more? Despair tried to raise its ugly head and she shoved the fear back down. Her teeth were bared in a snarl. Tentacles flashed in from her left—she dodged right—

WHAM!

Selene felt the blow hit her right shoulder. Pain stabbed into her from where one of the tentacles had impaled a pointed shaft above her right breast. *The suckers were barbed!*

The impaled tentacle held her fast, while another wrapped around her waist—and another around her neck.

She screamed.

KNIFE HELD OUT MENACINGLY, the alien had turned toward them, its face a mixture of rage and fear. *Why fear?* Patrick wondered. And then he saw that this alien wasn't as big as the other, more *warrior looking* aliens. This one was the alien equivalent of the helper class—the clerks, cooks, dishwashers, message runners. It held the knife like it was a strange object.

"Do I kill it?" Alex asked.

"Yes," Patrick replied.

The All-State Quarterback's arm flashed and the alien was suddenly knocked backward to the ground. A rock clattered onto the cavern floor and rolled to a stop. On the cavern floor the body quivered, blood seeping from a dent in the stunned alien's forehead.

"Now, the other!" Patrick yelled, his voice panicked upon seeing Selene suddenly wrapped in tentacles.

"Still think I'm worthless?" Alex challenged.

"No… just too slow!"

"Bite me!" Alex snarled, his old, familiar sneer making his mouth lopsided. Right hand whipped again and a rock flew across the cavern… and missed.

"Typical!"

"Nobody's perfect."

"Hit the bloody thing!" Patrick yelled.

The next rock slammed into the alien jellyfish's overly large head. Tentacles shook in violent spasms as the creature faltered, swaying downward. On either side, tentacles shot out and grabbed hold of stalagmites.

"Again!" Patrick shouted, handing Alex another rock. He was hunched close the cavern's floor, gathering rocks and feeding them to Lewisville's scion of athletic prowess. Patrick had to admit, Leach Junior was good—*really good.*

Another rock smashed rudely into the alien—then another—then a fourth and fifth; each in rapid succession. Tentacles whipped around. Beyond the creature, Selene was released, falling to the cavern floor in a shadowed lump.

"It's really pissed off now," Alex remarked. His right hand whirred again and the jellyfish-thing dodged left, evading the missile. "And it has a brain."

"Behind us!" Patrick screamed.

Torchlight had appeared thirty feet above them on the staircase. They were trapped between alien hunter and a tentacled beast maddened by pain.

Alex's voice spoke volumes. "Not fair."

BLOOD SEEPED FROM HER right shoulder and she felt her arm going numb. *Some kind of paralyzing venom,* her mind calculated. *Stupid creature needs to be killed—that hurt!*

"Selene?" The name echoed off the cavern's ceiling.

She lifted her head, recognizing the voice.

"Selene?!!!" Patrick's voice echoed again in the cavern.

Throat dry and raw from the foul air, she tried shouting but nothing came out but a croak.

"Move to your left!"

Her eyes blinked. *Left is good. Left works for me.*

"Uh… move now? Like, right now?!" Patrick's voice screamed. "Don't know how long we hold this thing off—"

"Have I missed yet?" That was Alex's voice—and the cockiness was such a familiar reminder of Lewisville that she actually felt hope blossom within her.

"Move now because kidnapper alien is moving in your direction," Patrick warned.

Looking right, her alien captor was sliding toward her. Dark fluid streamed down its face. It still held the torch and the firelight was reflecting off the knife in its other

hand. Murder was in its dark eyes as it stepped forward—
WHAM!—a rock slammed into her captor's jaw and he fell
roughly to the ground. His alien arms bent as he tried to rise
upward, unsteady.

"Rock… meet alien face," Alex said.

"Enough with the comic banter," she heard Patrick say.
"Just throw!"

Now or never, she thought. Selene struggled to her feet,
right arm moving but with thousands of pinpricks tingling her
skin. She was behind the alien jellyfish, its tentacles waving in
front of its body in a primitive defense agains the rock missiles
that flew in from across the cavern. A stalagmite jutted six
feet up from the floor to her left and she darted behind it—no
tentacles followed.

"Drangall!" Her alien captor was on his feet again,
crouching behind a stalagmite and wary of another rock
missile. "Drangall!"

Pressure on her left shoulder—Selene jumped in
surprise—

"You okay?" Patrick asked, kneeling beside her.

"Alive," she croaked.

"Not as many rocks over here," Alex complained from
the other side.

"Drangall!" the alien screamed… but this time it was a
scream of terror.

B AGUT'S ENTIRE PLAN had been ruined. He'd tracked the
intruder; captured it and brought the delicious
morsel—*at great effort*—to bring it as a gift to the
laargspurr. *Wasted effort!* But Bagut wouldn't be cheated.

"Drangall!"

Bagut's voice echoed around him. *The intruder was
there, behind his laarg. Drangall must have this gift!* He shouted
again. "Drangall!"

This time the laargspurr swiveled toward Bagut.

Pointing to where the intruder crouched, Bagut shouted. "Drangall, gamla vis et bislinger!"

Bagut had never ventured this close to the creature he'd found lurking in the old ways. *But this was different. This was a special occasion!*

"Drangall, gamla vis et bislinger—" Bagut began to say.

Tentacles lashed out. Bagut felt spikes enter his legs and chest. He was lifted off the ground and yanked forward— to where the gaping mouth ringed with jagged teeth opened wide, expanding outward.

Bagut screamed.

And screamed again as his head was torn in half by the force of Drangall's teeth.

ELENE CLOSED HER EYES. But the images in her mind matched the sounds of her captor's last moments of agony.

"Wow." Alex said with awe.

Bile rose in her throat and Selene started to wretch.

HE ZARTAKSU WATCHED the peasant filth being eaten by the laargspurr—one of the ancient evils that inhabited the old ways—and the warrior appreciated the efficiency of the creature's kill. Blue-green tentacles quivered in agitation. Blood sprayed from the bulbous head as its jaws expanded around the peasant's body. There was a loud crack and the peasant went still… limp.

The warrior moved forward. He would use the laargspurr's distraction as an opportunity for his own kill. Setting his torch on the stone floor, the warrior slipped into a stand of tall stalagmites. He'd seen his two intruders join a third—three intruders now.

Even better.

PATRICK WATCHED THE alien warrior creep from the staircase and move into the shadows to their left. Which of the two aliens was the more dangerous? It was a toss up. He looked behind them. More cavern. Stalagmites and stalactites stretched into the darkness and he shuddered. In this subterranean world they would be easy prey for this tentacled creature. What if there were more of its kind?

"Do these aliens ever give up?" Alex moaned.

Patrick turned and followed Alex's gaze to where the alien warrior moved silently in the shadows. The crunching sounds of the tentacled creature's kill continued. He was about to suggest moving deeper into the cavern when the warrior attacked just sixty feet away. It came at them in a blur of speed. Patrick snarled. "Now!"

From his knees, Alex faced the oncoming warrior. His right hand whipped forward—a rock flashed out in a blur—and missed; the warrior dodging casually aside.

Thirty feet.

Another rock. The warrior dodged the missile with ease, using a stalagmite for cover. The rock smacked and ricocheted into the darkness.

Twenty feet.

They were dead meat, Patrick's mind screamed.

"Drangall!"

The voice was Selene's. "Drangall!" she screamed a second time.

Ten feet.

Alien warrior lips parted in a snarl.

The snarl turned into surprise.

A tentacle lashed out—a second and then a third— a triad of dagger tipped suckers that impaled the warrior. It screamed in defiance, the alien warrior whipping a long blade in an arc that severed two of the tentacles. The laargspurr seemed to go into a frenzy, tentacles lashing out even as its own blood sprayed from severed stumps.

"HEY!" Selene's voice cut into Patrick's thoughts. "Now would be a good time to leave, don't you think?!"

They left. Quickly.

Chapter Twenty-One

Hall Of Bones

HEAVY FOOTSTEPS SOUNDED OUTSIDE—at least twenty—and then all was quiet again. Jeremy slowly exhaled. The sound of their breathing echoed in the cramped passageway. They were in darkness so thick Jeremy had to breath deeply just to mentally cope with feelings of suffocation. They'd evaded the alien hunters again, but Jeremy knew just how close it had been.

"Not so smart after all," Leo said with scorn.

"Thank god," Marissa panted, out of breath.

But Jeremy had seen intelligence in the eyes of the aliens. "Don't speak too soon—"

"Shhhhhh!" Marissa hissed.

There was a muffled sound outside and then a scraping sound. Jeremy groaned. Twice they evaded the aliens by finding secret passageways—how Jeremy found the passageways he wasn't saying, because even he didn't know what was going on in the tangled mess of his brain—but each time the monsters would pass by and then return. It was as if their sense of smell could penetrate the foot-thick blocks of stone. The scraping on stone became louder.

"It's like they have a homing beacon on us," Leo said.

"It's me."

There was silence… except for the scraping.

"They're tracking my scent," Marissa continued.

"No. It's all of us," Jeremy said reassuringly.

"Uh, sorry to disagree, lunkhead. Didn't you ever get the birds and bees lecture from your mother?"

"No. She died when I was just a baby."

"Er…sorry…"

"You're menstruating," Leo said clinically. "Having your monthly period, right?"

"Unfortunately. Watch any wildlife show on predators; what do they track?" Marissa moaned.

Silence. *Wow…the female reproductive cycle*—Jeremy tried to close his mind to the anatomical images from his biology textbook. "No matter," Jeremy finally said. *We will all get out of here alive,* he thought determinedly. He'd hoped they could rest a while. Marissa breathed in hoarse gasps. For the last ten minutes, she'd fought to keep up to the pace Jeremy was setting. *Would the aliens figure out the code to open the hidden door?* They stood in darkness as the sound of scraping intensified.

"What do we do now?" Marissa asked in a small, fragile voice.

"*We…* find a way out of this city," Jeremy reassured her. "Light."

Light pulsed on in hidden recesses to reveal a modern

passageway. Whatever ancient civilization had built this massive city had found ways to create subterranean bunkers and a network of passages.

"How do you do that?" she asked.

"It just pops into my head."

"Wish I had the *power*," Leo said mournfully.

Jeremy started them down the passage at a brisk walk, conscious of Marissa who was moving with obvious discomfort. The walls were coated in slimy, green algae. Cold, damp air mixed with the stench of decomposition made it difficult to breathe. They passed metal doors sealed by rust. The tunnel made several turns, and it was before a flight of steps leading downward that they stopped to catch their breath.

"Awesome... more stairs," Marissa panted.

"Shhhh," Leo hissed. "Listen."

From deep within the passage behind them came a sudden, distant crash... and then a chorus of alien yells echoed up the tunnel.

Jeremy grabbed Marissa's hand and pulled her down the stairs. "No time for thinking."

"I hate stairs," she moaned.

Leading Marissa downward, Jeremy sensed a renewed energy from her—*she wasn't a quitter.* The stairs led to another tunnel chiseled out of stone, except the way further was blocked by rubble. A huge, gaping hole had been cut into the passage on their left, jagged and raw, created by some form of violence. Behind them came the sound of footsteps.

"Come on," Jeremy said, and led them through the hole.

They entered a spacious hall with a colonnade of marble pillars. Light filtered down from windows high overhead—windows painful for Jeremy to look at, so long had they been in the dark. The colonnade led to an arched doorway.

A horn sounded behind them, shattering the stillness.

Marissa turned an exhausted face to look back. "Crap."

Twenty alien hunters poured into the hallway, weapons held at the ready.

"Run!" Jeremy shouted.

They sped through the arch and into a cavernous hall, once a place for feasting or maybe a great hall to receive foreign dignitaries, Jeremy couldn't figure out what. White objects were heaped in piles and others were scattered on a marble floor that was broken and in disrepair. Lying on its side was a huge statue—a knight thrusting a sword into a dragon.

Marissa tripped on one of the white objects and she fell hard to the floor. Jeremy whipped around, expecting the scything of a blade, fangs reaching for his throat—instead, *there was no pursuit*. The aliens were huddled outside the arched doorway, as if afraid to follow them inside.

"This is NOT good."

Marissa's voice brought Jeremy back around and suddenly he realized what the white objects were... *bones*. Hundreds of them, and most partially eaten. The source of the horrible stench that had assaulted their senses for the past hour became evident as they saw the bloody carcasses scattered amongst the bones. *Fresh kills*. Most of the carcasses were like those of the alien hunters, which explained why their pursuers refused to enter the great hall.

"Quick," Jeremy snapped. "To the other side."

They stepped gingerly among the carnage as they followed Jeremy toward another arched doorway at the opposite end of the hall. Leo's voice echoed as they moved.

"I'd rather not meet whatever, thing lives here—"

WHOMP.

They froze. Three heads turned to stare at a gaping hole in one side of the hall.

Light reflected off the shiny, metallic underbelly of the largest—thing—Jeremy had ever seen. Over twice his height, the monster reminded him of a dinosaur... the triceratops. It was staring at him with intelligent eyes. A large horn protruded from its forehead, and its open jaws revealed rows of teeth sharp as daggers.

Leo ran.

Before Jeremy could react, Marissa was following Leo in a headlong flight toward the exit door. He started after, but then—

"DON'T RUN!" Erik's voice screamed in Jeremy's mind.

The monster thundered into the great hall on its massive legs, letting out a bellow that shook masonry from the ceiling.

"Too late," Jeremy moaned and then he too ran after Leo.

Chapter Twenty-Two

Twists And Turns

 0:08:44

Evans flicked off the bracelet's clock and looked to where Keene was surveying the city with binoculars. "Barely one hour in and we've lost the boy."

"Not lost," Keene said indignantly. "Just *out of touch* for a time." The security man produced a small data pad with a shiny black screen. A red light pulsated on the screen. "He's alive and moving—"

"No thanks to your man," Evans said, glaring at Rudolf Hicks. The research director paced off to one side, away from the soldiers. Shirt tails hanging out, his pants sagging, Hicks was lost in thought, gazing ever so often to the city that rose upward toward the temple.

"Doctor Hicks is still useful," said Keene, following Evans' gaze. "We *will* have another Portal to deal with if we're going to make it back home."

Evans stared behind them, studying the canopy of forest that stretched downward from their vantage point. They stood on the barbican over the main gate of the alien city.

"Strange," whispered Keene.

Evans turned and shot a questioning glance at Keene, who was fidgeting with his data pad.

"The map we were given shows this location as a Portal," Keene said. His fingers touched the display and he gritted his teeth in frustration. "But there's no mention of a city."

"That data better be accurate," Evans spat angrily. "I'm getting a little tired of surprises."

Seven points of blue light showed on the pad's screen.

"What are those?" Evans asked.

"TerraGen base camps, Portals, cities... who knows?" Keene's finger pointed to one of the seven points of light, "This is the *away Portal* we have to make tracks for. It's called the *Tomb*."

"Cute. But... thirty days over unknown terrain..."

"We'll have an escort."

"You trust our contact?"

Keene let out a long breath. "I trust only one thing in the field." The veteran soldier patted the assault rifle slung on his shoulder.

"If we don't find the Austin boy," Evans spoke in low tones, "good luck getting back to Earth with that."

Lachlan Evans, once of the CIA, walked over to the edge of the parapet and wondered what had possessed him to agree to this crazy venture. His plans were spiraling out of control, and *control* was a commodity he valued highly. In the world of weapons and technology, Evans was a successful entrepreneur. He'd come to this planet to steal TerraGen's latest technology—not for the CIA or the United States Government—*for himself.* Grit crunched underfoot as he rested against the curtain wall. Above him the sky was crimson as the sun hung over the horizon. Two moons showed for the first time in the waning light.

"Would you look at that!" Rudolf Hicks' voice cut into the silence.

Evans turned to see Hicks pointing upward toward the city's bluff. Evans' breath caught in his throat. Straight out of the temple's roof, a shaft of white light shot into the sky above. *A signal?* He turned toward Keene, but the big man was staring into the heart of the city.

"There it is again," Keene said, as if in response to Evans' unspoken question.

He heard the drums—*BOOM, BOOM, BOOM*—echoing through the city. He shivered and eyed their escape route below where his squad of paid mercenaries was fanning out into the forest. Hicks was suddenly beside him, staring down at the soldiers disappearing into the trees. A furrow of worry suddenly wrinkled the researcher's forehead.

"The kids… uh, aren't we going back for them?" Hicks asked, his voice small and plaintive.

"Impossible now with an army of aliens multiplying like cockroaches." Evans voice was cold. The look of absolute shock on Hicks' face caused Evan's lip to curl up in distaste at the man's evident weakness.

The research director tried to gather his courage. "But… we can't just leave!"

"We have contingencies—"

"They're just kids!" Hicks' eyes bulged with indignation. "I gave them my word. And they didn't exactly seem prepared for a dangerous expedition like this—"

"*Enough… Dr. Hicks!*" Evans face showed the same

intensity as Hicks'. "Every one of those kids was embedded with a tracking chip. They are *all* alive and we *will* get every *one* of them back!"

"It's just..." Hicks voice was soft as a whisper, "they came to find their parents, and now they're lost as well. A pity and a shame."

Suddenly the distant roar of the monster sounded from the city and all heads turned. An image of the Austin boy flashed in his mind, but then Evans' attention was suddenly drawn to one of the soldiers moving down the bastion's stairway. The soldier's body suddenly sprayed blood before tumbling down to the ground below. Startled, Evans saw another soldier twist sideways, a bloody hole in his chest. Evans moved, narrowly escaping death as a projectile smashed into the stone beside him.

"Aliens!" came Keene's panicked voice, pointing down into the city.

From the shadows of a hundred doorways came alien warriors, each carrying weapons and spreading out in a pincer move to trap them at the barbican.

"Time for us to head west, yes?" Evans shouted at Keene.

"Only if you want to live!" Keene spat before racing for the stairway.

In the barbican's gate, a line of mercenaries had established a rear guard and were pouring fire at the aliens. In response, the aliens simply melted back into the doorways and alleys, leaving several of their own dead. Evans rushed past them toward the safety of the forest. With a stab of regret, he wondered if leaving the TerraGen kids behind was the first nail in his coffin.

THEY BURST OUT OF an arched doorway and onto a deserted city street, the fading sunlight almost blinding and the fresh air washing away the smell of decay from their lungs. Jeremy glanced over at Marissa, whose face was beet red and her breathing hoarse as she bent over with hands on her hips. "Skipping all those gym classes wasn't such a good idea after all," she panted.

"We have to keep moving!" Jeremy shouted with as much encouragement as he could muster. "Let's check that place out." He pointed to a tall structure a block away that rose high into the sky. It was the architecture that drew Jeremy's attention—it was older, but also more Earth-like in design. Wearily, they started forward.

Jeremy glared angrily at Leo as they walked, "Not such a cool idea to always run away and leave the rest of us to face the monsters. Not cool."

Leo simply shrugged, face bathed in sweat. "It's my weakness."

In the great hall of bones, they'd barely escaped the monster by fleeing into a smaller hallway. The petulant roar of the monster had echoed behind them as they fled. Now they were looking for a way out of this city of death. The tall building soon towered over them. A sound caused Jeremy to turn around—an alien stood in the arched doorway they had just vacated a hundred yards away. Aliens suddenly appeared through other doorways and the sound of running feet echoed in the air. "Our popularity never ceases to amaze," he groaned. "Inside!"

The aliens attacked.

An arrow sailed close to Jeremy's head and he ducked inside the structure. Light through the non-existent roof revealed a massive heap of rusted metal one hundred yards in length and standing over five stories in height. Beckoning to Leo he started forward, moving around the ancient machine and kicking up thick clouds of rust-colored dust.

"Wait."

The voice was weak and filled with pain. Jeremy turned and saw Marissa stumbling forward. She turned slightly, and Jeremy saw a feathered arrow protruding from the back of her left shoulder. With no hesitation Jeremy rushed to her, snapped the arrow shaft in two and picked the dazed girl up into his arms. He ran past a bewildered Leo and felt the girl's body growing heavier in his arms as she slipped into unconsciousness. *She's dying!*

Moving around the rusted hulk of machinery revealed yet another one: it's twin. Metal tubes the diameter of a small car rose into the air like fingers of a forgotten god; ducts connecting various parts of the machine sagged with disrepair; shattered pieces of machinery lay in dirty orange-brown heaps under the structure—Jeremy feared being crushed under the machine in an avalanche of metal shards. With painful breaths he kept putting one foot in front of the other.

Leo's labored breathing trailed close behind.

Rounding the second machine Jeremy skidded to a stop. "Not good," he moaned, adjusting Marissa's limp body in his arms—at the building's opposite end, several hundred alien warriors stood waiting.

The whispered footfalls behind them let Jeremy know aliens were covering their rear. Leo whimpered in fear… and this time there was no place to run.

"You must command the watcher," Erik's voice echoed in his brain.

"Command what?!" Jeremy demanded of the voice. "We're about to be alien meat—"

"Command the watcher or die!!!"

The aliens were moving closer, and Jeremy hesitated. Gripping Marissa tightly, he began moving backward. Glancing behind him he saw a score of alien warriors sprinting toward him and cursed—*we're trapped*. And then the side of the building shuddered and an explosion of stone swallowed the first of the aliens behind them. The monstrous beast entered through the gaping hole, horn cutting the air, head snapping with blinding speed and ripping through the remaining aliens like an excited child tearing open presents on Christmas morning. Red mist followed the violence of the beast.

Jeremy suddenly realized that Leo was no longer beside him. Between the two rusted machines he saw the pudgy form of Leo scuttling to the other side. For once Jeremy was glad of the boy's initiative and quickly followed after.

An arrow whipped past and he hurried his steps. Dust kicked up and he almost gagged, temporarily losing sight of Leo. Marissa's body slipped downward and he stumbled, struggling to stay on his feet.

"You must command Ranger!" Erik's voice screamed in his head. *Ranger?!* He looked around, expecting to see the government's commandos coming to their rescue, but not one mercenary was in sight. He saw that Leo had stopped, wild eyed and head turning in all directions. Beyond the scared boy he could see the dark forms of aliens, moving silently through the shadowed hulk of the machines. *Ranger? I had a dog with the name of Ranger. He disappeared when he was ten years old, but he was a top-rate guard dog.*

A prickling on his neck caused Jeremy to whip around. *Nothing that big could fly through the air—*

The world shook as the monster landed ten feet in front of Jeremy, metallic feet sending stone missiles into the air. Hot, fetid breath hit his face and his legs almost buckled. The monster seemed to be confused by *this* prey that wouldn't run or fight. With blood dripping from its fangs, the creature lowered its horns.

"Ranger must be commanded," Erik's voice crashed into Jeremy's consciousness.

The beast started forward.

"Stop!" Jeremy's voice echoed in the cavernous space.

The monster seemed to not hear. Instead, it crouched, eyes locked on Jeremy and its muscles tensing for the final rush that would kill both he and Marissa—

"Ranger, stop… NOW!"

The transformation was instantaneous. The beast's

head lifted and its muscles relaxed. The prehistoric beast suddenly became animated; its head cocked sideways, eyeing Jeremy with obvious delight, and the back of the creature even seemed to wiggle.

He turned to Leo who stood twenty yards away. "Can you believe it?"

The younger boy's studious glance at Jeremy was a mixture of awe and jealousy.

Towering over them, the beast bobbed its head, as if waiting.

"Tell your pet to kill the bad guys," whispered Marissa weakly.

A cavernous grunt came from within the beast, head cocking again.

"Ahhhhh!!!" The scream came from Leo as a group of aliens rushed toward him.

Jeremy looked at the monster. "Kill them all, Ranger!"

It snarled, deep growls echoing from within. Its muscles tensed, and suddenly the beast leaped over them. Its sheer weight crushed the first of the attackers, and then its massive jaws went to work. The sound of death caused Jeremy to cringe.

The aliens fled.

FINALLY...THE ALIEN WARRIORS were gone... for now. Alex couldn't remember a time since they got here when his stomach *wasn't* tied up in knots. Patrick had led them down one passageway and then another... and then another. *It was mind numbing!* Aliens had been tracking their party, closing in—and then they vanished. Alex had prepared himself for death and then, suddenly, the warriors were gone. Now they faced a dead end and waited in silence, expecting a trap.

Patrick used both hands to feel along a seam in the stone wall. A loud, distant roar shook the stone pavement underneath them.

"That's really getting old," Selene moaned, her feet unsteady. Alex glanced at the girl, noting how her right arm hung limply, paralyzed from the tentacled creature's poisonous barb.

"Good thing for us someone else has to deal with it," Patrick whispered, "because that monster's giving them hell."

"I thought you knew how to get out of this place?" Alex's voice was petulant once more.

"The blueprint in my head isn't the most accurate," Patrick returned. "Outdated, more likely." He stepped back to look at the entire wall.

"Open sesame!" screamed Selene.

Alex just glared at the girl, imaging the multitude of ways the aliens would cook and eat a moron like Selene... *roasted airhead with a glaze of honey...*

With a hiss of satisfaction, Patrick moved back to the wall and placed his hands on a rectangular stone. "It's metal!" he exclaimed in relief, and then pushed. The metal block moved an inch and then glowed, making Patrick's fingers glow pink and translucent. A loud rumble sounded, and Patrick quickly stepped away.

The entire wall moved backward and then slid sideways to reveal a tunnel that glowed dimly. A sheen of blue light covered the new exit, and Patrick tested it by poking his finger through it. Blue light danced around his finger and he shrugged his shoulders. "Hmmm. Something to do with security, I bet." Patrick stepped through.

"Is it safe?" Alex asked plaintively.

There was no answer; Patrick had already disappeared down the passage.

"Punk," Alex hissed.

"What do you think?" Selene asked, suddenly at his side.

"Let's see," Alex said, smiling. And then he pushed Selene through the blue barrier of light.

Selene stumbled to one knee on the other side and shot

Alex a murderous glare. "Bully!"

A rumble sounded—the stone began to move back into place. Alex leapt through and felt the stone slab thunder shut behind him. He breathed deeply and grimaced, his nostrils filled with the smell of dampness and vegetation. Light glowed from recesses in the ceiling. Looking down the passage, Alex saw Patrick silhouetted in a pool of daylight.

Patrick's voice echoed in the tunnel. "We're outside the city!"

They stepped through an arched opening at the end of the tunnel and found themselves in a wooded glade. Covered in vines, the city's wall merged with the flora of the forest, and the arched opening became a dark smear that blended as well. Above them, stone structures rose in weathered splendor.

Alex turned to Patrick, a thought nagging at him, "You're so quick to leave… but aren't you both worried that your parents are being held captive by the aliens?"

"In that city?" Patrick's voice held a note of surprise.

"Not a chance," Selene said with solemnity.

"They're out there," Patrick said, pointing out to where a set of distant mountains shone in the sunlight. He pulled the data pad out of his backpack and turned it over in his hands. "Just what I thought." His fingers traced shiny blocks that were now glowing in the sunlight. "Solar powered."

RANGER STOOD LIKE AN obedient dog in front a large blue sheen of light. Dark smears on its sharp horn were all that was left of the alien blood, but the huge monster was still formidable to look at. Prehistoric though the animal may be, it was still smart enough to know where to lead them. The large passage was obviously their exit from the hellish city of the aliens.

"Nice pet you've got there," Marissa said with effort.

Marissa leaned against Jeremy, and he was glad that the shock of her injury had worn off and the girl had regained some of her strength. A stub of arrow still protruded from her shirt, and he winced at the pain she must be feeling.

"What are we waiting for?" Leo shot Jeremy an impatient look and then walked through the barrier.

Jeremy and Marissa followed. Upon touching the blueish light Jeremy was suddenly paralyzed as a flood of data poured into his brain. His body tingled and froze.

"Relax and take it in," Erik spoke into Jeremy's mind.

Cities, towns, fortresses, rivers, mountains… races flooded into him as a complete map of the planet assembled like a jigsaw puzzle. He was unaware of the sweat pouring down his forehead; he felt only the intense buzzing, as if his brain was boiling.

"We'll be separated for a time yet, young brother," Erik said. "The table is set and your people await—just keep your eyes open and beware the goblin's kiss."

Data streams suddenly ended and he took a deep breath.

"Go west to Vorgal's Deep," Erik said, "where the future of Genesis rests."

Jeremy felt a deep sadness from his brother.

"So long for now. Within the mountain you'll find the key to saving this world. It lies within my tomb…" The light vanished and Jeremy found himself standing on the other side of the passage entrance.

His tomb?

Ranger gave a whimper, and he noticed the monster looking at him through the blueish sheen of light, head cocked with a quizzical expression on its prehistoric face.

"Come on, Ranger," Jeremy commanded, but Ranger simply whimpered again and lay on the ground, head on its hooves. "Ranger, come!" he commanded with as much authority as possible, but Ranger cocked its head to the other side.

And then he understood: *Ranger is the watchdog.* The beast was unable to leave because Erik placed it here to guard the Portal. "I'll find Dad and Erik and we'll be back," Jeremy vowed through clenched teeth.

Jeremy turned and headed after Leo and Marissa. The door closed behind him, and Ranger's howl of anguish reverberated in the passageway. A shaft of sunlight at the tunnel's far end beckoned them onward.

Chapter Twenty-Three

Thirty Days

THE LIGHT FROM THE SETTING SUN filtered through the tree branches. A breeze rippled the leaves, causing golden-orange flashes that provoked an annoying blinking of his eyes. A mountain range lost in shadow reached toward the sky opposite them and the valley between was dark and forbidding. Alex shivered.

"Wow! So cool!" Selene exclaimed. They had been hiking under a dark canopy of trees for the last hour, slowed from time to time because the Asian girl kept vanishing into the surrounding foliage. Minutes later she would return with pieces of shrubbery, mushrooms and other such nonsense.

"I'm making a poultice," she'd said when pressed, lifting her right shoulder which showed the puncture hole in her shirt that was crusted with blood.

"Poultice from what?" Patrick had asked.

"This and that."

Doubt the bricks for brains airhead even knows, Alex had mumbled on the inside.

"Don't you have to go to a school for wizardry for that?" Patrick had teased her. A blank stare was all that Patrick received in response.

Now they had reached a bare hilltop and had paused to get their breath. Selene was looking behind them, body trembling with excitement. "It's like something from a movie!" Both Alex and Patrick turned, gasping in wonder as their eyes took in the alien city rising up behind them in its faded, majestic glory. And yet, all three were glad to be rid of that hell hole. But the city wasn't what Selene was referring to. She held her left hand high and pointed her index finger to where a bright, beacon of light was shooting into the darkening sky from the apex of the city's top level. "I've seen those at movie premieres."

"We never should've left the city," Alex said bitterly.

"The aliens weren't exactly playing nice-nice," Patrick said.

"Should've gone back through the Portal."

"Too late for that." Patrick said, turning to Alex. "That beam looks more like a signal—an alien signal."

"It could be a sign of welcome," Selene offered.

"Yeah, welcome to our bellies," Alex sneered, his words dripping with sarcasm.

"Point taken," Patrick said. The slender genius turned his attention to the west. Alex noticed that the computer geek was taking special pains to hold his precious data pad where the sunlight could hit the solar panels. *Pathetic.* But the light hitting the data pad was fading, and now Patrick was staring gloomily at the distant sky where the sun hung over the rim of a mountain. Patrick spoke in quiet voice. "Prudence says we'd better find a safe place to hole up."

"Who's that?" Selene asked.

"Huh?" Patrick asked, eyebrows pinched in the middle.

"Prudence. Who is she?"

A smile played at Patrick's lips. "Uh… it's just a figure of speech," he said and then started down the slope. The other two quickly caught up.

"What I'd give for the Four Seasons right now," Selene moaned. "And room service. I'd order everything on the menu. A fat, juicy hamburger—chicken salad with almonds and spicy Thai dressing—"

"Enough!" Alex shouted in frustration. He felt his stomach rumble, and he suddenly realized how hungry he was. The shock of near-death had worn off and he was ravenous. His eyes traveled to Patrick's backpack. "I don't suppose you have food in that thing?" *It would be just like the nerd to hide a bag of trail mix,* Alex thought.

"Yes. To be rationed between us." Patrick's voice was hard. "First we need a place to rest for the night."

"Roasted chicken breast with a teriyaki glaze," Selene intoned, eyes lost in a daydream.

Patrick ignored her. "We need someplace out of the way… hidden. That signal light could be alerting the entire planet of aliens—"

"Like a dinner bell," Selene interjected.

"Precisely. If those aliens come looking, I want to make it difficult for them."

Alex bristled at the nerd's tone of authority. "Don't remember anyone making *you* team leader."

"No one told me I'd be running from a bunch of aliens, either!" Patrick said heatedly. "What about you? Back in the dungeons, I kept waiting for gems of wisdom from you—directions, a plan of action, anything, but—"

"What of it?"

"All I heard was crickets."

"I heard aliens," Selene added.

TWO HOURS LATER ALEX stood warming himself beside a fire in the mouth of a cave. Overhead, the smoke drifted through thick branches of fern and dissipated into the night sky. The remote location had been the *brainchild's* idea… and, for his part, Alex hadn't been able to think of a better place, and so he had remained silent.

"Almost done." Selene was crouched beside the fire, using a small twig to stir a watery substance that steamed above the fire. They didn't have pots or pans, and so the girl had used a thick, massive leaf that cupped in the middle. Now, a dark, greenish mixture began to bubble and Selene raised the leaf to her lips, blowing air to cool the liquid.

"Are you gonna drink that…filth?" Alex asked.

"Do I look stupid?" Selene flashed him an annoyed look. "It's a poultice."

"Whatever *that* is…"

"It's to go on my wound. It'll counteract the poison."

"And you learned this in biology class?" he asked sarcastically.

She seemed to think hard on his question, ignoring his scorn. Shrugging, she said, "I just know."

Wow. Straight from looney 'ville! Lips forming a sneer, Alex forced himself to ignore her. He began chewing the last of an energy bar as he examined the data pad he'd taken from Patrick's backpack—Mr. IQ was off scouring the woods for more food. His fingers traced the smooth surface of the data pad which remained dark, reflecting the starry, night sky.

"Give it to me." Patrick's voice was cold as ice. Alex looked up to see the nerd stepping in from the stand of trees that sheltered the cave from wind and from prying, alien eyes. There was a hardness to the boy genius that Alex had never seen before.

Alex's finger moved along the pad's edge and he found the power button.

Patrick moved closer. "I won't tell you again, Alex! Give me... the pad," he snarled.

Alex looked up and saw the threat of violence in Patrick's eyes. But still, his finger pressed the button. "Gimme a second." He moved deeper into the cave and gasped as a faint logo appeared on the data pad: TerraGen's lunar eclipse. A heavy club appeared in Patrick's hand and he moved toward Alex. And with a sudden air of indifference, Alex tossed the data pad toward the computer geek. "Don't get your panties in a wad," Alex sneered as he watched Patrick examine the data pad.

Like a crack addict needing a fix.

"I miss surfing the net," Selene moaned. She continued to blow air on the liquid mixture that sent up wisps of steam from within the leaf.

Patrick squatted on a rock and let his hands caress the data pad. "This may be our only hope in getting back to Earth," he said.

Alex silently crept behind Patrick and leaned closer for a better look. The TerraGen logo spun out of view and new words popped onto the screen with artistic flare: GENESIS: A NEW WORLD OF TECHNOLOGY . Four icons appeared: MISSION STATEMENT, TECHNOLOGIES , MAPS, and NOTES .

Patrick took a deep breath and said, "Let's find out where we need to go." His finger pressed the MAPS icon, and a three-dimensional map appeared, matching the one they'd examined in the TerraGen vault hours before.

"Is that us?" Selene gestured with her eyes to where a red light pulsated in a mountain range.

"A likely guess," Patrick mused, "but GPS technology needs satellites—"

"Or maybe... it's a higher *level* of technology," she said excitedly.

Alex hissed in frustration. "Just get us the heck out of here!"

Patrick chuckled. "Processing your order, Mister Leach Junior."

Stifling a sudden urge to hit the geek, Alex simply watched as seven pinpricks of red light appeared on the map, signifying what had to be TerraGen's base camps. Patrick double-tapped the icon nearest their location and the screen flashed: THE WELCOME CENTER.

"This is where we entered this world," said Patrick as his finger pressed further. The screen flashed and schematics of the *Arrival Portal* animated in three dimensions. "Strange... no mention of a city or aliens," Patrick's voice trailed off. His fingers moved and the seven red lights reappeared on the map.

"Just find the one with the Departure Portal," Alex said with restrained frustration.

Patrick swiveled and looked up at Alex. "Excuse me?" Alex had never seen the boy wonder look so confused, and he enjoyed the moment. Patrick's voice turned icy. "Come again, Leach?"

The sneer returned on Alex's lips. "There's only one Portal that sends us home—"

Patrick sprang off the rock in a heated rush. "And you're just telling us this now?!"

"What of it?" Alex feigned anger, secretly scared of the geek's recent aggressive behavior.

"What else are you holding out on? Did your dad slip you some secret information—?"

"My dad can go off himself—"

"Then how did a rancid jock strap like *you* hear about a Departure Portal?!"

"Keene," Alex spat. "Security Director Keene."

"What about him?" Patrick demanded.

"I overheard him talking with that research guy, Hicks," Alex said smoothly, his confidence returning, "which is why we need to go back to the city and find those guys. That data pad belongs to TerraGen... not you. They're the professionals. It's their expedition. They probably need that map to get us back home!"

"This computer belongs to me as much as it does Mr. Keene and his dangerous friends," Patrick stated flatly. "I trust myself to find this Departure Portal, *not them*."

"Then you better get to work... and fast," Alex warned.

"Why fast?"

"Well... thirty days to be exact."

"Thirty...?"

"Evidently we have only thirty days to get to the Portal."

"Or what?" Selene asked.

"Or we don't get back home."

"Nice to know!" Patrick laughed bitterly. "Thirty days to find a Portal on a strange planet—through unknown terrain we'll be lucky to survive—aliens chasing us—we might starve—thirty days! I don't like the odds."

Resting the cooking leaf on the ground, Selene began to stuff wads of spider webbing into the mixture. Selene turned and looked up to Patrick. "And you don't want to find Dr. Hicks? He was very nice."

An awkward silence ensued as Patrick looked from Selene to Alex. And then he simply shrugged his shoulders, "Hicks, Keene, the CIA guys... they don't work for TerraGen."

"Then... who?" Selene asked.

"A competitor, obviously."

Chapter Twenty-Four

Servant Of The Shadow

THE CHIRPING OF THE TRACKING DEVICE woke Benton Keene out of his reverie just in time to hear another of Morton's tirades.

"...poorly planned, no mention of aliens, no clear goals," Morton was saying, "and worst of all, no clear exit strategy."

"I was never informed of two separate Portals," Hicks said, trying to placate the Washington man. "Just like you! That was Mr. Keene's area of knowledge."

I'll kill that idiot researcher if it's the last... Keene shoved that thought aside as the tracking device chirped again.

The single-file line of soldiers had been moving steadily up the mountainside for the last hour. Darkness was like a cold blanket wrapped around them. Beams from flashlights bobbed up and down, bouncing off the huge trees that grew thick around them. Suddenly, the forested path gave way to a carpet of tall grass... grass that covered a huge swath of mountainside.

Two moons hovered in the night sky and their light revealed a medieval structure further up the mountain. Like the ancient keeps in England that once stood sentry for marauding Norsemen, this structure had been made of stone and its vantage point looked out across the deep valley to where another mountain range rose up, dark in the moonlight. Blueish light reflected off the smooth contours of the stone structure which was nothing more than a scattered collection of ruins. The remnant of a wall and fortress keep jutted out over the side of the mountain—pillars, stairs, and huge blocks of stone were ensnared in the carpet of grass.

The soldiers fanned out in their defensive formation, their light dancing among the grass, and they formed two groups that approached the ruins from two opposing directions. Keene never saw the deployment: his mind was consumed with relief at finding the ruins. It meant his map's coordinates were accurate and he hadn't brought the expedition on a wild goose chase.

"Is this the place?" Lachlan Evans' voice echoed in the dark.

"Our rendezvous," Keene responded.

"Rendezvous with who?" Morton asked, his voice filled with skepticism.

"Colonel Wilhelm Glass," Keene said. "Commander of the original expeditionary army."

"He's agreed to hand over the technology?"

"That's why we're here, isn't it?" Keene said flatly, trying extremely hard to force respect into his voice. As a former commander in the U.S. Special Forces, Keene knew how to put on the military face whenever dealing with superiors.

Morton turned his skepticism toward Evans. "You trust this Colonel Glass?"

"He's in line with our directives," Evans said.

"And do these *directives* line up with the plans of the United States?"

The question didn't faze Evans. He simply smiled, his teeth showing in the dim light. "Did you think the US would be the only party interested in TerraGen technology?"

Keene studied Morton and admired the government insider's moxy—if Morton was shocked, he'd put on a pretty good poker face. Morton's voice was harsh. "Just remember who wields the ultimate power, Mr. Evans. We don't like traitors."

They entered the ruins, its ancient walls towering around them. The stone slabs jutting into the night sky reminded Keene of his youth—stealing into the local cemetery at midnight to catch the ghouls at play. *Funny, never saw any ghosts or ghouls.* He banished that thought as well.

WHAP, WHAP, WHAP, WHAP! The sound of a hundred rifles slamming into shoulders made Keene snap his head around.

His group of mercenaries were training their weapons in one direction. From out of the gloom stepped a black horse. Its rider was clothed in black flowing robes that covered black mail armor. Where there should've been a face, there was instead a hooded cowl of deep shadow.

"Where's the boy?" the rider asked in a low and rasping voice.

Keene felt beads of sweat trickle down his face, and the feeling of fear returned.

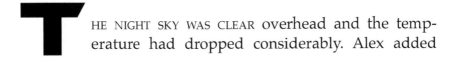 HE NIGHT SKY WAS CLEAR overhead and the temp-erature had dropped considerably. Alex added

more sticks to the fire while Selene squatted nearby, poking a single twig into the fiery coals. The sight of the two moons overhead disturbed Patrick. They were a reminder that Earth was a galaxy away, and it made him homesick. And yet, his dad was somewhere on this planet, and his longing for home quickly gave way to a cold determination, and he returned to the data pad.

Patrick was now an hour into Dr. Victor Austin's research—more specifically, Austin's discoveries in brain mapping: the ability to download and upload data to and from the neocortex with pinpoint accuracy. *He had actually unlocked the secrets of brain memory!* Jeremy's father was a genius. His discoveries in liquid memory and nanotechnology had resulted in thousands of patents that had made TerraGen a fortune.

"Scum bags," Selene said in a resigned tone. "Kidnappers."

"My father knew nothing." Reality seemed to have hit the son of Alexander Leach like lead weight.

"I feel violated," Selene continued.

"You're alive," Patrick said, "at least for the moment. Count your blessings."

"MetaUniversal Genetics," Alex repeated as if still trying to comprehend the enormity of the deception. "Meta…. Universal. Sounds like a bunch of pirates to me."

"Technology sharks, ruthless… not your mother's garden variety of philanthropists."

"Lunk-head pirates," Alex said through gritted teeth.

"They kidnap a bunch of kids and hire a couple hundred mercenaries, for what?" Patrick's mind had been working this over and over to the point of giving him a headache. "Stealing technology, obviously, but what?"

Frustrated, Alex threw a pile of sticks on the fire, sending sparks into the air. He looked at Patrick and the data pad. "Have you found our ticket home yet?"

"Yes, for the hundredth time," Patrick replied irritably.

No matter how many times he told the big jock, it didn't seem to penetrate his Cro-Magnon-sized brain.

"Where?"

"The same place I told you an hour ago."

"The Departure Portal?"

"Yes, for the hundredth time."

"You both sound like a bunch of five year olds," said Selene without taking her gaze off the fire.

Patrick shut down the data pad and placed it in his backpack. He studied Alex who stood at the cave's mouth, biting his fingernails in frustration. "Only problem, Alex, is that we don't know how far away the Portal is and what the terrain will be like."

"Not to mention thirty days," Selene said.

Patrick was about to voice his own doubts about finding their parents at the Portal when suddenly the moonlight around them flickered.

Something big. Something with wings. Flying overhead.

Air caught in Patrick's throat as he watched a giant shadow pass in front of Genesis' two moons.

JEREMY STARED AT THE CITY of death where it hunched in silent darkness like a black widow in its lair, black orbs searching, waiting for its next victim. From the highest part of the city, a beacon of light shot skyward, illuminating clouds and visible for hundreds of miles. A hacking cough turned his head and he moved back to where Marissa lay. In the dim light he could see that her left arm was criss-crossed with black, spider veins. Jeremy looked to where Leo sat watching. "The poison is spreading. We have to get that arrow out."

"Can't do it without water... and a fire," Leo said.

"She may not live long enough," Jeremy said, looking at the black veins traveling up Marissa's neck. Even with the dim light from the city's beacon he could see the veins appearing on her face that was bathed in sweat. Her eyes remained closed. Muscles twitched on her face. An internal battle was being waged inside Marissa and there was nothing Jeremy could do.

Suddenly, the light disappeared. Both Jeremy and Leo stared back at the city.

The beacon had gone out.

"Let's move," Jeremy said with a sense of foreboding.

Together, they struggled under Marissa's weight and managed to lift the girl to her feet. She seemed to wake, opening her eyes. Words fell out her lips, "Whhh.. whuh... doing?" she mumbled. Neither of them responded because it took all their strength to half-carry the girl.

"Marissa looks small, but she's heavy!" Leo said through gritted teeth.

The pudgy eleventh grader grunted, but was not backing down from the challenge. Jeremy couldn't remember ever seeing Leo with so much determination. "Coach Hayfield would be proud of you," Jeremy said.

"Coach Hayfield despised me," Leo sneered, not trying to hide his bitter tone. "The other coaches used to pick on me when I was a freshman. But then my dad threatened the whole lot of 'em and they backed off."

"Good for you."

"I hate P.E.," Leo spat. "Running, climbing, football… it's your favorite class, I'm sure."

Jeremy didn't respond, sensing that they had ventured into a dark area of Leo's psyche. Both young men were now breathing heavily, stumbling on roots and branches, and getting tangled in vines. Every step a huge exertion. With only the light from the two moons to see by, they often found themselves walking in thick darkness. They warily passed under trees. Branches gashed their arms and knocked against their foreheads. But they refused to give up. Marissa's breaths were very shallow—time was running out.

Stepping through another patch of inky blackness they

pushed through the low-hanging branches of a fern. Rocks rattled under foot, but then their sound vanished.

Jeremy instinctively stopped. "Back!" he shouted. "Back—back—now!"

Momentum carried Marissa's body forward, and Jeremy struggled to pull her back. Leo's shoes scrambled for traction. Marissa's limp body swayed... and then fell backward to the ground where they all landed. A swirl of dust and pine nettles coated them as they breathed deep the mountain air.

Jeremy's eyes sharpened and he caught a glimpse of the two moon overhead but in front of them, just inches from their shoes, was a dark chasm. Wind whistled past them as his eyes grew more accustomed to the darkness, and he picked out the faint reflection of moonlight on a river far below them.

They were on the edge of a cliff.

The river was just a ribbon in the distance, and Jeremy guessed they were hundreds of feet above the valley floor. *One more step, and...*

"That was close!" Leo said hoarsely. "Too close!"

Pain pounded in Jeremy's temples as he fought off the shock of near death. Sweat stained his forehead and he felt chilled to the bone. He craned his neck to see over the cliff's edge but all was black. His heart pounded in his chest, and he leaned back, staring up at the two moons that hung in the night sky.

Suddenly, movement. A winged shadow flashed overhead, just a hundred feet above them and the boys pushed back from the cliff in fear.

"What was that?" Leo whispered.

"I'd rather not find out," Jeremy responded.

"It was big."

Yeah, as big as a private jet. Fear was trying to tighten its grip on Jeremy when he suddenly realized he couldn't hear Marissa's breathing. His mind screamed the unthinkable: *She's dead!* He put his ear close to her mouth and heard the faintest of breaths. *Well, almost dead.* "Let's pull Marissa back...

under that tree," Jeremy said, pointing toward a gnarled fern that grew out of the rock.

"You're not leaving me!" Leo gasped, horrified.

"Just long enough to find some water," Jeremy said. "She's dying."

Painfully, they gripped her arms and dragged the girl's body away from the cliff, placing her body on a soft bed of fern branches. Leo plopped down next to Marissa, gasping heavily. Jeremy stood over them, and he studied Leo, not trusting the boy to stay with the stricken girl. "You *will* stay here and watch over her... promise, Leo?"

Leo glanced up at Jeremy and there was an awkward silence. "I won't leave," Leo said finally.

Jeremy turned and headed into the forest.

L ACHLAN EVANS HATED to be in the dark, and his current situation had nothing to do with the time of day.

Keene had lied.

"Where's Colonel Wilhelm Glass?" Evans asked, both to Keene and this mysterious black rider straight out a gothic horror novel. For the past year, Keene had assured him that Glass was a one hundred percent solid and reliable contact. Corporate espionage was expensive, and they had paid millions to Glass and his associates, a project now going on five years, and one that had started when MetaUniversal first heard about the Genesis project.

"Glass no longer exists," rasped the hideous creature in black.

Evans shot Keene a withering look. His mind was working overtime. The fate of their expedition hung on—

"The boy!" the rider shouted. "WHERE—is—he?!" The voice echoed in the ruins, and the force of it caused many of the soldiers to take an involuntary step backward.

"Where is Colonel Glass?" Evans persisted. "We had a deal for technology."

"TerraGen technology?" The rider laughed. "We've moved beyond them."

"We came clear across a galaxy!" Evans was losing his temper.

"Bringing an army of soldiers, armed for war—"

"A security detail!"

Laughter came from the hood again. "You were told not to bring weapons of any kind."

"We wouldn't have survived the city and its aliens!" Evans was trying desperately to reassert his authority over the expedition... and he was losing.

"The Austin boy was the key. He would've protected you from those predators."

"What about our deal?"

"You were told to bring the boy to me—here!" the rider hissed. "You failed!"

"Our deal was with Colonel Glass!" Evans' voice sounded pathetic.

"He would be disappointed, I'm sure."

"But we're tracking the boy!" Hicks blurted out.

HICKS KNEW HE SHOULDN'T have opened his mouth but he was upset. He stared with disbelief at this horse rider out of a nightmare—monster, aliens and now the *Grim Reaper*—what next?

But Keene had lied.

This wasn't an expedition to find TerraGen's missing scientists. It was corporate theft. Greed. Piracy. The betrayal stung the good Dr. Hicks deep into the core of the respectful, life-affirming, loyal researcher that he'd spent over fifty years perfecting. And now his wounded soul was transforming into anger. *Fool me once...* he thought, his lip curled in a tiny, rebellious sneer. The enormity of leaving Earth, his family and the security of his job at TerraGen... chills of fear went down his spine. *I'll be darned if you fool me twice!*

The hooded cowl of the rider suddenly swiveled toward Hicks. *"Tracking the boy?"* Hicks immediately regretted opening his mouth, but it was too late. "With what?" the rider pressed with interest.

Slowly, Hicks raised a finger and pointed toward Benton Keene. "He has a computer."

The black rider started his horse toward Keene, then stopped. The cowl, with its black interior, swiveled violently to one side—the rider completely ignoring them—head bent out of shape… listening.

CHAPTER TWENTY-FIVE

FOXES AND RABBITS

WHEN HIS HANDS FIRST TOUCHED the water, he felt a tingling sensation. It started in the very tips of his fingers and traveled upward. He had come to find water, and now his brain was buzzing with energy as if he'd just drank a hundred caffeinated soft drinks. One minute he was kneeling beside a mountain stream, and then next he was being sucked into a vortex of water and energy. Light flooded through his body, painful light that throbbed with power...

And then Jeremy connected.

A higher intelligence plugged into his brain like a dry

hose into a high-pressured flood of water, but the water was data, and it coursed through every cell of his body.

He *was* the stream—became *part* of it—traveling downward and combining with other streams that splashed over a waterfall as they joined a massive river that flowed south. Visions of glades, valleys, rock outcroppings, and ancient, man-made fortifications filled his mind. *His* mountain was part of a larger range of mountains stretching south and east, and farther on there was an ocean. What part of his mind was still his own realized one fact:

The higher intelligence was the planet.

THE BLACK HORSE PAWED its hooves at the rocky turf as if impatient, but the hideous rider continued to be distracted, his head cocked to one side as if listening to something far off. Lachlan Evans' temper was cooling in the mountain air, but his frustration was still mounting. Here was this cowled demon from the depths of whatever evil lived on Genesis—which gave TerraGen's name for this planet an ironic twist—who was threatening to renege on their deal. Glass or no Glass, the deal had been made, and he'd risked his reputation on the success of this expedition—not to mention the fact that he was millions of light years away from his home planet and the various bank accounts where Evans had stashed millions during his twenty years as a CIA operative.

And now Doctor Death was ignoring him. *How rude.*

But Evans held all the cards. He looked around at his soldiers—over a hundred of the most dangerous mercenaries culled from all branches of the military. They were killers. And it was now time to force the issue. "What happened to Dr. Glass?" Evans demanded.

The dark rider continued to ignore Evans, cowl still tilted in a listening position.

"We came here at great expense—we brought the Austin boy, per your request, and we *will* get the technology you promised!"

"You will get nothing."

At first, Evans thought he had misheard. The voice had echoed from within the dark robes, low and guttural, and combined with a sudden wind coming down from the mountain had caused the ex-CIA man to mistrust his hearing. "Where is the technology?!" Evans demanded again, putting more force behind his words.

The cowl slowly turned. "Excuse me. Did I hear the rabbit speak?"

"What?" Evans was beginning to think the rider was insane.

The cowl remained fixed on Evans. The voice within became deeper and filled with menace. "The rabbit said to the fox, 'Where is the forage you promised me?' The fox only laughed—he remembered how the greedy little hare had betrayed his fellow rabbits to the fox in exchange for a lifetime supply of carrots."

"Cute," Evans spat. The soldiers began to shift nervously.

The rider continued like a kindergarten teacher reading a nursery rhyme to a class of five year olds, "The fox had delivered bundles of carrots, and in return, he ate the other rabbits: friends, mother, father, sisters and brothers. The greedy rabbit turned a blind eye as he gorged on the carrots. Until one day the carrots stopped... because the other rabbits were nothing but bones, and the fox was hungry once again."

"The technology, if you please," Evans said sternly.

"What kind of deal do you think the rabbit made with the fox then?" the rider said, cackling in laughter which sounded like bones grating on bones.

"We're not here for bedtime stories."

"*You* are the bedtime story!" the rider shouted in a voice that seemed to shake the stone ruins. "One requirement—the boy—and you failed! There is no deal."

"Don't be so quick to—"

"Silence!!!" the rider's voice cracked, and the ground

shook underneath them—hands slapped stocks as the mercenaries struggled to stay on their feet.

Evans stepped backward to steady himself as he felt the ground move. *This guy should be in a freak show.*

The cloaked rider laughed again. He pulled on the bridle and his horse began to back up. "Don't worry, little rabbits. I won't treat you the way a fox would."

"We can take care of ourselves," Evans countered bravely.

"You asked where's the technology is?" the rider said, and then swept his hands wide, motioning to the surrounding mountainside. "It's all around you."

"You're crazy, old man."

"False bravado as you hide behind your pitiful weapons," the creature rasped again. His horse had stopped at the fort's entrance, but the rider continued to stare at Evans. "Lots of dangerous predators live in these mountains. Maybe your toy guns will protect you." The rider chuckled low and ominously. "But the animals aren't the only predators you should be worried about!"

A dark wooden rod appeared in the rider's hand—one of the soldiers instinctively raised his machine gun and opened fire. *Death*... a name befitting this creature... simply pointed the rod, and a bolt of bright light erupted from it, eviscerating the soldier in flaming white heat. Charred flesh fell to ground without the slightest whimper. Death's magic wand pointed downward, and the ground began to erupt.

A shockwave ripped through the soldiers and Evans was knocked backward to the ground.

They all were going to die.

 LASH.

Stone ramparts stretched for miles. Crowds in oldish, plain costumes filled the streets—

A large palatial structure overlooked the entire city like a diamond set in stone—

A medieval city.

Jeremy was inside a large, prosperous city out of the middle ages: with huge ramparts, towers, fortifications, and a population of 12,817… correction… 12,816—one of the soldiers normally stationed at the main gatehouse just died from alcohol poisoning.

Jeremy lost track of the towns, villages and cities he visited. There would be a blinding flash and his entire being would be pulled at light speed to the next destination. FLASH—another town. It was as if an energetic child was hurrying to show him the best and coolest places on the planet.

This was the third major city and it was the largest so far. The people couldn't see him and yet they were tantalizing close. Many times he tried to communicate with them but it was as if he were a ghost.

FLASH.

The city and its people vanished.

FLASH.

Jeremy was violently thrust back onto the mountain, still an observing specter…or see he thought. Earth and rock exploded into the air where an ancient warrior—a *man* filled with malevolent power—was causing destruction… and then a *vortex of evil* suddenly turned its attention to… *Jeremy*.

A black, hooded cowl. Two eyes that shimmered with energy… formless, yet looking right through him. Eyes that widened in recognition—

Jeremy ripped his hand out of the water, face sweating, drawing breath in large gasps. He had to get back to the others.

They had to run.

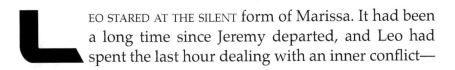

EO STARED AT THE SILENT form of Marissa. It had been a long time since Jeremy departed, and Leo had spent the last hour dealing with an inner conflict—

self-preservation or duty, run away like always or stay and be isolated.

Marissa was going to die.

Hello, Captain Obvious.

It was all so depressing. Nothing on this side of the Portal was how he had envisioned it to be. There was the mass chaos and the constant threat of imminent death—*which absolutely sucked*—and then there were the aliens. *Beyond scary.* And the hunger. He'd forgotten the last time food went into his mouth and down into his now-growling stomach. Marissa's pockets had been emptied of food—he'd debated for, oh, maybe ten seconds over whether to pilfer her clothes for anything edible—his search came up empty.

She was dying anyway.

He sighed and folded his knees close to his chest, shivering in the cold, evening air.

And then he saw the old man.

Standing half in shadow and half in the light of the twin moons, the man blended into the background. It was the man's eyes… no, it was the *feeling* of being watched that drew Leo's attention. Dressed in a dark robe with a hooded cowl, the man was silent and motionless.

Run!

But he couldn't. And obviously, Marissa wasn't going anywhere. So Leo remained still… and waited as the old man started toward him.

CAMPFIRES STRETCHED FOR MILES like a flotilla of fluorescent jellyfish in Caribbean waters. Patrick, Alex, and Selene were ensconced behind a rocky outcropping on a cliff that overlooked a wide valley. The valley lay like a dark abscess in a landscape bathed in moonlight… except for the hundreds of fires. Dim forms moved amongst the encampment where tents and pavilions could be seen in the firelight.

"It's an army," Patrick said. *A vast army*, he thought with dread.

"Ah... arrrr... are th-th-they friendly?" Selene asked, teeth chattering from the cold.

The warmth of the fire was long forgotten. The large shadow had passed overhead, and Patrick had immediately doused the fire. Once encased in darkness, the glow of light on the horizon had drawn them out of their hole like a beacon offering hope. But it was a deceptive hope—a trickster's trap—because the army they found standing around the fires weren't going to offer them safe haven—but something more sinister. The shadowed figures looked human...and yet, not human.

Selene's chattering grew louder. Her left hand pressed into her right shoulder, under which her shirt stilled showed dampness from the poultice underneath. She flexed her right hand constantly, the feeling returning and Patrick just stared in wonder. *Maybe he'd underestimated this girl?* He turned back to studying the army below. All three huddled close for the mutual warmth of their bodies, stomach's growling from hunger. All three were awed by the scene below.

Patrick grunted. "Nothing on this planet is friendly, just saying."

"Are your parents down there, you think?" Alex asked, voice filled with dread.

"I hope not."

"Wh... wh... why?" Selene stammered.

"Because I don't even think those soldiers are human." The nearest campfire was only a couple hundred feet below them, but not so distant that Patrick couldn't see details. His eyesight had always been as sharp as an eagle's. The beings moving in and out of the firelight had an unnatural way of moving, like furtive animals. *Wild.* "Whatever direction they're going," Patrick said in a whisper, "we need to be running in the opposite."

"Even I can figure that one out," Alex growled, his

arrogance unruffled by the freezing temperature.

"I'm freezing," Selene groaned.

Twigs *snapped* behind them. Alex and Selene ducked down behind the boulders, but Patrick didn't move, knowing that movement attracted attention.

Utter stillness.

The world around them had gone silent…as if all the birds, rabbits and squirrels had collectively decided to go into hiding. Which meant they feared whatever had invaded their home.

Behind them, one hundred yards of grass stretched away from their hiding place to the edge of the mountain forest. There was a flicker of moonlight and four alien hunters stepped into the open like silent wraiths. Each held bows nocked with arrows. Strange, Patrick thought. These aliens were shorter than the ones that attacked them in the city. And they were dressed differently, more woodsy. They almost blended with the background of the trees as they began moving swiftly along the tree line. All except one.

The single alien bent to the ground, head moving spasmodically in one direction and then another. *He was sniffing!* And Patrick knew what scent had attracted the creature's attention. He slowly lowered himself beside Alex and Selene, and they crowded close. He whispered softly: "Aliens."

Selene began to tremble.

"We need to run," he said, pointing to a stand of trees further down the cliff. "Run… now!!!"

They ran.

JEREMY MOVED SWIFTLY THROUGH the trees, retracing his steps back to Leo and Marissa. Brush and thorns tore at his clothes. He felt wetness on his hands and knew that his palm had been gashed open. *No matter*, he thought. *Must get back fast.* Panic had its hold on him, and all he could think to do was to get back to his friends.

WHAP! A branch smacked his face and he felt a burning in his lower jaw.

That's gonna leave a mark.

The trees thinned out and he was able to move faster. Fear coursed up and down his back and his legs felt weak. Energy had fled his body after his connection at the mountain stream. The opposite of his first encounter with the alien presence. When wrapped in the white light in the Portal—his entire being electrified as Genesis downloaded data into his brain—something had happened to the cells of his body.

Rejuvenation. Health. Healing.

Now, the exhaustion that had robbed his body of strength after his coma, had returned with a vengeance. His feet felt leaden. Breaths came a shallow gasps. His heart pounded in his chest and he feared it would burst.

There was a crashing sound to his left and he almost tripped. Breaking into a mountain glade he found himself running through grass and tall weeds, heedless of caution.

More crashing on his left and he heard the distinctive sound of...*snorting.* He glanced left and saw moonlight reflecting off a horse's coat. And then he saw the rider—a fearsome creature dressed in a black robe.

Jeremy ran faster.

CHAPTER TWENTY-SIX

PREY AND PRAY

"**J**UST GREAT," LACHLAN EVANS voiced bitterly for the umpteenth time, and again he looked for the cowed form of Benton Keene. "Keene!" The line of mercenaries snaked out of the ruined fortress and down the mountainside. Evans was convinced the security director was evading him. "*Keene!*" he shouted even louder.

A cold voice spoke behind him. "Mister Evans?" Benton Keene strode past several soldiers and fell in step with the CIA man.

"I want an exit plan!" Evans said angrily. "This whole mess is your fault, and I *will* hold you accountable." The threat in his voice was naked and raw.

"We have the exit Portal," Keene said, holding up his data pad.

"Without the boy?"

"Tracking him as we speak—"

"Where?!"

Keene gestured with his free hand. "Somewhere in these mountains—"

"He's left the city? Good!" Evans said. He was about to inquire of the Austin boy's exact location when a sudden chorus of shouts interrupted his thinking.

Shouts of pain.

The line of soldiers had been weaving in and out of the carpet of tall grass, following the path downward. Ahead, beams from flashlights began waving spasmodically.

Evans felt something brush across his pant leg. He stopped. A thin line. Liquid seeping out. He touched it and pulled away a flap of cloth, revealing a gash in his leg. *Strange.* He started forward again and felt another flicker of a touch… and this time there was pain. The back of his other pant leg had a similar gash—a gash where more blood trickled out.

"It's alive!"

Evans heard Keene's voice, but it didn't register. His brain was too busy working the puzzle of how he was suddenly bleeding.

The blades of grass began to move—wait, move? One blade flicked out and rapped against his boots, slicing the leather.

Screams sounded.

Looking up, Evans realized that the whole mountainside was alive with moving grass.

Alive and deadly.

 JEREMY RAN HEAVILY THROUGH waist-high scrub, passing huge boulders, driven by the sound of snorting and

crashing that followed close behind him. He was like a fox being hunted by some spectral lord from hell on horseback. A grassy clearing opened in front of him, and then suddenly there was emptiness. Trying to stop his momentum, Jeremy almost twisted his ankle, scrabbling at tufts of grass, his body spinning sideways, and then his lower body was hanging out over nothingness. He held on, thinking the grass would surely come loose... but he did stop and he dangled over a precipice that dropped away several hundred feet. He strained against rock and dirt, managing to pull himself up.

A horse snorted.

He saw the sheen of a horse's lathered coat and black robes that moved in the mountain air, and then a voice spoke—a voice that grated like iron on iron, low and deep.

"Jeremy... Austin."

Jeremy couldn't see anything inside the rider's cowl.

"No need to run." The rider's casual, commanding tone only terrified him even more.

Jeremy stood at the cliff's edge, facing this apparition on a black horse, knowing he was trapped.

SELENE TRIED HARD TO keep up with the two older boys who were running twenty yards ahead. *It's not fair!* Her father had always wanted a son, and now she would rather his wish had been granted. There was Patrick, a skeletal, muscularly challenged computer nerd, running stride-for-stride with Alex, a decorated athlete. Her feet hurt. Her right arm buzzed unhappily and she still tried to keep her poultice pressed in place with her left hand. Her Gucci pants were in shreds, and the constant up and down motion of running was giving her a headache.

Thank god I'm flat chested.

She ran harder.

Moonlight revealed a small glade and Selene dared to glance behind her without lessening her stride—

Four shadows moved under the trees. Light reflected off the long, metal blades they carried.

She ran even harder.

The three high school students from Lewisville were being tracked by aliens. Fighting down emotion, she focused only on putting one foot in front of the other.

I freakin' hate aliens!

THE SINGLE-FILE OF DISCIPLINE had disintegrated into a maddened rampage to find a safe haven from the wicked, green blades that sliced with sudden swiftness. Benton Keene was bleeding from deep cuts in his legs and arms. Nearby, a soldier clutched his right hand which was missing three fingers.

"Do not stop!" he shouted.

To stop was to die, because the long-bladed grass was alive and seeking their blood.

HIS HEEL TWITCHED AND ROCKS fell away, vanishing into darkness. Jeremy looked around; boulders blocked escape to his left, and to the right he saw a narrow ledge that moved down the face of the cliff.

The black rider moved closer. "We've been waiting a long time for you to come."

Jeremy made his break, darting right and hoping against all hope that the rocky ledge wasn't a dead end. It wasn't. He found himself on a game trail the width of his shoulders. He swiftly moved down the steep cliff face, taking care to avoid the tufts of grass and rock that jutted upward underfoot.

Empty space.

With a horrified groan, Jeremy realized his luck had run out: a section of the trail had eroded long ago, leaving a gap that showed empty blackness. Clouds moved in the night sky and covered the two moons, thrusting Jeremy into darkness.

Laughter sounded from behind him. "No need to keep running." The sound of hooves stepping on stone came from further up the trail. Something in the rider's presence emanated pure hatred. Hatred and power. Tendril webs of energy poured from the rider further up the mountain—foul energy—corruption like a cancer seeking to eat away his strength, his hope, and any resolve to fight back. The tendrils would probe at Jeremy, touch him from different directions—

"You're only delaying the inevitable, son of Austin."

Wind whipped at his hair, and suddenly light illuminated the ground as the clouds parted. The two moons appeared higher in the alien sky, and their light revealed a fifteen foot chasm on the path before him. Jeremy backed up, his mind calculating the distance.

A horse snorting sounded close behind, and fear stabbed his insides like an icy flame—he felt his bowels go soft. Stepping back further, he stopped, took a deep breath... then ran.

Fifteen feet—ten—five—he jumped and felt the emptiness of space underneath him. The other side of the trail came quickly, and he hit the edge chest-high with a sickening thud. Pain lanced through his ribs and he prayed that none were broken. Scrambling upward, he rolled over on the trail and froze.

Standing on the other side of the gap was the horse and rider.

The rider laughed.

SELENE TRIED HARD TO keep up with the two older boys who were running twenty yards ahead. *It's not fair!* Her father had

Leo studied the old man who stooped over Marissa. The cowl was pushed back to reveal long, silver hair tied in a braid. Lines wrinkled the man's face, yet he seemed ageless somehow, and radiated a sense of strength and power. The robe draped around his body shimmered with dark hues of blue in the moonlight.

"Wh… what are…. you doing?" Marissa moaned weakly. In the dim light Leo could see a network of black veins running up the girl's neck, and almost covering her face. The bloody arrowhead was lying nearby—the old man had twisted and pulled the alien arrow free and a wash of blood, puss, and poison had gushed out as a result. Now the old man tipped a vial of liquid into Marissa's mouth.

"I can't believe she's still alive," Leo commented, more out of fear of the old man and some need for reassurance that this mysterious figure wasn't going to kill them both.

"Gnome arrow," the old man said, "tipped with poison from the lands of Abaddon."

Marissa tried to spit up the liquid, but the old man held her mouth shut as he slipped the vial into the pockets of his robe. The girl fought for a brief second, and then swallowed.

"Will she survive?"

"Likely."

"Is that some kind of potion? Magic?"

The old man gave a grim chuckle. "Something like that. But not a moment too soon. This potion works fast, but another hour? Another hour would've been too late."

The ancient man turned to look at Leo, studying him. Perspiration beaded on Leo's forehead and he wished he was anywhere but here. Leo's throat was suddenly dry and he moved a pace backward.

The old man spoke again. "You're obviously NOT the boy they're looking for."

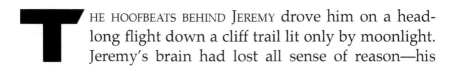

THE HOOFBEATS BEHIND JEREMY drove him on a headlong flight down a cliff trail lit only by moonlight. Jeremy's brain had lost all sense of reason—his only goal now was survival. How long he'd been evading the horseback rider he couldn't say. A half hour? Hour? Eternity was sometimes measured in seconds. No off-shoot of the trail had presented itself, no alternative course, and still the horse and rider came on like a pair of hunting dogs refusing to give up the scent. Worst of all, what little remained of Jeremy's strength was failing.

OK, Erik, now would be a great time for a little direction! But it seemed the voice of his brother had stayed behind in the Portal city along with Ranger, the pet behemoth. *Erik's talk of saving the planet—I can't even save myself, for crying out loud!* Exhaustion fueled his frustration with each step. Perhaps that hadn't really been Erik after all? Or maybe there'd been a gun to his head (off camera, of course)—*lure your younger half-brother to go on a suicidal expedition—fill his mind with crazy talk about arch villains!* Inwardly he cursed George Tobias, the attorney—*keep your videos and self-destructing data pads to yourself!* His breath was labored and he grunted in pain, stubbing his toe for the umpteenth time on a boulder hidden in the darkness. Nothing about his experience on Genesis had shown Jeremy to be anything other than a common, ordinary, nothing special kid.

Save the planet... Sheesh!

If Jeremy had anything to do with the fate of Genesis and Earth, well... forget trying to pay off that mortgage early because you're pretty much screwed. Just accept the apocalypse when it comes.

Save yourself, Erik!

Suddenly, the trail opened up and he felt the ground shift from rocky dirt to soft, tufts of grass that muffled the sound of his shoes. The grass was slippery from the damp night air. He was on a flat expanse of ground that jutted out... into blackness.

Another cliff!

His head snapped one way then another, looking for an escape. *Trapped!*

Empty blackness stared at him, mocking him for thinking he could escape…

Snort. Jeremy turned. The Grim Reaper and his might steed studied their quarry with a distain that both infuriated and scared the piss out of Jeremy. Dark and seemingly shrouded in evil, the horse and rider stepped closer, out of the gloom, moonlight rimming the hooded cowl. Jeremy pointed his finger at the rider defiantly. "What do you want from me?!"

Again, the rider laughed. "You have a role to play."

"No I don't. I'm just a kid!"

"You're older than you realize."

"I haven't done anything to you… uh, most high and mighty sorcerer."

A chuckle from the depths of the cowl. "Not yet."

A distant sound reached Jeremy's consciousness: the sound of rushing water. He glanced backward and saw moonlight glinting off a rushing river far below him. He faced the rider again. "Does this have anything to do with my father? Do you have him locked up somewhere?!"

"If only. No, little one. I am called the *Gnome King*, the *Mindbender*," rasped the rider. "My armies call me the *Dark Overlord*."

Rushing water—why is that sound jabbing at my subconscious? And why is my mind having conversations with itself while facing Death Rider and his horse, Killa'?! Jeremy backed away from the cliff, having chill spells just thinking about the emptiness behind him. His steps took him closer to *Death* and *Killa'*.

"I can make you a *great man* in our kingdom," Death rasped—*which is fitting because how else would Death speak? A high nasal voice? Or with a British accent—too obvious.* Jeremy fought to master his brain as Death—*no… the Gnome King,* continued. "Would you like to rule your own country?"

"No, sir. I'm not equipped for that kind of responsibility." *There. Done. Let's move on.*

"Rule in your own palace?"

"Sounds cold. Uninviting."

"Loyal subjects bowing down before your throne?" The voice of the Gnome King purred with temptation... and desire. "Beautiful maidens that will obey every wish you command?"

Hmmmm—beautiful maidens... Images danced in his head. Now that was a concept Jeremy hadn't thought about. *No! Banish images!* Jeremy shook the cobwebs of desire out of his mind.

"King Jeremy..." the voice rattled.

Evil seemed to wash over Jeremy—his mind fought to remain free. The enjoyable images of beautiful girls were suddenly replaced by images of death—*which is fitting—standard horror film trope—pretty, scantily clad girls distract hero as a chainsaw wielding maniac shreds his fellow classmates...*

"King..."

Something about the creature on the dark horse warned Jeremy of his own, impending demise. Power radiated from this man, and every cell in Jeremy's body tingled from its foulness. *Trust? This creature could not be trusted.* His mind fought back against the onslaught of evil.

The Gnome King's hand whipped upward, extending a wooden rod toward Jeremy. White heat lanced outward—Jeremy dove sideways as *time slowed* to fractions of a heartbeat, his eyes capturing the scene in strobe-like snapshots: white lighting flashing by, narrowly missing his ear; a jagged rock digging into his ribs and ripping the cloth of his shirt, his letter jacket whirling outward like a pair of monstrous wings; his body rolling over; gathering what strength was left and jumping to his feet to face—

White hot lightning slammed into Jeremy's chest.

Weightlessness. Falling. Darkness.

This is what's it's like to die, his mind screamed.

Not fair.

Chapter Twenty-Seven

Wizard's Duel

MOONLIGHT SILHOUETTED THE GNOME KING who stood at the cliff's edge, hand holding the reins to his horse. He stared down at the dark, snakelike waters of the Kallos River. The wand in his other palm still felt hot. *Hmmmmmm.* The Lord of Shadows would not be pleased. He sighed. Frustration was an emotion he rarely had to put up with and some innocent victim would pay for his blunder. *Too much power*, he calculated. *But the boy was a bit of a lightweight—almost like a feather, he reasoned...* his ego soothed just a fraction.

Except now the boy was gone… *escaped or fallen to his death.*

Moonlight flickered off a glistening rock underfoot. He smiled with satisfaction. Taking a cloth from one of the pockets of his robe, he stooped and swiped blood off the rock. Folding the cloth, he tucked it back into his robe while taking a small, metal tube from around his neck. Placing it to his lips, he blew three times. No audible sound was emitted. But the creature known as the Gnome King understood the science of sound frequencies—knew that the *grakken* would hear and obey. A smile of pleasure played at his lips.

Stepping back into the saddle he pulled on the reins and headed the horse back up the trail, wind whipping at the tails of his robe. There was still work to be done—

My old friend. Come to meddle in the world again.

He'd sensed the other's presence earlier, and confrontation was inevitable. His hand slid the smooth, dark wand back into his robe and patted it confidently.

LEO WALKED INTO THE TREES.

"The wizard told you to stay put, Leo," Marissa said, her voice gaining strength.

"Wizard… *really*," Leo spat derisively and turned to look back at Marissa. "You stay and take care of his pet." The girl sat with her back resting against the largest bird Leo had ever seen. The old man had called it a *roc*, and the bird stood well over ten feet tall, with massive, folded wings which trembled in the cold night air. Leo had never liked airplanes, and the ten minutes they spent flying on the back of this roc had made him almost soil his pants. Huge, sharp talons bit into the soft ground, and it was against one of the beast's legs that Marissa rested.

"You'll get yourself killed," Marissa feebly warned one final time.

Leo moved deeper into the forest. It was unnaturally quiet. The only sound he heard was his own breathing and the occasional twig snapping under his shoes. Moonlight filtered down in patches. After a few minutes passed, he started to have second thoughts. Any kind of predator could exist in these woods. He was a fool. And then the distant roar of rushing water reached his ears, mingled with the sound of voices. He slowed, gingerly stepping past huge evergreens and moving behind an outcropping of rocks. He peered over.

"You won't be able to control the boy," hissed a dark, evil-looking man mounted on a black horse. "He's already gotten a taste."

Leo then noticed the wizard standing in the center of the small clearing—his right arm was outstretched, and he pointed a small, wooden rod at the rider. When the wizard spoke, it was with a voice filled with such menace that it gave Leo chill bumps. "Tell your master that you failed, *King of the Gnomes*."

"He's already aware."

"The boy will *not* be perverted by your hand," the wizard said.

"That story isn't written... yet!" the rider said, whipping a small rod out of his robes. Lightning shot out of the Gnome King's wand, straight at the wizard. Leo tensed, as if to run, but the wizard stood, unharmed. His wooden rod was still upraised, and it absorbed the rider's lightning like a vacuum.

The wizard laughed. His blue robes billowed and flared as energy surrounded him. He seemed to recoil, body tensing as the rider's lightning suddenly vanished. And then he uncoiled, striking back with a beam of white light that shot out of the wizard's rod, hitting both horse and rider—and screams sounded from both as they glowed blue and white.... but the Gnome King remained. Tendrils of smoked drifted off the evil rider and his mount, and yet they looked unharmed.

The Gnome King's voice was cold. "I guess we've both evolved."

"You and your kind will be stripped of power and thrown—"

"Yeah, thrown into Abaddon's fires," the Gnome King laughed. "Another one of your old wives tales."

A shadow moved past Leo, and he stopped breathing. The smell of rot from the creature turned his stomach. No, two creatures. Each carried long blades and were completely silent in their stealth.

The Gnome King was no longer laughing. His voice was deep and filled with all the coldness of a mountain lake, "Lysander, my kind are doing just fine."

Leo's eyes blinked—not two shadows, but six, were closing in on the wizard. The old man seemed to notice; his head turned, ever so slightly, from side to side. One of the creatures passed into a shaft of moonlight, and Leo recognized it as one of the alien spawn. He shuddered.

"I will find the boy," the Gnome King said, "and there isn't a nation that can hide him from me. He *will* turn to the Shadow... like all the rest."

The wizard snarled defiance and raised his wand. "You were always weak in the mind, both you and your Lord." The wizard swept the wand downward and light exploded into the ground. A shockwave erupted outward, and Leo was knocked to the ground, his head striking a rock... all went black.

ALEX STARED BITTERLY AT the three aliens who had caught up to them. They stood fifty yards away, heavily muscled, eyes black and shadowed in the dim light, with bows drawn and arrows nocked. Three pairs of alien eyes watching them with contempt.

"I suppose they've seen us," Patrick said, breathing heavily beside Alex.

"Wow, good observation, brainchild!" Alex hissed with as much sarcasm as he could imbue the words with.

"That's what I'm here for."

Alex contained the shock at seeing the computer geek's utter coolness in the face of disaster. The three aliens remained motionless. "What are they waiting for?"

"Do you have any barbecue sauce? We could rub some on our meaty flesh—"

Alex wheeled on Patrick. "Cut the crap! You saw what they did to the soldiers."

Patrick shrugged, "I'm tired. I want this over with."

A moan came from below them where Selene knelt on the ground, shaking in fear. Whatever dark part of her mind the Asian girl had fled to wasn't going to save her from the real... the now. Alex returned to studying the aliens. "What concerns me is... where's the fourth?" Alex moaned. "I distinctly saw four."

"Three, four, what's the difference? We're dead either way."

And then the aliens began to move. Like big cats on the African plains, the creatures moved toward them in graceful strides, weaving through the trees and underbrush. To run was futile. The only thing left was capture and a violent death.

A tremor rippled underneath them.

Mid-stride, the aliens froze, their heads darting one way and then another like startled birds.

Suddenly, rocks started to move. The trees swayed as a massive shockwave tore through the forest. Alex felt himself lifted off the ground and thrown backward. *Wham!* His back slammed on the ground and he rolled and rolled before coming to a stop. Wisps of black hair blew across his face and he sneezed.

Selene lay beside him, their heads almost touching. She leaned up with difficulty, her left hand delicately pulling leaves and debris out of her hair, staring at him with eyes wide, pupils dilated. "We can't seem to catch a freak'in break on this planet! First aliens and now atomic bombs!"

Alex struggled for a suitable reply. Nothing.

And then Patrick was tugging at his shirt. "Come on! Look!" Alex, bruised and battered, rolled to his feet. He followed to pointing of Patrick's finger to where the three aliens had once stood, and were now gone.

"Grab the girl," Alex barked.

"I'm right here!" Selene growled. She struggled up on shaky legs.

Alex and Patrick exchanged looks—then each took one of Selene's elbows and then turned, tugging Selene and running in the opposite direction from where the predators had vanished.

Alex knew that the girl was a hindrance, but he needed Patrick to get off this planet from hell—*the nerd wasn't about to dump Asian Barbie*, he thought with frustration. *At least her shoulder was healing.* They crashed through the underbrush. Branches whipped at their heads and bodies, brush and dry limbs crunched underfoot, broadcasting their position to unseen aliens like a GPS locator.

Alex gritted his teeth, leading the way and pulling both Selene and Patrick to move faster. *If we could just put enough distance…* his mind calculated.

They broke from the trees into a small clearing to find the alien waiting for them, its hands raised with a wicked looking blade.

Purring. A deep rumble from within the alien. Jagged teeth flashing in the dim light.

Alex felt a sudden warmth run down his leg, and he realized he'd peed his pants.

L EO WAS PROPPED UP against a boulder and pain pounded his temples. He blinked and saw the wizard standing over him with arms folded. The old man wore a very stern expression. "Eavesdropping can be hazardous to one's self," the wizard said in a raspy voice.

"What happened to..." Leo paused, trying to find a suitable word for the hideous rider, "the, uh, evil warlock guy?"

"He's still around... but not feeling so confident, I would gather." The wizard leaned closer to Leo, studying his face. Leo wanted to run, to escape the old man's penetrating gaze. The wizard's face was emotionless as he continued, "Your father, where is he?"

"Dead," Leo lied. He feared the old man, and some instinctive told Leo not to trust the wizard. "I'm an orphan."

The wizard straightened and looked into the trees, and then back to Leo. "The warlock's name was the Gnome King. He rules over the race of Gnomes and is a lapdog of the Shadow Lord. His bodyguard are assassins, and we must be gone before they catch our scent."

"We're flying again?" Leo groaned, getting to his feet.

"A luxury few people have on this planet," the wizard chided. His blue robes swished as he moved past Leo, setting a brisk pace back to Marissa and the roc. Leo followed quickly, searching the woods for whatever Gnomes might show up.

Gnomes?

Chapter Twenty-Eight

Problems And More Problems

"**M**ETAUNIVERSAL GENETICS." The words tasted like acid in Hicks' mouth. The research director had pieced together the puzzle behind this expedition, and had discreetly approached Lachlan Evans.

Evans looked at the scientist and smiled. "Get used to it, Dr. Hicks."

"Stealing technology… it's unseemly."

"Fortune favors the brave?" Evans suggested.

Dr. Rudolf Hicks thought of TerraGen, Dr. Victor Austin, Dr. Korrapati, the years of hard work, the patents, the discoveries—his stomach roiled with revulsion at the man standing in front of him. Hicks' voice came out as a croak. "Barbarians get rich at the expense of science."

"Look at history, Hicks. Greeks, Romans, Vikings—the strong have always conquered the weak. Technology is just a spoil of war."

"Really?!" Hicks couldn't hide the distaste in his voice. "I don't remember any countries declaring war on TerraGen."

"Oh…war was declared—"

"By whom?"

Pounding his chest, Evans grinned broadly. "By me! The United States of Lachlan Evans!"

"You're just another Hitler. Murder, rape, pillage, theft—any technology you acquire will be wasted and the only beneficiary will be you."

"My men will be generously rewarded, that I can guarantee," Evans spat.

"Or dead," Hicks said, nodding his head to where several of the mercenaries lay dead.

"Risk and reward," Evans said, his eyes gravely studying the fallen men. "They knew the score—the odds."

"Serves them right… *invaders, interlopers, thieves—*"

"Soldiers," Evans said heatedly, his temper rising, "who were hired to protect *you*. Remember that, Dr. Hicks. If they bother you so much, you are welcome to go your own way."

The portly researcher glanced to where the mercenaries were binding their wounds, conversing in low tones. Many of the soldiers sat cleaning their weapons. There was a fierceness to these men that was beyond Hicks' protected world of research. *They belonged here*, he thought. He glanced into the forest gloom, knowing he could never survive on his own. "No. I find their company most agreeable."

Evans laughed without warmth. "Wisely said."

The rest of the expedition members consciously ignored the research director, and Hicks felt like a man adrift in the ocean. Robert Morton ignored Hicks as well. The Washington insider's eyes followed Evans like a an attack dog waiting for the command to kill.

Clouds drifted overhead. Somewhere from the mountain above came the sound of animals, and Hicks turned his head to listen. Soldiers grabbed weapons as demonic howls echoed in the trees.

Keene's voice sounded immediately, "We're moving out! On the double!"

THE KILLER GRASS HAD unsettled Benton Keene—*it was something out of the supernatural!* Now he was taking no chances. Weapons were snapped up and his men followed him quickly down the mountain slope. There was no shame in running. Nothing on this planet could be taken for granted, and he had no desire to meet up with whatever else was up on the mountain. He clutched the data pad in one hand and his assault rifle in the other. His legs moved rhythmically, boots searching for solid ground. They were out of the killing patches of grass, and the rocky terrain was a relief.

Howling sounded off to his left. It was answered by another set of howls from off to his right. It was a common tactic among the cowboys of the old west…except now, he and his band of mercenaries were playing the role of stampeding cattle. *They were being hunted.*

Soldiers streamed around a line of huge boulders and scrambled down a steep embankment on the other side. They entered a valley where a mountain stream wound through its center. They were halfway into the valley when two monstrous shadows dropped from the trees and slammed into a column of men. Metal flashed in the moonlight. Two soldiers quickly fell to the ground, minus their heads. Men screamed in terror as the metallic blades spun in wide arcs.

No shots fired. Only screams. Fear—terror—agony—

screams and more screams. Not one soldier had the presence of mind to fire a shot.

Keene tucked the data pad into his waistband. Gripping his rifle with both hands he ran to where his mercenaries were being slaughtered. The men had scattered in all directions, heedless of cohesion. Already a dozen of his soldiers were dead on the ground. Keene raised his rifle and tried to follow the path of the attackers. One creature stopped in a shaft of moonlight, and he could see it was easily seven feet tall, larger and heavier than the creatures they fought in the Portal city, with small pointed ears, a flattened nose, and eyes as black as night. The large blade it wielded was like an ancient scythe, slightly curved and longer than a man's arm, and dripping with dark fluid. Keene lifted his rifle, but the alien moved out of sight, blade swinging… followed by another scream.

Gunfire sounded behind him. Keene turned around, gun raised. Panic gripped most of the rear guard except one squad that opened fire together. An alien was blasted ten feet into the air before crashing in a bloody heap. At least some of his men were fighting back.

A scream jerked Keene back to the front. One of his lieutenants stumbled toward him, trying to mouth words, but failing. And then Keene saw that the man was missing his right arm. A cold anger swept over him and he moved past the grisly sight.

Ferns slapped at his legs as he pressed forward, searching. Keene's anger had gripped him, obsessed him, and he failed to notice the hulking figure detach itself and move in behind him. His mercenaries had lost all semblance of training during their first battle, and that could only reflect on Keene's leadership.

Instinct saved his life.

He sensed the movement of air and ducked. The swish of a blade passed over his head. He threw himself sideways, rolled, and came up in a crouch with his gun leveled. Twenty years as a sergeant in U.S. Special Forces didn't prepare him for the beast that towered over him. This creature was almost eight feet in height and weighed well over three hundred pounds—an alien killing machine. Its curved blade was already swinging downward.

Heart racing, Keene waited for death.

The armless lieutenant saved his life. Delirious, the man stumbled into the alien's path. Curved blade met with hapless human, and the lieutenant was neatly divided into two parts.

Keene opened fire.

The vicious snarl of sharp teeth disappeared in a spray of blood as the alien's face exploded in a hail of bullets. Keene breathed in ragged gasps and chided himself for hesitating.

More screams echoed in the woods.

CHAPTER TWENTY-NINE

THE GIFT

JEREMY FELL FOR WHAT seemed like hours—though in reality it was only seconds—down and down through pitch blackness toward the roaring waters below. He slammed into icy, cold water—breath bursting from his lungs and the shock of it buzzing loudly in his brain. Breaking the surface, he struggled for breath as he was swept downstream. Water rushed into his mouth and nostrils and he gasped for air. Massive dark shadows whipped past— huge boulders that threatened to crush him like a tin can.

Light flooded into him again.

The dark shadows coming toward him suddenly

became geometrical designs: boulders, rocks, tree branches—
even the water itself—all became computerized data in his head.

He was *connected* to whatever magical source ruled
this planet... and he was no longer afraid.

The river was not his enemy—he knew every rock,
each tributary, the shallows, rapids and waterfalls.

FLASH.

Again he was taken to a city, but this time he could see
the people. They were of a race he'd never seen before, tall,
with pointed ears.

FLASH.

Another race of people: short but stocky, and well
muscled.

FLASH.

A huge race, taller and larger than the others, rooted
in evil.

FLASH.

WINGS FLAPPED IN THE DISTANT sky, the shadowed
form bisecting both moons before wheeling
downward. Astride his horse, the Gnome King
watched the *grakken* descend like a faithful pet. Equally as big
as the roc, grakken were Shadow spawn mounts for only the
most powerful of dark lords. *Makksis* had been the Dark
Overlord's airborne transportation for almost a century. Part
bird and part reptile, Makksis had leathery wings like a bat
with an elongated head that was made even longer by the
massive jaws that jutted out. Sharp teeth studded upper and
lower jaws—teeth made for ripping and gashing its prey.
Grakken were an ancient breed and very rare.

Scrawwwwwk! Makksis screamed its cry of recognition
as it floated down toward its waiting master.

"Easy, girl" the Gnome King said with warmth.

Air whipped at Mindbender's cloak as the grakken
swooped in, it's massive wings beating rapidly as the leathery

body and taloned feet lightly touched down beside horse and rider.

Scrawwwwwk!

Makksis was a bird of prey and seemed to guess her master's intentions. Her dark eyes blinked, head cocking sideways in anticipation, waiting for the command to go and kill. She wanted to hunt—the swipe of talons—the spray of blood—the glistening of fresh meat—these drove the grakken to madness.

"Yes, my darling," the Gnome King's voice soothed. The great beast bent forward, head lowered and the Gnome King placed his right hand on the grakken's leathered skull. "You're in for a rare treat."

A gloved hand reached into the dark robe and came out with a piece of cloth—cloth stained with blood.

Makksis immediately lifted its head, sniffing excitedly. Her body shook with a tremor, eyes blinking, beak reaching for the tiny cloth her master held out. More snuffling sounds.

"Makksis always longs for the taste of human flesh," the Gnome King purred. "Gnomes and Trolls are so mundane… common—of course, the random deer is rather tasty. But human? She loves."

The massive head of the grakken bobbed up and down, talons gripping turf in preparation for flight. More tremors. A cooing sound rumbled from the beast's throat.

"Find the boy. Gut him like cattle. And while you're feasting on his innards, make sure he's alive to watch!" The Gnome King cackled a booming laugh and placed the bloody cloth against the grakken's beak. Drawing a deep breath, the grakken's head turned inquisitively sideways, waiting. "Go, my darling. Go to the hunt!"

Massive wings reached for air. Makksis' legs thrust upward and the great beast soared into the night sky, wings beating rapidly, causing Mindbender's horse to skitter sideways. In seconds, the grakken had disappeared to the west.

Laughter continued to bubble up from within the Gnome King as he tucked the cloth back into his robe. He pictured Jeremy Austin flat on his back with the great beast ripping at the boy's stomach.

Pity, he thought, *it would've been a nice coup to have subjected the boy to the Shadow Lord's will. Oh well…*

H E LAY IN THE TALL REEDS beside the river, chest heaving, taking in deep gulps of air while his mind cycled downward, trying to recover from the tremendous amounts of data that had flooded into his brain. It throbbed. Jeremy reckoned he had ingested the Genesis equivalent of a Rand McNally atlas, the Encyclopedia Britannica and the entire Smithsonian collection—names, places, histories, battles, treaties—just adding it all up made his mind hurt. The visions had disturbed him—most horrified him.

But his connection was still intact.

"Dad," Jeremy whispered, "where are you?"

The only reply was a sudden wind that whispered in the trees above. A chill rippled through him and he sat upright, arms hugging legs for warmth. The loneliness of his predicament was overwhelming…abandoned by his father *and* his brother. He fought back sobs and struggled to his feet. He'd never counted despair as a friend, but right now, it was definitely putting on lipstick and a touch of rouge—*despair* working its wiles to be his next conquest. Jeremy felt sick. The nearness of the rushing water drew him back, the power of the river calling for him.

His head ached. He'd had enough of the planet's history. *Smithsonian…go off yourself!* Jeremy turned and began walking in the opposite direction, away from the river's siren call, and into the forested hillside.

One thing was certain: Jeremy, Patrick, Marissa, Selene, Leo—his entire group of TerraGen kids—had been brought to this planet for a purpose. And he knew their parents had something to do with it. Maybe Dr. Austin or Dr. Korrapati hadn't directly forced the TerraGen Universal Corporation to bring the five of them on the expedition, but their parents had definitely prepared for the possibility of their coming.

But *why?*

What great plan was he and the rest supposed to fulfill?

Their parents were lost, their expedition an apparent disaster. What role must he and his friends play in finding them? This was an alien world with an ancient history. Jeremy was just one person... and powerless to help even himself.

"Sorry, Erik." He spoke into the air as he walked. "I am *not* your savior. Mr. Gnome King and Mr. Shadow Lord, also called Malca...Malcontent—whatever—*they* have all the power. I'm just an average jock from an average high school. I have no powers—no special destiny—for these evil, sorcerer *dudes* to fight over. None!"

The terrain became steeper and he began hiking uphill. A chuckle rumbled from deep within him. "If I'm the savior of planet Genesis..." He let out a burst of laughter—*what a joke, right?* "If Jeremy Austin is supposed to vanquish the dark lord of the shadows then planet Genesis is in for a world of hurt." He put one foot in front of the other, hands pressed against his ears in a futile gesture to shut out the information that kept trying to enter his brain.

Hours passed.

His breath came in painful gasps. Turning, he looked down to where the river wound through the countryside, a ribbon of roiling darkness far below. Around him the terrain had become more rocky, with mountain ferns dominating the foliage.

The twin moons hung lower in the sky, peeking through the branches overhead. Jeremy breathed easier, his strength returning as he entered a mountain glade with even terrain. Leaves and branches crunched underfoot as walked through a forest of ferns and pines. Data flicked back and forth in his brain, his magical connection to the higher intelligence a constant buzz. He tried to shut his brain down, but the effort was pointless. A bird flew overhead—a hawk seeking prey—and Jeremy's mind was violently pulled into the hawk's brain. Suddenly he was flying through the upper trees.

"Die, bird!" he shouted, yanking his brain back into his own consciousness. He'd lost count of how many times his mind had been hijacked. The constant pulling one way then another was *really* annoying.

Two squirrels raced down a huge oak tree, darting, running, and jumping frenetically. "Where's a shotgun when you need one," he lamented. His mind was violently pulled into the brain of the squirrel being chased—jumping, scrambling, leaping high for a branch—

"Get lost!"

The squirrels immediately stopped. They looked down at him from the tree, and, like obedient children, went back up to their nest.

"Finally, some peace," he moaned. The forest was quiet and the only sound was his footfalls echoing softly. He stopped. Nausea and fear flooded into him in a wave that emanated from the forest.

Danger...

Through the trees he could see a glade filled with moonlight. Reflections of light glimmered in the grass.

Pain. Violence. Death.

Waves of horror wafted into his body from the glade. Mist hovered over the ground, shifting, moving in the night breeze. He forced himself to walk forward.

The scent of death is so strong.

Jeremy knew that some horrible act of savagery had occurred in this glade, despite the peaceful way it looked in the moonlight. The mist shifted, and he jumped backward. A dark alien lay prostrate on the ground by his shoes, legs and arms bent at odd angles. Dead.

"Gross!" Jeremy said, seeing gashes in the alien's stomach and realizing the mass of twisting tubes that tumbled out like used radiator hoses... was actually intestines. Gingerly, he moved around the carnage, averting his eyes—

Another alien... also dead, with three arrows protruding from its chest. Its hand still clasped a strangely designed sword where dark matter encrusted the blade. A fanged mouth was open wide in a rictus of pain.

Jeremy looked up. The mist, clinging to the ground like a gray blanket, was suddenly swept aside by a gust of wind. Bodies—more than a hundred—lay clumped in a wide semicircle that ended at the far tree line.

A battle—vicious and bloody—had been fought in a wooded glade the size of a strip mall parking lot.

Aliens by the dozens lay in a variety of positions— some on top of each other—each with swords, spears, helmets and shields strewn on the ground or held in a death grip—the entire tableau a vicious battle frozen in death. Jeremy stopped counting the aliens after twenty.

A long spear had pierced an alien through its chest and then pierced a second alien behind. Both corpses lay in tandem. Gripping the spear's haft was a hand.

A human hand.

Frozen fast to the wooden spear, the hand was protected by a metal glove. The warrior's arm was covered in metal—his entire body protected by medieval-style armor, like a knight on display at Windsor Castle in England.

"I've traveled through time to the middle ages!" Jeremy mumbled in awe.

A wooden stick—wait, *not* a stick—the haft of an axe jutted up from the warrior's helmet. Tips of the axe blade showed from where it was embedded in the human's skull. Dark, matted blood blended with a gray matter below the helmet. Jeremy turned away in revulsion—*the man's brains!*

Another human warrior lay on his back, gripping a sword in two hands, arms limply stretched above his head. He was a big man, arms thick with muscle and well over six feet in height. The dead warrior's helmet lay askew because the man's left eye had been pierced by an alien arrow. His other eye stared lifelessly upward. Who was this knight? What kind of world was Genesis that men wore medieval armor and fought with swords and spears?

"No offense," Jeremy murmured, looking down at the fallen knight, "but I'll stick with Uzi's."

His eyes blinked as he surveyed the glade of death. Dozens of knights lay dead in a much smaller semicircle. *A last stand.* Each of the warriors wore tunics over their mail, each tunic emblazoned with a blindfolded eagle in flight, holding a sword in its talons. Alien corpses surrounded them in dark clumps. Jeremy breathed in deep the cold, mountain air and caught the smell of decay and winced. Stooping, he examined the warrior whose head had been fitted with the axe. *No bloating. No visible decay.* Jeremy wasn't a rocket scientist nor a cast member of a popular TV hospital drama… but the lack of decomposition said that this battle had been fought very recently.

A shiver of fear swept through him.

Maybe there's more of the aliens… *watching him right now.*

Whinnying. A horse's whinny.

Jeremy felt a surge of animalistic pain and fear enter through his neocortex. *Neocortex? I actually know what that is!* He marveled once again at the data and information that would bubble up as a result of his bonding with the planet's magic. Another *whinny*. Again, fear and pain flooded through his brain like an unwanted visitor.

A flash of white showed in a group of trees choked with underbrush at the back of the glade where the semicircle met the tree line. Jeremy cautiously approached. His eyes searched the dark woods beyond for aliens. *Every shadow looks like a freakin' alien,* his mind shouted. The branches shook violently and his eyes snapped back to the blur of white. Moving closer, he saw that it was a horse—a horse unlike any he'd ever seen before. It was beautiful and dangerous at the same time. A white mane flowed across a flawless white coat. But long branches had wrapped around the beast like a nest of vipers. The more the animal struggled the more the branches wrapped tighter. The horse's wild, white eyes suddenly produced a pair of pupils that saw Jeremy. The horse trembled violently and began thrashing against its bonds, trying to break free.

Jeremy placed a single hand on the horse's flank, seeking to quiet the—

FLASH.

Like magic he was inside the war horse, seeing every detail of the great stallion like a repairman opening the back of a Swiss pocket watch… that is, if the repairman could also feel the watch's emotions… which now shouted *TERROR* in a loud voice. Jeremy wanted to calm the horse but didn't know how. Tiny tremors rippled through muscles and suddenly the horse's inner structure was translated into schematics—like three-dimensional MRI scans. Jeremy reached with his mind, searching but finding no injuries. Fear rippled through the horse again.

Fear… but not for the stallion's own safety, but for his—

Master.

Jeremy pulled his mind from the horse… and saw the hiding place at once. The stallion, wearing a saddle and bridle, suddenly calmed and stood at attention with eyes focused on a tangle of brush a dozen yards away—eyes riveted like an army private waiting on orders from his sergeant. Crossing over bodies of fallen knights, Jeremy approached the cluster of leaves and branches, noticing how they lay one on top of the other unnaturally as if concealing something.

Concealing what?

Hands trembling, Jeremy took hold of a large branch and lifted—

Aaaaargh!!!

A loud snarl sounded from the shadows beneath, the tip of a sword blade jabbing between two of Jeremy's ribs and sending a stabbing pain that caused him to jerk backward. The sword point remained pressed into Jeremy. Looking down, he counted himself lucky that it hadn't broken the skin. The blade began shaking and then fell with a tiny clatter on the branches beneath. Jeremy almost dropped the large branch but stopped upon seeing a pair of eyes, human eyes, that stared up at him in relief.

"Thought you were a *slinker*," a voice rasped. "My apologies. Hope you're not grievously wounded."

Slinker?

Jeremy ran a finger across a small rent in his shirt and it came away with a trickle of blood. "Just a small cut," he said without thinking. He blinked away tears that had appeared after the initial eruption of pain. The sword's tip had glided between the folds of Jeremy's Lewisville High School letter jacket and the shock of the sudden violence caused Jeremy's legs to wobble. With a loud grunt, Jeremy threw the large branch aside.

"Fortunate for you I'm close to death, otherwise I would've skewered you," the man said… for it was a man that stared up at him.

"Uh… yeah… that would've been bad," was all Jeremy could say, still shaking. Quickly, Jeremy pulled away more brush. "A pretty good hiding place!"

"Wasn't my idea."

Encased in armor, the man wore the same tunic as the other fallen knights showing a blindfolded eagle in flight holding a sword. But this man had ribbons and a sash with strange designs. *A general, perhaps?* An ornamented helmet lay amongst leaves behind the man. Jeremy stared down at the man's thigh from where a stream of blood flowed from a large gash. "We need to bind that wound."

A bitter laugh escaped the man's lips. "No use. Severed an artery. I've managed to live this long…" A pause as the man's eyes blinked. Jeremy noticed how pale his face was, even in the dim light of the twin moons. A ragged breath…

then, "Lived this long because of my great constitution. But no matter." Eyes blinked again. This time, Jeremy realized the man was studying him. "A hunter? Trapper?"

"Excuse me?"

"A damned fool, obviously." The man suddenly glared at Jeremy. "You're not part of the king's retinue, are you boy?"

Jeremy didn't know what a *retinue* was and so blurted out the first words that came into his head. "Should I be?"

"Retinue, hah! A bloody herd of boot lickers that should never have left the palace. And... a complete waste of my time." The man's eyes blinked and went vacant. Jeremy glanced at the man's chest and was reassured by the slow rise and fall of his chest. Lips moved, now more slowly and with effort. "Kenghas Arga has claimed a king and an army. The von Drokken line has met its end in the ancient city. Thought we could make a successful retreat... but, we were too slow." The last words came in a rasp. The blind eagle holding the sword on his tunic rose feebly.

"You speak English," Jeremy blurted out... and then cursed himself, seeing the man was on the verge of dying.

Eyes snapped open and suddenly the man was studying him with a new intensity. Upon seeing the Lewisville Raptor emblem on the front of Jeremy's jacket the man's eyes widened, his voice suddenly infused with a new strength. "Boy... you never said *where* you were from!" It wasn't a question, but a demand.

Jeremy blinked down at the man who continued to examine every inch of Jeremy's clothes and hair. Forcing down a feeling of alarm, Jeremy jerked his thumb over his shoulder. "Back there."

"Where?!"

"Old... dead city—with aliens—did you see the beacon thing? Big light in the sky?"

"Aliens?"

Jeremy jerked his thumb again, toward the glade of corpses. "Like these..."

The man tried lifting himself up to get a better look at Jeremy, eyes incredulous. "*You* were the one who set off Paladin's beacon?"

"Uh... yeah... the big light," Jeremy stammered. "Probably hit a switch, sir. Didn't mean to, really."

The man fell back, eyes staring into the sky above Jeremy. When he spoke, his voice came in the smallest of whispers. "After all this time..."

An awkward silence ensued. Unsure of what else to say, Jeremy began to clear more of the brush away, trying to avoid the man's eyes. A sigh escaped from the knight and Jeremy stopped.

"Lord Wilmot, commander of the Knights Aequitas, your humble ser—"

Eyes fluttered and Wilmot seemed to pass out. Frustration flooded through Jeremy and he looked around for a canteen, jug, *anything* with water. But no canteen or jug lay in sight. "Is there water close by?" Jeremy asked.

Eyes fluttered again and Wilmot asked in a hopeful voice, "You have water?" He looked up at Jeremy expectantly.

"There isn't any, sir, unless you know of a source—"

"Beer—ice cold—that would be better!"

"Uh... beer," Jeremy groaned, hoping the man's demise wasn't going to turn into a scene of raving lunacy. "I'd get you a doctor, but—"

"On this planet, a reliable physician is as scarce as good beer," Wilmot spat. Wind moaned through the trees, stirring the damp hair that hung around the knight's forehead. Jeremy guessed the man's age to be in his forties and now Wilmot was staring up at Jeremy like he was seeing an old acquaintance. "Haven't had an ice cold beer since"—Wilmot raised a finger and pointed toward the big 'L' on Jeremy's jacket—"since the day I left Lewis-ville." He enunciated both parts of Lewisville as if it were a distant memory. Jeremy's jaw slowly dropped from shock.

Lewisville?

Jeremy's eyes blinked, not believing his ears.

Lewisville?

"And your name would be?"

Speechless and dumb. Jeremy couldn't even move his lips for a response. *How does this medieval knight know of Lewisville?*

"You came a long way, boy. Don't go all shy on me now. Your name!"

Jeremy cleared his throat. "How… uh, d-d-d-do you know about Lewisville?" Jeremy stuttered.

"My son…" Wilmot's voice faltered and then came out strained. "My *son* graduated from your high school, that's why."

"What was his name?"

"I asked you first," Wilmot rasped, "and time is running out." Jeremy noticed that the knight's breathing was coming in wheezing gasps.

"Jeremy Austin."

Wilmot's eyes narrowed. "Any relation to Dr. Victor Austin?"

"Father."

Wilmot regarded Jeremy thoughtfully. And then a look of pleasure came over the man's face. "A great man."

"You know him?" Jeremy blurted out.

"Know him?" Wilmot chuckled. "My soldiers knew me as Lord Frederick Wilmot, commander of the Knights Aequitas, defender of the Freedom Wall, slayer of Shadow scum." The knight sighed, eyes glazing over for a fraction of a second before refocusing on Jeremy. "I came to this land just like you—but as Wilfred Littencott, security advisor to the TerraGen Universal expedition. And your father is a great leader—"

"I have to find him!" Jeremy declared. The hope of reuniting with his father was like a jolt of electricity racing through every nerve in his body. "Is he close by?"

"Hard to say," Wilmot/Littencott said.

"Where are all the other members of the expedition?"

"Scattered...many dead," Wilmot whispered, eyes staring blankly toward the sky. His lips curled with distaste. "Your father was betrayed. Many of the expedition were murdered. It was only Victor's quick thinking that allowed the rest of us to survive." Wilmot's eyes fastened back on Jeremy. "And now, here you are."

"What of Erik? He came *months* before me?"

Another wave of pleasure crossed Wilmot's face and he only whispered one word: "Legendary." Sudden concern chased the pleasure from the knight's face. "Why are you here?"

"To find my father!" The words poured from Jeremy in a storm of pent up frustration. "We brought men—with guns—"

"Foolish," Wilmot said derisively.

"We came to rescue you!" Jeremy was shocked at Wilmot's attitude.

The knight's face became cold and the eyes even colder. "There won't be any rescue on this planet, even your own. Your father has many enemies and now you'll be hunted down for slaughter—"

"Yeah, I know. I've already met one."

"And survived. Lucky you."

Jeremy shrugged. "If you consider throwing yourself off a cliff *lucky!*"

Wilmot chuckled and then winced in pain. A fit of coughing wracked his body, back arching with pain. Exhausted, Wilmot lay still, eyes clenched tight, jaw muscles taut from the pain. He relaxed in sudden relief and spoke, eyes still closed, "If this body wasn't expiring I would take you to the great Victor Austin."

"Could you point me in the right direction?" Jeremy felt guilty even asking the question but he was lost on this planet and the only man who could help him was bleeding out. And then Jeremy realized that Wilmot's eyes were fixed on the sky above. Dead. *Crap-ola.* Jeremy reached out a hand to mercifully close the eyelids—

Eyes shifted to Jeremy. *Not dead! You've got to kidding!* "Grakken..."

Jeremy's eyes blinked in confusion, still surprised at Wilmot's sudden return to the living.

"Grakken!" Wilmot croaked.

"I don't know what that is—" Jeremy began but Wilmot interrupted.

"They've found you already! Just...*run,* son of Austin! And pray there isn't a rider."

A shadow passed over them, casting the knight's face into darkness for the briefest of seconds.

"Run!!!" Wilmot croaked louder. And then in a whisper he said it again, "Run..." Air escaped from Wilmot's lips as his head lolled to one side, eyes staring blankly into the sky— this time *really* dead.

A loud scream. Branches raking back and forth.

Jeremy wheeled to see the white stallion thrashing against the small trees and vines that still held the great horse like chains. It screamed in terror, sending shivers down Jeremy's back.

Darkness. Danger. The beating of air.

Spinning, Jeremy sensed the attack—a massive shadow—and dove sideways. Great talons came within a razor's edge of his head. Air blew passed like an eighteen-wheeler on the highway as Jeremy rolled over on the ground. A massive force impacted against pine and fir trees, snapping branches and shaking the towering trees that guarded the dead Wilmot's body. Jeremy gained his feet and stared in horror—

Bat-like... no, prehistoric... his mind tried to comprehend the creature that thrashed amongst the branches and shook a hail of pinecones that dropped to the ground in a staccato of *plops.* Elongated jaws that reminded him of a chainsaw snapped viciously at its bonds. A dark, leathery head swiveled toward him and black eyes saw Jeremy. Over ten feet tall, the beast's wings, like the stallion, were trapped in the tangle of vines and branches.

Scrawwwwwk!

Jaws parted in the beast's cry to reveal jagged, fang-like teeth that snapped at Jeremy. A dozen yards away the stallion also snapped at its bonds—fear and terror from the horse assaulted Jeremy's mind. He crossed the distance toward the horse—three, four, five strides—and began clawing at the vines that had wrapped around the stallion's legs, hooves and chest. But the horse's own terror made the work almost impossible. The thrashing of hooves almost took one of Jeremy's fingers. This was a war horse trained for battle and the violence it sent against the vines and boughs knocked Jeremy to the ground. Still, he was able to free one hoof—then a leg—then another hoof and leg—a loud scream from the stallion sounded in his ear—not from terror, but warning—

The grakken.

Jeremy jerked his head back toward the final resting place of Wilmot—darkness and violence shook the trees in a cascade of pine needles and falling branches. Like a hideous demon from the underworld, the grakken beat and hammered against the smaller trees and branches that still wrapped around its leathery body. It jerked backward. Vines snapped. A smaller fern shattered. The bat-like beast—*a hundred times larger than a bat, even the vampire version*, Jeremy's mind noted—had the power of a whole chariot of horses.

Jeremy's hands scrambled to pull another vine free from the stallion. Three legs had been untangled. A blur of movement around his head and he realized the stallion was snapping its jaws and pulling at branches. Fear and panic were transferred back and forth between horse and boy. A quick glance to his right—

The grakken was almost free, violently tugging with one wing wrapped in vines.

Loud *shrieking*—blasting his left ear drum—

"Okay, okay!" Jeremy shouted at the stallion who continued to neigh in panic just inches from Jeremy's ear. "I'm focused!" His hands ripped at a branch and the horse's fourth leg was free—

WHOMP!!!

Jeremy fell to his knees as the earth moved. The grakken had pulled free of its last bond and crashed to the ground. It lay dazed. Leathery head rested on a mountain boulder where a small stain of blood spread. *It's not supernatural,* Jeremy realized with a small kindling of hope.

The hope was quickly dashed as the creature stirred.

Not supernatural but very resilient. A weapon. I must get a weapon or I'm dead meat, Jeremy's mind calculated. Wait... I'm on a battlefield. Weapons here are like boy band cd's at a collector's store. He left the stallion and moved into the glade of death. An axe showed—*too small.*

CRASH!

Jeremy jerked around—the grakken stirred but was still moving lethargically on the ground as if drugged. It was the stallion who'd made the loud noise and now sat back on its haunches, free of its wooded bonds after a final, violent pull at the branches.

Hissing. Cold, dark eyes focused on Jeremy like laser points of doom. The grakken rolled and came up on two clawed feet. *The axe would have to do,* Jeremy grimaced. Grasping the handle, he raised it and marveled at the weapon's weight— *more than marveling, actually. This sucker's heavy!* Hissing sounded again and he realized the grakken was stalking him, head lowered, a long, red tongue flicking over jagged fangs, feet taking small, careful steps as it moved toward Jeremy.

Coach Hayfield had always told him he had a great arm to be quarterback but the accuracy of a five year old girl with dyslexia—hence, his role as a wide receiver because catching footballs was no problem. Twenty yards separated him from the grakken, and it could've been two feet because he knew the creature had tremendous leaping ability.

Can't wait to be clawed to death, his mind warned.

Lifting the axe, he said a quick prayer and then let if fly, using all of his strength. Tumbling end over end, the axe defied his coach and the five year old girl and accurately thudded into the grakken, partially embedding the blade into the creature's chest. *Scrawwwwwk!* The grakken thrashed in a pain maddened circle, trying to dislodge the axe. It balanced on one leg and used its other talon to grasp the axe's handle. With a loud scream of pain, it pulled the axe free and let it drop to the ground. Cold eyes jerked back to Jeremy—

"Really?!!!" Jeremy shouted without thinking… then turned and ran.

He felt the pounding behind him. His bowels turned liquid, arms churning, knees flashing up and down, his feet dodging mounds of the dead, eyes searching for the next weapon—

Hot, fetid breath washed over him from behind.

THUMP!

The impact came at the middle of his back—the feeling reminiscent of being nailed by a defensive back just after making a catch—it catapulted Jeremy forward and his body flew fifteen feet through the air. He hit a mound of turf and rolled instinctively. Pain lanced up from his back and side. His right hand dug out the object that was digging into his ribs and turned up a knight's helmet. His eyes blinked… eyes that saw light reflecting off a long, metal object.

WHOMP—WHOMP—WHOMP—

Jeremy jerked around, rising to one knee. The huge bat monster took slow, measured steps, not afraid of losing its prey. Possessed by a killing frenzy, the grakken's jaws snapped over and over again, saliva flying in all directions, eyes focused on its next victim… Jeremy. Obviously a master of the skies, but on ground, the creature was at a disadvantage. It shambled through the mounds of dead knights and aliens like a doe on newborn legs.

Struggling to his feet, Jeremy's eyes again noticed the

light reflecting off a long object—a long *bladed* object—the long blade of a knight's sword. Grasping the sword's pommel with both hands, Jeremy raised the blade and pivoted—

Well... he tried to pivot but the weight of the sword caused his arms to lag behind. His mind screamed in frustration, *guys actually fight with this?!* And then terror filled him as the grakken thundered toward him. Over three feet in length, the sword was difficult to raise but Jeremy managed it—just barely, the tip wavering unsteadily.

Scrawwwwwk! Another wave of fetid breath blasted his face. Jeremy snarled at the grakken as the creature lumbered to a stop just yards from him. Ten feet of prehistoric creature stood over him, black eyes glancing from the Jeremy to the sword. It hesitated.

"Taste this!" Jeremy snarled, waving the sword closer to the grakken's long, razored jaws.

Hissing came in reply. The leathered head lowered and the jaws parted as it *hissed* again. The beast's head cocked sideways, eyes still flashing from the sword to Jeremy, calculating...

The attack came suddenly.

With blinding speed the grakken's head flashed past the tip of Jeremy's sword and he twisted out of reflex—his reflexes were good—razored fangs snapped air close to his right elbow. He tried to bring the blade down on the creature's head but he was too slow. The grakken's head jerked back up... and then cocked sideways again. *It's just playing with me—playing with its food, more like it!* He panted and tried to will strength back into his legs which had gone weak from the sudden violence.

Hissing. The grakken's head feinted left then came back around the right—

Jeremy threw himself backward, desperate to escape those jaws.

Jaws that snapped air.

The grakken leapt into the air, talons raised for tearing.

Jeremy frantically raised the sword. Massive wings beat the air and the grakken slewed sideways to avoid the sword's point. Jeremy rolled sideways and came up in a crouch. He tried to raise the sword but the claw of one of the creature's leathery wings slammed down on the sword blade and Jeremy felt it ripped from his hands. Jaws came forward, white fangs flashing—

Diving sideways, Jeremy felt the heat of the grakken's breath. He rolled and came back to his feet. A shadow rose in front of him as the great beast rose up on its legs, wings flexing on both sides, claws twitching. It slowly took one step forward… and then another.

Jeremy knew his end was near. The cold eyes assessing him would be the last things he would see before those jaws ripped him open as easily as a knife through butter.

Another step.

There were no regrets. Just terror. He could smell the beast's foulness—like rotted flesh with a touch of reptile for added flavor. Jeremy threw himself backward, hearing the squish of liquids and knowing he'd just landed on a bloodied corpse—his own corpse would be added to the battlefield shortly… or eaten—*eaten? Really???*

Two steps. *Hissing.* It was like a dance… of death.

The grakken's head flashed forward. Jeremy threw himself backward and this time he slammed against a whole pile of corpses. The grakken's jaws snapped and he felt a sharp pain through his left shoe. Panic raced through his brain. Prehistoric jaws had his foot in a vise of pain. He kicked—over and over—landing blows on the leathered snout but the grakken's fangs were fastened like a petite woman finding a size five shoe at a Black Friday, 7 am, one hour only sale. More kicks. More useless kicks. Jeremy's face was bathed in sweat and his breath was ragged. Another pain, higher up his leg—

One of the grakken's talons had latched onto his left calf just inches above its jaws—the jaws released his shoe and the beast seemed to grin expectantly, saliva dripping. It held his left leg like a trophy. A low growl rumbled out of the creature's chest.

This is it…

Jeremy waited for the flash of fangs and the unbearable pain that would follow.

Scrawwwwwk!

The grakken screamed—not a scream of triumph—but pain… it screamed in pain! Jeremy's eyes blinked.

Scrawwwwwk! He felt a release as the grakken let go of his leg.

And then Jeremy saw the white muzzle of the stallion's jaws that were clamped onto the grakken's neck. Leathery beast and white horse thrashed sideways as the grakken tried to dislodge the stallion. The horse held on, it's own weight tilting the grakken sideways—*holding on for how long?* Jeremy pushed against his corpse backstop and rolled up to one knee. He searched the area around his feet, eyes darting from dead knight to dead alien—knight to alien—knight—

Another sword. Greedy hands grasped the sword hilt and Jeremy pulled it out from under a fallen knight.

Thrashing behind.

Jeremy spun around—and this time is was a *for reals* spin because the sword was vastly shorter than the other one—topping out at just two feet in length.

The grakken crouched, the horse still fastened to its neck, and then exploded upward like a bucking bronco at a cowboy rodeo. And like a good cowboy the stallion stayed in the saddle, relatively speaking—the stallion's jaws remained clenched deep into the grakken's knotted flesh. Blood frothed the horse's mouth, showing dark in the moonlight. Jeremy crept forward, knowing he couldn't run, knowing he couldn't leave the horse to be killed by the much heavier grakken, knowing that if he ran, the winged beast would just hunt him down anyway.

The decision is practically made for me, he thought grimly.

The grakken's head lifted and black eyes saw the

new threat as Jeremy crept to within a few feet of the two combatants.

"Enough is enough, you prehistoric pain in my—" Jeremy began.

Bucking. Twisting violently. The grakken violently leapt upwards and spun in a half-circle. To Jeremy's dismay, the white stallion's jaws lost their grip and the horse was flung sideways. White horse, mane and saddle slammed into a collection of alien corpses with a resounding *THUD!*

Jeremy didn't hesitate. He rushed toward the grakken, arms extended, sword blade aimed for the creature's heart. Sensing the attack, the grakken twisted, wings billowing outward, one talon rising from the ground. But Jeremy was quicker—the same quickness that would've made him an All-State wide receiver (if he hadn't been in a coma). He felt the resistance as the sword's tip penetrated the creature's hide—felt the resistance and then the sudden rush of metal through flesh. His hands were bathed in hot liquid as the sword hilt met the grakken's hide—

But not where the creature's heart was located. His eyes blinked and he cursed the five year old, dyslexic girl that had missed the mark by *two whole inches*.

Razored jaws snapped at his face. Jeremy jerked backward, escaping the fangs and rancid breath and the sudden beating of the grakken's wings. Landing on his rump, he stared up. The grakken was in full terror mode, twisting one way and then another, jaws snapping as it hopped on one foot while trying to dislodge the sword with the other. Red liquid poured from where the short sword had penetrated under the left wing. The sword's tip was bright red where it protruded from the beast's upper back.

Jeremy backed further away, scooting his rump over the pile of corpses and trying not to think about the gore underneath. The winged creature never even looked in his direction, filling the glade with its screaming agony. It began spinning clockwise in a vain attempt to dislodge the sword.

It was mesmerizing to watch the alien creature in its death throes. A loud *whinny* snapped his head around.

Standing on wobbly legs, the stallion was looking at Jeremy. It *whinnied* a second time... *from impatience!* The white horse, its flowing mane fluttering in the night breeze, had turned his body and was taking a step away from where the grakken continued to thrash and spin. The horse shook his head, beckoning.

"Are you asking me out for a ride?" Jeremy shouted to the stallion.

It whinnied in response, shaking his head up and down and stamping his front hooves into the turf.

"I accept."

Jeremy skirted the grakken's throes of pain and approached the stallion. Grasping the pommel, Jeremy put one foot in a stirrup and pulled himself up and into the saddle. He barely had time to grasp the reins before the stallion began trotting toward the western side of the mountain glade. Weeds and small brush whipped past. As young man and horse left the scene of carnage the foulness of decay was replaced with the scents of pine and mountain ferns. Wind whipped his hair and he zipped his letter jacket to shut out the cold.

"I'm alive and I have *you* to thank!" he said to the stallion, patting its neck. His mind replayed the horror of the last few minutes. *I'm alive! I've survived a prehistoric killing machine and the Grim Reaper!* The image of the dying Wilmot floated into his thoughts and his final words came back.

My father was betrayed. His enemies want to kill me.
Welcome to Genesis...

EPILOGUE

PREDATOR AND PREY

S HE THRASHED CONTINUALLY for an hour until finally collapsing with exhaustion. Grakkens had been designed for stamina but not for having shafts of metal thrust through their flesh with the resulting blood loss. Makksis had long forgotten about killing her prey, forgotten about the directives of Mindbender, her master, but she hadn't forgotten about the shaft of metal that *said prey* had deposited underneath the grakken's left wing. Her life force poured out of both sides of the wound.

Scrawwwwwwk!

Her cry was heard by no human or alien.

Scrawwwwwk!

Pain wasn't something foreign with the grakken, just inconvenient. Her flesh had tremendous healing properties—the beast screeched her cry more out of anger than pain. After an hour of biting and clawing at the sword—causing new waves of searing pain—the grakken had managed to pull the blade halfway out. The sword protruded a good foot and a half and wobbled up and down whenever the beast moved. The grakken placed her right talon onto the sword's pommel, claws snapping around the metal... then pushed. With a loud *slurp* the blade came free and clattered onto a discarded warrior's shield.

Scrawwwwwk!

The cry echoed off the surrounding trees and died away in the wind that swirled leaves around the fallen bodies. There wasn't an answering cry.

MetaUniversal Genetics. *Corporate sharks. Technology whores.* Robert Morton had overheard Lachlan Evans' earlier conversation with Hicks, and he'd done his best to control the fury that burned inside. This expedition was funded by *his money*—millions of dollars siphoned from CIA bank accounts around the world—and damned if he would continue to watch the expedition be led by the MetaUniversal mole, Lachlan Evans. Besides, Evans' venture was an abject failure so far—they were no closer to finding Victor Austin's original team of scientists, and he suspected Evans was lost.

Morton stalked over to where Evans, Keene, and Hicks huddled in conversation. Men had died—a score at least—and now their company had regrouped. Many of the mercenaries had suffered injuries. Many would never leave this valley alive. Morton approached the *cabal*—the traitorous MetaUniversal leaders—who glared at him as he stepped inside a huge ring of boulders that rose up on either side.

Beyond the boulders, the ground dropped away several hundred feet to a valley that twinkled with hundreds of fires. A sound reached Morton's ears—*drumbeats—thousands of drums*. It made his skin crawl.

Evans and Keene, both bandaged and bloody, seemed mesmerized by the vast army camped in the valley. Hicks' voice trembled with nervousness. *"They came out with all their troops, a huge army, as numerous as the sand on the seashore—*Joshua, chapter eleven."

Great, Morton thought with exasperation. *Things must be desperate if we're quoting Scripture.* The CIA man looked down at the fires dotting the valley floor and wondered just how they were going to make it off this planet alive. "If that army is any bit as good as the four creatures who just killed half of our men... I suspect that *meeting our deadlines* will be the least of our worries. Just what other surprises do you think are in store for us, gentlemen?"

"Adaptation takes time," Keene said defensively.

Lachlan Evans glared at Morton. "Our men will do better."

"Our men... or MetaUniversal's?" Morton asked coldly.

Evans moved away from Keene, but said nothing.

"I gave you millions of dollars, and I expected a well-trained, and *loyal* security force—loyal to the United States!"

Evan's face went hard. "Enough already—"

"Correction, Mister Evans." Morton was losing his temper, but he didn't care. "I have lost all patience with your poor results and obvious treachery." He could see the momentary shock in Evans' eyes and felt a surge of triumph. "I paid for this excursion and I say it's time for a change!"

Silence... except for the echo of drumbeats. Morton watched as Evans and Keene exchanged looks.

"I don't like to be played, Mr. Evans." Morton's voice sounded almost petulant. He cursed himself inwardly.

"You had no intention of giving all of the technology to

the government," Evans said.

True. Very true. But this is my expedition and this pup needs to be put down. Confidence soared into Morton and he opened his mouth to speak—and then confidence drained off his face—

Evans was pointing the muzzle of a gun at him.

"This expedition has *always* been MetaUniversal's," Evans said without emotion. The pistol in his hand was unwavering. "We're taking over this world. And we thank you for generously providing our budget."

"Now, see here, Evans—"

Morton saw the gun's muzzle flash.

E VANS STUDIED THE BLOOD seeping from Robert Morton's temple with detached interest. *Finally, the overbearing power broker was silenced... and dead*, he thought with cold relief.

"What are going to do now?" Keene's voice broke the tension.

Evans put the pistol back in its holster. "We adapt."

"How do we get back home?" Hicks voice was small, almost childlike.

Evans looked at the research director, wanting to shoot him as well. But the scientist, with his computer programming skills, was a necessary thorn in his side. "We find the Austin boy. Our adversaries want him, and that makes the boy valuable... giving us leverage."

"Do you suppose gun shots can be heard in the valley?" Hicks said, leaning between two boulders and staring down the mountainside.

Drum continued to echo up from the valley floor.

"Aliens *might* have pickets," Keene's graveled voice said begrudgingly. Keene turned and barked an order to the assassin, Duarte Vega. "I want to be ready to travel in five minutes. Stretcher the wounded as best as possible—"

Vega walked into the cluster of boulders. He sneered, "I *could* shoot them."

"Where's your sense of camaraderie, Mr. Vega?" Keene said with humor.

"Lost it decades ago in Libya," Vega replied. "Along with my patriotism."

"Let's not eat our own... just yet," Evans suggested coldly. He had also considered killing the severely wounded. Speed would be a life or death factor if the aliens returned in larger numbers. Still, a soldier with a shattered leg could still wield an assault rifle.

"For now..." Vega said.

29:20:11. The numbers shown brightly on Evans' bracelet. He flicked it off, mind working... and then noticed Dr. Hicks staring at him just a foot away.

"Less than thirty days to find a boy, evade an army of alien super warriors and..." Hicks motioned with his hands as if to include the entire planet of Genesis, "locate a Portal in a world more hostile than anything I've read about in books. My powers for unbridled optimism are failing me right now."

"Yes..." That was all Evans could say in response. The enormity of their task would paralyze each member of the expedition if dwelt on for too long. *Action*—action was the only solution for a problem so depressing that a cyanide pill was seen as a favorable solution.

Hicks wasn't finished. "Still, the brightest minds in science went on the first expedition."

"And probably dead, judging by the natives—"

"Oh, they're not dead."

Evans blinked. "And you know this... how?"

The portly research director smiled with his old enthusiasm. "Victor Austin was brightest of them all. If anyone could outwit aliens and sorcerers, it's him!"

Evans could only grimace. "I'm sure." He turned and walked out of the boulders and breathed relief to be away from the Pollyanna researcher.

THE SMILE FADED FROM HICK'S face as he watched the ex-CIA agent stride away. Lachlan Evans... *the tyrant takes me for a fool.* Hicks wasn't a cunning man, didn't possess a devious heart, trusted others too easily—and yet, now he smiled. Victories on this planet and with these mercenaries were small and few. He relished this one little victory. Morton's body lay just feet away, growing cold in the mountain air. *No one even pays attention to Dr. Rudolf Hicks,* the research director thought with satisfaction.

He didn't like morgues, hospitals, anything with dead bodies.

Except now.

He bent down and ignored the sightless eyes of Robert Morton. He kept his eyes from the stream of blood from the hole in Morton's forehead—blood that had dried and was now turning black. Like a surgeon performing a delicate surgery, Hicks' fingers slid the bracelet timer off the wrist of Morton, slipping it smoothly in his pants pocket. Standing up, he smiled and walked out of the ring of boulders, giving himself a mental pat on the back.

I *THOUGHT I LEFT CHRISTMAS BEHIND,* Marissa moaned inwardly. A thousand firelights twinkled below... but they weren't putting her in the holiday spirit— more like a *Tolkien nightmare.*

"Gnomes?"

Wind whipped at her hair and she patted her face— her cheeks were frozen—*where was the flight attendant with the extra blanket... just sayin'.* She pulled the wizard's cloak tighter against the chill of a thousand feet above sea level— *I guess this planet has seas,* her razor sharp wit reasoned. *And Gnomes.*

"Gnomes? Really?"

"Slinkers—scabs—man-eaters—bogeymen—were-men—the scourge of Kankor," the wizard's voice rattled off.

"Scourge?!" she shouted. "There's a whole lot of scourges down there!"

"I hadn't noticed." The wizard's voice was thick with sarcasm.

"Ha ha. Funny old wizard!"

"Wait until you get to know me better."

They were flying over the army of the Gnome King. Thousands of fires meant thousands of killer aliens. Her knees gripped tighter to *big bird*—the wizard's roc—*whatever*—and she was thankful.

"I appreciate the flyover," she yelled over her shoulder to where the wizard sat, leather reins in hand, driving—*scratch that*, piloting a giant bird like a character out of an alternative reality, medieval punk-like graphic novel.

"Fly… over?"

"Your scourge—I mean, slinkers—"

"Just say Gnomes, Marissa!" Leo shouted from behind the wizard. The pudgy son of Kaiser Tyrannus was straddling the wizard at the rear and holding on, white knuckled, to the old man's waist as if he were on a ride at an amusement park.

"Let's just say, up close and personal, your Gnomes scare the tee-tee out of me!"

"And yet you survived," the wizard quipped, his sarcasm still on full throttle.

"Uh… arrow in the *shoulder!*" Marissa growled.

"Still breathing—"

"Thanks to a little of your wizarding magic!"

"On the inside, I'm taking a bow," the wizard said with a hearty bowl of cheerfulness. "On the outside, I'm getting a little tired of your prattle."

"*Scant survival* might best describe my last experience with your Gnomes," Marissa shouted with her bowl of spitefulness. "But from now on? I'd prefer to keep a good distance from the aliens! A thousand feet above… works for me. Thank you!" She looked down at the thousands of campfires below and jerked back from the sudden vertigo.

She glanced over her shoulder at the wizard, "Yo, captain my captain…"

"Another question," the wizard groaned.

"Just one."

"Perhaps I let the roc do a rolling maneuver and let you have another face-to-face with *your* alien friends."

"It's the last question, scout's honor—"

"Five—four—three—"

"Why the big army?" Marissa screamed. "Are you and the good fairies in some kind of war?"

"What's a fairy?"

"Loaded question, wizard!"

"I mean it! What's a fairy?"

"Gnomes, fairies—it's rhetorical! Seriously, what kind of war have we stumbled into?"

"Marissa, you ask the craziest questions!" Leo shouted over the roaring of the wind.

"What war?!" she repeated stubbornly.

Clouds suddenly covered the twin moons and the wizard's face was cast into darkness, giving him an ominous look. The old man's voice added a touch of menace. "The first Gnome army in centuries has marched out of the south. Their general is the Gnome King. But the real power behind Mindbender and his minions is the Shadow Lord. *He* controls this army and *he* is only interested in one thing."

"Killing stupid humans from Earth?" Marissa suggested.

"Actually? Yes."

BARKING AND THE GNASHING of teeth followed a stream of guttural speech that sounded like dull saws biting through wood. The response was violent: lots of shoving and clawed hands grasping knives and strange, alien blades. Tension filled the dark woods high in the mountains. Three aliens faced one defiant rebel—the fourth alien who now had hold of Selene's wrist.

"You think he wants to eat her?" Alex whispered the question to Patrick, who dutifully rolled his eyes. Alexander Leach, Junior was the scion of Lewisville's wealthiest family but he easily could've been the dumbest pick from a litter of St. Bernard puppies—and that's being generous.

"I doubt he wants to take her on a date," Patrick hissed. He couldn't take his eyes off the over-sized alien hand that was swallowing Selene's wrist. It pissed him off. Pissed him really, really off. His hands lifted as one... and the fact that both his hands were bound tightly made his anger, in all practicality, impotent.

To her credit, Selene remained calm.

"I think he wants to eat me," she said to Patrick in full voice, not bothering to whisper. "And he smells." Her captor suddenly stepped backward, barking a snarl at her and jerking Selene violently around. "That was rude," she added, matter-of-fact.

But the action had brought an immediate response from the alien's leader—a loud rumble of a growl that sounded like an African lion before killing its prey. A head taller than the rest, the leader faced the rebel alien; the remaining two warriors stood behind, splitting time between watching Patrick and Alex, and glaring at the incorrigible alien who wanted to sample the exotic, captured food.

There was a metallic scraping as the leader slowly drew a knife. Up to that point, he'd taken up a posture of scorn, arms folded across his chest as if the rebellious alien was too insignificant to warrant his attention. But now, the leader had obviously lost patience.

Fear filled the rebel alien's eyes. Pupils darted from the leader to the other two warriors, then nervously back to leader. Taking another step backward, the rebel thrust Selene in front as a shield. Wayward, nervous eyes studied the knife. A guttural language infused with fear poured from the rebel, saliva spraying, eyes darting from the knife to the leader's face. He pulled violently on Selene's wrist and the girl let out a cry of pain.

"Do something!" Patrick shouted at the leader without thinking.

The leader suddenly turned and thrust a face marred by battle and a set of teeth marred by the misuse of genetics. And then the leader snarled at Patrick—

"Siiii-lence ooo-mun!"

It was deep voice. A raspy voice. An alien voice. And yet it was a voice speaking the English language. For some reason that filled Patrick with more horror than the thought of being eaten by these creatures.

"I'm gonna be sick," Selene mumbled weakly.

Brown, yellowed teeth—teeth looking like a handful of golf tees having fallen on the ground and pointing in all directions—these formed a defiant smile in the face of the rebel alien as he flashed a challenge at the leader. Selene whimpered again as the rebel alien pulled her backward.

A flick of the wrist.

It was so fast Patrick only saw the movement as a blur.

And then blood was dripping down Selene's forehead, down her nose, a stream of dark red falling onto the forest floor. Her eyes opened wide and then slowly moved upward... to where the leader's knife protruded from the right eye socket of the rebel alien. Rebellious lips closed and the smile faded. The remaining left eye's pupil dilated and then rolled upward a split second before the alien tilted backward and fell—dead before hitting pine needles and brush.

"I think—" Selene began and then bent over to vomit. Except most of her vomiting was nothing more than a dry heave because half an energy bar didn't amount to much.

"Nice shot," Alex mumbled in awe.

"They speak our language," Patrick whispered, eyes unable to leave the alien leader who sauntered toward the fallen rebel. A quick *slurp* of liquid and the knife came out of the skull with ease.

"We're not in Kansas, Dorothy," Alex shot back under his breath.

Patrick winced at Alex's attempt at wit.

Selene was yanked back to her feet by the leader who then unceremoniously shoved the girl into Patrick's arms. He felt her weight as she slumped against him. Her shoulders heaved and shook and he realized that this fashionista of Chinese descent was crying. "They're going to kill and eat us all," she said in the barest of whispers.

"Uh... not... right... away," Alex said, his voice shaking.

Patrick looked at Alex. The jock's eyes were wide and his lips quivered. He was staring at the scene of conflict and Patrick followed his gaze. Patrick's own bowels began to turn to liquid.

Sounds of metal slicing through flesh were followed by *gnashing* and *slurping* noises.

They were *eating* the rebel alien.

Like a food truck parked in the midst of a hungry mob, the dead alien was being dismembered and eaten by the other three. The carnage and violence caused Patrick to turn and vomit. Beside him, Alex was doing the same. Patrick's chest heaved, taking in deep breaths. His mind worked furiously for an escape from this horror.

But there was no escape.

Three high school students from Lewisville were separated from their expedition and captured by aliens.

Captured by cannibal aliens.

I would like a do-over, please. He meant it as a prayer. But it was a prayer with no hope.

Patrick did something totally out of character: he began to cry.

Their stone perch was cold underneath. Marissa felt a tug on the wizard's blanket and realized Leo was trying to greedily pull more of the warm covering over to his side. She pulled back. Beside them, the wizard sat serenely smoking a long, wooden pipe. *Looks like a geriatric former child star finally escaped his Disneyland gig,* she thought. "How much longer are we gonna sit here?" she grumbled.

"Long enough for Berengyle to finish his hunt," the old man responded with just a hint of impatience.

"But I'm freezing *now!*"

"You're weak."

"I thought wizard's were kind and protective," she growled acidly.

"Those kind end up dead."

Marissa pulled her feet underneath the blanket while shifting her weight on the cold surface of the ledge. The wizard and his two earthling guests sat against a mountain cliff, the sheer stone walls blocking some of the hated wind that would occasionally blow down from the freezing upper reaches of the mountain. Light from the twin moons filtered in and out the clouds that moved swiftly in the upper atmosphere. Hundreds of feet below lay a wooded land with hills and valleys through which a ribbon of water wound like a silvery snake.

"Who is he hunting?" Leo asked.

The wizard blew a ring of gray smoke. He glanced down at Leo and there was an uncomfortable silence. Finally the wizard spoke. "Berengyle hunts an old foe."

"And that's more important than us finding a warm bed and hot food?" Marissa asked sweetly.

"If it's what I think it is—"

"What you *think?*" Marissa pressed—she was cold, hungry and to be perfectly honest... afraid of this land where Gnomes had armies and wizard's rode the night sky on the back of really big birds. And when she was cold and hungry her mouth had the tendency to run on overdrive. "Big bird is, well, really big. And has really big claws. What could possibly challenge him?"

"Many things, child."

"Like... what?"

He puffed harder on his pipe and growled. With a sigh, he spoke again. "The Shadow Lord—"

"Really bad dude. The Gnome army marches like puppets and he's the puppet master... check!"

A stream of smoke puffed angrily into the air. Marissa stole a glance and saw the wizard rolling his eyes for the umpteenth time, almost swallowing the long pipe in frustration. "He is a warlock of incredible power. Through magic and sorcery he's birthed creatures that would give your nightmares goose pimples."

"More powerful than you?" The question came from Leo.

Exhaling slowly, the wizard stared into the valley below. "In some ways, yes."

"Wonderful," Marissa moaned. "I guess we're all royally screwed."

Laughter rumbled from the old man. "Does everyone give up so easily on your... *Earth?*" He pronounced *Earth* like it was a home for incorrigible kindergarten students.

"We don't like to be on the losing team."

More chuckling from the wizard.

"Wizard? You never said *who* Berengyle was hunting," Leo suggested in a persistent voice.

"Not a who, boy," the wizard snapped, "but a *what.*"

AIR BEAT UNDER HER WINGS, and she slowly lifted skyward. Her healing prowess had seen the closing of both sides of the sword's thrust but the pain remained. As one of the ancient grakken, Makksis could function with pain. But the injury wasn't without its consequences. She could fly—her wing beating furiously and giving her lift—but without the power that made her one of the deadliest hunters of the sky.

Wind hit her from the northeast and she was blown

sideways, one wing clipping the top of a tree. Makksis was flying low and trying to blend with the dark canopy of forest underneath. She knew how far north her master had sent her. She'd hunted in enemy territory and knew that carried risk because other predators lived in these mountains. And she was injured. Trusting her radar-like senses to see oncoming obstacles, she flew just over the tree tops in a south-easterly direction.

Bank *right — left*—she narrowly avoided the dead hulk of a large oak tree that towered above the forest canopy.

Pain lanced briefly in her left wing and then settled back into a dull, persistent ache.

GHOSTING OVERHEAD, WINGS SPREAD wide and riding the upper currents, Berengyle saw the grakken narrowly miss the tree. On some level of the roc's intelligence he frowned with disappointment. Berengyle wasn't a subservient *mount* for the wizard—*snort... like a horse*—but a partner in the fight against all Shadow spawn. Roc's were infused with a high level of intelligence. They were smart *and* deadly. When a roc partnered with a rider like the wizard there was a symbiotic relationship—ideas and opinions flowed back and forth. Which is why Berengyle had informed the wizard that he'd heard the cry of an ancient foe... the grakken.

Grakkens were a rare foe and it had been decades since the roc had fought one, the wizard rarely venturing into the south where the Shadow Lord's power reigned. Now, Berengyle was relishing the opportunity to test his mettle against one of the Shadow killers.

Except this grakken was injured.

Hrrrrrmmmmffff... The roc snorted in disgust. Berengyle was tempted to let the Shadow spawn go without a fight... He watched the grakken glide past a towering crag of rock then bank left toward the east. The roc banked left without effort, now just a couple hundred feet above his prey. The grakken's head twisted left and right and then returned to looking straight ahead, satisfied it wasn't being hunted.

It did have two serviceable wings, the roc observed. *It wasn't entirely defenseless.*

Berengyle let out a war cry.

The grakken's head jerked and then it's wings folded up and it disappeared in a steep dive behind a wall of trees. The roc's wings were also folded and he flashed downward at tremendous speed, reveling in the thrill of the hunt and the spilling of Shadow blood.

 *CRAWWWWWK...*

The cry was faint and battered by the howling wind but all three humans heard it. Marissa glanced at the wizard—he huffed with satisfaction and then shoved a wad of tobacco into his pipe. Fingers flicked and a small flame appeared which the old man shoved into the pipe, puffing contentedly as small red sparks danced around the tobacco. He cut his eyes sideways and wasn't too pleased to see Marissa studying him. "Are all maiden's from your Earth as relentlessly inquisitive as you?"

"Don't get me started," she snorted. She motioned to the east. "You definitely heard *that*, right?"

"Berengyle at work, more like it."

"Hunting a… *thing?*"

"Not just any thing—a grakken!" he said with a resolute puff of his pipe.

"Sounds creepy."

"Shadow spawn and very deadly."

"A guess you see one of those every day?" Leo asked.

"A grakken hasn't been seen this far north in almost five hundred years," the wizard spoke so softly that his voice was almost lost in a burst of wind coming down the mountain.

"Release the grakken!" Marissa shouted into the wind.

Silence. Neither of her companions got the reference and Marissa just hunched down, biting her lower lip in a sullen huff. The wizard exchanged a withered look with Leo. "One more outburst like that and I will push the girl off this mountain myself," the wizard growled.

"She has a talent for making people lose their mind," Leo said matter-of-factly.

"Obviously," the wizard said. And then he turned his back and moved a few feet from the two Earthlings. A series of puffs announced that the old man had returned to his pipe.

"Five hundred years is a long time," Leo ventured. "Why now?"

Marissa glanced at the wizard and her mouth bent in a lopsided grin as she watched the wizard roll his eyes in frustration and groaning, "More questions—"

"Then... why?" Marissa inquired, giving the wizard her most serious stare.

"Are you deaf as well as daft?" the wizard snarled.

"Just curious," she retorted.

"Right now the Gnome King is hunting one of your own—an Earthling—probably a friend of yours, if it's possible for a witless fool to have friends. And while you joke and make laughter under my protection he's out there running for his life!" The wizard paused, the heat of eyes causing Marissa to shrink away.

"Hunted by this grakken?" Leo asked.

The wizard sputtered in disbelief. "Haven't you been listening?"

Shame... with a healthy dose of remorse. The realization of what the old man was saying finally dawned upon Marissa's mind. As she spoke, her voice sounded hollow in her own ears...

"Jeremy."

Acknowledgments

IN PREPARING THIS NOVEL I have been greatly influenced by the works of Michael Crichton--*Jurassic Park* provided a great blueprint; JRR Tolkein--in **War World** Books 2 & 3 the influence of Middle Earth will show itself more and more; Terry Brooks--the *Sword of Shannara* was my introduction into the world of fantasy; and, Bernard Cornwell--Richard Sharpe, Uhtred of Bebbanburg, Thomas of Hookton, Nathaniel Starbuck, and Nicholas Hook are just the handful of incredibly well crafted characters set in worlds vividly painted by a master.

Research into black holes, portals, wormholes, quantum theory and other science was done with enthusiasm and the best of intentions. Bending space via wormholes is an often fantisized dream of both scientists and readers of science fiction and this reader...er...writer is just one of millions.

However, this book is entirely fiction, and the views expressed here are my own, as are whatever factual errors exist in the text.

Jeremy and the rest of the TerraGen teenagers will continue their quest to find their parents, escape certain death and return to planet Earth as the series continues with...

For more mysteries about planet Genesis check out:
www.warworldseries.com

Turn the page for a sneak peak.

CHAPTER ONE

WIZARD'S TALE

RIDING HORSEBACK WAS HARDER THAN IT LOOKED. Three or four times he'd almost fallen off the war horse's back, a dangerous proposition considering the steep mountainside and jagged rocks. But Jeremy had always been athletically gifted and through sheer grit he'd hung on. The fear of an aerial attack had faded as the hours passed. He shivered, remembering the *scrawwwwwk* of the *grakken*, the foul stench of its breath, the loud hiss as razor-sharp talons whipped by his head. Over ten feet in height with twice the wingspan, the grakken was a man-eating bird straight out of a Jurassic nightmare. *I'll say 'no' to seconds on that one*, he thought wryly.

Ears twitched and the horse whinnied a deep, baritone rumble, as if sensing Jeremy's relief. The magical connection to the war horse allowed them to work together… noble steed and hapless rider. This wasn't Houdini magic nor the *saw a hot model in two* Vegas extravaganza—that was all illusion. This was a real, electricity coursing through your veins, mind screaming in terror… magic. His mind knew every cell, every muscle, every fiber of the horse underneath him. Connecting to the horse's thoughts? *Well, nothing to write home about there.* Jeremy could only understand vague concepts like: *flee; flee now; flee now really fast!* So it wasn't exactly a melding of equal minds. But how many people can say they share a consciousness with a war horse? *Yeah. Exactly.*

A night breeze whipped at his hair, his ears picking up the distant roar of swiftly moving water. For several hours they'd picked their way along the shadowed bluff overlooking the river, following its course. Falling hundreds of feet from a mountain cliff into the waters of that river seemed a lifetime ago… yet, it had been earlier this night. The scent of pine needles and the smell of forest damp filled his nostrils. Jeremy was unconsciously making for a tall promontory that jutted out over the river. It commanded a high view of the surrounding country, and he hoped it would point him toward a civilized town.

"Come on, boy," he said, patting the horse's neck. It's white mane flew into his face as the horse gained speed. The horse had the amazing ability to sense dips, rocks, and hidden depressions that might break one of its legs. The twin moons hung over the far horizon.

The promontory was a massive slab of rock the size of a football field. It had a tree line on one side and sheer cliffs, which dropped hundreds of feet down to the river below, on the other side. Only a few trees were able to bury roots deep into the rock slab's crevasses. Jeremy tied the horse's reins to a fern and walked to the promontory's edge. Far below, the river was now much smaller and its roar barely discernible. Upriver he saw the dark shapes of mountains in the distance. His friends were in those mountains—*if they lived*. Somewhere in those dark peaks was a city of death—a city guarded by a man-eating beast—a city with a Portal that connected light-years to the planet called Earth. No beacon showed in the gloom. No city was visible.

"Nice horse thou hast."

The voice jolted Jeremy, and he whipped around. His hands fumbled for a knife, sword, any weapon, but in his haste to flee the grakken he'd left all the weapons lying back at the glade where a battle of human and aliens had been fought. A dark figure stood by the white horse, patting its lathered neck. "Travel far?"

"Far?" Jeremy stammered. "Uh… I guess"

Another dark figure appeared to his right, holding a large war bow. "I recognize that steed. Its trapper and saddle belonged to Lord Wilmot."

"True. Very true," said the first man. "How didst thou come by the horse, stranger?"

There was a threat in the man's voice, and Jeremy suddenly felt trapped against the cliff's edge. Escape was futile. So he walked toward the horse. "I found him in some trees. Trapped, you see, sir."

"Alone?"

"Of course," Jeremy stammered. "Everyone else is dead!" More dark figures emerged from the line of trees, some with swords, others with large war bows, and all with the look of medieval knights. Standing just ten feet from the horse, Jeremy was soon surrounded.

"I think thou lie… *thief*," the first man said. He was older, dressed as a medieval warrior with a face scarred and fearsome. "By thy strange attire, I guess thou to be a gypsy. A gypsy used to crawling under fences and down chimneys by the look of thy clothes."

"I found the horse—" Jeremy started to say, but his voice was cut off as two sets of hands grabbed him from behind. The warrior smiled grimly, and Jeremy felt a stab of fear.

"Lord Wilmot was my friend," the warrior said, "and he was a tough man to kill. So… I think thou stole this horse." He turned to the second man holding the war bow. "Aelgar, get the rope." He grinned coldly at Jeremy, "Back up on thy steed, master thief!"

"He wished me—"

WHAM!

A fist slammed into Jeremy's face with a thud. Stars danced in his eyes and there was a loud *whinny* as the war horse reared up on its hind legs.

Minutes later, Jeremy sat on the horse with a noose hung around his neck, the rope looped over a tree branch overhead. Jeremy shook with fear, and was afraid he would urinate in his pants. He twisted his head from side to side; the rope's noose itched terribly.

"Guilt bothering thou?" asked Kayell, the warrior—Kayell, Aelgar, and Sully—all names new to Jeremy, names that belonged to men who were now his executioners. The young archer, Aelgar, moved with a catlike grace, but was the butt of many jokes; he took them lightly and retorted just as often. Sully was the large, portly axe man who held his horse's bridle and whose fist had silenced Jeremy's protest. The big man stood watching him with indifference.

Kayell dominated them all. Easily in his forties, the scarred warrior leaned against a tree, clearly pleased with the evening's festivities. "We haven't heard thy confession as to wherefrom thou stoleth the horse," Kayell said.

"Not stolen," Jeremy rasped. "He gave himself to me."

"Lord Wilmot?"

"Not actually. He was a good man… uh, but he's dead," Jeremy said.

"Enough of thy mockery," Kayell said, and then looked at Sully. "Give the beast a good whack on the rump. Let's see if our young thief finds humor in his hanging."

Sully cracked a smile on his huge, bearded face as he walked past Jeremy. With a violent swing of his arm he gave the horse a loud *whack* on its flank.

The horse didn't move.

"Lost thy firm hand?" Aelgor quipped with a smile.

Flushed with embarrassment, Sully gave the horse another whack. It didn't flinch or move a muscle. Jeremy allowed himself a tight grin. *The magic worked.* He was deep inside the horse's mind, and they were as one.

Aelgor laughed. Sully turned on the young archer, who mockingly held up his hands in surrender. Sully pulled Aelgor's sword from its sheath. "I'll make the beast move!" He turned back to the horse and raised the flat of the sword's blade.

"Enough!" came a new voice. A horse stepped out from the trees carrying another knight. Black hair moved above the handsome face of a man in his thirties whose dark eyes studied Jeremy. "I feel slighted. Executing a man while I'm out relieving myself! Unforgivable!" He dismounted.

For a brief second Jeremy felt a surge of hope… and then that hope was quickly snuffed. The new warrior stood below him, looking up at Jeremy as if judging him guilty on the spot.

Sully looked at this man with respect, "Sorry, Captain. Thou seemed grievously disposed."

"Constipation again, Lord Hilderberg?" quipped Kayell with a grin.

"Painful," the Captain said without mirth. He still looked up at Jeremy. "Horse thief?"

"Yes, Fergal," Kayell said.

And then he saw the horse for the first time and his eyebrows lifted. "Lord Wilmot's charger?" His men nodded. He turned back to Jeremy, eyes flat and cold. "I shall slap the horse myself if thou speaketh not on how thou camest to be riding him."

"Already slapped the horse… twice," Sully admitted with shame. "The boy said the horse was a present."

"From Lord Wilmot?" Fergal asked, a confused look on his face.

"Nay," Sully said, "but the noble steed presented himself to the boy."

Snickers of laughter sounded amongst the other men, but Kayell didn't smile. "Wilmot is two days late, Captain. I would know how this thief came by such a valued mount."

Fergal turned back to Jeremy, no longer smiling. "Lucky thou stumbled upon a most benevolent horse. Did he give thou a name?"

"His name is Adjudicator."

A look of surprise registered on Fergal's face. "Thou saw naught of Lord Wilmot or his retinue?"

"He must one of the local guides turned opportunist," Kayell accused.

"Lord Wilmot would've wished me to have his horse! I spoke with him!"

"Lies! Trying to save thy neck from a proper hanging!"

"Lord Frederick Wilmot of the Knights, uh, something or other. Except, that wasn't his real name—"

"Touched in the head, my Lord," Sully croaked, and then belched.

"The only other live human I've seen on this planet was a creepy old guy riding a black horse," he said. "Called himself the Gnome King, and a few other names—"

More laughter went up amongst the group. Kayell left the tree to stand next to his Captain and there was murder in his eyes. "The boy mocks us."

Fergal's eyes remained on Jeremy. "Did thou see a bright beacon of light earlier?"

"Beacon? Sure… but it came on by itself—"

"By itself?" Fergal asked with naked scorn.

"We had nothing to do with it. The… uh, Lord Wilmot, mentioned a Pal-a-thingy beacon" Jeremy's voice trailed off. Nothing had gone right since they walked through the Portal. Nothing.

"Put a flame to the bonfire," Fergal said, looking at Kayell. "The old wizard may have need of this dirty thief." He looked up at Jeremy. "Thou escapeth the noose, but don't get too hopeful. The blood of many a valiant man has been laid at the wizard's hands."

FLAMES LEAPT SKYWARD, SENDING forth a shower of sparks that floated red hot in the night air. Jeremy sat against a rock, sullen and mindful of the young archer smiling at him from across the clearing. Aelgar sat cross legged with his bow across his knees, arrow nocked just in case Jeremy decided to make a run for it. Captain Hilderberg commanded a troop of twenty knights, he learned, and they had camped out on this promontory on orders from a powerful wizard.

Faces turned suddenly skyward. "He cometh," Aelgar said. The archer looked at Jeremy and winked. Jeremy followed the man's gaze upward. A dark silhouette flashed into view from above the trees—a winged creature the size of a small jet airplane. Apprehension filled Jeremy's mind. Wings flapped, and the sound rippled the air. Down came the largest bird he'd ever seen. It landed with surprising grace, its huge talons spread. Its wings folded to the side as a shadowy figure climbed down from the bird's back.

Fergal stepped forward. "Master Lysander, thou cometh quickly." The old man, robed in blue, merely nodded in acknowledgement. He'd seen Jeremy from the first, and his eyes were locked on Jeremy's as he slowly approached. Fergal seemed out of sorts, and followed the wizard. "He says naught of who he is or where he cometh from. Me thinks he's a thief, and not a clever one—"

"Jeremy Austin."

The old man had spoken his name, and Jeremy was in shock. The wizard stood above him and continued to stare at him, appraising him.

"Thou knowest yon thief?" Fergal asked, looking at Jeremy with new interest.

"The boy's no thief," said the wizard called Lysander in a voice low and measured, cool and confident.

Fergal looked from Jeremy to the wizard. "But he rides Lord Wilmot's charger—"

"I'll vouch for the boy," Lysander said. "I have no doubt he came upon the horse honorably." The wizard held a hand out to Jeremy. "Come. Let's get you acquainted with this world and answer the questions wracking your brain. But I'd prefer sitting by a warm fire."

Jeremy clasped the hand and was suddenly yanked to his feet. The wizard might have looked a hundred years old, but his strength was that of a young athlete.

They sat near the bonfire, the wizard holding court and surrounded by his retinue of knights. Jeremy sat opposite the old man, who'd thrown back his hooded cowl to reveal long, silver hair woven into a braid. Lysander continued to study him, and Jeremy felt the wizard's eyes boring straight into his mind.

Lysander spoke solemnly. "You've been having flashes? Headaches?"

"Maybe," Jeremy replied cautiously. He still didn't trust this man, nor his *friends*.

"You set off the beacon?"

Jeremy felt a flush of heat in his face. "Probably."

"Thou denied it earlier!" Fergal said angrily.

Jeremy shrugged his shoulders innocently.

Laughter rumbled from the wizard. "Easy now, Lord Captain. Our young charge here is unaware of his own talents."

"He hast a talent for thievery," Sully said with mock seriousness. "He steals only the most obedient horse flesh." Laughter sounded amongst the other knights.

Jeremy sensed they no longer wanted to kill him, and he relaxed. He looked straight at the wizard and for the first time saw… compassion. "What are these flashes?"

"Magic."

Duh… Jeremy thought darkly.

There was a sudden stillness amongst the group. Jeremy found each of the knights looking at him—some looked at him with new interest, but others stared at him as if he was diseased.

"Pah!" Kayell muttered with suspicion. "Magic has long died out—save thou, Master Lysander, no offense intended," he recovered. "I meant amongst commoners."

"True," Lysander agreed.

"But he hath the gift?" Aelgar asked.

Lysander looked at Jeremy and smiled. "Only a person of magic could set off the beacon at Kenghas Arga."

"I was one of several hundred," Jeremy protested. "Besides, that beacon probably lights up every Christmas!"

"Not for over a thousand years," Lysander corrected, eyebrows lifting.

"What hath a Christmas?" Sully asked.

Lysander ignored the question. "You also have flashes—"

"Headaches only!" Jeremy continued his protestations.

"Talks with horses," Sully ventured with a smile.

"You have flashes because the magic is connecting with you," Lysander explained with sudden seriousness. "You may deny your gift or pretend it never happened, but your greatest enemy won't be so dim witted." The harshness of his last words shrouded the smiles.

"What enemy?" Jeremy asked.

"Is thou a foreigner from across the ocean?" Fergal asked with honest surprise.

"Thou hint of dark forces long dead," Kayell said with a sneer.

"I hint at *nothing*," Lysander said, his deep voice silencing any dissension. He looked gravely at Jeremy. "A hundred souls might have been present when you set off the beacon. But only one person was pursued by the Shadow Lord's most trusted commander, and that person was *you*, Mister Austin."

"Thou speak as if the Gnome King were alive!" Fergal exclaimed. "His last army was defeated over a half century ago. Surely he rots in his grave!"

The wizard leveled his eyes at Fergal, "This is a land of magic, and dark magic has served to give long life to the Shadow's servants." Lysander's eyes swept the entire group of knights. "I myself dealt with the Gnome King after the boy escaped him." A few murmurs went up among the men.

"Myths and fairy tales," Kayell spat with contempt. "Five hundred years have passed and naught has been seen from the Shadow Lands."

"I have to agree with my compatriot, Master Lysander," Fergal said respectfully. "Thou speak of villains from fairy tales, dark fables spoon-fed to every child to make them behave."

"Why the Shadow Lord has lain silent these five centuries I do not know," the wizard said gravely. "The beacon awakened him from slumber. The Gnome King's appearance was just evidence that things are about to change."

"The beacon was a signal?" Fergal asked.

"A signal? Yes," Lysander said. "But not for the Shadow Lord." The wizard paused and a hush descended over the group of warriors. "For centuries upon centuries, the free nations of this world—mankind, Dwarves, and Elves—have stood against the warlock known as *Malcator*. All have sacrificed their lives because to *not* take a stand would mean slavery. The armies of the Shadow Lord have attacked, and the free nations have always managed to fend off disaster. And yet, Malcator has never been threatened in his own lands."

"No king had the courage to attack the necromancer!" Fergal said bitterly.

"I don't blame them," Lysander said.

"Bunch of women," Fergal muttered.

The wizard sighed. "Evil awaits any man who travels the Shadow Mountains, so our kings have preferred to build up their defenses and promise to raise even larger armies. Unscathed and safe in the strongholds of Abaddon, the Shadow Lord devises new schemes and bigger armies of his own. But after his last defeat at the Valley of Kings he pulled back from the free world. Some say he awaits the return of King Servas—the great Redemptor King—others say he awaits the *Paladin*, the inheritor of King Servas' power."

"And a great warrior," Kayell said with a hint of awe.

"So which is it, wizard?" Fergal asked impatiently. "And what part hath this boy to play in this drama?"

The wizard stared into the night sky that was already growing brighter with the approach of dawn. *"He will come, unheralded and without recognition; into a land hungering for truth he will bring the sword of light. The sign above Arga will signal his arrival, and from Kenghas' lair he will shape the planet."* Lysander went silent and turned to gaze at Jeremy. All eyes followed the wizard's.

Redness flushed Jeremy's cheeks—he wanted no part in saving a planet. "You've got the wrong guy," Jeremy said weakly.

"Him? The Paladin?" Hayell pointed to Jeremy in disbelief.

Suddenly the air was split with a loud roar. The giant roc, the wizard's bird, was staring in the direction of the distant mountains that hid the dead city of Kenghas Arga. The roc opened its beak and screamed again.

Lysander hastily stood to his feet. "The Shadow Lord isn't wasting any time. Already his minions search for the boy. We must be going."

52120226R00219

Made in the USA
San Bernardino, CA
12 August 2017